Praise for the nov

"Mona Shroff does it again, with a beautifully engrossing tale of family, forgiveness, and finding the courage to follow your dreams."
—Tracey Livesay, author of *Like Lovers Do*

"A sweet romance with a ton of he... pages until the heartwarming end. —Farah ... ...raged

"The best storytellers know how to keep the tension in the story threads taut as they weave the strands together, by turns compelling, by turns beckoning. Mona Shroff is one such storyteller and *Then There Was You* is a fascinating story." —*Frolic*

"A sweet, angsty romance with a second chance for two people struggling to overcome the harsh mistakes of their past."
—Sonali Dev, author of *Pride, Prejudice, and Other Flavors*, on *Then, Now, Always*

"Shroff manages to make several of romance's most enduring tropes feel fresh in her cute contemporary debut.... [This] sweet second-chance romance is rendered with nimble prose, quick plotting, and rich cultural details, making it clear that Shroff [is] a writer to watch."
—*Publishers Weekly* on *Then, Now, Always*

"Mona Shroff weaves a sweet and heartwarming romance of forgiveness and second chances, and the lies we tell in the name of love. Sam and Maya are utterly unforgettable."
—Falguni Kothari, author of *The Object of Your Affections*, on *Then, Now, Always*

"This was the kind of story that lives and breathes with you...the kind where the characters stick with you long after you're done. The fact they looked like me made it all the more real."
—Shaila Patel, author of *Soulmated*, on *Then, Now, Always*

Also by Mona Shroff

Then, Now, Always
Then There Was You

The Second First Chance

MONA SHROFF

HQN

ISBN-13: 978-1-335-45346-4

The Second First Chance

Copyright © 2022 by Mona Shroff

For questions and comments about the quality of this book, please contact us
at CustomerService@Harlequin.com.

HQN
22 Adelaide St. West, 41st Floor
Toronto, Ontario M5H 4E3, Canada
www.Harlequin.com

Printed in U.S.A.

To my parents, Ran and Sudha Sharma.
Everything parents should be and more.

The Second First Chance

one

DHILLON

A dark brown Lab-pit mix puppy raised its head to look at Dhillon as he entered the exam room. Dhillon's joy was instant, which was why he loved his job. His nurse, Shelly, was right behind him with the brief introduction.

"Dr. Vora, this is Scout. She is being brought in today by Firefighter Ian Walsh. Scout was found abandoned at one of their scenes and is currently under the care of the Howard County Fire Department."

It was at the word *firefighter* that Dhillon tensed. He made eye contact with the man and extended his hand, anxiety flooding through his system, increasing his heart rate and beading sweat on his upper lip.

Shelly threw him a worried look. He ignored her.

"Good morning. I'm Dr. Vora." Dhillon found his voice but focused on the leashed puppy as the man's walkie-talkie emitted an irritating squeal. "Everything okay?" Dhillon nodded at the walkie-talkie. "We can reschedule if you have to go."

The Lab-pit puppy twitched her ears and raised her head at the squawk. Shelly made a cooing sound and went over to pet their patient. Any remaining anxiety Dhillon might have had melted away as he took in the befuddled pup. The firefighter didn't even look at the puppy.

"Nah. It's all good. I'm supposed to get the pup tended to, so let's just do it." The firefighter shook his hand.

Dhillon nodded to Shelly as she moved from the dog's side to the computer so she could enter the information they had so far. He got down on the ground where the puppy had lain. "She looks like my Lucky."

"You mean that older dog out front? With the scarring?"

"Mmm-hmm." Dhillon picked up Scout and let her climb into his lap. He played with her a moment. He held a small treat out and watched her track it as he moved it from side to side. She lifted her mouth to grab it, but Dhillon made her wait another second before letting her have the treat and a scratch under her chin. Best part of being a veterinarian. He glanced at Walsh, who watched him with a scowl. "Lucky was caught in a house fire." Dhillon tried to keep his voice neutral. It wasn't this man's fault that Lucky was burned. He stood, bringing Scout with him.

Her coat looked almost pure black, and her big brown eyes reminded Dhillon of Lucky's when he'd been a puppy. For a moment, Dhillon was dragged back to the day he brought Lucky home from the SPCA. Best day of his life. Well, maybe second-best.

"The vet at the time was the previous owner of this practice. He did excellent work. Shelly here used to work with him. That scarring barely reflects how bad his injuries were."

Dhillon laid Scout on the rickety old exam table that stood in the middle of the room. Nice shiny coat, alert and playful. "How old is she?"

"Uh…maybe ten weeks. I'm not entirely sure. We just got her. Our station's new recruit found her on scene, no collar, nothing. She hasn't even been chipped yet, as far as we know. We're keeping her at the firehouse for now until we find her a home." Ian shook his head and pursed his lips.

"Why not take her to the SPCA? They can help find her a home."

Ian shook his head again. "Our new recruit insists that's not necessary. She thinks someone's going to claim the little thing." He shrugged. "My experience says not likely."

Dhillon turned to Scout, the sight of the puppy putting a grin on his face again. "I know someone who'd say the same thing." Or used to know, anyway. Sadness flitted through him for an instant before it was replaced with resignation. He'd given up his chance to keep knowing her long ago.

Dhillon scratched the puppy's belly. "I can chip her today." He held out a small treat and softly said, "Sit." Scout flipped over and sat on the table. He rewarded her with the treat.

He looked in Scout's ears and checked her teeth and paws, dictating his assessment to Shelly as he went along. The puppy looked cared for, healthy. Maybe three months old. Obviously, the guys at the firehouse had cared for her. "Does she eat well?"

Ian shrugged. "We have her dog food, but a lot of the guys spoil her, slipping her a bit of meatball, steak, hot dog. Not me, though. You can believe that."

"Can any of you take her home?"

Ian shook his head. "But there's always someone at the station because we do twenty-four- and forty-eight-hour shifts. She works out with us. The new recruit is teaching her to sit, stay, come. Even to go fetch gear. Like that's practical." Ian shrugged, as if taking care of a dog was really not his idea of firefighter work. "You know anyone who would want her?"

Dhillon had a thought flash through his mind. Nah. She was likely too busy, and honestly, she might even have a dog already, for all he knew. Running into her occasionally outside the house didn't really give him much information about her life. "No. But I can keep an eye out." He continued with his examination, prepping Scout's shots as Shelly held her.

"Are you Indian?" Ian asked.

Dhillon sighed, knowing the reason for this question. Ian knew someone who was Indian. "Yes. Well, my parents are from India, but I was born here." Dhillon barely afforded Ian a glance. He approached Scout and administered the shot. Scout gave a small yelp.

"It's okay, sweetie," Dhillon cooed softly. "Just one more."

"Just asking because the new recruit—who's all about this dog—she's Indian."

She? Dhillon snapped his attention back to Ian and could not refrain from raising an eyebrow. Interesting. An Indian woman firefighter? Didn't see that every day.

"Maybe you know her?"

Dhillon did his best to not roll his eyes as he focused on administering the second shot, but a sigh escaped all the same, as did a small *hmph* from Shelly. Just because he and this firefighter were both Indian didn't mean they knew each other. "I doubt it." He ran a gentle hand over Scout's head and body as if to soothe away her discomfort.

If someone he knew was a firefighter—male or female—he'd already know.

Scout turned a full circle, sniffing, then promptly peed on the table.

Ian scowled at the puppy and stepped back. Shelly made a move to grab the paper towels, but Dhillon was closer. He shared a look with Shelly as he cleaned up the mess. "Potty training can take some time. Helps if she has a crate, where she feels safe."

Ian shook his head and put out his hands. "I saw a crate in the bunk area. Desai would know."

Dhillon's heart skipped a beat. "Desai?" It couldn't be. Desai was a common-enough Indian last name. Could be anybody. Right?

He stared at Ian, who continued, completely unaware of Dhillon's rising panic, as blood pounded through his body, his heart rate increasing. "The new recruit. Who wanted this dog. The Indian girl. Riya Desai."

Of all the names Ian could have said, that was the absolute last one he wanted to hear.

It couldn't be *her*. The Riya he knew would never run into a fire. As far as he knew, she had the same reaction to anything fire-related that he did: panic and anxiety.

But then again, he didn't really know anything about her, did he? They never really talked anymore, outside of uncomfortable pleasantries when they were forced together. Riya avoided him, and he avoided Riya.

Dhillon's heart hammered in his chest, and the blood drained from his head. He fought to maintain professional composure as he continued his examination of Scout. "It's a common name." Dhillon tried to sound casual, as if he really believed his own words. He needed to believe them.

"Brown skin, dark brown eyes."

Really? That was his description? Dhillon took a breath so he wouldn't lay into this guy. He fought fires, after all. Saved people.

Some people.

"She's a paramedic, too. Which helps because we have to do EMT training."

Dhillon's stomach plummeted, and his head spun. It *was* his Riya. Dhillon clenched his jaw. Well, it was the Riya Desai that he knew.

She'd never been *his*.

He should have picked up on it when Ian said she was teaching Scout to get gear. It was exactly what she had taught Lucky to do when they were young teenagers. Go get their backpacks or books or whatever they had forgotten. Lucky would do it, too. For her. Even though Lucky was really *his* dog.

What the fuck was she doing going into fires? She'd never bring back what they'd lost.

Ian was still talking. "Between you and me? She's hot. She has the sexiest mole just below her ear, and she is stacked." Ian put his hands in front of his chest to indicate large breasts, and Dhillon saw red.

"You know, I actually do know her." He stared Ian down. "She grew up next door to me. So you'll want to shut up now." He didn't usually talk to patients this way, but this guy was asking for it, and technically Scout was his patient. And she seemed fine with it.

"Oh, dude, sorry. I didn't know she'd be like a sister to you."

"She's not a sister to me. Just a neighbor." Dhillon had spent too much time imagining kissing that mole to look at Riya like a sister. "Either way, isn't she your colleague? Maybe show a little respect?"

Ian waved him off. "Whatever. She won't last long. Doubt if she can do the job."

Oh, she could do the job. Riya and Dhillon may not be best friends anymore, but one thing he did know was that Riya Desai was fantastic at whatever she put her mind to. If she was the rookie in the department, that meant she'd made it through the academy. Since she made it through the academy, Dhillon knew she had put her mind to becoming a firefighter a long time ago.

Dhillon finished up with little Scout and—reluctantly—handed her back to Ian. "Scout will need another set of shots in one month." His mouth moved as if by rote as he doled out instructions, but his mind was spinning.

What the fuck had Riya got herself into now?

two

RIYA

Sweat dripped from every part of her body onto the parking lot outside the fire station for Engine and Ladder 52, and it had nothing to do with the fact that it was June in Maryland. Well, not entirely.

Riya was in full turnout gear: jacket, pants, gloves, boots and helmet, the oxygen tank strapped to her back, finishing the *requested* fifty push-ups. At least the gloves provided padding from the gravel where they were ending today's training. The sixty pounds of gear on her body simply got heavier with each push-up. And hotter.

"What's the matter, Desai? Too much for you?" Her lieutenant, Jeff Ambrose, stood in front of her. He was also in full gear, and he had finished his push-ups. He was calling the count for the rest of them on this shift: Bill Schultz, Ian Walsh, Marcus Evans and Alejandro Alvarez. But he only called out her name. She was the rookie. And the only woman.

"No, sir!" she shouted.

"Down!"

She went into the lowered push-up position, her body hovering a couple of inches above the ground.

Lieutenant Ambrose stood in front of her. All she could see were his boots. Riya almost wished the alarm would sound and they had to take a call. Though, Ambrose would probably make her stay in this position until they got back.

She concentrated on her breathing and not on the ache in her muscles. Or the sweat dripping off her face, pooling in various parts of her body.

"Up!"

She pushed up. One more.

"Down." Lieutenant Ambrose knelt in front of her as she hovered again. Her abs and shoulders were screaming. "How's it going, Desai?"

"Great, sir!"

"You feel that?" He stood as if addressing them all, but Riya knew he was talking to her. "Your whole body is screaming. Your muscles are spent. But if one of you falls, your whole team starts fifty push-ups on a count of one. That's how it is on scene. Everything you do affects the man..." he paused significantly "...or woman, next to you. Up!"

There was general groaning, but Riya didn't make a sound. She wasn't about to show even the slightest amount of weakness. They'd never let her live it down.

"Down." Lieutenant Ambrose spoke in a normal tone again. "Dismissed. Get cleaned up."

Riya collapsed on the spot, removing her gloves, helmet and oxygen tank, not oblivious to the chatter of the other guys, who were complaining about the extra hard workout and somehow blaming her for it. Didn't they need to be in shape regardless of whether she was there or not? She reached for her water bottle. The water was hot from sitting in the afternoon sun, but she didn't care. She closed her eyes, lay on her back a moment and enjoyed the hydration. Cars whizzed past on the highway behind them. The firehouse had four bays, two engines and one ladder truck. There were offices in the back, along with sleeping quarters and a kitchen upstairs. This was Riya's home away from home. She loved it.

A small tongue licked at her face, and she grinned. At least someone here liked her.

"Scout! That's gross, licking up my sweat." She opened up her turnout jacket, imagining a slight breeze to cool her. She brought the puppy close. She needed a shower, but with only the one locker room and that with open showers, she would have to navigate around the men who had already gone in to clean up. She wasn't exactly a prude, but she wasn't getting stark naked in a shower full of men she worked with.

In between calls, they maintained the truck and all the equipment on it. Riya made sure she was always busy, always doing her share, be it maintaining the equipment, cleaning the engine or cooking and cleaning the firehouse. She knew she was the probie, and as such she did the scut work. She loved firefighting in a way that was different from the way she loved being a paramedic, so this probationary period was just another rite of passage for her.

Didn't hurt that she was a good cook.

A few of the men hadn't bothered to hide the fact that they doubted her ability to do the job based solely on the fact that she was a woman. Those same men seemed to have no trouble eating her food, however.

There was no point in fighting them. Her work could and

would speak for itself. She had excelled at the academy, and her first few shifts here had gone well. It would be a couple of weeks before she was able to do twenty-four-hour shifts. *She* knew she could do the job. The guys would just have to see for themselves.

Right now, though, Riya squeezed her eyes shut and laughed as Scout climbed onto her stomach, preventing her from standing. She was grateful for the excuse to lie still for a moment. "Hey, Scout. Hey, there." She patted the pup's head. "How're you doing?"

"Took her to the vet today." Ian approached from her periphery.

She was sitting in an instant, closing her turnout jacket over her tank top almost instinctively. "Yeah, where?" Whenever she was in Ian's presence, her muscles tensed, and the hairs on her arms stood on end. She focused her attention on Scout and those big brown puppy eyes.

"You know that old building on the corner, opposite the bar? A new vet took over the practice." He paused. "He seemed to know you."

At this, Riya glanced up, the summer sun making her squint at Ian. Her heart raced as she tried to maintain the appearance of mild interest. "Oh, yeah?" She continued to pet Scout almost as if the puppy was a shield against the bomb Ian was about to drop.

Riya didn't know many vets. In fact, she only knew one.

Before Ian could say anything, a very familiar cold nose nuzzled her hand. Riya smiled and greeted the newcomer even as her stomach bottomed out. "Lucky?" She leaned in toward the older dog so he could lick her face. She held Scout with one hand and petted Lucky with the other. She hugged him and tousled his fur, automatically assessing the older dog's scars.

"Lucky, what are you doing here?" It was a ridiculous question because of course Lucky couldn't answer it, but it was something to say, as she knew his owner wasn't far behind. Clearly he was the vet in question.

Which meant he knew that she was a firefighter. Which meant he was pissed, though he hardly had a right to be. She was a grown woman. She could do what she wanted. Didn't stop her stomach from clenching in anticipation of seeing him.

Riya swallowed hard as black sneakers entered her view.

"I could ask you the same thing." A deep, soft rumble that was foreign and familiar all at the same time. She had known that voice before it had gained the smoothness and timbre that made it so irresistible now.

Riya cleared her throat and stood to face the man behind that knee-melting voice.

Dhillon Vora.

He stood a few feet from her, his hands in his pockets, his dark-eyed gaze raking over her and hardening as he took in the gear she still had on. The scruff on his jaw that she'd seen last month was now a trim beard. It suited him. At the sound of a newcomer, Scout wiggled out of her arms to go to him. She released the puppy. Without taking his eyes off Riya, Dhillon bent down and scooped Scout up, muscles stretching his dark T-shirt. He called to Lucky, but the older dog stayed at Riya's feet.

His hand shook slightly as he stroked the fur on Scout's back. He was holding the puppy to calm himself. Clearly, even standing in the parking lot of the fire station was challenging for him.

"Dhillon Vora." She used his full name because she hoped it would irritate him. Her reward was an eye roll so minute she'd have missed it if she blinked.

"What the hell are you doing?" He stepped closer to her and laid into her as if he had the right to barge in and demand these answers when they never even really talked anymore. Even when she checked in on Lucky when she visited her parents every week, they barely did more than exchange pleasantries. Which Riya tried to avoid at all costs.

"I'm working." She fixed her eyes on his. They watered in the blinding sun.

"As a *firefighter*? Seriously?" He said the word like he couldn't stand having it in his mouth.

She inhaled, squaring her shoulders and lifting her chin to fill every bit of her full five feet six inches. Dhillon still towered over her, even more so when he stepped forward and crowded her space. She didn't move back. Simply tilted her head and raised her eyes in as bored a fashion as she could muster. "Yes."

God, he smelled good. Like soap and disinfectant and cologne. And she probably stank of sweat and more sweat.

"How can you possibly have anything to do—to do—with—with—" In his anger or disbelief or both, the usually calm, steady Dhillon Vora was sputtering. And he didn't bother to lower his voice.

"Fire?" she offered, unable to keep the smirk from her voice or her face. Ruffling Dhillon's feathers had once been a favorite pastime of hers. Nice to see she still had it.

"Yes. How can you possibly be fighting fires?" Dhillon regained some composure, but not enough to hide his anger.

"How could I not?" She pressed her lips together, narrowing her eyes. It took no small amount of discipline to ignore the soft shuffle of feet and the murmur of men's voices behind her. Her colleagues had conveniently finished showering just in time for the show and were clearly trying not to be seen or heard so they could eavesdrop.

Surprise or shock at her response played on his face for just a split second before he masked it again with anger. Or was that pain? Riya couldn't tell anymore.

"Don't tell me I have to remind you of what was lost—"

"No!" she snapped, cutting him off. "No, you do not need to remind me of anything." In a motion that revealed more than she was willing to share, she reflexively clutched at her neck. But the necklace wasn't there. She couldn't wear it on duty.

"Then what the fuck are you doing?" He was nearly shouting now, which was so not Dhillon. Well, maybe it was. She had no idea what was typical of her former best friend anymore.

"I'm doing a job that needs to be done." She clenched her jaw. She would not reduce herself to yelling back at him in front of her colleagues. No matter how badly she wanted to scream at him that it was her life to do with whatever she damn well pleased.

"Riya," he said, his voice softening on her name, "you're running *into* fires."

"I'm *fighting* fires."

She could have sworn she heard a derisive noise from behind her. She'd deal with the guys later.

"What about your parents? How could you put them through this? After they lost Samir?" he growled.

At this, her gaze faltered. She had lost Samir, too. He'd been the perfect older brother.

"You haven't told them?" He shook his head at her. "Un-fucking-believable!"

"Lucky, come," Riya commanded, her eyes never leaving Dhillon's. The dog came to her, and she rested her hand on his head. "Go with Dhillon." Lucky whimpered, but he went. "I'll take Scout."

Dhillon handed her the puppy. Scout wiggled in her arms

a moment. He had no business coming here and spitting out the past for all to hear. She steeled her voice. "The showers are free. I'm going to clean up."

"Do they know?" He jutted his chin at the men behind her. "Do they know about the fire?"

Riya leaned toward him so she was in his space, forced to take in even more of his scent. She spoke through her teeth. "Leave. Now."

Dhillon grunted, but she did not miss the heavy gaze he rested on her before he turned. He mumbled to Lucky, and Riya watched the dog lumber beside his master as Dhillon strode off, confident in his anger, punctuating his aggravation with each step.

Riya lingered a moment, watching Dhillon's infuriated but magnificent form retreat to his car with Lucky. She gathered her wits and turned to face her department, chin high, mouth set, eyes hard. Show no weakness. They were watching her, some grim-faced, some curious, some sympathetic. All expectant.

"Is that how the dog was injured? House fire?" Schultz looked her directly in the eye. This was more than simple curiosity.

Schultz had been at this station for a couple of years. He was one of the few guys who had shown her kindness in her first days on the job. She met his gaze. "Yes."

"You were in a fire?" Ambrose narrowed his eyes at her. "Is that why you're here?" The accusation in her lieutenant's voice was clear.

"No, sir. I'm here because I worked my ass off." She raised her chin at them, same as she had with Dhillon, and spoke with authority born of a paramedic, of a survivor. "I did exactly what you all did to get here. I passed every test. Content. Physical." She paused. "Psych." It had been brutal. The content she learned. The physical training had had her puking more than once, but she got stronger and stronger. She was lean and muscular and strong, and she was damn proud of it.

The psych had been the hardest part. They wanted her to come to terms with the house fire that had scarred Lucky and taken her brother. As if.

"Seems like you got some major issues if your boyfriend didn't even know you were a firefighter." Lieutenant Jeff Ambrose was a few years younger than her, and he'd been in fire service since the age of eighteen. He was her immediate boss, and he made no secret of the fact that Riya was going to have to prove she could do the job.

"Everyone in this room has an issue with fire, Lieutenant." Schultz spoke up.

"He's not my boyfriend," Riya said evenly.

Never was.

"Whatever." Lieutenant Ambrose did not back down. "You have an issue with fire, you better deal with it. I'm not thrilled about going into a fire with someone who's likely to lose it because they haven't dealt with their issues."

Riya fumed but did not lower her chin. It would take more than her closed-minded lieutenant for her to doubt herself. She could do the job. Including carrying out all two hundred and twenty pounds of Ambrose, if need be. She'd been making slow progress with some of the guys. Dhillon's little show had just set her back.

"What happened to you? In that fire?" Ambrose spoke to her as if he had the authority to ask. Lieutenant or not, it was none of his damn business.

Riya continued to stare him down. Her own family didn't talk about the fire. She wasn't about to discuss it with him, or any of these guys, for that matter. *None of their damn business.*

After a moment, Ambrose stepped back. "I'm watching you."

Riya said nothing, though her stomach churned and her blood boiled as she watched him walk away. Damn Dhillon. What the hell was he thinking coming down here like that? And why? For years, they'd barely spoken to one another, so what did he care what she did for a living? He'd never cared when she was a paramedic.

She marched toward the locker room, taking off her gear as she walked. She'd thought the showers were empty, but she still heard some of the guys in the area and decided she'd just clean up at home. She went to the single bathroom and washed her face and exchanged her sweat-soaked T-shirt for a clean one. She'd forgotten to bring an extra sports bra, so she'd just have to deal with the dampness.

As she attended to her duties, the normal chatter and clamor of the firehouse returned. There was always a good amount of laughter. The guys had bonded through the experiences of saving lives. Riya envied their bond and knew full well she'd have to earn her way in. Once they saw that she was more than capable of doing the job, things would be different.

Schultz brought out a box of supplies as she restocked. He was about her age with buzzed blond hair and friendly blue eyes. Scout had followed him to the truck and now sat between them as they replaced used inventory.

"My wife was not happy when I decided to do this." His voice was deep and kind, and he had a slight drawl she couldn't place.

Bill and his wife, Angie, had been married a couple of years, and whenever Schultz talked about her, it was clear that he was still smitten. The guys teased him. Riya thought it was wonderful that even after being married for a time, he still flushed when he said his wife's name.

"Angie worries, but she gets it. She knows it's a part of me." Schultz smiled at her, tipping his head toward the parking lot where they'd had their workout. "He'll come around."

"Oh." Her heart hammered, and she flushed. "I was telling the truth. He and I are not together. We grew up next door to each other." She looked away. "Raised Lucky together. That's it."

Schultz eyed her a moment. "Okay... Whatever you say." He put a few things away. "But that dog *was* burned in a fire, wasn't he?"

Riya snapped her gaze to him. "Yes. He was." Lucky had been just a couple of years old at the time. It was part of the reason Dhillon had become a vet.

They had both made decisions based on that fire.

three

DHILLON

Dhillon pulled into his half of the shared driveway, jolting forward as he hit the brake harder than was necessary. He stared at the garages, not really seeing them.

Riya was *going into fucking fires*. Of all the jobs in the world that she could do. The way she had looked at him, full of defiance, like *he* was the outrageous one. He shook his head. He had waited for the crew to finish their exercises before getting out of his car. Riya was clearly physically strong. Every one of her push-ups looked perfect. And that was after she'd done whatever else before he got there.

She was swimming in her gear. How did she manage to move in it? He could only imagine the ice-cold welcome she was getting from her coworkers. Not to mention the asshats like Ian. Everything about this screamed danger. But that was Riya: no thought, ever, for her own safety.

Riya's mom's car was parked in the other half of the driveway. Their houses were townhomes with one shared wall. Sometimes, in his mind, he could still see the flames in the window above the garage that looked into the family room. And then in the window above that which looked into a bedroom, where his father had been. Because the townhomes were mirror images of each other, the flames had been similar on Riya's side.

The acrid stench of smoke came back to him, and like a movie reel, he could watch the events play out. He shook his head as if to clear it of the memories. He knew how the scene ended. No need to see it through.

"Come on, Lucky." Dhillon got out of the car.

The dog didn't move. "Lucky!"

Whining, Lucky heaved himself up and out the door.

"Good boy." Dhillon rubbed the fur on Lucky's head, instantly feeling his heart rate slow down. He tried not to notice the white hairs in his dog's once-beautiful black coat, tried to ignore how slow Lucky's gait had become in recent weeks. He couldn't believe how much the dog still listened to Riya, even though technically Lucky was *his* dog.

The jingle of a bike bell interrupted his thoughts as a child from the neighborhood rode by, training wheels still on, his father jogging behind. "Hey, Dr. Vora! Dad said I can get a puppy!"

Dhillon felt a bubble of excitement, as if he was the one given permission to get a puppy. He raised his eyebrows at the dad. "Is that so?"

"Jacob did everything he said he would, and he's taking responsibility."

"That's fabulous, Chris," Dhillon called out. "Let me know if you need anything."

"You can count on it," Chris called back as he followed his son.

Dhillon had wanted a dog his whole young life. His parents had put him off and put him off for years. He and Riya had played with the neighborhood pets every chance they got.

Then finally, just after his thirteenth birthday, his dad took him to the local animal shelter, saying that this was his lucky day. Dhillon's excitement had mirrored Jacob's. Of course, Dhillon's father had also made it clear that Dhillon was to be responsible for the animal. He would have agreed to anything at that point. He already knew he would name the dog Lucky.

He and Riya had trained Lucky together, reading countless books on dog training, and arguing about which approach was best, but somehow Riya was always able to get Lucky to do what she wanted.

He and Riya had been best friends.

A professional eye was not needed to see that Lucky was on borrowed time. Dhillon pushed aside those thoughts. He couldn't think about losing Lucky any more than he could think about Riya running into burning buildings.

He removed his shoes in the small, tiled area just inside the door, changing them out for his well-worn house slippers. "Hey!" he called out. "I'm home."

"Whoop-de-doo." His sister, Hetal, was on the sofa, staring at her laptop, buried under a pile of books, her sarcasm spot-on but weary. Her dark hair was pulled up in a ponytail that bobbed as she spoke. Lucky plopped himself at her feet. "Took you long enough to get home."

Hetal worked with him in the clinic office from time to time while she went to college, but she hadn't been in today.

"Wait." He narrowed his eyes at her. "Is that my UMD T-shirt?"

Hetal opened another book and feigned concentration. "No. Why would I wear your T-shirt?"

Dhillon took a step closer. The short sleeves came almost to her elbows. "That's my favorite one! You had to have gone into my closet for it."

Hetal looked up at him, all wide-eyed innocence. Her eyes were the same honey-brown their father had had. "I would never do that. That would be an invasion of privacy."

Dhillon narrowed his eyes further. "Uh-huh."

"Too bad no one gets privacy in this house. But if someone who already had a job would move out, some of us wouldn't be tempted to go into others' closets. Then you might be able to keep some of your T-shirts." She grinned at him before turning back to her computer. "Just not this one."

Dhillon shook his head to dismiss her comments. He couldn't move out yet: he had to make sure she was settled into her graduate program first. She wanted to be a vet. "What's going on?" He jutted his chin at her computer.

She scowled. "O-chem exam tomorrow."

"Ugh. The absolute worst." He plopped down next to her. "Show me."

Hetal showed him her problem. They went over it together, until she understood. She went back to her computer, and he dropped his head onto the back of the sofa. "Where's Mom?"

"She's meeting a guy for coffee. Then she has a shift." Dhillon could almost hear his sister's eye roll. "Hiral Mama sent her a text about dating. Again."

Dhillon's stomach tensed. Between his mom dating and his uncle having a fit about it, not to mention Lucky's age—and now Riya fighting fires—he was going to need a dose of antacid. "What did he say?"

"Well, let's say that our *mama* is being less than supportive of our Mama."

He shook his head at her wordplay. She especially loved mixing the Gujarati words with the English ones.

A few months ago, their mother, Sarika, had told her older brother that she was going to start dating. It was time. Well past time, according to Hetal, because Dhillon's father had been gone for close to fifteen years. Hiral Mama, Sarika's brother, was really all the family she had left, as their parents had already passed. According to Sarika, she figured that since she and Hiral lived in the same town, he was bound to find out anyway.

Dhillon wasn't overly thrilled with his mother being on shaadi.com, either, but his concern was that she would get hurt.

"She looked really sad," Hetal said.

"Who's the guy?"

"A new one. Lawyer." She side-eyed him as she worked. "You should try it."

"Nope. Not going to happen. I'm good."

"So you enjoy being alone, living with your mom and sister, pining over a girl you've never even made a move on?"

Damn, his sister was feisty. Where'd she get that from? "Don't you have some big test tomorrow?"

She stuck her tongue out at him. "You'd have to tell Riya Didi you like her for her to go out with you. It won't happen by magic."

The best move here was to ignore his sister. She was constantly trying to fix him up with someone, and she had long ago figured out how he felt about Riya. Hetal just didn't understand how complicated his relationship—or nonrelationship—with Riya was. "What are we doing for dinner?"

"It's your turn to do the rotli. I did the dhal and shak."

Dhillon stood and put some distance between him and his sister before he answered her. "Yeah, but is it edible?"

"Better than what you come up with," Hetal shot back.

He started up the stairs to change out of his work clothes, his mind wandering back to Riya. Even soaked in sweat with all that heavy gear hanging on her, her facial expression one of complete frustration, she had looked incredible. There was a part of him that reveled in the fact that she had focused on him for once. Even if that focus was simply in annoyance. Or possibly even anger.

He'd seen her in passing last week when she was home for her weekly visit to her parents. Lucky had escaped through his dog door when he heard her roll up. Dhillon had watched them through the kitchen window. He inexplicably landed on the memory of her from a couple of months ago at their families' yearly remembrance. She had been dressed in a simple light blue salwar kameez, her hair loose from the long braid she favored and flowing past her shoulders. She was as beautiful that day as she had been today, covered in sweat and wearing oversize gear. She'd hardly even looked at him that day. She had stayed for the prayer but slipped out before the mandatory meal.

It was believed that the family members who had passed on enjoyed food through their loved ones. So once a year, the two families, the Voras and the Desais, held a small remembrance ceremony. Riya's brother, Samir, and Dhillon's father, Kishore, had both been lost on the same day. In the same fire.

The families made their favorite foods and ate them together. All except Riya. She left as the meal was being warmed. No one ever commented on it, simply accepting that Riya would do as she pleased.

As she always had.

Dhillon pulled on shorts and a T-shirt for his evening run. The sky was overcast, promising an early summer downpour.

The image of Riya glaring at him popped back into his head. He needed that run. He grabbed a hoodie and bounded out the door, only to be greeted by the rumble of a motorcycle.

Speak of the devil. Riya had purchased that bike years ago, claiming that it was economical and practical. But Dhillon knew she rode it for the thrill. For the danger.

Riya pulled up alongside her mother's car. Dhillon placed one foot on a step and leaned forward, gently stretching his hamstring, as she removed her helmet and dismounted her bike. Her long dark hair was still pulled back in a braid, revealing the mole beneath her ear that had mesmerized him more than once. She almost always wore her hair in the simple braid, complaining that it got in her way otherwise, but she never cut it short, either. She appeared to be preoccupied with adjusting something on her bike, but Dhillon knew she'd seen him standing there.

Before he could say anything, he heard the door behind him slam open, and he was nearly knocked over by his sister bounding out.

"Riya Didi? I thought I heard the bike."

Riya stood and flashed a rare smile as Hetal ran toward her. "Hey, how's it going?" Riya opened her arms and wrapped them around his sister in a huge bear hug.

His sister adored Riya, and with good reason. After the fire, she'd done almost as much babysitting as he had when his mom worked. Hetal had actually learned how to make dhal from Riya. Irritation warred with warm, fuzzy feelings as he watched his sister with Riya. Riya loved Hetal as much as he did.

His sister squeezed Riya back. "Okay, I guess."

"Ready for that big o-chem exam tomorrow?"

Riya knew about the exam?

Hetal shrugged. "We'll see."

Dhillon spoke up. "Surprised to see you here."

"Are you, though?" She spared him a glance. He ate it up.

"I'm going for a run." Get her out of his system.

"I'll still be here when you get back," she spit out at him, the familiar throaty rasp of her voice tinged with anger.

Dhillon didn't move. *She* was pissed at *him*? His agitation returned with a vengeance.

Hetal looked from Riya to Dhillon and back to Riya. "Okay...well, I have an exam to study for...so I'll catch you later." She backed away from them as if the tension in the air was a physical thing. "See you, Riya Didi."

Riya broke her stare, turning to smile and nod at Hetal. "Good luck. You'll be fine."

Hetal moved toward the house, and Riya held Dhillon in place once again with her glare. As soon as the door shut behind Hetal, Riya uncrossed her arms and leaned toward him.

"When did you become such a caveman?" she hissed quietly. Cleary, she did not want to be overheard.

Caveman? What the—

"You had no business coming down to the station and chewing me out in front of my coworkers!" she whisper-shouted. "Do you have any idea how hard it is to be the rookie? Not to mention a woman? And then some guy comes around and implies that I may have made my career decision based on some traumatic event? You undermined me in my first week on the job! What the hell is your problem? Why do you even care what I do for a living?"

Was she serious? He might be stern at times, but he wasn't a monster. But when he thought about it, he felt a pang of regret. Okay, reaming her out in front of the department had not been the best way to handle the situation. It was too late to change that, so he addressed her other accusation. "Why wouldn't I care? You're—" he lowered his voice "—running into fires. It's dangerous. I can't imagine why you would want to do such a thing."

"You don't have to imagine it." She stepped closer, and he took in her hair, matted to her forehead. She had changed into civilian clothes, with just a hint of her usual floral scent. "You can't just come down and yell at me. I'm fighting for respect, and you just put doubt in their heads," she continued in a stage whisper as she backed up, her breath coming heavy. She turned to go into her parents' house. "Thanks, Dhillon," she snapped, before slamming the door.

Dhillon stared at the door. No one infuriated him like Riya Desai.

She was going to be the death of him.

And he was completely in love with her.

four

RIYA

Riya watched from her parents' window as Dhillon left for his run, his form perfect. Long legs, even stride; he was broad and muscular, yet he ran with power and grace he didn't seem to be aware of.

The aroma of mustard seeds mixed with curry leaves and asafetida sizzling in hot oil drew her attention to the kitchen, where her mother was starting dinner. The spicy aroma and the sound of the seeds popping instantly took her back to her childhood. When she still had Samir. When her mother still knew she existed.

She shouldn't be watching Dhillon anyway. He was the single most infuriating person on the planet. She'd had a thing for him when they were teenagers, but that was a long time ago. She had tried to pursue him, but he had changed after the fire. Every time she thought she had successfully moved on from him, he inserted himself back into her thoughts. And right now, he was all she could think about.

She walked toward the kitchen, closing her eyes as she passed the garlanded picture of her brother hanging on the wall, opening them when she knew she'd passed it. "Hi, Mom." As long as Riya could remember, her mother kept her long hair in a braid straight down her back and wore a cotton salwar kameez when she cooked. The outfit brought back as many happy cooking memories as the food itself.

Her mother startled, her hand at her chest. "Array, Riya!" She turned. "Why are you sneaking up on people?"

"Good to see you, too, Mom." Riya sighed. "Sorry. Didn't mean to scare you."

Her mother shook her head. "No. It's fine. I was thinking something and did not hear you."

Riya kissed her mother's cheek. It was perfunctory. She rolled up her sleeves. "I can do the rotli, but I need a shower."

Her mother nodded. "Sure." She did a double take. "Why so sweaty?"

"Um…well, it's very hot, and we had a lot of outside calls today," she lied. Wasn't the first time she'd lied to her mom.

Her mother shrugged and went back to the shak. Riya quickly went upstairs and showered. She had kept some clothes at her parents' house for just this reason. She was back in the kitchen in twenty minutes, her wet hair braided to the side. It was great to finally feel clean.

Riya found the big bowl they used for making the dough for the rotli at the bottom of a stack of various-sized bowls. She put in the wheat flour, salt and a touch of oil and started to make the dough with warm water, mixing by hand. It really was the only way to know if the dough was being made correctly.

"What brings you by today?" Her mother's voice was guarded.

Riya frowned and shook her head. "Nothing, really. Just stopped in to check on you and Dad." And she needed to yell at Dhillon and find out if he was going to tell everyone where she was working.

"You were just here."

Riya widened her eyes. "I know. Can't a girl come see her parents?"

Her mother frowned and tasted the cooking vegetables. "Sure. But you don't."

Silence fell between them. It was true. She wanted to be there for them, especially as they got older—they were her parents, after all—and she was all that they had. She just couldn't live here anymore, so Riya stopped by once a week to check on them. However, she always managed to have an important errand to run or an appointment to get to, which more or less advertised that she stopped in on them out of a sense of duty.

A bark at the back door caught her attention. Her mother smiled and shook her head. "Someone is always looking for you."

That someone was Lucky. For as long as Dhillon had had Lucky, the dog had always come to Riya when she needed him. When they were kids, Dhillon and Riya had convinced their parents to install doggy doors. Then they trained Lucky to go back and forth between their houses. Lucky had always managed to show up at Riya's when she'd needed a friend. Especially after the fire.

"Lucky, come!" And sure enough, Lucky's collar jangled as he slid through the doggy door and trotted into the kitchen. That jangle alone lifted Riya's spirits and put a smile on her face. The total opposite of how Dhillon affected her. She was either going toe-to-toe with Dhillon or ignoring him completely. Neither was effective at tamping down her misplaced feelings for him.

She turned to find Lucky lying on the tile, clearly exhausted from the trip from Dhillon's. Riya ignored the pang in her heart as she realized how old Lucky was getting.

She washed her hands and got on the floor to cuddle him. "You always know when I need you, don't you, boy? Even now." He sniffed her thoroughly and whined. She laughed. "You still smell that little puppy on me?"

Oh, shit. She shouldn't have mentioned the little puppy. Maybe no one would notice.

"Hi, Radha Auntie!" Hetal walked in and hugged Riya's mother. "Oh, here he is." Hetal nodded at the dog.

"Hello, beta." Genuine affection filled the space between Hetal and Riya's mother. Riya hadn't seen her mother that relaxed in a while. "All ready for that exam?" Then she looked at Riya. "What little puppy?" Nothing wrong with her mother's hearing.

Riya waved a dismissive hand as Hetal picked a piece of potato out of the pot.

"I hope so," Hetal managed to answer, around the piece of hot potato.

"Don't pick." Riya's mother playfully smacked Hetal's hand. Hetal giggled.

They acted like mother and daughter. She might have been jealous, but it was a pang of regret that sparked in Riya. When was the last time her mother had been that relaxed around her? When was the last time Riya had really shared her life with her mother? *I should tell her.*

Riya hid her feelings by concentrating on Lucky. "It's good to see Lucky. I'll drop him off later." It was the way things were when Riya had lived at home. Lucky spent half his time with Riya. She missed him. And he clearly missed her.

Hetal nodded and said her goodbyes as she left.

"You know about Hetal's exam?" Riya vented the remaining steam from the pressure cooker before opening it and mashing up the cooked lentils in preparation for the dhal.

Her mother nodded, gave the potatoes one last stir. "She sometimes comes here, and we cook together." She pulled out a small frying pan for the vaghaar for the dhal. She poured in a few tablespoons of oil, and while it heated she gathered the mustard seeds, cinnamon stick and clove she would be tempering for the dhal.

Riya nodded. It had been her own decision to move out. She let her gaze wash over the kitchen. Everything was the same as it had always been, from the elaborate Ganesha clock her parents loved to the small Formica table pushed against the wall.

Her mom tossed the mustard seeds into the heated oil, and a satisfying sizzle emitted from the pan. The tantalizing aroma was always a comfort to Riya, reminding her of better times.

"Need me to grab the laundry?" Riya asked. The washer and dryer were in the basement, which meant that her mom or dad had to carry the laundry down two flights of stairs and then back up again.

"It's in the dryer. You can bring it up before you go," her mother said.

Sometimes, Riya could still smell the smoke or see the charred remains of the furniture after the fire had been doused. She closed her eyes against the memory, and Dhillon's angry face replaced it. She sighed and opened her eyes, forcing herself to focus on making the small balls that she would roll out for the rotli.

"Where's Dad?"

"He should be home shortly." Her mother's gaze landed on the clock. It was overly ornate, a wooden filigree piece painted gold, with a full-color painting of Ganesha in the center. The clock face was just above his ample belly, the face of the clock around the elephant-headed deity. The Remover of Obstacles. Since the fire, after losing Samir, every room in the house sported some form of this image. "Are you staying for dinner?"

"I have an early shift." Her reply was automatic.

Her mother's eyes clouded over for a second, but then she nodded.

"But I can stay to eat," Riya added. Guilt was a powerful motivator.

Her mother jerked her head up to look at Riya.

Riya widened her eyes as if she changed her mind all the time. "What?" *Tell her.* Dhillon's admonishment that she hadn't even told her parents weighed heavily on her. But what would she say? *"Mom, I'm a firefighter"*? If Dhillon's reaction was any indication, her parents would never understand that choice. As it was, they had a hard time understanding her decision to be a paramedic. *Why not just be a doctor?*

Every decision she made for her life just seemed to put another layer of space between her and her parents. The hardest was when she had moved out. It didn't matter that she had been twenty-eight. Tradition dictated that she live at home until she got married. *Why would you want to live alone? Even Dhillon is still at home.* The concept was as foreign to them as eating steak. Dhillon was still at home because he *wanted* to be. He wouldn't leave his family until he was sure they were okay. What *okay* looked like, only Dhillon knew.

Riya had moved out because she couldn't be in the house anymore. She would have left the minute she turned eighteen, but her parents had seemed so fragile she couldn't do it. She finally made the move two years ago when she realized that her presence wasn't really doing anything for her parents. At least, not that she could see. She had also started training for the academy at that time.

Now she found it hard to even have dinner here.

"Nothing," her mother managed. "Good." She smiled.

"Hello," her father called from the front door.

"Kitchen!" her mother responded. She had added the cinnamon and clove, and the kitchen smelled like comfort.

Slow, uneven footsteps as her father made his way to the kitchen. Slower than she remembered. It seemed to take forever for him to get to the kitchen. Riya looked at her mother, a question on her face.

Her mother shrugged but offered no information.

Riya glanced at the doorway as her father's steps got closer.

"Riya!" he boomed from the kitchen doorway. "I thought I saw the bike." Her father was taller than her, with a slight belly and thinning black hair. This was in contrast to her mother's shorter, slightly rounder stature, which made them look mismatched at times, when nothing could be further from the truth.

Riya noted but ignored her mother's tight mouth at mention of her motorcycle. Just another item on the never-ending list of things her mother did not understand about her.

He beamed at her and kissed her on the cheek while she rolled out the flatbread. "How's it running?" While her mother had never approved of what Riya was doing with her life, her father had simply changed his expectations. He didn't like that she rode the bike, moved out and worked all hours as a paramedic, but he accepted that his daughter was living her own life.

After Samir had died, her father had taught her all the things a father like him might have taught a son. How to change a tire, change the oil, mow the lawn. Riya wanted to believe that he would have taught her these things even if Samir had lived. She did know that during these teaching sessions, he was thinking about Samir, fulfilling some fatherly obligation, imparting his wisdom. It had to go somewhere. Why not to Riya? She had eaten up the attention and the knowledge. If nothing else, it now gave them a platform from which to start a conversation these days.

I really should tell them.

"It's fine, Papa." She smiled. He winked as he stole a hot, freshly buttered rotli from her stack.

"Go, change your clothes!" her mother reprimanded him as he bit into the bread.

"Delicious," he whispered to Riya as he approached his wife. "I'm going. After I eat this." He kissed his wife on the cheek, and she flushed despite herself. Riya watched this exchange, as she had many times before. Things had been rough after Samir died, but their love had remained ever strong. She should be so lucky. Her thoughts turned back to Dhillon. She sighed and pushed those thoughts away. No sense in going there.

Her father returned from changing his clothes and pulled out a bottle of her favorite red wine.

"You keep that here?" Riya asked, as she finished buttering the last rotli.

"Of course!" He opened it and poured three glasses.

"Helloo," a masculine voice called from the front.

Riya's heart instantly went into overdrive. As if it recognized Dhillon's voice before her brain did. She cursed her traitorous heart, quickly washing her hands and occupying herself with cleaning up. There was nothing as comforting as fresh, hot rotli, but making it made a huge mess, for which she was now grateful.

She glanced at Lucky, who looked at her like she was an idiot. She rolled her eyes at the dog. "He's come to get *you*," she explained. *Not to see me.* Lucky plopped his head back down onto his paws.

"In the kitchen!" Her father pulled out a fourth glass and poured wine into it.

Great, now he'd be having wine with them. Her stomach fluttered in a happy way she wished she could ignore.

Dhillon's footsteps were unhurried. Riya had her glass at her lips when he reached the kitchen. Damn. The man could fill a doorway. His head nearly grazed the top, and his broad shoulders leaned effortlessly against the frame as he folded his arms across his chest. He must have showered after the run, because his hair was wet and slicked back, and he wore loose basketball shorts and a fitted T-shirt.

Riya took a gulp of her wine.

"Hi, Karan Uncle. How's your leg?" He leaned over and kissed Riya's mother on the cheek. "Auntie." He greeted them comfortably and took the offered drink. "Started drinking without saying cheers, did you, Riya?" His voice took on the tone of irritation she'd become familiar with over the years. It was like he rehearsed it. "It's bad luck."

She grimaced and held her glass out, clinking it against the others. "Cheers." The word was deliberate, like a sassy teenager making a point.

This earned her a raised eyebrow over dark mocking eyes. *You're still mad?*

She gave a one-shouldered shrug, into which she tried to put the full force of her anger as well as the depth of his offense. *You were wrong.*

He sighed. It wasn't an apology, but she read the regret on his face. Her father was discussing his sister's upcoming visit in August. She lived in India, and the two of them hadn't seen each other in a few years. He was talking about all the places he wanted to take his big sister and all the things they wanted to do. His excitement was contagious, and Riya's mother was equally thrilled. Riya loved her foi very much and was excited to see her, but the timing of her visit put Riya on edge.

Her father's sister was coming for Rakshabandan, which was at the end of August this year. It made complete sense for brother and sister to be together for the holiday that celebrated the sibling bond, but as Riya no longer had a brother, she generally chose not to even acknowledge the day.

She felt Dhillon's gaze on her during this discussion but ignored it. She didn't trust herself to look at him with Samir's memory hanging between them.

Dhillon chatted amiably for the length of his glass of wine with her parents, which meant she did not have to interact with anyone. She was grateful, knowing he did it not to help her but because he genuinely cared for her parents. Just as she cared for his family. They'd been neighbors for close to twenty-five years, after all.

Her thoughts wandered to Rakshabandans past. When she and Samir celebrated. She remembered the first time she had actually made his rakhi.

She had been about seven. Her mother had got her some embroidery floss and taught her how to make a simple braid. She had practiced and practiced until she had made a rakhi she was proud of. It was blue and pink and she just knew her big brother would love it. She had helped her mother make some sweets, too. When the day arrived, Riya could barely contain herself. She couldn't wait to tie her rakhi. As per usual, they got together with the Vora family. That year, Auntie's brother, Hiral Uncle, had joined them, in addition to Rumit Mama, Riya's mother's brother.

She had already shown Dhillon her rakhi, and he had approved, saying it was awesome.

Hiral Uncle sat on the floor first, and Sarika Auntie tied his rakhi. Then she untied it because Hiral Uncle said it was too loose, so she tied again. They fed each other a small piece of peda, after which Hiral Uncle presented his sister with an envelope with cash as her gift.

Rumit Mama and Riya's mom had been next. They tried to stuff each other's mouths with as many sweets as possible, while everyone laughed around them. Rumit Mama gifted his sister a book she had been coveting.

Then it was Riya's turn. She had worn a beautiful blue-and-pink salwar kameez that Rumit Mama had brought for her. Samir was dressed in his cream-colored tunic and matching pants.

They sat on the floor, legs folded, across from each other. They blessed each other. Then Riya pulled out her homemade rakhi to tie on Samir's wrist. It was entirely too long. Her face fell.

"That's okay, Riya," her brother had said. "Just wrap it around a couple times."

She wrapped it around twice, and it fit perfectly. She chanted the prayer that wished him a long and happy life and tied the rakhi tight. She beamed as they fed each other sweets. Samir hugged her and presented her with a gift, a stuffed elephant toy. It was soft and fuzzy, and Riya slept with that toy for years. It had been a perfect Rakshabandan.

Some days later, her mother was called into Samir's school. Riya had to go with her. When they got there, Samir had a bloody nose.

"What happened?" asked their mother as she approached him outside the principal's office.

"This kid was bugging me about my rakhi. Making fun of it." Samir sounded angry. "He pushed me when I told him to shut up about it. So I punched him." Samir grinned. He caught Riya's eye and winked.

"Samir." Their mother had not been impressed. "Hitting is not the solution."

Both boys were given detention, and they had come home after meeting with the principal. Their father had pressed his lips together when he heard the story and saw his son's injury.

"Tell him, Karan. Tell your son violence is not the way." Riya's mother was beside herself.

"It is not the first choice of action." Their father had turned to Samir. *"And I do not advocate hitting. But sometimes it becomes necessary to defend yourself."* He had given Samir a small smile and dismissed him to his room.

Young Riya had knocked on his door, mortified that her gift to him had resulted in this. *"Bhaiya,"* she started when he opened the door, *"I'm sorry—"*

"Don't be sorry. It wasn't you. It was him. He's just…" Samir had looked at her and shaken his head. *"Never mind. He deserved it, trust me. And I love my rakhi, okay?"*

Riya had nodded, relieved. Samir eyed her. *"Do you know how to throw a punch?"*

She had shaken her head. Of course not.

"Well, it's time to learn." Samir nodded at her. *"Okay?"*

"Okay," she replied.

"Make a fist."

Riya sipped her wine and grinned. Samir hadn't even really got into trouble beyond being sent to his room. And he had taught her how to throw a proper punch. A skill she used often.

Dhillon narrowed his eyes at her, one eyebrow raised. She shrugged. Let him wonder what the smirk was about.

"How's your mother?" Riya's mom was asking Dhillon. "I haven't seen her in a few days."

"She's at work."

Riya's mother narrowed her eyes at Dhillon. "And?"

"And nothing, Radha Auntie."

Her mother stared at him, her lips pursed. "Dhillon, beta. Don't even try. What are you hiding?"

Riya glanced at her mother. She had lied to her not thirty minutes ago, and her mother suspected nothing. Dhillon made a little face, and she knew he was keeping something from her. Riya's heart ached a bit that her mother didn't even know when she was being lied to by her own daughter.

Dhillon sighed and shook his head. "And…she's on another shaadi.com date."

"That's wonderful," Riya's mother said and smiled.

"Your mom's dating?" Riya said at the same time.

Dhillon shrugged at them both, raising his eyebrows in a what-can-I-do? gesture.

Riya's eyes bugged out. Good for Sarika Auntie.

"Dhillon Vora," her mom said, "your mother is barely fifty-five years old. She deserves to have a life outside you children." She turned back to the stove to stir the dhal.

It amused Riya that her mother referred to a thirty-year-old man and his twenty-year-old sister as *children*.

"Of course she does, Auntie. It's just—"

"Just what?" She pointed her spice-covered spoon at him.

Dhillon eyed the spoon and took a small step back. "She could get hurt."

Riya's mom waved the spoon at him and shook her head like Dhillon was five years old. "Of course she could. But she could also find someone who adds to her happiness."

Dhillon nodded politely, but everyone in the room knew he didn't believe that for a second. "Also, Hiral Mama sent her an upsetting text about it."

"Well," Riya's father chimed in, "Hiral has always been a bit extra conservative, not to mention he's always concerned about what everyone at the mandir will say. All the more reason she needs your support." He raised his eyebrows pointedly at Dhillon to drive his point home.

"Okay. I got it, Uncle." Dhillon grinned at him, rolling his eyes slightly. Like a son.

Dhillon finished his wine, giving his empty glass a quick

rinse before placing it in the sink. "I'd better get going." He looked at her parents. "My turn to make rotli."

Riya saw him do a double take at her neat pile of rotli before meeting her eyes. They had both learned how to make rotli together. Right here, in fact. He had asked her mother to teach him so he could surprise his parents. Riya broke his gaze, unable to look at him and think about happy times before the fire.

"Lucky, come," Dhillon said as he stepped out of the kitchen.

Lucky lifted his head but stayed put and raised one eye at Riya. She smiled and shook her head. "I'll bring him over. You know how he is."

Dhillon simply nodded.

"Come, Lucky," Riya called as she left the kitchen. Lucky followed, and Dhillon brought up the rear. The sun was just getting ready to set, and the sky was a summer shade of violet. The heat from the sun was gone, but the air was as sticky as ever. They walked single file like this all the way to Dhillon's door. Neither of them spoke as Dhillon moved in front of her to enter his house. Why did he smell so good? More to the point, why did she keep noticing?

Before he went in, Riya needed to know if Dhillon was going to tell everyone about her job. "Dhillon," she said to his back.

He turned to face her. Suddenly, he smiled a bit. His teeth were slightly crooked, but only if you studied them, and—sadly—she had. But he had the perfect mouth, and when he stretched it into a rare smile, it was breathtaking, refreshing to see. "Do you remember when you broke your arm?"

Riya smirked. "Which time?"

"The time when you just *had* to get that cat out of the tree and you fell?" His tone was a mix of pride and frustration.

"My sister thought you were freaking amazing. I heard about your heroism for weeks!"

She wrinkled her nose in a grimace. "It was the worst. I couldn't ride my bike for, like, six weeks."

"Remember what you did as soon as the cast came off?" His smile widened.

Riya giggled. It was an almost foreign sensation as it rose from deep inside her. She had forgotten about the incident until he mentioned it. "I got back on my bike the minute I got home from the doctor."

"She had specifically told you not to do that. To let it keep healing."

Riya put her fingers to her lips in an attempt to hide her guilty smile. "But I had been off it for *six weeks*."

"You fell off within minutes. And rebroke that arm." He chuckled.

Now Riya laughed out loud, wincing at the memory. "That hurt so bad. You helped me up and took me right to my parents." She recalled the pain vividly. But more than that, she recalled being petrified that her parents would be mad that she had so blatantly ignored the doctor's orders. She stopped laughing and focused her gaze on Dhillon. "You told them I had tripped over a toy your sister had left out. You lied."

"I didn't want you to get in trouble." The laughter was gone from him. Even in the waning light, she could see the intensity of his gaze. "I didn't tell then. And I won't tell now." He paused. "I'm not sorry I yelled at you. But I am sorry I yelled at you in front of your team."

Riya relaxed. "Thanks." He was still her secret keeper. Even though they never traded secrets anymore. Something soft and familiar passed between them.

Dhillon spoke into the silence, his voice an intimate whisper. "Lucky always needed you to walk him home."

Riya warmed at the memory. They had no idea when that had started, but one day they realized that Lucky would only leave Riya's house if she walked him over. She ruffled the fur on his head and bent down to hug him. "He's getting old."

"I know."

Remnants of her anger with Dhillon dissipated into the night. Sometimes she was just angry with him out of habit. She also remembered that the cat she had pulled from the tree had been injured. It had been Dhillon who had treated the injury and found the cat's owner.

She looked up at Dhillon and found him intently watching her and Lucky. His shoulders sagged, his arms hung limp by his sides, he bit his bottom lip, and his eyes had almost no fight in them.

"He'll be all right, Dhillon. Lucky's too stubborn to die."

"You know you're lying to us both?" His voice was low and soft, dreading the inevitable.

She nodded, unable to speak.

Dhillon opened the door and entered the house, Lucky close behind.

five

DHILLON

"Sit." Dhillon reached into the pocket of his scrubs, pulled out a small cracker and placed it in front of the dog's snout. "Good girl!" The German shepherd–husky mix crunched up the biscuit with a wag of his tail and looked to Dhillon for another.

"That's enough, now, Hobbes." His owner, a college kid, tugged at the leash. "Time to go." With a small whine of protest, the dog walked over to his owner and waited. "Thanks, Doc," the kid said. "See you next time."

"Take care." Dhillon waved him out and then headed to his office in the back to work on charts. His desk was nothing more than an eight-foot fold-up table. He didn't need more than that, he told himself, just a place to put his computer and a picture. There were no paper files anymore, and buying a real desk was not a priority right now.

The photo was of him, his mom and his dad. It was from before Hetal was born. It was Dhillon's first ski trip—actually, it was everyone's first ski trip. His mom and dad had had their first ski lesson right along with Dhillon. Dhillon had loved that day, watching his dad learn to ski, so they could do it together.

He was well into his charts when Shelly poked her head in his office, her short blond curls bouncing. "Good night, Doc. You should go home. Been a long day." She yawned.

"Thanks, but I have to finish these charts before I head over to the soccer field." He glanced at the time on his screen. "I have an hour." He tapped a few keys and looked at her. "And you know you don't have to call me Doc when the patients are gone."

Shelly had been the one who trained Dhillon in all the operations of the office when he worked the desk after school as a teenager, and she'd been thrilled to stay on when he came back from school and bought the practice. She knew how to run the day-to-day, and Dhillon found her invaluable to his team. Not to mention that she was amazing with the animals.

She shook her head and leaned against the door frame, her petite body barely filling the space. "Whatever you say, Doc."

Dhillon grinned. "I do want to have a meeting about how we can improve the flow of the office without doing a major overhaul."

"You want to modernize? About time. Let's do it!" Shelly's blue eyes lit up, and she started pacing, talking about a new office she had seen that had all the bells and whistles and—

"Shelly. Just baby steps. I don't have the money for an entire redo."

Shelly froze midstep. "Take out a loan."

"Not right now." Dhillon shook his head. "Hetal is still in college. I still have a loan on this place."

Shelly deflated. "Okay. You're the boss. But I do think it's high time you found yourself a nice girl and settled down." She eyed him, as if appraising him. "You're handsome, but you're not getting any younger."

Dhillon grimaced at her and turned back to his computer. "You know, I have a mother at home."

"Clearly you need a mom here, too. You can't live alone forever."

"I'm not alone. I have my family. I have my practice. I have you." His life was full. He loved his work, and he had people he cared about. Riya popped into his head.

"It doesn't have to be Riya." Shelly sighed.

"Good night, Shelly."

Shelly turned, saying goodbye to Hetal, and left on another sigh, her sneakers gently squeaking on the tiled floor.

Hetal came into his office, removed her lab coat and sat down across from him. She said nothing. Just watched him, her dark eyes fixed on him, her mouth set in a line. The last time she had done this was to tell him their mother had opened a profile for herself on shaadi.com.

He continued his charts for a few more minutes until he could no longer ignore his sister's eyes boring into him. Defeated by her silent insistence, he sighed and turned away from his monitor. The lights flickered. "Is Mom getting married?"

"What? No. That last guy turned out to be married. Mom called his wife." She pursed her lips and dipped her chin before breaking out into a huge smile that was almost the exact replica of their father's, except that Hetal had perfectly straight teeth. Dhillon's heart ached with a sad happiness he could never really put into words.

"The lawyer? Huh." Dhillon allowed himself a moment of

pride for his mother as well. Do not cross Sarika Vora. "Okay, Mom's not getting married. So why the stare-down?" He glanced at the monitor.

"You work too hard." Her ponytail bounced, adding emphasis to her statement.

"That's not a thing." He tapped away for a minute, adding notes to a chart.

"Yes, it is. You should at least take a break, go out, have some fun. Call Ryan. Or better yet, go out on a date." Her voice rose in pitch.

"Stop talking to Shelly." Dhillon pursed his lips and pointedly maneuvered his screen between them. If she wanted to talk dating, she could talk to herself. He didn't have time for that right now. He had a business to run, patients to see, debt to manage.

"I made a profile for you." She bit her bottom lip.

He narrowed his eyes at her over the screen.

She let it sink in for a moment. "I haven't posted it or anything. It's just ready for when you are. Mom approved. And Shelly."

"You're going to put me on shaadi.com? Where Mom goes?" He shuddered. *Eww.* But at least Hetal seemed to have dropped the Riya idea.

"So what? We know your type."

"You know nothing about my *type*." But he did. She was about five-six, with luxurious long dark hair and dark brown eyes that could pin you to a wall. She was strong, inside and out, but good luck breaking that barrier. He'd almost broken through once. But that was a long time ago, and when he messed things up, Riya had put that wall up fast and strong. He went back to his electronic medical records, or EMRs, as they called them in the office.

"I'm just saying it's been, like, three years since…you know…

the *breakup*." She used air quotes. "And, yes, you have a type. It's the opposite of Sharmila." She rolled her eyes as she said his ex-girlfriend's name. "But a lot like Riya Didi."

He'd almost been engaged. Just as he was making plans to buy a ring and pop the question, Sharmila had dumped him. Something about him being too serious. He didn't really understand it, but he wasn't as torn up about it as one might have thought. If he remembered correctly, his sister had never really cared for her, either. That should have been a red flag. Even now, he had no feelings about their breakup either way.

"If you want to talk about my social life, call Ryan. He's trying to set me up, too. You can all have a blast while I work and don't go out," he grumbled. Though there was a small part of him that thought he should at least consider it. Pining away for Riya Desai was no way to live life.

Riya had moved in next door when they were both five. Being a boy, Dhillon had been drawn to playing with Samir, who, at the ripe age of ten, was the coolest boy Dhillon had ever met. Samir, while a doting brother, wasn't going to spend all his time with five-year-olds.

Riya, meanwhile, had been content to play by herself. Her imagination was vivid, and she was fearless. When Dhillon joined her to play, she accepted him without question, and Dhillon's little five-year-old heart warmed to her instant acceptance. They took Samir's scooter and pretended they were in space. They went to the playground across the street (where Samir was supposed to watch them) and jumped off the swings, pretending they could fly.

As an only child at the time, Dhillon relished having playmates and was in awe of the bond that Samir and Riya clearly shared. Both Riya's and Dhillon's extended families were still living in India at the time, so the Voras and the Desais did what immigrant families did: they made their own extended families. They looked out for one another, shared meals and childcare, among many other things. They also got together for all the holidays: Diwali, Thanksgiving, Christmas, Rakshabandan.

The last one was always a bit awkward for Dhillon, as his sister wasn't born until he was ten. The Rakshabandan when he and Riya were nine was probably the weirdest.

"Riya," Radha Auntie had said gently, her eyes flicking to Dhillon, "why don't you tie a rakhi on Dhillon?"

Panic had flushed through Dhillon because even at the age of nine, he had known that Riya was most definitely not like a sister to him at all.

Riya had coolly passed her gaze over Dhillon, then turned to her mother. "Mom," she had stated with the patience and attitude of someone who was explaining something to a toddler, "Dhillon is not my brother. He's my best friend. Samir is my brother."

Young Dhillon had sighed in relief.

"Maybe I will call Ryan." Hetal's response pulled him back to earth. She was undeterred. All Voras were like this. Stubborn and focused.

A few more minutes into his EMRs and Hetal was still sitting there, her fingers tapping on his makeshift desk, still biting her bottom lip. Okay…so she didn't want to talk about his social life. He moved the monitor away again and faced her.

"What's up, little sister?"

She sat up straighter and placed her hands on the table. "Don't get mad." She reminded him of when she was little and had got caught doing something she shouldn't have been doing.

"Okay. I won't get mad." Experience had taught him that he needed to keep his voice even. Much like dealing with a scared animal.

"Promise?"

"Hetal, what's going on? Are you pregnant or something?"

She screwed up her face. "No, Bhaiya. I'm completely capable of not getting pregnant."

Dhillon squeezed his eyes closed and squirmed in his seat. His sister's sex life was not something he cared to think about. "Then what? Spit it out."

She widened her eyes. "I'm not sure…I want to be a vet."

Dhillon stared at her. She'd wanted nothing more than to be a vet for as long as he could remember. He pushed aside the blip of disappointment that popped up. This was not about him; it was about his sister and her future. "Okay, so what do you want to do? You're a sophomore. You still have time to check things out."

"You're not mad?" She seemed surprised.

"No, I'm not mad." He smiled. "But you need another plan."

Hetal's face brightened, and she became animated again. "Well, I still might want to be a vet. I mean, I love the animals, and I love working here… It's just… I'm not sure. A lot of my friends are clear on wanting to go to med school or grad school or whatever. I'm not sure I have that clarity, you know?"

"Don't worry about everyone else. They have their doubts, too. Trust me." He leaned toward his sister. "If you want to investigate and find what excites you, you do that."

She nodded, a small smile on her face.

"What do you want me to do?" he asked.

"Not be mad."

"Listen, it was your idea to be a vet. I never told you that you had to. It's your life."

"You're not disappointed?"

He grinned at her. Their age gap, and losing their father, meant Dhillon trod the line between father figure and brother, and the lines were always blurry. "Of course not." He walked around his desk and hugged her. "Do you know how hard I had to work to get my degree? The loans I took out to buy this place? Being a veterinarian, having this practice—that has been my dream for as long as I can remember. I'm living my dream. There's nothing else I'd rather be doing." Except gutting this space and putting in place more efficiency and modernization. "But it's *my* dream. It doesn't have to be yours. Do what makes you happy. Do what calls to you. Everything else will fall into place." He lowered his voice. "That's what Dad told me."

She smiled, relief brightening her face. "Thanks, Bhaiya. You're the best." She paused. "At least if I become a vet, I know I have a job here."

Dhillon walked back around to the monitor, out of her range. He shrugged, his eyebrows raised, his mouth in an exaggerated frown. "That depends on how good you are."

"I'm your sister!"

"Whatever. I only hire the best." He put up his arms in defense of the smack that he knew was coming his way.

Instead, a smirk crossed her face. "Let's talk about getting you a girlfriend."

He would have preferred the smack.

six

RIYA

Riya was jolted to her feet by the station alarm. Even after a month of this, her adrenaline pumped, pounding blood to where she needed it, and she thrilled at the excitement. She was up to doing twenty-four-hour shifts now, and she slept in the dorm with the rest of the guys on shift. The dorm had twin beds lined up side by side with half walls in between each to separate them, which gave her a modicum of privacy. The team pretty much slept dressed in case of a call, and the increased time at the station was letting her get to know her colleagues better.

Marcus Evans was the reason the station kept getting asked to do a firefighter-themed calendar. With flawless dark skin, hazel eyes and a smile that radiated joy, it was no wonder he was the station's charmer. It turned out that Evans was also quite the carpenter. He had built many of the shelves and cabinets at the station. They were sturdy and beautiful, with intricate carvings to accent them. If anything needed to be built, he was the guy. He also had a brother who was a firefighter in another house. Schultz was the firehouse mechanic, and he knew everything about the rigs since he was the engine driver as well. Schultz could also bake like a boss, so the house frequently smelled of homemade cinnamon rolls, which Riya found herself indulging in more often than not. Alejandro "Do Not Call Me Alex" Alvarez, with his dark curly hair and creamy brown skin, towered over them all. His six-foot-five frame and semiperpetual scowl could be intimidating to anyone. But Riya was getting to know that scowl was just a show. He was known to pull out his guitar and play in between calls and was also in a band that played each week at a bar in Baltimore that Riya used to frequent with her paramedic friends. And when he sang, his face lit up, and there was no sign of the tough guy. He was also their resident electrician and plumber.

Ambrose, their lieutenant, came from a family of firefighters and had hit the academy as soon as he was legally able. He was the only one who did not seem to have some sort of hobby. He wasn't often in the common room, but when he was, he was quiet or watching sports with everyone else. He didn't say much during their off time, but it was clear that everyone respected him and deferred to his rank and experience, regardless of his youth.

They ate their meals together, family style, and it was at these meals that she saw her tough lieutenant relax, even crack a small smile. Riya's contribution to this family was that she was an excellent cook. And not just of Indian food, which seemed to be a hit, but of all her food.

She'd started cooking in earnest after Samir had died, when her mother was too grief-stricken to do so. At first, she resented it, like many things during that time, but she quickly found it soothing. She would lose herself in the way the flavors blended together, in how her rotli would turn out depending on how much she had kneaded the dough or in how the dhal would change depending on how long she boiled it. She fed her parents, but soon that became her only connection to them as she started sneaking out of the house at night to meet new friends she knew her parents would not approve of. She smoked and drank and met up with boys. Her parents would have been horrified had they known. But they hadn't. And they didn't ever seem to make an effort to find out what she had been up to.

Only two people knew what she was up to. One was Dhillon. She knew this only because she'd seen the light on in his room and him peeking out as she sneaked out the back door, but he never told on her. The other was her cousin Roshni. And she only knew because she sometimes tagged along.

Roshni was Riya's mother's sister's daughter and the closest thing to a sister Riya had ever had. Born only nine months apart, they did almost everything together. So on the nights that Roshni spent with Riya, they sneaked out and headed for the tree house. Riya appreciated the company, but the tree house was never as much fun as when Dhillon was there.

All the firefighters took turns making food, but cooking was her thing. She had most recently made kati rolls, a kind of Indian street food that resembled a burrito, and the guys were still talking about it.

With the blare of the alarm, the whole team was on their feet. Riya controlled her breathing and focused completely on gathering her gear and making her way to the engine. The department was organized chaos as everyone readied themselves, only taking seconds to do so. In less than four minutes, they were on their way, sirens wailing.

Details of the fire came through the comm, and Riya quickly understood that this fire was bigger than the ones she had fought so far. This was her chance to prove that she could do the job as well as any of the guys. As the dispatcher spoke, her lieutenant evaluated her with unabashed judgment. Adrenaline continued to pump through her body, and she swallowed hard and masked her face. Lieutenant or not, she was not going to let him intimidate her. She belonged here, and she knew it, heart and soul.

She smelled the smoke before she saw it. Upon arrival, sure enough, thick smoke billowed into the already-humid July air. She and her colleagues immediately got to work. Their captain, a tall, solidly built man in his forties, called out orders, and they rushed to fulfill them. Riya was assigned to the hose alongside Ambrose and Evans. She fastened her oxygen tank to her back and tightened the straps of her self-contained breathing apparatus, or SCBA, and helmet. They entered the smoke-filled building and began dousing flames. Riya, as the rookie, walked behind the other two and fed them hose. They moved as a unit, attacking the flames. Sweat immediately soaked her through, dripping into her eyes. She blinked to remove the sting. Their efforts were working, but the flames were still eating away at the building when Riya heard a voice from inside.

She turned to the man closest to her. "Lieutenant, did you hear that?"

"Hear what?" Ambrose concentrated his attention on the hose.

"It...sounds like someone calling for help. Over on the other side." She indicated with her head where she had heard the voice come from. "We should go."

Ambrose spared her a glance. "You can't go alone. We need you here to feed the hose. Hang on. I'll grab someone." He spoke into his radio. "Requesting assistance. Need someone to hold the line—"

"Sir—" Riya started.

"Desai! Stay put," he ordered. She heard him mumble. "Last thing I need is to have to go in after a rookie."

Riya heard the cry for help again. "Well, fuck that." Without waiting for a response, Riya dropped the line and bolted for the other side of the house. This was what it meant to be a firefighter. Saving lives, not protecting fragile male egos.

She wasn't going to let someone die because she was following protocol. The heat hit her like a wall: it was incredible she didn't melt right there. The thick smoke slowed her down, impeding her vision. She moved toward the sound, calling out as best she could. Ambrose came up behind her. "Desai! We have to work as a team."

She heard the scream again. She ignored whatever Ambrose was trying to say and called out to the voice. "Hello! Hello!"

"Over here," someone said roughly.

Riya followed the sound of coughing and found a young girl, maybe twelve years old, sitting in a corner. "I'm coming." The girl was shaking and crying. "It's okay." Riya was able to skirt the closest flames and reach the girl. She gently pushed the girl's head down close to the ground to help her breathe. "Can you walk?"

The girl shook her head, fresh tears filling her eyes, as she indicated her foot. "It hurts."

Riya swept her gaze over the injury. The girl's foot was at an odd angle. Didn't need a paramedic to diagnose that. "What's your name?"

"Christi." Bright blue eyes shone from her grimy face.

"Okay, Christi. I'm going to pick you up, all right?"

Christi nodded, clearly holding back a sob.

Riya picked her up like a baby. "Put your arms around my neck."

The girl did as Riya asked but paused to look at her first. "You're a girl."

"Mmm-hmm." Riya focused on finding the safest route out for them.

"Cool." Christi buried her face in Riya's shoulder as Riya ran.

The fire roared around her, and she focused on getting out, wondering for just a second where Ambrose had gone. She looked around, just as a loud crack split the air and a beam fell in front of her, just missing them. Christi shrieked. Riya's heart pounded way too fast. Her head was light, and her vision blurred in and out as nausea gripped her. Determined, she took a step, but the ground felt unsteady, and she faltered. A strong hand caught her, and she looked up to see Lieutenant Ambrose at her side.

"Come on, Desai," he grunted and took Christi from her. "Before you pass out."

"I got this." Her feeble protest barely made it past her mask, and she was unable to hold on to the child anymore. She forced herself to follow Ambrose out of the house, barely able to stand.

The three of them navigated the fire and made it out. Riya made it as far as the hose before collapsing to the ground. She ripped off her SCBA and welcomed the humid air into her lungs.

She was fine. Ambrose had been out of line.

A paramedic approached her and began assessing her, though she attempted to brush them off. Ambrose stood with Christi, a paramedic assisting the little girl. Once she could breathe, Riya laid into him.

"I was fine. You did not need to come after me. Just because I'm a woman." She coughed.

"I came in after you because we don't go anywhere in a fire alone. You know the rules. Two in, two out." Two firefighters in the danger zone, in touch with two firefighters outside the zone at all times. The lieutenant grunted at her. "And you're a rookie."

"I was fine." She coughed and cursed her body for betraying her.

Ambrose spoke plainly. "You were not. You didn't see that beam coming. You could have hurt her as well as yourself."

"I heard you, *Lieutenant*." Damn the extra rasp in her voice from the smoke. Wasn't the SCBA supposed to prevent that? She narrowed her eyes at him and brought herself up to her full height. "I heard you mumble to someone you didn't want to have to come in after me."

Ambrose gave her a withering stare. "I'm not going to apologize for that. If you can't follow orders, you're a liability. Not to mention you lack experience."

"I can do the job as well as any of you." That beam could have fallen in front of anyone. *Right?*

"Not from what I saw today." Ambrose walked away.

"Fire's still live. Anyone want to fight it?" the captain's deep voice growled from behind her, and her stomach clenched. *Fuck. How much did he hear?*

She spun around. "Captain Davis, sir, I…"

He turned to go but pivoted back. "I'll be seeing both of you in my office after this is over. Desai, feed hose to Evans. Ambrose, go help Walsh."

Chastened, Riya scattered to the hose to do her job. Evans glanced at her, dark eyes piercing her with disapproval. "Get your gear back on, and let's get to it."

★ ★ ★

At the station, Riya attended to her duties as usual, but her stomach roiled. Scout followed her around, looking adorable and snuggling her while she tried to do her postfire tasks. Even the scent of Schultz's homemade cinnamon rolls wasn't enough to settle her stomach. It was only a matter of time until—

"Desai!" Captain Davis bellowed. "Hand off the dog, and meet me in my office."

"Yes, sir." She handed Scout to Evans as he passed her on his way out of the captain's office.

Ambrose followed her. She turned to glare at him.

"What the hell is going on here?" Captain Davis demanded. More than a few gray hairs poked through the black, speaking to years in the trenches, fighting fires. His deep-set, dark brown eyes were dead serious, and right now they were fixed on her.

She and Ambrose remained silent.

"Someone better speak," the captain grumbled.

"Desai heard a scream from the opposite side of the building from where we were. She wanted to go in and investigate. I asked her to wait so we wouldn't leave Evans alone on the line. She proceeded without me."

"Of course I did. Someone screamed for help! We didn't have time to get *coverage!*" She appealed to her captain, death stare be damned. "Captain, sir, he literally said he did not want to have to come after me. He thinks I can't do the job. I need to be able to have opportunity if I'm to show what I can do."

The captain shook his head and looked from one to the other. "Desai, you do know we have a protocol? No one— male or female—goes into a rescue situation alone." He arched an eyebrow at her. "Particularly a rookie."

"Yes, sir."

"That protocol applies to you and to Ambrose, here, equally." He turned to Ambrose. "Do you have an issue with Desai being a woman?"

"No, sir. I do not."

"He absolutely does have a problem with me, sir." Riya spoke up.

Ambrose inhaled and fixed Riya in his ice-blue glare. "I have a *problem* with a firefighter who has a chip on their shoulder. Desai has one the size of a boulder."

Well, the good lieutenant would, too, if he had to prove himself every minute of every single shift just because of his gender.

Captain Davis turned to Riya, eyebrows raised. "Is this true?"

She met her captain's gaze. No good would come from complaining about it; besides, she could handle these guys. Her words were icy. "I'm fine."

The captain stared her down for a moment, and she matched his glare. He turned his gaze to Ambrose. After a moment, the man stood. Easily six feet tall, over two hundred pounds of muscle, he was an intimidating figure.

He managed to seem like he was looking down at both of them, even though Ambrose was the same height. He turned first to his lieutenant. "Everyone in this department went to the academy, had the same training." He waited until Ambrose nodded acknowledgment.

He turned to Riya. "Everyone in this department works as a team. We have a hierarchy, and I need my people to follow orders. If that falls apart, I have chaos. And chaos does not put out fires. Or save people." He waited until Riya nodded that she understood.

"I'm watching you both. Go. Play nice. Dismissed." He

waved a hand at them, as if they were his children having a squabble.

Yeah, right. As if any of the men here would ever see her as an equal.

Riya left the office and rounded on Ambrose the instant the door shut. "You think I have a chip on my shoulder? You're damn right I do. I'm a woman in a male-dominated field. I have to be twice as good to prove I belong here, even though I graduated at the top of my class. Not to mention the asshole that constantly leers at me. You're going to have to come to terms with the fact that I'm staying."

Ambrose just stared down at her, anger flickering in his blue eyes for a moment. "You just have to learn to be a team player. We're brothers here. That makes you a sister. We're a family. We work together, have each other's backs. You're not a team player, Desai. That's the real problem here. And just so we're clear, every rookie here has had to prove themselves. Every. Single. One. Me included." He paused for breath. "And who the fuck is leering at you?"

"I can take care of myself." Riya narrowed her eyes to hide the tears that burned behind them at the word *sister*. "And I'm nobody's sister anymore."

"Desai, whoever is leering at you," he said as his hands fisted at his sides, "sexual harassment is grounds for dismissal." He pointed firmly to the ground they stood on. "We are a team. And that kind of behavior has no place on my team." He leaned in closer, and Riya caught a flicker of concern in his face. "Who?"

Riya opened her mouth to retort, but she caught sight of Dhillon.

What the hell was he doing here—*again*?

seven

RIYA

Scout was nestled contentedly in Dhillon's arms, but his body was stiff, and a thin sheen of perspiration covered his face as he tried to keep himself together in a place associated with loss and fear.

All her anger at Ambrose melted away and refocused on Dhillon.

"What the hell are you doing here? Come to yell at me again?" She headed for the locker room to grab her stuff, Dhillon trailing behind her. She was ridiculously aware of his presence in a way she wasn't of anyone else's.

"No. I'm not here to yell. Riya—"

She stopped at the entrance of the locker room and called out, "It's Desai. Everybody decent?"

A chorus of *yes*es reached her.

She entered, Dhillon still behind her. The guys were in various stages of undress, but everyone was indeed decent... except Walsh. Ian Walsh was walking around stark naked.

Dhillon growled low next to her and took a few steps in the naked guy's direction, his free hand fisted by his side. Scout wiggled as he clutched her closer. Riya reached out and pulled him back. He looked at her, and Riya's breath caught.

A vein throbbed at his temple, his jaw clenched under his beard, and a red flush burned under his brown skin. What stopped her was the hard coal-black of his eyes. Gentle, steady Dhillon was ready to do some serious violence to this man.

"Jeez, Walsh. I asked if everyone was decent." Riya had averted her eyes for her own preservation. She didn't want to think about this guy naked every time she saw him. Though, clearly, that was what he wanted. She fought to keep her voice steady. She wasn't about to let him get to her.

Dhillon did not stand next to her, but at her silent request, he did not advance, either. He simply stood a step in front of her. A shield, should she need it.

"I'm decent. This is how I walk around at home." He grinned.

Anger and defiance raged inside her, but she wouldn't give him the satisfaction of letting him see that. "Well, I feel sorry for your girlfriend, because that—" she turned toward him and ran her eyes down his body, a mild scowl on her face "—is a *chota lund*." Dhillon let out a small groan only she could hear.

"English, Desai." Walsh's eyes darkened in anger.

She widened her eyes, all innocence. "Oh, sorry. Translation, *small penis*."

A low chorus of *oooh*s went around the locker room, and she heard Dhillon suppress a laugh.

Walsh's face darkened. "You little—"

"Exactly," she quipped, and the other guys burst into laughter and went about their business. Walsh headed for the showers.

Her heart raced from the confrontation, but she had more important things at hand. She turned back to Dhillon and the emergency that had brought him here. "Why are you here?"

He was still staring at Walsh, passing an angry gaze over the whole locker room. He turned to focus on her. "Your mom had a heart attack." Scout wiggled again, and Dhillon glanced at her, as if only just now noticing that he was holding her. "Oh, sorry, girl," he murmured and let her down. She stayed at his feet.

"What?" Riya's heart thudded against her chest, and she froze in the middle of taking off her suspenders. Her turnout pants dropped, leaving her in leggings. Her stomach turned. Dhillon was braving the firehouse because something awful had happened. She should have expected it; Dhillon wouldn't come in here for anything less. She shoved what she could into her locker and grabbed her bag without changing clothes.

Dhillon brought his attention back to Riya. "Is this the shit you deal with from these guys?"

"Not all the guys. Just him." Riya tried to sound matter-of-fact, but the reality was that sexual harassment of any kind was not matter-of-fact. "Other guys," she mumbled, "have other issues."

"You should report that one. He's trouble."

Maybe she should. But she was new, she was the only woman. She'd deal. "I handled him just fine, don't you think? Even taught him a couple new words."

A smile flickered at the edges of his lips, and Riya knew she'd impressed him. He shook his head, raking his gaze over her, and she was suddenly conscious of how fitted her clothes were. She opened her mouth to explain when Dhillon spoke again.

"Shoes."

"What?"

He looked at her face. "You need shoes."

"Your mom's in the hospital?" Schultz approached, as she opened her locker and grabbed her sneakers.

There really was not much privacy.

Dhillon answered. "Yes."

Schultz's face filled with concern. "Jeez. Go ahead, Desai. We'll get the rig. I'll tell Ambrose. Shift's about over anyway."

Her heart filled with gratitude for him, and she slipped on her sneakers and grabbed her backpack. "Thanks."

"Come on. I'll fill you in while we drive." Dhillon was already on his way out. He was in a black T-shirt that fit tight around his back and very defined biceps. He must be doing more than just running.

Riya followed close behind. "I have my bike."

As soon as they exited the firehouse, Dhillon's body relaxed, and he inhaled deeply, as if there hadn't been any oxygen inside the building. His voice no longer held anger and irritation but warmth and caring. "Come with me." He took her hand, and against her will, Riya relaxed into its strength.

Blood drained from her head, and she was uncharacteristically light-headed as she squeezed his hand. Odd. Being a paramedic, she was used to dealing with this kind of thing.

As if reading her mind, he said, "It's different when it's your mom, Riya." He tugged on her hand to get her moving. She nodded and followed.

"I'm taking water out of your vet-to-go bag," she told him as she dug through the bag and found a water bottle.

"No problem. Just be careful," Dhillon said, wincing, "of all the meds in there."

"Yeah, okay." She rolled her eyes and chugged the water. "Where's my dad?" She pulled out her phone. She had ten missed calls from him and Dhillon and as many text messages.

"He's already at the hospital. He sent me to get you when you didn't answer your phone." The air-conditioning was on in the car, and it felt good to be properly cool for a bit. Her phone buzzed. Roshni.

She held up a finger to Dhillon as she answered. "Hey, Rosh."

"Oh my God, Riya, what the hell is going on?" Her cousin's voice was filled with concern. "Dhillon called—"

"Rosh, I was at work. At the firehouse." Riya paused. Roshni had been the only family member she'd been able to tell when she'd entered the academy. Their mothers were sisters, and though Riya and Roshni were cousins, they really were more like siblings. Roshni not only kept her secret but supported her unconditionally. "My mom had a heart attack."

"Oh, shit. Okay. I'll tell my mom and try to keep her home until we know more, so we don't clog up the waiting room." Roshni paused. "How about you? You're with Dhillon?"

"Mmm-hmm," Riya said, glancing at his profile as he drove. He was singularly focused on the road, his body tense, his movements calm and controlled. The only indication that something might be amiss was the slight furrow in his brow. She suddenly felt an overwhelming amount of gratitude for him and his calm under pressure.

"Lean on him, if you need to, Riya." Roshni's concern came through the phone.

"I'll be fine."

"You don't have to be fine. Dhillon's a great guy, and he cares—"

"I'm good, Rosh." She didn't want to hear how Dhillon cared about her.

"In any case," Roshni sighed, "if you're not alone, I'll catch up with you tomorrow. Seb is at the restaurant, and I have Anand. Keep me posted." Roshni hung up.

"Roshni says hi," Riya said, sighing, and turned to Dhillon. "Tell me what happened."

Dhillon shook his head. "I'm not sure. Your dad called me, saying your mom had collapsed. He had called 9-1-1." He paused. "Your dad had been expecting you to show with the ambulance."

"They always think that." She rolled her eyes. "Like the ambulance I worked on was the only one that existed."

"So you're in trouble?" Dhillon glanced at her.

"What?"

"At the fire station. You were in with the captain and the lieutenant. I heard you arguing."

She sighed. She really didn't want to do this right now.

"Are you not a team player, Riya Desai?" Dhillon asked, as if he found the idea of her being a team player ridiculous.

"Well, I can't play if the team doesn't want me."

"Make them want you."

"I shouldn't have to make them. It's up to them to realize that I am part of the team, regardless of the fact that I'm a woman." She sighed again. "Besides, I saved a little girl today."

"Doesn't sound like a bad thing." Dhillon sounded cautious.

"It's not." She tried to sound confident.

"So what's the problem?"

"I went alone." As she said it, she knew he was going to flip.

"You went alone? Why would you do that?" The accusation as well as the panicked concern in his voice were clear. "Isn't there some kind of rule against that?"

"You know what? Just because I'm a woman doesn't mean I'm not capable." She turned on Dhillon. Yes, there was a rule. No need to confirm that for him.

"You're telling *me*?" His eyes bugged out, and a smirk fell across his mouth. "I've known you since we were five. If there is anything that's true about you, it's that you can do whatever you decide to do." He side-eyed her. "What is also true is that you're not a team player."

"Whose side are you on?" Honestly, Dhillon could be such a pain. Just once, could he take her side? "Not that what I do at work is any of your business."

"I'm on the side that keeps you safe." Dhillon's voice went back to being calm and even, annoying Riya even more.

"I am perfectly capable of going into a fire and bringing someone out."

"I don't think that's why you were in with the captain. You were in trouble because you didn't act as part of a team."

"Just drive. My mom's in the hospital. Why is this the moment you choose to lecture me?" Riya turned away from him. He didn't understand. She had to prove herself capable of doing this job.

"And what the hell was that locker room?" Now he sounded agitated.

"There isn't a separate women's locker room. Because there haven't ever been women at this department. I'm the first." She felt more than a little bit of pride at that. "It'll be fine. I can handle them."

Dhillon shook his head. "You shouldn't have to."

She stared out the window, not really seeing anything. The locker room was the least of her current worries. Her mother's health was bad. How had she not seen this coming? She'd just seen them a couple of days ago. Sure, her mother was on high-blood-pressure meds, but her diet was good, and she exercised. She should have known something was off when she'd last seen them. Shouldn't she?

"You know, you don't have to prove you can go into a fire.

But ever since we were children, you have *always* been the hero, Riya." He shook his head again. "You were the one to stand up to bullies, the one who climbed trees for errant cats. Even playing kickball in the street, you had to score the most runs, make the most outs. No one on your team ever got any action. You had to do it all."

"That's not true!" *Is it?*

"Why do you think Tommy Higgins never let us up in his tree house?"

"That's why?" Her eyes bugged out at this revelation. That was stupid.

Dhillon rolled his eyes as he parked the car and turned to face her. He placed his hands on either side of her face, making her look at him. "Stop trying to always prove yourself. Your abilities speak for themselves." She made herself ignore how secure and warm it felt to have him touch her like that.

He'd done so only once before, years ago. They'd been teenagers—hardly more than kids—and best friends. At least until the night of a school dance, when he'd held her face like that and looked at her with pure joy in his eyes. Right before he kissed her.

"You made it out this time, Riya. What about next time?" There was genuine fear in his voice that left Riya speechless.

When she said nothing, Dhillon pulled away from her and got out of the car. "My sister and mom are here with your dad," he said calmly, bending down close to her ear. "My mom was on shift in the ER when Auntie came in."

Riya inhaled deeply to settle her nerves before entering the waiting room. Funny, she'd had no such apprehension when she'd gone after Christi, but put her mother in the hospital and she was a basket case. She spotted her father, who was pacing, and went directly to him, stopping just short of throwing her arms around him. He stopped and looked at her. She took his hands. She needed to do something.

"Papa," she said gently, as if she were talking to a child. "Papa. I'm here. What happened?"

He looked at her for a moment, his eyes sad and distant. Then his eyes went hard. "She didn't feel well. I called 9-1-1. Mario and Leigh came." His gaze searched her face. "You said you had a shift. But you weren't there."

Riya nodded. This was not the time to explain that there were many other ambulances in the county. "I'm here now. Tell me what happened."

"She felt nauseous. We thought she had a stomach bug, but then she collapsed. I called for an ambulance, then you. Then Dhillon. Riya, where were you?" Her father leaned toward her, inhaled. "You smell like—" his eyes darted to hers, horror forming in them "—smoke. And your face…" He brushed her cheek. "Oh, beti!" His voice rose an octave. "Were you in a fire?" He ran his hands along her arms and stepped back to assess her.

She squeezed her eyes shut. She had left in such a hurry, she hadn't even washed the ash off her face.

Just then, her radio crackled and spit. Voices confirming a fire location crackled through in the silence of the waiting room. When Riya opened her eyes, she found four pairs of eyes staring her down.

Sarika Auntie was the first to speak. "That's a firefighter's radio, isn't it?"

Riya remained frozen, her gaze locked into Sarika Auntie's. Dark brown, like Dhillon's, they were the safest eyes in the room. Had Riya been willing to tell anyone, she would have told Dhillon's mother.

Auntie continued. "You're fighting fires?"

Riya nodded as she kept her gaze on Dhillon's mother,

too scared to see the look on her father's face. Had she really thought she could keep this from her family? She should have told them outright and faced the consequences then. This was worse, because now she had lied to them on top of everything else.

The look on Sarika Auntie's face softened, and Riya took a breath and faced her father. His eyes were wild and glassy, and a vein throbbed on the side of his head.

"What does that mean, *fighting fires*?" he barked, the frightened concern evaporating from his face, replacing itself with a frenzied look.

"I'm a firefighter, Papa." Her voice was soft, willing him to understand.

"You…go…into burning buildings…" He left the rest unsaid. Riya wasn't sure if it was because he couldn't say it or because he didn't want to. Either way, it was hurting him. Which was why she had wanted to keep it a secret.

Riya's heart broke. She nodded.

"But how…? Why?"

It was too much for him right now. It was too much for *her* right now. "Papa, we can talk later. Let's find out how Mom is doing, okay?" She squeezed his hands, and with sad eyes, he slowly pulled them away from hers.

"Yes. Yes, of course. Sarika Ben, what do you know?"

Sarika Auntie jerked her gaze away from Riya and focused on Karan. "Not much more than before. I'm sorry." Her voice was soothing, a balm for all the hurt in the room. It was Sarika Auntie's superpower. She was always calm. Riya couldn't remember the woman ever raising her voice or being agitated. Even after she lost her husband and was raising two children alone. Had to be from working in the ER all these years. Now she rested her warm gaze on Riya. "She has had a heart attack. I believe they are putting in a stent as we speak.

We'll have to wait for the surgeon. She has Dr. Waller. He's one of the best."

Riya nodded at her, and her father sat down. He put his chin in his hands and leaned over his knees, staring at the floor. Riya sat beside him, wanting to reassure him, but he wouldn't look her way.

"I do not understand this. Your brother and Dhillon's father— lost in fire." He shook his head. "Dhillon?"

Dhillon raised his hands in helplessness and shook his head.

Anger bubbled up inside her. Would it have killed him to take her side? To tell her father she was good at what she did? She raised her chin in defiance as she had so many times before.

It was Hetal who broke the silence. "That is so cool!"

Riya snapped her gaze to the girl. What was she saying?

Hetal started shooting questions at her. "What's it like in a fire? How long have you been keeping this secret? Have you ever saved anyone? How long was the training?"

Riya was still processing the fact that the girl was looking at her like she was some kind of hero when the surgeon came out.

"Mr. Desai?"

Her father turned. "Yes. That's me."

The young surgeon's smile was fatigued but genuine. "Your wife is out of surgery. She did very well and is just coming out of anesthesia now. I'll send someone out when you can see her. She'll need to stay in the hospital for a couple of days, then rehab for a week or two. But she's going to be fine."

"Thank you," her father responded.

The doctor did a double take as he noticed Riya. "Riya Desai? This isn't... Was it your mother I just saw?"

Riya nodded. "Hey, Doc. She's my mom." She remembered him being the surgeon for more than one of the cases she'd brought in on the bus. Anytime they had spoken, it was for the transfer of a patient. She didn't think he'd remember her.

"Haven't seen you bringing anyone in lately. You still working?"

"Actually, I'm firefighting now." She couldn't help the proud smile that fell across her face.

"Seriously? Very impressive." His gaze lingered on her.

"Thanks." She found herself flushing a bit under his scrutiny.

"Well, good to see you, Riya." He shook her hand, lingering maybe a bit longer than necessary. He looked at her father. "You should be very proud. She's one of the best paramedics I've seen. And I'm sure she's an amazing firefighter."

Her father furrowed his brow but nodded. Riya couldn't even be sure that he heard the compliment. Her phone buzzed. Text from Roshni. Sorry. I tried to stop her. Riya started to text her back when the door to the waiting room crashed open.

"Okay. Don't worry. I am here. How is my sister?" Riya's aunt, Varsha Masi, was no more than five feet tall and maybe one hundred and ten pounds, but she dominated a room like no one else. She barreled into the waiting room, her arms filled with not one or two but *three* brown shopping bags that Riya knew held enough snacks and food to feed an army. And forget that it was late at night: for sure there was a thermos (or two) of piping hot chai.

"Why is everyone staring?" she called as she bustled into the room. "Take the bags," she said to Dhillon. Then, "Riya, take out chai for everyone." Varsha Masi made a beeline for Riya's father, pulling him into a hug, assuring him that all would be well.

Dhillon grabbed the bags and caught Riya's eye with a smirk. Riya shook her head and shrugged. "Thank God. I could use some chai."

eight

DHILLON

"Can you work Tuesday and Thursday evenings throughout the summer?" Dhillon asked Hetal as they sat at his makeshift desk, working on the schedule. He needed to hire another person in the fall when she would be in school full-time, but right now, he was just trying to get some coverage.

"Yes. My class meets from eight till noon." Her thumbs flew as she entered the days into her phone.

"Hey!" Shelly popped her head into the office. "Got that new one for you, Hetal. The one you spoke with on the phone?"

Hetal looked up from her cell. "Oh, right."

Dhillon donned his white coat over his scrubs and followed both women up to the front to meet their next patient, a very anxious pit bull mix. The owner struggled to hold her dog as he barked and lunged in their direction.

Hetal's face lit up as she walked around to the front of the desk and knelt on the floor. "Well, who do we have here?" she asked in a high-pitched, singsongy voice.

Dhillon grinned and watched his sister work. She may think she didn't want to be a vet, but she was a natural. He was going to have to let her figure that out for herself. He and Shelly exchanged looks of pride.

"That's our girl, Doc," she whispered.

Hetal looked up at the owner. "Ms. Harris, let the leash go just a bit." Her voice was even and calm.

Ms. Harris's eyes popped open wide. "You should know that she has bitten someone in the past."

Hetal nodded. "I remember from our phone conversation." Hetal reached in her pockets for treats. "She's been diagnosed with separation anxiety by your behavioral specialist, correct?"

Ms. Harris nodded.

Hetal smiled. "Loosen just a bit." She tossed a treat just out of Sandie's reach. Ms. Harris loosened the leash a couple of inches. Sandie gobbled the treat, and Hetal tossed another, all the while speaking softly to the dog. She started tossing the treats closer and closer to herself, until Sandie was in touching distance, but Hetal did not reach out to her. She simply allowed Sandie to decide when she wanted to get closer. It took close to twenty minutes, but Sandie finally ate treats from Hetal's hand. Her tail wagged, the lunging and growling stopped, and she even sat when Hetal commanded.

Ms. Harris was thrilled. "How did you…? She's only that good with us…not strangers."

Dhillon beamed. "My sister is a dog whisperer." He held out his hand. "Dr. Vora. Let Hetal get Sandie's weight and settle you in the exam room, and I'll meet you back there."

While Ms. Harris followed Hetal, Dhillon went around the back hallway to meet them in the exam room. When he got there, Hetal was waiting for him outside the door.

"You're amazing." He smiled at her. "Good thing I taught you everything I know."

She rolled her eyes. "As if." But then, in an instant, his sister was all business. "Listen. I'm going in with you. Sandie will need extra time and patience so she decides to trust you. I blocked off extra time for this one."

"Seriously?" Dhillon stared at her. "You know I went to vet school, right?"

She raised both eyebrows. "Trust me."

"Famous last words." Dhillon sighed and motioned for her to open the door. When she was in the zone, there was no arguing with her.

Things went smoothly with Sandie, and before Dhillon knew it, he was on the last patient of the morning, a very sweet Great Dane.

"Buster has a mild case of hookworm, Mrs. Perlman," Dhillon said as he signed off on the bill for the Great Dane and shook the owner's hand. "Hetal will get you the meds, and he should be fine in a few days." Dhillon ruffled the hair on the large dog. "Isn't that right, Buster?" Dhillon was rewarded with a nuzzle. This really was the best job.

Lucky lumbered by and took a seat at Dhillon's feet, and Mrs. Perlman bent down to pet him. "Beautiful dog, but he's getting old, Doc."

Dhillon nodded, a slight pain in his heart. "Too true, Mrs. Perlman, but Lucky is hanging on."

"Right this way, Mrs. Perlman," Hetal called out. "We'll settle up and get Buster his meds."

That was his morning. He refreshed his coffee on the way to his office and gave Lucky a few treats. The dog curled up at his feet and snoozed while he ate lunch and worked on charts. He was only halfway through his sandwich when Hetal came back.

"Hey." She sat down and opened her lunch.

"Hmm." He did not look up from his work.

"So, Auntie will be okay?" She took a bite of her sandwich. "Wow. Chutney sandwiches. My favorite." She grinned and batted her eyelashes. "You do love me."

Dhillon pursed his lips and afforded her a quick glance. "It used to be the only thing you would eat."

"Not true," Hetal said, defending herself.

"Guess again, Miss Finicky. Six months straight of chutney sandwiches for lunch. With the crusts off."

Hetal took another bite and shrugged. "What can I say? I have good taste. Better than dhal for six months straight."

"We eat dhal all the time. Different kinds." Dhillon rolled his eyes. "And I never ate it six months straight."

"You totally did," Hetal insisted, her mouth full.

"Whatever." Dhillon bit into his sandwich and turned back to his computer. *Little sisters.* "Auntie has to recover, then maybe rehab for a week or so. Then home."

Hetal swallowed. "So Riya will be next door again."

Dhillon stopped chewing as he tried to calm the unwanted excitement that rushed through his veins. "How the hell would I know what Riya is doing?" he grumbled. The image of that doctor squeezing Riya's hand a couple of nights ago popped into his head again, making his stomach roil.

"I'm telling you that Riya's moving back home. At least for a while." Hetal grinned. "Isn't that sooo cool? I mean, it's not cool that Auntie had a heart attack, but that Riya will be next door again, you know?"

Dhillon knew that Hetal adored Riya and had missed her terribly when she moved to her own apartment.

But Hetal was extra bubbly today. "I've been thinking about what she does for a living. Saving people."

Dhillon narrowed his eyes at her, an alert going off in his head at the tone of his sister's voice. It tamped down the spike of happiness. "She saved people on the ambulance, too."

He'd practically raised his sister, so he knew her too well. Hetal's voice was off right now, reminding him of the numerous times she had tried to evade telling him the truth about something. He turned his monitor away from him.

"What's going on?"

"Well, I was talking to Riya the other day…" She ripped small pieces of her napkin.

"Yes." He put down his sandwich. Anything having to do with Riya was going to affect his appetite.

"And I think it would be great to be a firefighter." She spit the words out quickly. She'd known he wouldn't be happy. She was right.

She was also out of her mind. "Absolutely not." He turned his screen back to him. Conversation over. No doubt in his role today. Today he was the firm father figure.

"What do you mean, *absolutely not*?"

"What part do you not understand? The *absolutely*? Or the *not*?" He typed with extra vigor.

"I am twenty years old and fully capable of deciding what I want to do with my life."

"Clearly not," Dhillon spit out, more the older brother now than a reasonable father figure. He didn't care. "And Riya does whatever the hell she wants." Without really considering the risks to herself. Or what it might mean to the people who cared about her.

"There's nothing wrong with being a firefighter."

"You're right. There isn't." He kept typing. "It's a noble profession. I have no problem with it. For other people. Not us. We have already sacrificed plenty to fire." Like their father. Who really should be the one having this conversation with her, not him. But that was no longer possible.

"Well, Riya said she would help me," Hetal said, as she finished the last of her sandwich.

Dhillon stopped hammering his keyboard, blood pounding in his head. "She *what*?" Was there no end to the ways in which Riya Desai could manage to upend his world? He was going to have a word with her. It was one thing if she wanted to risk her own life—which still made Dhillon panic—but encouraging his sister? No. Line crossed.

"She said she would help me. Like a mentor." His little sister said this like it was a normal thing, when it was anything but. What was normal about supporting a young girl in her desire to put herself in constant danger?

"No. That's not happening." Fear grew heavy inside him as he envisioned his sister running toward flames. He couldn't keep Hetal safe if she were a firefighter. Every cell in his body screamed *Shut it down! Shut it down NOW.* "I don't care what she says. This will kill Mom."

"Mom's tougher than you give her credit for." It was a fact as much as it was an accusation.

"I know Mom's tough—"

The front door jingled, announcing their first afternoon patient. Hetal chugged the last of her water and gathered her lunch box. "Duty calls."

"Hetal." Dhillon narrowed his eyes at his sister. "This isn't over yet."

"Says you," she spit at him as she whipped around and left his office.

Ten minutes later, Hetal popped her head in his office, a light in her eye and a smirk on her face as she spoke. "First patient waiting for you in Exam 1."

Dhillon nodded as he stood and grabbed his lab coat. He entered the exam room to find Riya sitting there with Scout in her arms. She was smiling, her face and eyes soft as she scratched Scout under the chin. Riya glanced up as he walked in, and some of the softness left her face, replaced by a mask designed to hide her vulnerability. A pang of regret reverberated through Dhillon's body, reminding him that he had allowed that to happen. He had allowed the distance between them to creep in and take hold when he was a teenager mourning the loss of his father, convinced that Riya couldn't possibly still want him. Even though he had known that she mourned, too.

The pang was gone as quickly as it came, as Dhillon took in Riya's firefighter blues, the Howard County Fire Department emblem over the left breast. She was going to help his sister run into fires, too.

Not if he had anything to do with it.

She spoke first. "Hey."

"Hey." He glanced at Scout and felt a smile at the edges of his mouth that he couldn't stop. Well, he wasn't mad at the puppy.

Riya seemed to lower her guard and soften again as his smile widened.

Dhillon couldn't move. He was angry with her, at the same time that he was taken in by how gorgeous Riya was when she wasn't trying to prove something.

"Dhillon? Dhillon?" She scrunched her face in concern. "You okay?"

Dhillon shook his head as if he was shaking off the Confundus charm. "Yeah. Yes." He moved toward Scout, and she nearly leaped into his arms. "Hey, there," he laughed, as Scout wiggled free of Riya and climbed into his arms, trying to lick his face.

"She needs shots," Riya said, giggling. "Or so I was told."

Dhillon held Scout under one arm like a football. "She does." He pulled up her chart on the computer. "Just the one." He made eye contact with Riya, and his heart raced as she held his gaze. "Hold her. I'll go get it."

Normally, he would ask Shelly or Hetal to get it, but he needed to be away from Riya for a moment. For so many reasons, it didn't matter how he felt about her. The least of which was the fact that nothing would ever happen between them. They'd had their chance, and the fire had burned it away. He found what he needed and returned to the room to find Hetal talking to Riya.

Riya was typing on her phone. "I'm sending you the link to sign up. Take a look, see what's involved. Firefighting is hard. There's a test to get into the academy, then another one for placement."

Dhillon's anger returned instantly. "You aren't seriously encouraging her to do this, are you?"

Riya's head snapped up. "I'm supporting her."

"Supporting her to risk her life!" Dhillon barked. He approached Scout, who was content in Riya's lap. "Hold her still," he grumbled.

"I'm supporting her right to do what she wants," Riya shot back.

"I'm sitting right here," Hetal piped up.

"The next patient is here," Dhillon snapped at his sister. Now he was her boss, not a father figure. "Go prep."

Hetal stomped from the exam room.

"You can't do this," Dhillon said furiously.

"I have to. She wants to do this, so she should have a mentor." Riya stood, still holding Scout.

"Hold her," he said, getting closer and administering the shot.

Dhillon had been wrong. Riya was every bit, if not more,

beautiful when she was trying to prove something. But that changed nothing. It didn't change the fact that there had been an electrical fire in both their homes that night they'd come home from the dance. It didn't change the fact that life for them had been irreparably changed by that fire. Dhillon's father would never come back. Neither would Riya's brother.

There was no point in wondering what might have been. That was all in the past.

"She shouldn't be doing that. You should be discouraging her."

"Damn, Dhillon. I never took you to be the *You have to be a vet* kind of guy." She was shaking her head at him, disappointment oozing from her.

He narrowed his eyes at her and forced himself to not shout. "I don't care if she's a vet or not. She can be whatever she wants."

"Except a firefighter." She smirked at him.

"Damn straight."

Riya simply glared at him. He met her hard gaze without flinching.

Shelly poked her head in. "Uh, hey, Doc. Buddy's ready in Exam 2."

"Be right there," Dhillon grunted, his eyes never leaving Riya's.

"Okay." Shelly flicked her eyes between the two of them before leaving. "Sure."

"You can bill the station," Riya said as she turned to leave.

"Fine."

nine

RIYA

Riya dismounted the engine and was heartily greeted by a tail-wagging, attention-seeking Scout. There was no choice but to get on her knees and cuddle the puppy. Playing with Scout was de-stressing, but it wasn't enough to take the edge off her lieutenant's comments.

"You and that dog." Ambrose shook his head at her.

"What about me and the dog?" She was immediately defensive.

"Takes up a lot of time is all I'm saying."

"I get my work done." She continued to play with Scout.

"That you do. But we can't keep her here, Desai." Ambrose's voice was gentle, something she had not heard before.

Riya snapped her gaze up to him. "What do you mean?"

He squatted down next to her. His mouth was set in a line, but sadness flicked through his blue eyes. "I mean you need to find her a real home." He stood and walked away.

She cuddled Scout, cradling the puppy's little head in her hands. "What am I going to do with you?" She could take her back to her parents' after shift tonight, but then what? Put out an ad on social media? No. Too risky. Scout might end up with someone abusive. The best thing for the puppy was for her to ask Dhillon. He knew his patients' families and knew who would be able to take in a puppy. Her heart sank at the thought of Scout being with a strange family. Maybe her parents wouldn't mind having Scout, temporarily. But maybe not the best idea while her mother was recovering.

She needed a shower and a change of clothes before she headed over to the rehab center to see her mother.

She walked into the locker room and was met with a round of *Hey*s and *Whoa*s, not to mention an eyeful of half-naked firemen. That may not sound bad to most women, but these were her coworkers. She squeezed her eyes shut and turned on her heel. "I'm leaving," she yelled.

She refused to apologize. It wasn't her fault there was no women's locker or shower. The problem was that now she would have to wait to get in the shower.

"I don't mind if you're in here!" That would be Walsh. Gross.

"Yeah, well, I do!" she called back.

Riya went back to the bay to clean the rig and was teaching Scout some new commands when she spotted Hetal wandering around.

"Hey! Did I know you were coming here?" Riya hopped off the engine.

"No. I just knew you had a shift and took a chance." Hetal

glanced around, her face shining with excitement. "This place is amazing! I've never been in a fire station before."

Scout was wagging her tail, trying to get Hetal's attention. Hetal laughed as she knelt down to greet the puppy. Riya shook her head. "Dog whisperer all the way."

"So did you just get back?" Hetal asked, giggling as Scout licked her face.

"Yeah." Riya looked down at her gear. "Just waiting to use the locker room."

"They don't have a women's locker room?" Her eyes widened in shock.

"Or shower. The guys got in first, so now I wait." She sighed. "Not a lot of women in firefighting."

"Can you show me around?" Hetal asked as she stood up. Scout simply gazed at her with pure adoration.

Riya was thrilled to show off the station to Hetal. She was proud to be a firefighter, and Hetal was the only one who seemed to understand and support that. Plus, if she was serious about firefighting, Riya wanted to help guide her, so she wouldn't have the same obstacles she herself had dealt with. Like any big sister would.

Schultz was the first of the guys out. "Hey, Desai, sorry about that. They're almost done."

Riya was grateful for Schultz's almost immediate friendship. "Thanks. Meet my neighbor, Hetal."

"This is the vet's sister?" asked Schultz.

Hetal laughed. "Yep, that's me. I'm actually interested in becoming a firefighter."

"Oh, yeah?" Schultz grinned. "Want to be a hero like Desai, here?"

"A hero?" Hetal repeated.

"I'll let her tell you. I need to get my report written so I can get home. Haven't seen my wife for two days." He smiled and waved as he walked away. "Nice meeting you. Don't let Desai leave out the good parts."

"What happened?" Hetal asked excitedly.

"Well, I did pull a young girl out of a fire last week, all by myself." Riya couldn't help but brag a bit.

"You did?"

Riya nodded. She left out the part where she had got in trouble for risking herself and how she hadn't been prepared for that beam falling in front of her. And how her lieutenant was the one who had helped her. "Her foot was broken, and she couldn't walk, so I carried her out."

"So cool!" Hetal's face shone with adoration. "I took a look at that link you sent me the other day."

Riya tried to keep her face neutral. The way Dhillon had looked at her in the office that day was seared into her brain. It was as if he hated her for helping Hetal. She'd watched a lot of emotions cross his face over the years, but hatred at *her* was definitely not one of them. Until then. She shook her head to clear it from her mind. It didn't matter. Anything she and Dhillon could have had was long gone. She focused instead on the girl in front of her.

Hetal's amber eyes shone bright with excitement, and she babbled on about the recruitment website Riya had sent her. Riya was reminded of the first time she'd helped in a fire as a paramedic. It was a high she couldn't explain, but it was pure passion. She'd known in that moment that firefighting was her calling, and she'd never looked back.

Riya described the process from application to testing. Hetal bombarded her with questions, and Riya answered what she could. Clearly Hetal had done her research and was serious about this. Good for her. She wandered around, looking at all the equipment, asking more questions, fascinated with everything. Scout never left her side.

"We're EMT-trained, so my background as a paramedic gets me to most scenes," Riya explained.

They ran into Ian Walsh as he was leaving the locker room. He stopped and ran his gaze up and down Hetal's body. Riya made a fist at her side—she'd love to punch him, but she held off.

"Well, hello," he said.

"Back off, Walsh," Riya said, staring him in the eyes.

"What's the matter, Desai? Jealous?" He stepped closer to Riya as if he couldn't see the hatred in her face, and Riya nearly choked on the scent of him. Cologne and more cologne.

"Hardly." She lifted her chin and narrowed her eyes. "Step aside before I make you."

"I'd love nothing better." He smirked at her, and her skin crawled. She flexed her fisted hand, but he stepped aside and let them enter the locker room.

"What was that?" Hetal asked as they walked to Riya's locker.

"That's one of the downsides of the job. Men who think women are only good for one thing." Riya shook her head. Every run-in with Walsh made her want a shower. "You'll get that no matter where you work." Though that didn't excuse it.

Hetal nodded knowingly, and a small piece of Riya filled with sadness that this girl was aware of such misogyny at her young age.

Riya had just started taking off her turnout gear when Lieutenant Ambrose emerged from the showers, a towel around his waist.

"Lieutenant." Riya snapped to attention. "I thought everyone was out."

"You thought wrong." He was rubbing his head with a second towel, but stopped as he spotted Hetal.

"We can go, give you a minute." Riya started for the door

but found Hetal frozen to her spot, unable to take her eyes off a half-naked Jeff, as if she'd never seen a man before. Granted, Ambrose was an attractive man if you liked the tall, muscular, dark-haired, blue-eyed, chiseled-abs kind of look. Not that Riya hadn't noticed, but he was her boss, and quite frankly, she didn't fall for every pretty face.

"Hetal!" Riya called out in an effort to break her trance. "Let the man get dressed."

Hetal nodded, her eyes never leaving Ambrose. "Um, yeah. Sure."

Ambrose smiled at Hetal, and Riya realized she had never in all this time seen him smile quite that way. It changed him completely. His features softened, and his youth became apparent. Maybe that was why. He was quite young to be a lieutenant: he needed to maintain composure to have authority.

"It's okay, Desai. My locker is on the other side, anyway." He shook his head and left them standing there, Hetal unabashedly watching him.

"No wonder you like this job." Hetal looked back at Riya.

"Yeah, no. He's my boss." Riya shook her head. "And the rest are my colleagues, anyway. Not interested."

Hetal pursed her lips, a knowing smile forming there. "Duh. Of course you're not interested in *him*."

"What does that mean?"

"He's your boss, right? So *of course* that's the reason. Not because you're into another guy." Hetal rolled her eyes. "Are you changing or what?"

"Yeah, okay." Riya furrowed her brow. What other guy? She couldn't mean— No. There was no way Hetal could know how she felt about Dhillon. No time for a shower now. She changed her clothes and pulled out her necklace.

"You don't wear that to fires?" Hetal asked.

It was true: Riya was usually never without this necklace.

But she shook her head. "It's metalwork. Not safe in a fire. It gets exceptionally hot on scene."

"I know I've said it before, but it's gorgeous." Hetal admired it. "Samir really was talented."

"Yes, he was." Riya kept her voice neutral.

"Why was he going to engineering school, then?" Hetal asked.

Riya shrugged. "Engineering was a solid field, that's why." Their parents had probably convinced him art wasn't a real job. She didn't want to bad-mouth her parents to Hetal, so she did not elaborate.

She eyed the necklace and put it on. Hetal was her little sister in every way that was important, except that they did not share blood. "Follow your heart. Do what makes you happy. Fuck everything else. Seriously. That's why I do what I do. Life is too short."

Hetal beamed at her. "You are absolutely right, Riya Didi. Absolutely right."

Riya wrinkled her nose at the antiseptic odor of the rehab center. Her mother had been moved here this morning. "How are you feeling, Mom?"

"Okay." The weakness of her reply belied her response.

The room had stark white walls, and some of the paint was peeling, but it was clean and functional. There wasn't anyone in the other bed just yet, so maybe her mother would get the room to herself for a bit.

"I brought some flowers to cheer this place up, and I brought you some tepla for lunch." She set up a plastic water pitcher as a vase and arranged the bouquet of mixed flowers in it. That added some color, but the place still felt like it was infested with Dementors.

"Thanks, beta," her mother croaked. The bed was propped

so she was somewhat sitting up. Riya draped another white hospital blanket over her.

"You gave Papa quite a scare. How are you feeling?" Riya sat on the bed next to her mother.

"Is it true, beta?" her mother asked. Her arms were tucked under the sheets, so only her head and neck were visible. It really only served to make her look more frail.

"Is what true?" Riya feigned ignorance, though she knew what her mother meant.

"Is it true that you are a…firefighter?"

"Who told you that?" Avoidance might be the key here.

Her mother shook her head slowly, her eyes closed. "Fires cannot be fought. Only tamed. A fight with fire results in loss." Sadness oozed from her, which would not help her mother's healing.

"That's not true. I can help people."

"You cannot bring back Samir." She looked her daughter in the eye.

Riya broke her gaze. "Mom, I don't want you worrying about all that right now." Riya cleared her throat. "I need you to rest so you can get better."

Just then, her phone buzzed in her pocket.

Her mother shook her head, sadness filling her eyes before she shifted her gaze to look out the window. Riya checked her phone. A text from her cousin Roshni put a small grin on her face. Sorry I missed you at the rehab center. Had to get to a meeting. She had added a sad-face emoji. Of course Roshni had a meeting. She always had some kind of meeting. But that was how it was when you ran your own online clothing business. Her degree had been in fashion, which Roshni's parents had had some serious doubts about at the time. But now that Roshni was the CEO of her own very successful online store, all doubt was forgotten.

No problem. Just hanging out for a bit.

Great. Mom is on her way with more food. Roshni had added an eye-roll emoji.

Riya responded with a thumbs-up emoji, but the three dots popped up, indicating Roshni was typing.

You're going to have to move in, you know that?

Riya sighed. She did know that. Her stomach churned. The last thing she wanted was to be back in the house. Too many memories. She responded with another thumbs-up and returned to her mother.

"Listen, I'm coming home for a bit." She forced a laugh. "So you don't have to eat Papa's cooking. He tried, but it wasn't pretty."

"You're coming home?" Her mother's head snapped up. Riya caught the initial look of panic in her mother's eyes, though it was gone in a flash. It matched the panic in her own stomach.

"Well, yeah. I can work my shifts around Papa's schedule. You have rehab for a few weeks, and the house is much closer to the rehab facility than my apartment," Riya pointed out. "So I'll also be there when you come home," she finished softly.

Her mother nodded, a small grin on her face. The two of them were in complete agreement about how they felt about Riya coming home. But neither wanted to admit it.

"Hey! Why so sad here?" an upbeat voice called from the doorway.

Both Riya and her mother turned to face the newcomer, the tension immediately easing in the air around them. Riya caught her mother's eye and found her relief reflected there.

Riya stood and greeted her mother's older sister with a huge—and grateful—hug.

"Varsha Masi!" Riya inhaled the scent of her masi, a mix of drugstore perfume and whatever she had cooked. Today, Masi carried the comforting aroma of chai spices. She must have ground the chai masala fresh today. "So good to see you."

"You, too, beti." Her aunt grinned. "You, too." She squeezed Riya again and met her eyes with a meaningful gaze.

She knew.

Riya clamped her mouth shut. Her masi bustled past her in a cloud of flowers and spice. "Radha, seriously, you must take better care of yourself." Varsha Masi spoke with an accent, as did Riya's mom. And when they got going, they mixed English with Gujarati.

Riya stepped back, biting the inside of her cheek, to suppress the smile that was fighting to poke through. Her mom was about to get it.

"You need to eat better—forget all this samosa, pakora, poori business. No more fried food." Varsha Masi spoke with the authority that older siblings seemed to take as their God-given right.

Riya's mother opened her mouth to say something, but her sister kept on, oblivious of anything. It would not matter to her masi that her mother rarely made any of the delicious fried foods. "And you need to exercise. I know you can't just yet. But we will have to step it up."

Varsha Masi whirled around the room as she spoke, her shoulder-length hair swaying behind her, until she stopped and fastened it into a small bun with an elastic band from her wrist. She continued taking out plastic containers of varying sizes and setting them up. By the time she was done with her little speech, an entire spread of fruit, yogurt and nuts, complete with steaming hot chai, had appeared. To Riya's disappointment, all the fabulous deep-fried snacks that usually accompanied chai were missing. Maybe her mother couldn't have those snacks, but she could.

It was no wonder Roshni was such a nonstop, energetic force. She got it from her mom. Varsha Masi poured them each a foam cup of chai and held up hers as in a toast. Riya and her mom followed suit.

"To my sister. Thank God you are okay." They tapped cups and sipped chai. Riya was a definite coffee drinker, but when she had chai, she always felt wrapped up in warmth and love. Maybe because she usually had chai with Varsha Masi. Her aunt had added fresh mint to today's brew, and the freshness hit the spice just so, causing a smile to spread across Riya's face.

"Excellent chai, Ben," her mother complimented her sister.

"Hmph." Varsha Masi pouted and threw her younger sibling a skeptical look, as if she were in the hospital on purpose. She shook her head and closed her eyes and bent down and kissed her mother's forehead. "Get better, Ben."

It took exactly three sips of chai before Varsha Masi turned her attention to Riya. "So...you are doing a man's job?"

Riya rolled her eyes. "It's a job, Masi. And anyone can do it. Man or woman."

She arched a perfectly threaded eyebrow. "Then let someone else do it. You'll give your poor mother another heart attack."

"Masi! What about all those stories you used to tell me about how women can do what men can, that you should go for your dreams?" Riya asked indignantly.

"Sure. Be a doctor, lawyer, whatever." She tilted her head and held up her free hand. "Don't do dangerous things."

"Masi, I'm happy. I make a difference in people's lives," Riya continued, knowing her mother was listening. "Sure, it's dangerous, but it's what I'm drawn to."

Riya felt her mother's eyes on her.

Her masi tilted her head at her. "Why don't you make a difference in someone's life by marrying them?"

"Oh my God, Varsha Masi." Riya dropped her head into her hands.

"What? You. Are. Thirty." She emphasized Riya's age as if she were an old lady. Which, as far as her masi was concerned, Riya was. "Roshni has a three-year-old and one on the way."

If not for the fact that Riya loved her masi so much, she would have bristled and possibly left the room. "I haven't found anyone yet."

"That can be easily remedied, huh?" Varsha Masi's eyes held a gleam that Riya did not care for.

"No. No." Riya shook her head. This conversation was taking a turn she didn't want. Maybe they needed to talk more about Mom and her fried food. "I'm not ready."

"Think about it, Riya. We know you have dated, and we said nothing. After all, you grew up in this country, and that's how things are done here. But now? Now it is time to try the Indian way." Varsha Masi raised a finger to silence Riya as she opened her mouth to protest. "What is the harm in a simple introduction? Meeting for a coffee? That's how Roshni met Sebastian."

"Sebastian was the barista where Roshni went for coffee every day in college!" Riya protested.

Varsha Masi waved a dismissive hand. "Whatever. Coffee was involved."

Riya pressed her lips together to suppress her laugh as she caught her mother's eye. There was laughter in her mother's eyes, and she too was clamping her mouth shut. Varsha Masi had started to list all the eligible young men she knew who might be interested in Riya, even if she was a firefighter.

Riya was not going to win this. She figured Varsha Masi's list of men who wanted to be married to a firefighter would be short. She sighed, resigned. "Fine. Whatever." It might not kill her to have coffee with a guy, whereas this argument might. Besides, it wasn't like anything was ever going to happen with Dhillon. And it would make her mom happy. It would be a nice change to do something that actually made her mom happy.

Varsha Masi grinned wolfishly. "Aren't there single men at the fire station?"

Oh, fuck.

ten

DHILLON

"So just try a bit of plain rice with boiled chicken for tonight, and see how it goes. If she's not better in the morning, call the office. We'll squeeze you in," Dhillon said into his phone as he entered the rehab facility, nearly bumping into Riya as she was leaving. He nodded at her, and she stopped. The sick dog's owner was worried, so he was asking questions, and it was another few minutes before Dhillon was able to calm him enough to end the conversation.

Riya fidgeted with her wallet, keys and phone while she waited for him to finish his call. He was surprised she had waited, considering their argument the previous day.

"Hey. Sorry. A patient." He analyzed her face as he had so many times before. He would like to be able to say he could read her completely, but the truth was she was still an enigma to him. He might be able to read her expressions, but only the ones she was unable to shield from him. Though, right now, she looked distracted, apprehensive. "How is she?"

"She's recovering well." She spoke to his shoulder, her voice clinical. Not a good sign.

"But...?" He dipped his head, trying to catch her eyes with his.

"But nothing." Riya shrugged, still not meeting his eyes.

"What aren't you saying?" He softened his voice and moved closer to her.

Riya shook her head but did not move away from him. "I'm fine." She sounded more like she was trying to convince herself. She still wouldn't meet his eyes.

"You don't have to be fine. Your mother just had a heart attack." The urge to wrap his arms around her and hold her tight fell over him in a tidal wave, but he stopped just short of actually touching her. She didn't need him.

"She's going to be okay. I understand that. I'm fine." She paused. "I think I'll need to move home for a bit, however."

And there it was. "I assumed so."

"You did?" Her surprise sounded genuine. As if she believed that he didn't think her capable of caring for her mother.

"Of course." He grinned. "You *are* her daughter."

If Riya was at all put off by his proximity, she did not show it.

"Mom seemed surprised." She looked at her fingernails. "Like she was nervous about me being home."

Dhillon nodded, a small smile on his lips. "Your past haunts you."

She finally made eye contact with him. Pathetic man that he was, his heart actually leaped for a moment even though she was glaring at him.

"What?" He held up his hands in surrender and grinned at her. "It's not a secret that you don't care to be home. She probably doesn't want to put you out. And honestly, are you excited about moving home? Even temporarily?"

She shrugged, her face softening. "Not really."

"So the feeling is mutual."

This insight earned him a smile. "I suppose."

That smile warmed him to the core as it always did, no matter how irritated he was with her. It was her magic bullet, and she didn't even know it. He forgot about staying in control of his feelings and wrapped his arms around her, pulling her close. She didn't even resist, melted right into him.

"It'll be fine, you'll see," he murmured into her hair.

She nodded and pulled back to look at him. "She's still awake, if you were going to stop in. I have a shift. You just missed Masi. Your mom's in there, though."

Dhillon nodded. "Ooh—did your masi bring chai?"

"Of course." Riya grinned. "There should be some left." She started to walk away but turned back. "So. Scout."

"What about her?" His face darkened with apprehension as he recalled their conversation when she'd brought Scout to his office. "Is she okay?"

"Oh, she's fine." Riya paused. "It's just…she can't stay at the station. And since I brought her in, I need to find her a home."

"So?" Dhillon smirked. She needed his help and he was going to make her ask directly.

"So. You're a vet."

He nodded, widening his eyes in innocence. "I am."

"You know people. People who like pets."

"Sure."

She stared at him, expecting him to get it.

"What?"

She sighed. "Can you help me find a home for her?"

He grinned. "Of course I can. But why don't you just keep her?"

"I can keep her for a bit while I'm at my parents'. But once I go back to my apartment, she'll be alone all day." Her eyes lit up. "You can keep her. Take her to work with you!"

He shook his head. "No. Lucky cannot handle a puppy. Especially that little one. She's a handful. I'll put the word out and see if anyone is interested."

"Sure. Thanks." Riya was smiling, but there was sadness in her eyes.

He located the room and found his mother there as well as a doctor he had never met. Must be Auntie's doctor-in-charge at the rehab facility. He was Indian, and he had a bit of gray sprinkled through the black of his hair. Perfect: if he spoke Gujarati, then Auntie would feel very comfortable here.

"Hi, I'm Dhillon." He offered his hand to the new doctor. "How is she?" He nodded at Auntie.

The older doctor shook his hand. "Dr. Rohun Shah. But I'm not her doctor here." Dhillon saw the doctor gaze at his mother. But her expression remained unchanged as she focused on Radha Auntie. Dr. Shah cleared his throat.

"Oh, I'm sorry. Who is her doctor?" And why was this guy here and looking at his mother that way?

"She just left. But she did say that Radha was doing well, and that she could start physical therapy in the morning," Dr. Rohun Shah informed him.

Dhillon nodded, but he still had no idea why this Dr. Shah was there.

"Hey, Mom," Dhillon said. His mother was still in scrubs, her hair in a low ponytail, so she must have stopped over on a break from work. "Did you meet with Auntie's doctor?"

"Yes. Everything is fine," she answered. His mother turned back to her friend, leaving Dhillon with this Rohun Shah.

"You're Sarika's—Mrs. Vora's—son? The veterinarian?" Dr. Shah asked.

Dhillon looked from his mother to this doctor. Who *was* this guy? "Um, yes."

"I have a new puppy. I really have no idea what I'm doing." Dr. Shah chuckled and glanced at Dhillon's mother again.

"What kind of dog?" Dhillon responded, almost on reflex.

"No idea. He's a rescue." Dr. Shah pulled out his phone and showed Dhillon pictures of his new arrival, like any proud papa.

The puppy looked like a hound mix. Quite adorable. Dhillon handed Dr. Shah his card. "Send me an email. I'll send you links for classes."

Dhillon finally went to sit by Auntie, but not before he noticed that the good doctor was hesitant to leave, glancing more than once at his mother. She gave no indication that the doctor was still in the room.

"It was good seeing you…all." Dr. Shah waved as he started to leave.

Radha Auntie waved back. "Thanks for stopping in."

Dhillon's mother nodded, and the good doctor left.

The instant Dr. Shah was out of earshot, Dhillon turned to his mother. "Mom. What the hell was that about?"

Auntie smiled. "My cardiologist is smitten with your mother."

His mother flushed, playfully tapping her friend's hand. "Stop." She looked at Dhillon. "Don't look so shocked. It's been known to happen."

"Wait." Dhillon stared at both women. "That was Dr. Shah from the hospital? He came here? To the rehab center?"

Auntie grinned at him, nodding.

"You're not even in his care anymore." Dhillon gaped.

Auntie looked at his mom, giggling. "I know! He knew she'd be visiting me, and he came just to see her."

"Stop it." His mom laughed, sounding like a young girl, as she squeezed her friend's arm.

Now they were giggling like teenagers. Dhillon shifted his gaze from one woman to the other. *Seriously?*

"Mom."

"What?" Her cheeks were flushed, and her eyes danced.

He paused. He wanted to say so many things. *Be careful. Don't get hurt. Do a background check on this guy.* "Nothing."

"You worry too much." She stood. "Radha, I have to get back to work. Let me know if you need anything. And don't worry about your daughter. She'll be fine. I'll see you at home, Dhillon." She squeezed his shoulder as she left the room.

Dhillon nodded and turned back to Auntie. "I hear Riya's coming home."

Auntie's smile faltered just a little. "That is what she said."

Dhillon chuckled. "It'll be fine."

"She should quit this firefighter thing. It's too dangerous."

Dhillon nodded, a pit carving its way into his stomach. "She won't. You know how stubborn she is."

"I know how stubborn you are, too. She'll listen to you, Dhillon." Her eyes widened. "Remember when she wanted to go into that boy's tree house when he wasn't around? What was his name? The Higgins boy?"

"Tommy." Dhillon remembered him well.

"Yes, Tommy. He wouldn't let you two up there to play, so Riya wanted to go when he wasn't around. You convinced her not to, remember?" Auntie looked hopeful.

"Yes, I remember." He sighed and looked at his hands.

"What?"

He shook his head, laughing again. "It's not quite the same thing. She went up there anyway. And she dragged me with her."

"That's because you would do anything for her." Auntie shook her head. "She will listen to you."

He would've done anything for her back then. Now? Now,

he didn't know. She had gone to the tree house again after the fire. She'd left him a note in his backpack to meet her, but he never went.

"Not this time, Auntie," Dhillon said, fidgeting.

"I can't lose them both." Her voice caught. This was not good for her recovery.

"You're not going to lose her. She's too stubborn." He attempted a smile, willing himself to believe his own words. "She's quite good at her job. She's trained well, and when have you known Riya to not be good at something she loves?" Was he convincing Auntie or himself?

"Talk to her, Dhillon, please. She always used to listen to you." Tears filled her eyes, and Dhillon found himself nodding.

He squeezed her hand. "Auntie, you know I've tried."

She squeezed his hand back and rested her gaze on him, almost examining him. "Dhillon." Her voice was soft, and her eyes slowly lit up as if gaining a new understanding. "You still love her."

Dhillon dropped his shoulders. It was one thing to deny his feelings to his sister. It was another thing to lie to himself. But to hear Radha Auntie—the woman who had helped raise him, his mother's best friend and, yes, Riya's mother—affirm it was another thing entirely. He had no idea what emotion his face showed, but it didn't matter. There was no masking his feelings in this room.

A tear escaped Radha Auntie's eye as she nodded at him. They shared the same fear. That they would lose Riya in the worst possible way.

In a fire.

eleven

RIYA

Riya climbed the ladder to the third floor of the apartment building with the hose on her shoulder. The flames were a floor below. She and Schultz were going to attack from above, while Ambrose and Evans came from below. Schultz was behind her on the ladder, Alvarez right behind him.

As the sun beat down on her, Riya stayed focused on her goal. This was what she trained for, and she was ready. Her focus was solidly on the live fire she needed to fight now. Sweat stung her eyes and dripped down her back. She blinked away the sting and continued up the ladder, balancing the hose with each step.

"How you doing there, rookie?" Schultz asked from behind.

"Fine." She opened the window of the apartment and announced herself. "Fire department! Anyone here?"

A small voice answered her. "Yes!" She turned to see a woman in a wheelchair. "My husband, he went to the store."

"I got a woman here, midsixties, wheelchair," she reported to Schultz behind her. She called out to the woman. "Can you stand?" Riya handed the hose to Bill as she climbed through the window. Her turnout gear was bulky on her, but she managed.

"No," the woman replied, panic in her voice.

"I'm in," she told Ambrose and Evans through the radio. "We have a woman in a wheelchair here."

"Great. Get her out. We still have flames," her lieutenant instructed.

Riya approached the woman and pointed to the smoke coming from the front door. "We're going to have to take you out the window, okay?"

Schultz emerged from the window and started laying out the hose to the door.

The woman nodded but did a double take. "You're a woman."

"Yep." Riya nodded as she wheeled the chair closer to the window where Alvarez waited. She prepared to lift the woman and hand her off to Alvarez.

"I'd rather have him help me." She pointed at Schultz.

"I assure you that I am perfectly capable of—" Riya started to explain.

"No. You'll drop me." The woman gripped the sides of her wheelchair.

"Ma'am—"

"I said I want him!" the woman interrupted, placing her hands under her legs, refusing to cooperate. Smoke was filling the room in earnest now. They had to move.

"Is she out, Desai?" Ambrose spoke through the radio.

There was no time for this. Riya knelt down in front of the woman. "Ma'am, I assure you that I am more than capable of picking you up and handing you to my colleague." She glanced at the door, at the smoke coming through the cracks. "We don't have much time. I can pick you up with your co-operation or without."

The woman glanced at the smoke and hissed at Riya, "Fine, but if you drop me, I'm suing."

Riya lifted her through the window where Alvarez waited to carry her down. She weighed less than the hose Riya had carried up the ladder. Lawsuit threats continued as Alvarez carried her down.

Riya quickly folded up the chair. "The chair's up here, Alvarez." She spoke into her radio.

"Yeah. Okay. This lady's pretty pissed at you, Desai." He chuckled.

Schultz came up behind her. "Sorry about that."

She spared him a glance. "Not your fault." She shrugged as if it didn't bother her, but her blood boiled. Even a woman trapped, her life in danger, thought that only a man should be doing this job. "Didn't have time to argue with her."

Riya focused her energy on picking up the line, then turned the nozzle, soaking the door. Alvarez joined them after delivering the chair to the woman. Schultz opened the door, and they entered a hallway thick with smoke. There was one other apartment on the floor. Schultz and Alvarez checked it for survivors, but everyone was out. The three of them headed down the steps to the continuing flames on the floor below.

"We're through the door, in the stairwell. I see flames below," Riya reported to Ambrose.

"Did you get the woman out?" Ambrose's voice crackled through.

"Affirmative."

"Come down here, and we'll check out the rest of the place," Ambrose said.

Flames met them in the second-floor hallway, and they activated the hose to douse the flames. Ambrose and Evans were on the other side doing the same. Once the flames were out, Ambrose sent Riya and Evans in to check for any sparks, while Schultz and Alvarez checked behind the drywall. They all came up empty, satisfied that the fire was out and wouldn't restart.

As they exited the building, they greeted the fire investigators as they arrived to determine the cause.

"Desai, gather up the hose. Schultz, check the surrounding area," Ambrose barked. "Let's load up."

After they gathered their gear, they climbed onto the rig and proceeded back to the station. Helmets were off, turnout gear open, but the heat wouldn't stop. No sooner did Riya wipe away her perspiration than she was drenched again. She stopped bothering.

They were going over the call when Ambrose turned to her. "Schultz told me what happened up there." His mouth was set.

Butterflies fluttered inside her as she set her own jaw in preparation for his reprimand. She had done what she thought was right. She couldn't be arguing with people or giving in to their prejudices while trying to save their lives.

So they could go on living and thinking their prejudiced thoughts.

"She can't really sue, can she?" She hated that her voice sounded weak.

Ambrose shrugged. "Maybe."

Panic shook her. "No." Riya looked around at her colleagues. "She can't sue for that, can she? She'd have taken in more smoke. I had to get her out of there. Schultz was busy."

Not to mention she couldn't be giving in to those demands when time was of the essence.

The guys all shrugged, none of them making eye contact.

"She's going to try to sue the department, right?" Riya was talking fast now. "I'll take responsibility. It was me up there. Not any of you."

She'd had no idea this would be so much trouble. Anger built inside her. No one sued when a man saved their lives. "She can't win, though, right? She's alive."

The guys were looking anywhere but at her. Evans and Alvarez were shaking, their heads bowed.

"Right?"

Evans finally looked up at her, his hazel eyes dancing, and burst into laughter. Alvarez joined him, then Schultz. Even Ambrose let out a chuckle.

"What?" she demanded.

"You," Evans finally said. "You're a goddamn firefighter, and you saved that woman. Who cares if she sues? You were doing your job. And you did it damn well, Desai."

Relief eased the tension in her muscles, flooding through her body. "What's so damn funny?"

"You should have seen your face!" Alvarez said, another fit of laughter taking him. He raised the pitch of his voice. "'I'll take responsibility.'" He sobered, allowing a small scowl onto his face. "As if we would let you take the fall." He shook his head.

Lieutenant Ambrose caught her eye, an approving smile on his face. "Good work today, rookie."

Riya relaxed into the laughter and camaraderie, grinning at the guys as they continued to poke fun at her. She couldn't imagine ever doing any other job than this, and she kicked herself for not following this dream earlier. Schultz expertly parked the rig in the station, and they all disembarked, immediately beginning the cleanup routine.

Today Riya was in charge of maintaining the line. She got to it, Evans helping her out. She'd always liked him. He'd always treated her like part of the team as opposed to a rookie or even a woman.

Ambrose ambled over. "Evans, I want you to go over the Jaws with Desai."

"Yes, sir." Evans grinned at Riya.

Ambrose passed his gaze over Riya as he walked away, a nod and grin where there had once been skepticism.

Riya snapped her gaze to Evans. "He means the Jaws of Life, right?"

Evans shook his head at her. "Yeah, the Jaws of Life. What the hell other *jaws* could there be?"

"Awesome." Excitement pumped through her. This was incredible. If Evans could teach her the Jaws, she'd have another skill to offer on scene.

"We got a guy coming in, couple days from now. But I can show you a few things ahead of time."

"You would do that?" She narrowed her eyes. "Wait. Why would you do that?" She was suspicious. Thoughts of Ian Walsh flashed through her mind.

Evans shrugged. "You have the potential to be a great firefighter. Clearly Ambrose thinks so, too. Or he wouldn't have suggested it."

Riya bit down on her excitement in an effort to remain professional. She failed as her eagerness came through in a huge smile she couldn't hide. The more she learned, the better things would be for her. She was a woman in a man's field. It would do her well to know everything there was to know about firefighting. And be the best at it. "Thanks."

"I'll go over it with you next shift."

"So, Evans." She paused as they finished up the hose. "What do you think about me starting a mentor program for young girls getting ready for the academy? Kind of showing them the ropes, so to speak?"

Evans shrugged. "Never been done. But doesn't mean it shouldn't be."

"Yeah. That's what I thought." Riya grinned. She really loved this job.

Riya finished out her shift without getting a shower. The guys had all jumped into the locker room, so when Riya parked her bike in the driveway of her parents' home, all she wanted was to feel clean.

She looked for Scout as she entered but then remembered that Dhillon had taken her while she was on shift.

She caught a glimpse of her father on the phone in his office and her mother asleep in her room.

When she closed her eyes in the shower, she saw the fear in the rescued woman's eyes as she had picked her up. Fear that Riya might not be able to save her. She also recalled the respect her fellow firefighters had shown her for saving her anyway. And how often did her lieutenant tell her she'd done good work? She smiled to herself as she turned off the water. And, even better, she was going to learn how to work the Jaws of Life.

She got dressed in her old bedroom, which had not undergone a renovation. There was still pink paint on the walls as well as all of her posters of Johnny Abraham and Leonardo DiCaprio.

Riya grabbed her smoke-reeking clothes and took them down to the basement laundry room. They needed to be clean and fresh-smelling before her father noticed.

Her heart was still light and bouncy from Lieutenant Ambrose's comments, and she was bursting to share the news with someone. It was the kind of thing you shared with a best friend or a lover. Thoughts of Dhillon flashed through her mind, but she dismissed them before they could take hold. He was neither of those things. Maybe she'd call Roshni.

She nearly bumped into her father on her way down.

"Ah, you are home." He inhaled deeply, looking up at Riya. "Firehouse?"

"Um, yeah." She avoided his eyes. "I only do one shift a week on the bus. Varsha Masi will cook on the days that I do my twenty-four-hour shifts." *Just keep the conversation to scheduling and move on.*

He squinted at her laundry. "You know, it scares us. Because we lost Samir..."

She nodded. "I know, Papa." She could just tell him that was why she did it, but it wasn't the whole truth. Firefighting called to her. And it had since the fire. She tried to move past him.

"How do they treat you there?" her father asked, his brow furrowed with genuine fatherly concern. "The other firefighters. I assume mostly men?"

"All men." She sighed, shrugging. "It varies. I have to earn their respect."

He straightened. This, he understood. "And have you?"

"I'm working on it. Today—" she couldn't help the smile "—my boss said I did good work."

Her father nodded. He didn't smile, but his brow was no longer furrowed. "I would expect nothing less. But, and I've told you this before, you are a woman, minority in the field you have chosen. You will have to work very hard to prove yourself and earn that respect."

She met his eyes and damn if she didn't see a bit of pride there. "Of course." She did move past him this time. "I'll get

Scout back from Dhillon's, but she'll be with us until I find her a home. Is that okay?"

"Of course."

She nodded and continued to the laundry room. Apparently, it was possible to share these things with her father. "Let me throw these in. Then I'm making khichdi."

"Okay," her father called down.

Khichdi and shak was the ultimate in comfort food, as far as Riya was concerned. Just add a dab of ghee to the steaming rice and lentils, with spiced vegetables on the side, and she was in heaven. She glanced at the Ganesha clock.

"Papa," she called, "can you get Mom's meds to her?" She glanced at Scout's empty bed in the corner of the kitchen. She'd have to go next door and get her soon. The idea excited her a little too much.

A jolt of happiness and a flush of embarrassment heated her as she recalled Dhillon coming over just as she had been getting ready to leave for her twenty-four-hour shift. He'd walked into the house, his arms full of puppy toys.

"What's all this?" Riya had been folding laundry.

"Just some toys for Scout." A stuffed lamb fell out of his too-full arms.

Riya smirked as she bent to pick up the toy. "Just a few, huh?"

Scout had grabbed it in her mouth and taken off with it. "Well, Lamby is a hit."

Dhillon laughed as Scout tore into the stuffed toy, destroying it with gusto. Bits of fluff flew everywhere. Riya laughed, too. She couldn't remember the last time the two of them had done so together. Dhillon was relaxed and happy, and that was as contagious as his laughter.

"See? She needs toys," he'd insisted as he stood in the doorway, a doggy Santa Claus in the middle of summer.

"She does. And that one is going to be her favorite." Riya found a small basket in a corner of the room. "Let's put those in here."

Dhillon emptied his arms of the various squeaky balls and chew toys into the basket. Riya had opened her mouth to thank him and send him on his way, but he slipped off his shoes and came in.

"She's doing really well." He glanced at Scout with a professional eye for a moment, then came over and started folding towels.

"Oh, you don't have to do that," Riya insisted. "I can do it."

"I know you can. But you probably have a ton of things to do before Auntie comes home tomorrow." And damn if he didn't fold a perfect fitted sheet. They sat on the sofa, the laundry basket between them.

She nodded and kept folding. T-shirts next. "I'll be on shift, but Papa can handle it."

"What about Scout?" He picked up one of her navy blue firefighter T-shirts and folded it, glancing at the emblem. But he made no comment.

"What about her?" She continued folding, her mind racing. She had already cooked enough food for a couple of days, her mom's room was ready for her, and now the laundry would soon be done.

"She's a puppy. That's a lot for your dad while he's trying to bring your mom home from rehab."

She paused in her folding. He was right. She knew she'd been forgetting something. Whatever her expression was, Dhillon grinned.

He reached into the laundry basket, his eyes on her. "Don't

worry. I can take her for one night. Mom's not on shift until the evening, so she'll be home with her."

Riya sighed in relief. Of course he would take Scout. Her relief was short-lived as she noticed that the last garment Dhillon had grabbed from the basket was her underwear. Her lacy, powder blue thong.

"Um… I'll just take that." She reached out just as his eyes widened and he realized what he was holding. She snatched it from him and balled it up in her fist as if trying to make it disappear. Heat made its way up her neck and into her face. She couldn't even look at him, afraid that he'd see that embarrassment wasn't exactly what she was feeling.

Silence seemed to float endlessly between them. "Well," she finally managed, "that was a bit awkward, but it's just laundry. Clean laundry." She was babbling. She needed to stop before— "It's not like I was wearing it or anything." Oh, God. Did she just say that out loud? She closed her eyes. She'd just given him a visual of her in nothing but a powder blue thong. Not really where she'd wanted to go.

Or was it?

He cleared his throat, and she opened her eyes to find him watching her, his mouth open and his eyes more than a bit glazed over. "I should go." He nearly jumped up to standing. "You seem to have *the laundry* all under control."

"Yep. Uh-huh."

Dhillon walked to the door. "Just drop Scout off on your way to work."

Riya bobbed her head. "Will do."

But Dhillon left without his shoes and then had to come back and get them. Would awkwardness never end? Even now, Riya flushed as she recalled the incident.

Her father's footsteps brought her back to reality. He let his gaze sweep over the kitchen as he filled a glass with water. "Smells wonderful, beta."

"Thanks." She scooped some of the potato-and-pea shak next to the khichdi. "I'll bring some up for Mom. Just get her to walk in the hallway a bit first."

"Making her work for her meal, are you?" he said, joking.

"It's good for her," Riya insisted.

"I know." He paused. "Beta, it is good to have you here." He kissed her forehead like he used to when she was a child, and Riya felt secure and warm in her father's love once again. How long had it been since she had felt this way? Too long. "You keep working hard at the station. Those men won't know what hit them."

Tears filled her eyes at his support. She had hardly expected it, but now that she had it, she realized how much she had missed it. Her heart was filled with gratitude. "Thanks, Papa. Now, go. Mom needs those meds." She shooed him from the kitchen, wiping her eyes when he turned his back.

Riya was just adding a scant half spoon of ghee to her parents' khichdi when she heard her name being shouted from the door.

"Riya Didi!" Hetal came running into the house. "Riya Didi!"

"In the kitchen," she called out.

"Riya Didi! You have to come." The girl's breath came hard, and her voice shook.

Riya spun around to face Hetal. Her eyes were glassy, and her lip trembled. "What's going on? Is someone hurt?"

"It's…it's Lucky." Hetal's voice caught.

A pit hollowed out Riya's belly. She knew Lucky was on borrowed time, though there was a part of her that had believed he would live forever. She washed her hands, made sure everything was turned off as she nodded at Hetal. She followed Hetal to the door and called up to her father.

"Papa, I'm going next door. Something's wrong with Lucky."

Her father appeared at the top of the steps, shock and concern on his face. "Should I come?"

"I need you to stay with Mom."

"Riya…" He nodded at her.

Her lips quivered as her heart started to sink. "I know."

Her father went back to her mother.

"Let's go." She turned back to Hetal. "Where are they?" She knew Lucky would be with Dhillon. They were almost never apart these days.

"They're here. At home."

Riya burst through Dhillon's front door, just like she had countless times as a child. She found Dhillon sitting on the floor, still in his scrubs. Lucky lay next to him, on his side, his tongue hanging out, breathing shallow. Scout was curled up next to Lucky. Sarika Auntie stood and made room as Riya barreled into the room.

Her heart fell into her stomach. "Do something, Dhillon!" Panic and dread vied for space inside her, making her shiver despite the heat. "Why is he lying there like that? Do something!"

Dhillon met her frantic look with red-rimmed eyes. His scrubs were crumpled, his hair tousled as if he'd been running his hands through it. "Riya…" The intimacy with which he said her name brought her back in time.

"Don't say it." All the years they hadn't spoken melted away in this moment.

"There's nothing…" His voice croaked.

She shook her head violently as she made her way to Lucky's side. "No!" she negated once again, as if the force of the word could ward off the inevitable. As if she could hold back death by sheer power of will. "There has to be something." Her demands were unreasonable, and she knew it. Tears burned behind her eyes. She was as powerless to fight them as she was to save Lucky. "Dhillon-V." It had been years since she'd called him that—the nickname she'd had for him when they were kids—and it fell out of her now with a sob. She gripped his hand.

He squeezed her hand and pulled her close, letting go of her hand and wrapping his arm around her shoulders. She leaned into his chest as she reached out to touch Lucky. His fur was soft, familiar and still warm. She ran her finger along his burn scars as she listened to Dhillon's heartbeat. Dhillon ran his hand back and forth across Lucky's snout, an action the dog had always loved. Riya managed life-and-death situations every day, but here she was, falling apart at losing a dog.

Lucky was more than a dog: he had been her friend, even when Dhillon wasn't anymore. Lucky had been there for her when Samir died. When she'd got in trouble for staying out too late, for not doing well in school, Lucky had been there for her unconditionally.

Lucky's chest continued to rise and fall under her hand.

Until it stopped.

She gripped Lucky's fur just as Dhillon did. She leaned toward the dog, laying her forehead on his side, as Dhillon removed his arm from her. Emptiness fell over her at the loss of his closeness. She heard him shuffling around, checking Lucky's vitals. She knew he wouldn't find any.

She stifled a sob and looked up. Dhillon shouldn't have to do this, but he'd never put Lucky into the care of a colleague. "Dhillon-V."

"Riya-D," he whispered, almost automatically, just as he used to. He looked at her, a clinical mask hiding his feelings. "Let me finish." Grief made his voice low and gravelly. He confirmed Lucky's death and then glanced at his watch. She reached her hand out to him, and once again, his hand in hers was strong and warm. Secure and familiar.

Riya knew his face almost better than she knew her own. His pain was just beneath the surface, and she saw it peek through in his dark eyes. He blinked, and the pain was suppressed. He wasn't trying to be brave or macho; he simply wanted to deal with the business of death before his thin mask failed him.

twelve

DHILLON

Dhillon had known Lucky wasn't going to last much longer, but he thought they'd have a little more time. He hadn't even had time to take Lucky to the clinic. His mother and sister sat around them. Riya stood beside him. She hadn't stood beside him like this in years. In unity, in support, in camaraderie, a united front where they each knew the other's thoughts, where they were almost...one. They hadn't stood beside each other like that since the fire.

He missed it. He missed the easy familiarity, the unmistakable bond.

He missed *her*.

But right now, Lucky's body needed to go to the clinic.

Sarika sniffled. "He was just a baby when we got him from

the shelter. Even though Dhillon took him out every hour, Lucky still had accidents." She shook her head. "Honestly, I thought he'd never be trained."

"Second-best day of my life," Dhillon murmured.

"What was the first?" Riya whispered.

Dhillon shifted his attention back to his mother.

Before he could answer, Sarika said, "Riya stayed over for a few days back then, remember, Dhillon? You two were so little then." She looked from her son to Riya, shook her head, a small smile on her face.

He remembered. They hadn't been that little. They had been thirteen. He grinned at the memory, caught Riya's eye.

"Mom had specifically said Lucky could not sleep in the bed with me. And the first thing you did was put Lucky in bed."

Riya smiled through her tears as she remembered, too. "She said he couldn't sleep with *you*. She didn't say anything about me. I took the bottom bunk. And Lucky."

"And he liked you best ever since." Dhillon rested his gaze on her. Riya smiling was a rare and beautiful thing.

"He had good taste." Tears accentuated the rasp in Riya's voice. Sarika wrapped her in a hug. "Plus, he knew you'd always be there for him. I was the wild card."

"I need to take him to the clinic," he said. No one would be available to get Lucky's body until morning.

She wiped her eyes and nodded at him. "Let's go, then."

There it was again. The familiarity, the bond, the knowing that of course she was going with him. That neither of them would have it any other way. His Riya-D.

He nodded. "Mom, you and Hetal watch Scout."

"No problem, Bhaiya."

Riya's face became a mask of professionalism that matched his as she helped him lift Lucky's body into his car.

As they drove the twenty minutes to the clinic, they talked about Lucky and recalled stories that were amusing and touching.

"He was a good dog," Riya said with a sad smile.

"The best," Dhillon agreed. "He's the reason I became a vet."

Riya looked at him, pride in her smile. "Wrong. You were always going to be a vet. Lucky gave you the courage to do so."

Silence fell between them. They both knew it was Lucky's injuries from the fire that had spurred Dhillon on. "He may have had a soft spot for me," Riya continued gently, "but you were the animal whisperer. You always knew what he needed. You're a natural."

In spite of his grief, Dhillon was buoyed. Riya hadn't let her guard down with him in years.

Dhillon parked the car right by the front door of the clinic, unlocked the door and turned off the alarm. "Grab the lights?" he called out to Riya.

"Sure." He heard the click of the switch, followed by Riya's soft curse when the lights didn't go on. He heard the click again and light flooded the empty office. Without the bustle of animals and people, the office was just tiles and drywall in the eerie light.

Riya propped open the door with a chair and waited for him. He nodded at her, and they went to retrieve Lucky's body from the car. They both took care of storing his body. There would be no formal service. Lucky's ashes would be dropped off at the office in a few days, and then they would scatter them.

"Too bad Lake Kittamaqundi isn't moving water," Riya said, as if they'd been having this conversation out loud. "It would be perfect for scattering his ashes."

"He did love that lake." Dhillon grinned. "He enjoyed Sandy Point Beach. Remember?"

Lucky had taken to the water like a natural. The days they

spent with him on that beach, both families bringing a picnic and whiling away the time, were some of Dhillon's most treasured memories. They had been complete families then, with his father and Riya's brother still with them.

Riya nodded, the memory flashing a smile across her face. "Sandy Point then."

Dhillon had taken Lucky to the beach after the fire, but Riya had never come along.

"I need to do some final securing. Wait for me up front." Dhillon waited for her nod, then walked to his office to email the company about picking up Lucky's body and texted Shelly so she was up-to-date.

Dhillon returned to find Riya staring into space. She caught his eye, and her face crumpled, a sob escaping her. Before he even thought about it, he was at her side, enveloping her in his arms as his own tears fell. She held on to him and sobbed. He held her tight, not speaking, but allowing his grief to join hers.

This may not have been the time to enjoy having her in his arms, but he did nonetheless.

She calmed down a little, sobs turning into sniffles, and pulled back slightly, but not out of his arms. She looked at him with a small, teary smile. He cupped her face and wiped away her tears with his thumb. She closed her eyes and leaned into his touch. She hadn't needed him like this in forever. He hadn't allowed himself to need her like this, either, since he'd lost his father. Right now, though, there wasn't anyone in the world he'd rather be with.

She rested her hand on his jaw, drawing her thumb across. "What's with the scruff?"

He shrugged, unable to tear his eyes from hers. "It's a look."

She nodded. "Not bad."

Silence floated between them, comfortable and calm.

Suddenly Riya smiled, mischief in her wet eyes. She cocked her head. "Let's go."

He was on immediate alert. It had been a long time since he'd seen this look, but he knew exactly what it meant. "What do you mean, *let's go*?"

"Don't be so suspicious. C'mon." She found a tissue and wiped her eyes before grabbing his hand and leading him out the door.

Dhillon allowed himself to be led, pausing only to set the alarm and lock the door.

"Keys." She stood by the driver's side with her hand out, that mischievous smile still on her face.

Dhillon could argue, but that would only delay the inevitable. When she got like this, it was best just to go with it. He handed over the keys. Her smile spread, wide and free, jolting his heart.

She drove them to Baltimore and parked in front of a bar. The red neon sign in the window read Phil's Place. Other than that, there was nothing remarkable about this specific bar except that there was a small sign in the window advertising karaoke night. Which was tonight.

"Oh, no, no, no." Dhillon shook his head as they got out of the car. It wasn't quite dark yet; the sun was just setting over the harbor. "I'm still in scrubs."

"What? It's just a bar. A bunch of my paramedic friends and I used to hang out here after shifts." She shrugged, all innocence. "The beer's good, the food is great, and we should toast Lucky."

"Uh-huh." Dhillon knew better.

"One drink. Promise." The smirk on her face said anything but.

Dhillon sighed. This was going to happen no matter what he said. He pulled on the wrought iron door handles and motioned for her to enter. Music—if you could call it that—assaulted them as soon as they entered. Some poor soul was belting out "I Will Survive" with tremendous heart and feeling that did not match their talent. The aroma of cream of crab soup made his stomach growl. They hadn't eaten. The place was already crowded and dimly lit, save for the so-called stage, which was really just a back corner that was sectioned off.

Riya turned and grinned up at him. "They started karaoke a few weeks ago, one night a week. Pretty cool, huh?"

He could deny the excitement building in him, but he'd be lying. Instead, he rolled his eyes and squeezed in at the crowded bar to order a couple of beers. The bartender, a woman about his age, greeted him with a friendly smile. "You're here with Riya?"

"Excuse me?"

The bartender nodded behind him. "Riya. She's the paramedic turned firefighter, right? She's amazing. She and my fiancé can talk for hours."

"Is your fiancé a firefighter?"

She shook her head. "An ER nurse and a helicopter flight medic. But he was really supportive of Riya becoming a firefighter." She looked behind Dhillon. "Here he is now."

Supportive of Riya becoming a firefighter? Dhillon's excitement dampened. He turned to see a man, also in scrubs, approach the bar. When he got close, the bartender reached over the bar to kiss him, then turned to Dhillon. "This guy is with Riya."

Dhillon flushed. "Well, I'm not *with* Riya. We just came here together. Actually, she brought us here. I just sat in the car." He was babbling. "Anyway, I'll just have two beers and a couple bowls of the soup."

The fiancé smiled and put out his hand. "Daniel Bliant. Riya's great. However you're here tonight."

The bartender went to get the beers. Dhillon shook Daniel's hand. "Dhillon Vora. It's…complicated."

"Isn't it always?"

They turned and saw Riya seated at a high-top near the stage. *Great.* "I'll stop over and say hello in a bit." Daniel smiled. "And bring the soup over."

"Yeah. Sure." The guy was entirely too handsome, and if he hadn't been engaged to the cute bartender, Dhillon might have wondered about his interest in Riya being more than professional.

The bartender returned with Dhillon's drinks. "Tell her Annika says hi."

"Will do." Dhillon grabbed the beers and made his way over to Riya.

"Just ran into friends of yours. Daniel and Annika?" He was facing the singer, as if all he wanted was to listen to someone butcher a song, but he couldn't stop himself from turning to face Riya. To see if she reacted to Daniel's name with any sign of attraction or interest.

He really was a sad, sad case.

Her eyes did widen with excitement. "Daniel's here? Awesome. I wanted to talk to him about something."

"What?"

Riya averted her gaze to the stage and shook her head. "Just a work thing."

That she wouldn't talk to him about, because he did not approve of her work.

They sipped their beers without talking for a few minutes, his thoughts jumbling around between Lucky and Riya. The air was on inside the bar, but it was only just enough to take the edge off the heat. Just as he was relaxing into the possibility that they were not going to have to sing karaoke, a man with a fair amount of gray on his head and in his beard announced Riya's name. And only her name. Dhillon relaxed some. She was sparing him.

He raised his glass to her as she hopped off her stool and headed for the stage. She looked completely at home in the spotlight in her cutoff shorts and loose T-shirt. Dhillon took in the muscles in her legs and arms. The level of comfort Riya had with her body was evident. The song started immediately, and Riya began singing.

Riya was wonderful at many things. She was an amazing cook, she could bake like a pastry chef, she saved lives. Singing, however, was not one of the things she was good at. At all. Not that her lack of talent kept her from the microphone. She sang her heart out, oblivious to how bad she sounded, her gaze intent on him. In it, he saw her pain over losing Lucky, and her desire to do something other than wallow in it.

The song ended, Riya took her bow to moderate applause, and she turned that mischievous smile on him.

Oh, no.

She leaned into the mic. "I'd like to invite my once-partner-in-crime to join me on stage for this next number." She brought the mic close to her mouth and deepened her voice. "Dhillon."

He shook his head as if that would somehow alter the fact that he had to go up there.

"Please join me on stage, Dhillon-V," she pressed, and the crowd applauded. That was the third time tonight that she'd used her name for him.

When they'd first met, as five-year-olds, they had been introduced with first and last names. Riya had a cousin named Dylan. So, to differentiate, she'd called him Dhillon-V. He, in turn, called her Riya-D, which had seemed extremely logical to his five-year-old brain. As they got older, those were the names they called each other.

Until they stopped addressing one another completely.

When she'd used it earlier, he didn't think she'd even realized it. And even now, it wasn't a manipulation: it was coming from her heart.

And Dhillon-V never could refuse Riya-D anything.

He inhaled and downed the rest of his beer. She immediately started applauding. "I'd also love for all of you—" she
pointed to the patrons "—to pick our song."

No, she didn't. Yes. Yes, she did. Just great. Blood rushed to
his face, and he was ever-grateful for dark skin and the scruff
on his face that would hide his flush. He focused on Riya and
approached the stage to great applause.

She glowed, and though her eyes were moist, her face was
filled with sorrowful joy. Her laugh as she hugged him was
victorious, and she handed him the mic with a smirk. He
melted. The crowd shouted out song titles until the DJ picked
one and started playing it. The music started, and the words
flashed on a screen in front of them. He was first.

Of course it was a classic by Sir Elton John begging someone to not break his heart.

Riya watched him as she sang the next line, in which she
promised she wouldn't.

And so it went.

He could thank Sir Elton John for this moment with Riya.

The twist here was that he actually could sing. He'd never
had formal lessons, but he could hold a tune. This surprised
the onlookers, and a whoop of cheering went up as they realized he had some game.

He concentrated on Riya as he sang. They were in sync,
a team again. They sang a second song, and by the time that
was done, Dhillon's heart was light. No thoughts of firefighters or work or loss. He was in the moment. And the moment
included no one but his Riya-D.

They took their bow, laughing and holding hands as they

left the stage. Her hand molded perfectly to his, warm and soft and strong. She squeezed his hand as they made it back to their table. Daniel came around as they sat down and deposited their soups.

Riya looked at Dhillon and spoke softly. "You ordered the soup for us?"

He shrugged and picked up his spoon. "Neither one of us had dinner."

"Nicely done, Riya!" Daniel laughed.

Riya laughed, too. "You know I'm awful. But this guy—" she pointed her soupspoon toward Dhillon "—he has skills."

Dhillon shook his head and ate some soup. He nearly groaned in pleasure it was so good.

"Fabulous, right?" Daniel was grinning at him. When Dhillon nodded, Daniel turned back to Riya. "How's that injury?"

Dhillon snapped his head up at Riya. She was hurt? But Riya seemed focused on Daniel, not Dhillon. And that wall started finding its spot between them again.

"It's fine. Simple sprain. You were right," Riya said quickly.

"Glad to hear it. Common job injury for you," Daniel continued.

Dhillon started to open his mouth to question Riya about it, but she pressed forward.

"So, Daniel," Riya said, sitting back in her stool, turning her body away from Dhillon, "can you put me in touch with Katie?"

"Katie the firefighter?"

Dhillon tensed. Riya threw a fleeting look at him before nodding at Daniel.

"Um, yeah. Sure." He looked from Riya to Dhillon, as if sensing the sudden tension in the air. "What's up?"

Dhillon saw Riya flick her eyes in his direction again and

hesitate. He stood, gazing back at Riya. "I'll just go get more beer."

Dhillon waited at the bar while Annika went to fill his order. He couldn't help himself: he watched Riya talk to Daniel, quite animatedly. Whatever they were talking about was obviously exciting to her.

"This is how they get when they talk about work." Annika set down his beers and grinned at him. "Wonderful how excited they are, huh?" She watched them fondly, but Dhillon's body remained tense with apprehension.

Riya did look very excited, very happy. He picked up the beers and went back to the table.

"It's a great idea, Riya. It's a fabulous way to give back," Daniel was saying as he left. "Nice meeting you, Dhillon."

Before Dhillon could ask *what* was a fabulous way to give back, a man approached Riya, completely ignoring the fact that Dhillon was seated across from her.

"Hey, Riya? Right?" The man reeked of alcohol and had a glazed look about him.

Dhillon sat up straighter.

"Yes…?" She narrowed her eyes and turned her head, making eye contact with Dhillon. She clearly didn't know who the man was.

"You don't remember, do you? It's all right. We met here. You were with your paramedic friends." He eyed her up and down. Dhillon was ready to rip the man's eyes out. "Very sexy."

A flicker of recognition lit Riya's eyes, and she shifted in her seat and cleared her throat. "It was a very long time ago." She looked at Dhillon again. "I was a different person."

"That was some night." The guy drew his hand across her forearm, and blood pounded through Dhillon's body. Whatever had happened between Riya and this guy in the past shouldn't matter, but the way the man was touching Riya brought unexpected feelings of jealousy to the surface.

Riya stiffened, removing his hand. "Well, as I said, that was a long time ago." She nodded, dismissing him. "Enjoy your evening."

"Come on, now. Is that any way to treat an old friend?" He reached for her arm again.

Dhillon stood.

Riya stared the intruder in the eye as she stood, too, and spoke through clenched teeth. "Let go of my arm. Now."

The guy was at least a head taller than she was. He did not let go of her arm. *What the fuck?* Dhillon stepped forward, reaching for the man's shoulder, but before he landed, Riya had twisted her arm around the man's and pinned his arm behind his back, speaking loudly. "I said, let go and leave." She pushed his arm farther up his back. "Am I clear?"

He grunted and nodded, his eyes shifting about at the onlookers.

Riya continued, not bothering to lower her voice. "I'm going to let you go, and you're going to leave. Got it?"

The man grunted and nodded again, clearly humiliated by the fact that a woman had him pinned.

She released him. The man made eye contact with Dhillon, a sneer coming across his face. He opened his mouth as if to say something. Dhillon clenched his jaw and made to step into the man's space, but before he could, Riya stepped forward, her hand fisted. She didn't even need to say anything.

The man ran his gaze over her, flicking his eyes to Dhillon, a look of disgust coming over his face. "All yours," he spit out before finally turning away, as if he couldn't be bothered.

Dhillon watched the man retreat, his heart pounding, rage flowing through his body.

"You going to stand there all night?" Riya was seated back at the table, sipping her beer as if nothing had happened.

He stared at her.

"What?" Riya rolled her eyes. "We were having a decent evening. Don't let that asshole ruin it." She nodded at his beer.

Dhillon shook his head, his rage subsiding. He shifted his focus back to Riya and sat down. "Wouldn't dream of it." He sipped his beer, unable to rip his gaze away from her. Everything she did amazed and impressed him. Well, almost everything.

Daniel stopped by, interrupting Dhillon's reverie. "Everything okay?"

Riya nodded. "Nothing I couldn't handle."

Daniel grinned. "I don't doubt it." His grin faded, and his face darkened. "Phil won't be letting that guy back in. And your tab is on the house today."

"That's not necessary." Dhillon reached for his wallet.

Daniel held up his hands in surrender. "Phil insists."

"Thanks, Daniel," Riya answered. "We're going to get going, anyway."

"Excitement just follows you around, doesn't it?" Dhillon chuckled at her as they walked to the car. He opened the passenger door for her.

"I'm still driving," she said, leaving him standing there as she got into the driver's side.

"What do you mean? We're going home, right?"

"I mean I purposefully did not finish that second beer, because we're not going home." She wiggled her eyebrows at him. "Come on, Dhillon-V. Get in the car."

He did as he was told. "Riya. I have to work in the morning, and you've just been on for twenty-four hours."

"Relax. You weren't going to sleep well tonight anyway," she said quietly. "Neither one of us would have."

That was true. They both would have just tossed and turned. Her eyes were almost black in the streetlight, and her skin glowed. A playful smirk played at her luscious lips.

"You know we're going to the lake. Fighting it will only delay the inevitable." She was staring straight ahead at the road as she spoke. Her complete certainty was as attractive as her mouth.

He shook his head as his own smirk played on his face. "Yeah, well. God forbid Riya-D doesn't get her way."

She laughed, and it was a musical thing. Dhillon had forgotten how her laugh had used to make him feel. Light and happy and like anything was possible.

"You should sing more," she said, as they hit the highway.

He shrugged. "I'm not an in-public person."

"Could have fooled me—and everyone in that bar. I had to drag you off the stage."

He shook his head at the absurdity of the statement.

"Sooo..." Riya started.

"What?"

She shrugged. "So whatever happened with Sharmila? You know, the fiancée?"

If Dhillon didn't know better, he would have thought Riya had flushed as she asked him the question. Maybe she had. He and Sharmila had been over for three years, yet she'd never asked him about it before.

He did the one-arm shrug thing. "She was never actually the fiancée. But she simply wasn't the one."

"Well, no shit, seeing as how you aren't married. But what happened?"

Dhillon inhaled deeply. He really had no idea. And that was probably why Sharmila had left. "She broke up with me." He glanced at Riya. Her eyes were focused on the road, but he knew she was listening. "The truth is that I wasn't fully invested in that relationship. Sharmila was smart enough to see that when I wasn't." He shrugged. "I was checking off a box."

"So you would have just married her anyway, even if you didn't love her?" When Riya said it, it sounded like the ridiculous notion that it was.

"At the time I thought I loved her. So it was the next logical step." He had been trying to live the life that had been expected of him. Not to mention Riya would never have had him.

"I couldn't do that." There was no hesitation in Riya's voice.

"What? Get married?"

"No. I could get married." Did she flush again? Hard to tell in the semidarkness of the car. "But I couldn't do it to check a box."

Dhillon rolled his eyes. "You don't say. Riya Desai won't do something she doesn't want to do? Just because it's expected of her? Color me surprised."

"Is that how you see me? Not doing what's expected of me?" Something in her voice made him look at her. Her lips were pursed.

"Well, yes. You do what you want. You always have." They drove in silence for a moment. "Much wiser than doing something you know is wrong for you. Sharmila and I would have been divorced by now."

Riya tilted her head toward him in agreement, a small smile on her face.

"Who was that guy, anyway?" Dhillon knew who he was; he simply wanted to hear it from Riya. He wanted to hear that he was just a one-night stand. That the guy had meant nothing.

Not that Dhillon wanted to think about Riya having one-night stands.

"Just some guy." She didn't look at him.

"Wow. That just cleared everything up. Thanks, Riya-D."

"What do you want, Dhillon? It was some guy I…" She stared out the window, clearly embarrassed. Which was saying something, because nothing embarrassed Riya. Nothing.

She had gone through a fairly long party-girl phase that had stretched, as far as Dhillon knew, from college until…now. "Some guy you slept with?"

She glanced over at him. "Yes. It was a long time ago. It was a one-night stand."

Relief flushed through Dhillon's body with a speed that was almost embarrassing.

"I was a different person. Clearly, this guy did not get that memo and didn't understand a polite turndown. What an asshole." She sighed. "I haven't been that person in a long time."

Silence floated for another moment between them.

"Not going to lie, Riya-D. I really wanted to punch him." The words were out before he thought about them.

She snapped her head up to look at him, then back at the road. "Because I slept with him? That is the most—"

"Because of the way he looked at you," Dhillon growled. The memory of that man's eyes on her sent adrenaline pumping through him. "He looked at you like you were…a plaything."

Her jaw clenched.

"You are a lot of things, Riya-D. Smart. Sassy. Tough. Stubborn. Pain in the ass. But you are not anyone's plaything."

She looked at him again. Then back at the road. Then back at him. As if she couldn't believe what he was saying. A smile tugged the edges of her lips. "Pain in the ass?"

Dhillon grinned. "All. The. Time."

She smiled wide. "I saw the look in your eyes. You might have killed him. I simply wanted him gone."

★ ★ ★

Riya pulled up into the center part of town and parked the car in the lot beside Lake Kittamaqundi. A few dim streetlights lit the walking path and outdoor amphitheater. At this time of night in Columbia, the streets were empty, and the town center was all but deserted. The night was thick and hot, without a breeze to be felt.

Dhillon followed Riya in the moonlight as she strolled past the picnic area and toward the dock where paddleboats and canoes were moored. For a small fee, people could take them out during the day and enjoy the lake. Riya leaned over and started to unravel the rope holding one of the canoes to the dock. She stretched and her shirt rode up, revealing her strong, bronzed torso. He should look away. He did not.

"Um, I don't think we're supposed to be doing that."

She looked at him over her shoulder and chuckled, her teeth gleaming in the moonlight. "No one's here. It'll be fine."

"So we're stealing the canoe?"

"Borrowing." She got into the canoe with the grace of an athlete and grabbed a couple of oars. "Get in."

He did as he was told—with much less grace, however, nearly tipping the canoe. His clumsiness earned him the sweetest laughter, which eased his soul. He sat down across from her.

They paddled together in silence, automatically in sync, until they reached the middle of the lake. The water was black lacquer, the ripples they had made slowly dissipating. Night insects provided a soundtrack. A slight breeze lifted Riya's flyaway hairs and provided them both small relief from the thick moisture in the air. Dhillon was facing her, their knees touching.

The moonlight hit Riya's skin, making her glow. She had no makeup on, her hair was in a ponytail, and Dhillon was once again completely mesmerized by her. No wonder she'd got him to agree to borrow the boat and paddle it out to the middle of the lake.

"Lucky really loved swimming here," Dhillon said into the silence.

The boat stilled and floated softly on the calm water. The soothing sound of water splashing the sides of the canoe mingled with the insect orchestra.

"He really did." She met his eyes, sending a jolt through his body.

"Thanks. For tonight." Dhillon watched her, his heart thundering at being so close to her, the moonlight giving him glimpses of her as she watched him.

"I needed it, too." Her voice was soft, barely a whisper as she avoided his gaze and looked out into the black night.

Silence again.

"You always loved sneaking out at night." He pressed his knee against hers in the dark.

She did not move her knee away. "I guess I did. It just seemed more exciting to do things at night."

"When you weren't supposed to."

"Duh." She rolled her eyes like she used to when she was a teenager.

"Remember when you took us up into Tommy's tree house? At midnight?"

"Well, he was mean and wouldn't let us up there during the day." She sat up, her mock indignation amusing him.

"True." Dhillon nodded into the darkness. He sighed. "We were best friends."

"We were." She spoke quietly, leaned her elbows on her knees so she was closer to him. He caught a whiff of her fruity shampoo mixed with beer from the bar.

"Things changed." He looked at her.

"Things changed." She met his gaze, her voice low, with that smoldering rasp.

Dhillon leaned on his elbows as well, bringing his face within inches of hers. "You remember that tenth-grade dance?"

"I do."

"I'd never seen you in a dress before. You were the most beautiful girl I'd ever seen." He moved closer, decreasing the distance between them, his gaze drawn to her mouth. Was it the moon, the water? He had no idea. All he could think about was kissing her.

thirteen

RIYA

Dhillon Vora was going to kiss her.

Again.

They were fifteen. She had worn a pink dress and the necklace that Samir had made for her for Rakshabandan. Samir had taken the photos. She and Dhillon were young, carefree and light. She was with her best friend and all their friends.

She recalled thinking that Dhillon looked so superhot in his suit. The way he had looked at her had made her feel all warm and safe inside. The school gym was stuffed with balloons and crepe paper and even had a disco ball in an attempt to transform the space into a beautiful getaway for a dance.

It worked, at least for Riya. She imagined it was one of the most romantic places she'd been. She and Dhillon had enjoyed hanging out with their friends, dancing to the bands of the day. When the DJ played a slow song, it had seemed natural that they came together to dance.

Dhillon had placed his arms around her. She had quite enjoyed the feel of his hands on her back. Strong and secure, even then. Her arms were draped lightly around his neck. She felt him looking at her, and she turned to him.

He had been watching her, and when she made eye contact, he had simply grinned, like having her look at him was all he'd ever wanted in life.

Then he kissed her. His lips were soft, hesitant. She kissed him back, and he became more sure of himself. It was the first kiss for them both, and when they parted, Riya knew her face reflected the joy she was feeling. But she hadn't been afraid to be vulnerable back then. Dhillon was her best friend. She trusted him completely.

Just then, the slow music changed back. She had rested her hand against his cheek, trying to absorb the fact that she and Dhillon had just kissed.

Dhillon had been fixated on her, looking at her in a way she had never seen. They were frozen, just for a minute, as the world around them dropped away. Then, in a rush of music and laughter, they were back. Their friends had rejoined them, and the moment was gone.

Now Dhillon's eyes were soft as they slipped to her lips. He smelled of the beer he'd had and the last remnants of his cologne. She felt that armor loosen around her heart, reminding her needlessly that she still had feelings for this man.

Kissing Dhillon would be reckless. He was grieving; he simply needed comfort. Well, so did she. Where better to get that comfort than from the one person who knew what she was going through?

The right thing—the safe thing—would be for her to simply sit back from him and enjoy the night.

She leaned in closer.

When was the last time she had actually done the safe thing? She could feel his breath on her mouth.

Dhillon brushed his lips gently over hers, and she let him. She held back for a minute, enjoying the sensation of him wanting her. Then she gently pressed her lips to his. Dhillon took over. He moved closer to her. Pressing his lips hard against hers and brushing his tongue across her lower lip, enticing her to open her mouth. She did.

Their legs were now entwined together. He rested his hand on the back of her neck, tilting her head to deepen their kiss.

Riya would never be sure how long they stayed like that; she simply knew it would never be long enough. Somehow he grounded her, yet made her feel like she was floating at the same time. The fact that he still wanted her—after all they had been through—was everything.

She pushed as close to him as the canoe would allow, wanting as much of him as he was willing to give. Slowly, almost painfully, he kissed her into oblivion. She'd always suspected he'd be an amazing kisser, but the reality was beyond anything she could have imagined.

When they pulled back for air, both of them were breathing heavily. She opened her eyes. His black gaze was as glassy as the lake, and his lips were swollen. Riya couldn't believe she had the power to throw straitlaced Dhillon off his stride.

Or that straitlaced Dhillon could throw her off hers.

"Riya." His voice was gruff and low.

They were grown, consenting adults, and her apartment was a ten-minute walk from here. She was a fool if she thought she could have everything she'd ever wanted from him. They'd grown apart since the fire. They had been best friends, but when she'd needed him, he hadn't been there. He had shut her out of his life back then, and he'd likely never let her back in, but she could have him for tonight. That should be enough.

"Dhillon." Her voice cracked.

He raised an eyebrow.

"Paddle fast." She grabbed her paddle and started propelling them, a grin on her face.

And paddle fast they did. They quickly secured the canoe, Dhillon dropping some cash at the rental hut, Riya rolling her eyes at him.

They walked hand in hand to her apartment, each afraid to say anything that would break the spell.

Dhillon had barely shut the door behind him before he had her in his arms, kissing her, making all her limbs feel like they were melting.

He kissed her like he'd been wanting to do for years, but Riya couldn't think about that. She had to stay in the moment. It was all she would ever get. She wasn't the type to ever do what was expected of her, and she wasn't going to start now.

She wanted to remember what his mouth felt like on hers, what his tongue felt like wrestling with hers, how hot his lips were on her body. So lost was she in every sensation he created, she was mildly surprised when she realized that he had navigated them to her bedroom.

"Riya-D." Dhillon paused. Her Dhillon-V. "I...have wanted *you* for so long."

She put her fingers to his lips. She couldn't listen to that. It was everything she wanted him to say, but she was afraid to hear it. "I want you now," she said. Her body hummed with desire for this man. Her fingers shook as she pulled at his scrubs.

He covered her hand with his and shook his head, a wicked smile on his face. He removed her hand and reached for the hem of her T-shirt. He lifted it up over her head. She raised her arms to allow it. She was exposed to him, and she loved it. Her gaze never left his, watching him watch her. He ran his fingers gently over her face, moving to her neck, her shoulders. Her skin nearly buzzed.

Riya basked in the attention, living in the moment. She had learned to do that the last time Dhillon-V had kissed her. He had kissed her that night at the dance, and they had never had a chance to talk about it because their world had gone up in flames that night.

Her eyes never leaving his, she removed his scrub top and finally got a good look at all that muscle he hid all the time.

She stepped closer to him, pressing her body to his, gasping his name as her skin touched his.

He kissed her neck and tugged slightly on her shorts, glancing down at the powder blue lace that peeked out just above the shorts. He caught her eye. "I was hoping you'd be wearing that."

fourteen

DHILLON

Her skin was softer than he could have imagined. He intended to touch and kiss every inch of it tonight. And honestly, he'd been curbing even more of these thoughts since he'd helped her with the laundry the other day. He might never get another chance. This was Riya-D. As much as he wanted her, as much as he loved her, she would never settle down. Least of all with him.

She left him completely speechless. What could he possibly say that wouldn't reveal his true feelings for her? If she knew, she would run, and he wouldn't even have tonight. Her body melted against his. Her silken hair was scented with something fruity. He was all instinct. He loved her, and it was going to show, but he wasn't going to say it.

She tilted her head up and kissed him, a groan escaping her throat as he reached back and released her hair from its ponytail. He ran his fingers down the length of her hair, following her dark tresses as they tumbled over her shoulders, losing his hands in it as he drew her closer.

She placed her hands over the drawstring of his scrubs. He covered her hands with his and removed them. She moaned against his lips.

He pulled back and leaned down to kiss her jaw, her neck, that mole that teased him so. "Not so fast. We're going to take our time."

Her lips parted as if getting ready to protest.

"Trust me." He simply covered her mouth with his and kissed her as if she was the only woman for him.

Because she was.

Dhillon woke, disoriented, to the sound of his phone vibrating. Riya was snuggled up to him, sound asleep, her arm snaked possessively around his naked torso and her head on his chest. It was glorious.

He carefully reached for the cell so as not to wake her. God forbid she wake up and decide she needed to get back to her parents' place. He was in no hurry to leave this bed, and he'd deal with the family in the morning. He'd have to make something up, but he was thirty years old, for God's sake. He could do what he wanted. And what he wanted was to wake up in the morning and have more Riya before the fantasy ended and they had to go back to their lives.

He looked at his phone. Hetal. He was immediately alert. What was happening?

"Hey."

"Bhaiya, where are you?" Her voice was teasing. "It's two in the morning."

"I'm out. Having a drink with…Ryan." No way was he telling his little sister exactly where he was at this moment.

Riya shifted slightly. *Damn, she's awake.*

"And will you be drinking all night with Ryan?" Her sing-songy tone was seriously irritating.

"No. I'll be home soon," he blurted out. Why didn't he just say *yes*?

He felt Riya get out of bed. He hung up.

"Hey, sorry. That was Hetal…"

Her beautiful, strong back was to him. "No problem. We should probably go anyway. Work tomorrow." She stood and grabbed her clothes, not turning to face him.

"I just didn't want her to know—"

Riya turned her profile to him. "Of course not. It's just a onetime thing, so why confuse the family?" She pulled on the sexy blue lace fabric that he had so enjoyed removing, then her shorts and T-shirt.

"Well, I meant—"

"It's fine, Dhillon." She fixed her hair back into its pony-tail, still not turning to look at him. "We're grieving. Emotions were high. One-night stands happen."

His heart plummeted somewhere deep into his stomach. *Of course.* As much as he'd tried to guard himself, tell himself it was only tonight, there had been that damn hopeful part of him that said Riya would never treat *him* as a one-night stand. That Riya wanted him as much as he wanted her… But what did he know? He had been ready to marry a woman he didn't truly love.

"Yeah. Sure. Okay." He stood with his back to her.

After everything they'd just shared, they were now su-premely self-conscious. He had been vulnerable with her like he'd never been before, but now he couldn't even make eye contact. He dressed and turned back to face her. She was beautiful. Her cheeks still held the flush he had put there; her lips were still swollen from his kisses. But her eyes had gone hard. The walls were back up, and she was unreadable.

She stared at him, and Dhillon wanted to believe she was studying him, just as he had studied her.

"Ready?" That rasp he found completely irresistible now sounded almost cold.

He looked around the room for his belongings, his gaze raking the unmade bed. He grabbed the sheets on his side and motioned for Riya to grab her side. She sighed but did so. They made the bed, tucking the sheets in nice and tight.

When they were done, there was no evidence of what had happened in the bed.

None at all.

fifteen

RIYA

The car ride was silent and tense. Of course it was. Dhillon was in a hurry to get home, probably ready to forget this whole night. He couldn't even tell Hetal where he was and who he was with. Even if it had been for only one night. It was appalling.

She had been all set to spend the night with him. She hadn't felt so whole and loved since before the fire. Clearly, she had read the whole thing wrong. Straitlaced Dhillon was not about to start a relationship with her. She was too wild, too...not what he needed in his planned life. Plus, she was a firefighter, and he hated that, too.

She had allowed herself to believe just for that time that Dhillon loved her, that they could be together. That they could find a way. She'd been a fool to allow that fantasy for even a few minutes, but she had.

Reality was a bitch.

Dhillon parked in the driveway of their houses and turned off the ignition. Without a word, or even a glance at her, he got out of the car. She did the same.

"You know, Dhillon…" She looked him in the eye, which was easier now that they weren't looking at each other over a bed where they had just expressed things with their bodies that they could not—or would not—with their words. "Let's not make this weird."

"Okay. It's not weird." He couldn't even meet her gaze. Did he think she didn't know when he was lying?

"Great. So we're…good." Now she was lying. Yet another reason to not be together. They were both willing to lie to each other.

Dhillon shrugged his shoulders. "Sure. We'll just pretend this never happened." He seemed irritated.

"Okay." What the hell was he so annoyed about? He was the one who couldn't stand to admit who he'd spent the night with. "Good."

He watched her over the hood of the car. A flash of something fell across his face. Regret? His expression softened, and he opened his mouth as if about to say something. But before he could, she heard her father's voice.

"Riya? Is that you?"

She turned her head toward him. "Yes, Papa," she answered, feeling every bit the teenager.

"Okay. Dhillon is with you?"

"Yes, Papa. Dhillon is with me."

The same conversation used to happen every night when they were kids. When they were still friends. Her parents had always taken comfort in the fact that Dhillon was with her, keeping her safe.

The door clicked shut, and she turned back to Dhillon. But he was gone.

She couldn't help thinking about the last time he'd kissed her, at that tenth-grade dance. Her fifteen-year-old self had been thrilled that he had liked her *that way* because she didn't ever think he would. She'd gone to bed that night dreaming about him, waiting to see him again the next day.

"Riya! Riya!" Samir was shaking her. "Wake up. Fire! We have to get out!"

She sat up, and Samir grabbed her hand. Smoke was everywhere. Riya coughed and jumped out of bed, letting Samir lead her out.

"Where's Mom and Papa?" she shouted.

"Not home yet." She and Samir were almost down the steps.

They ran outside and found Dhillon there with his mom and sister. Samir deposited Riya with them and charged back into the house.

Riya tried to follow, but Sarika Auntie's hands held her back, even as she shouted for Samir to come back. She and Dhillon had locked their gazes for a moment. Their kiss from earlier that night was simultaneously the most important and the least important thing in their lives.

Sirens sounded in the distance just as Riya saw her parents' car pull up. She ran to them.

"Samir is inside."

Her father ran into the house.

The next time she saw Samir, he was being carried out by firefighters, clutching her necklace.

He had died later that night from smoke inhalation.

That necklace was all she had left of him.

A few weeks after the fire, Riya left Dhillon a note in his backpack to meet her at the tree house. They still weren't living at home.

Her parents were walking zombies, and she missed her brother like she was missing a limb. She needed to feel alive, if only for an hour.

Dhillon never showed.

When she did see him, he was busy, distracted. She knew he was taking care of his family, that he had given up on soccer so he could work more hours at the clinic after school. She helped out by baby-sitting Hetal, helping her mom cook for the Voras, but as time wore on, she and Dhillon drifted further from each other, not closer. All she wanted was to be close to him, but he had put up a wall between them. If it hadn't been for Lucky popping over regularly, she would have collapsed from loneliness.

She had started taking her nighttime adventures on her own. She made other friends, but she quickly realized that the only person she could count on was herself. Before she knew it, she and Dhillon had drifted so far from each other that they basically only saw each other at the yearly remembrance their families held, and even then they barely spoke. She put up her own walls and reinforced them with behavior she knew would terrify Dhillon.

Those walls had crumbled a bit tonight. But not enough.

Flames had taken part of her house, her brother and her heart. All things she would never get back.

sixteen

DHILLON

There simply wasn't enough coffee to wake him up or improve his mood today. He was groggy from sleep deprivation, and even though his schedule was packed, it did little to distract him from thoughts of Riya or Lucky.

"The layout of this clinic doesn't make sense," he complained. "We need two separate entrances and maybe a back door. The surgical unit needs to be in the back, away from regular patients. And each exam room needs two doors." He was gesturing and talking, but no one was really listening.

"It worked for Dr. Halstead," Shelly piped up.

"It's antiquated."

"So change it." Shelly shrugged. "What you're saying makes sense."

As if things could just change because he wished them so.

While Shelly was efficient, she was also nosy. "Late night, Doc?" she asked as they closed for lunch. She was the same age as his mother and equally as interested in his social life. Or lack thereof.

"He didn't get home until after two." Hetal smirked.

Shelly raised her eyebrows, interested. "You know, Doc, if you had your own place, you could have had a sleepover."

Yep. Well, for that to happen, Riya would have to want to sleep over. Which she did not. "We've been over this, Shel." He threw Hetal a glare.

"I know, I know. It's the Indian way—"

"It's an excuse. He doesn't have to live at home."

His sister was really pushing it today.

Shelly glanced between brother and sister. "I'm going to run a few errands. I'll be back in time for afternoon patients."

Hetal sat engrossed in something at the front-desk monitor. He looked over her shoulder. "Are you applying to be a firefighter?"

"Yes."

"Do that on your own time," he snapped at her.

"This is my own time." She looked up at him. "You're, like, extra grumpy today. Maybe don't stay out so late *drinking with Ryan*." She used air quotes.

"I don't pay you to look for work elsewhere," he barked.

She rolled her eyes. "Fine. But you're only saying that because you don't approve."

"You're right. I don't approve. I actively disapprove."

"Whatever. You know Riya saved a woman's life the other day?"

"Did she also tell you she got into big trouble with her captain for trying to be a hero?" Dhillon headed back to his office.

Hetal followed. "That's her job."

"Her job is to put out fires and help people. It's not to be a hero. And it certainly does not need to be yours." Dhillon started to walk away from his sister.

"Well, I guess you didn't hear how her boss told her she did good work yesterday."

Dhillon froze. She hadn't mentioned it.

"Well, he did."

Fine. Good for Riya. She'd had a compliment from her boss and never mentioned it. Just like she never told him whatever she and Daniel had been talking about. Her career was progressing.

The pathetic part of the whole thing was that he was actually happy for her.

Dhillon pulled into the driveway to the sight of Riya wiping down her motorcycle, Scout running around the small yard on a tether. The summer sun was still strong, though it was evening, and the air was as thick as ever. Her hair was tightly braided, though some loose strands had escaped. She was wearing scrub bottoms and an old T-shirt, grease smudging her cheek. She'd never looked so sexy. Images of her from last night flashed across his mind. Her singing karaoke, her in the moonlight, her next to him in bed.

Dhillon took a deep—and hopefully cleansing—breath before exiting his car. Her living next door for the next few weeks was not making this any easier.

The sight of the motorcycle stirred an irritation inside him. She had got that right when she'd moved out. Her parents had forbidden it while she was living at home, but as soon as she'd got the paramedic job, she'd bought the bike and moved out. No, that wasn't right. She'd moved out two years ago, and she'd already had the paramedic job for a while. Riya had moved out when she started training to be a firefighter. The motorcycle irritated him even more now.

It was one thing for Riya to fight fires, but not Hetal. Anger built up inside him—a feeling he could actually understand. Anger at Riya was familiar, sadly comfortable. All those other feelings were new and overwhelming. He got out of his car and slammed the door. Riya looked up.

"Hetal was filling out an application for firefighting today," he said, as if they were continuing a conversation. Scout ran to him. He unleashed her and picked her up, holding her close. She calmed him, but not enough.

"Okay. Well, that's a first step. Needs to be done." She turned her attention back to her bike.

"No, it does not need to be done."

"If she wants to be a firefighter, it does." She picked up a wrench and made adjustments to her bike.

"How about you tell her how dangerous it is? Make her not want to do it. Tell her how it's an unnecessary risk, instead of telling her what a hero you are."

She turned to face him, scowling. "I didn't tell her I was a hero."

"She has always looked up to you. Remember that cat? And how you punched that kid in seventh grade because he was teasing someone? You're a freaking legend to her. And besides, you told her you saved a girl, didn't you? That you went into a fire and pulled her out? To her, that's heroic," Dhillon finished breathlessly.

"The girl's foot was broken. I had to carry her out. It's part of the job."

Dhillon could swear she was being extra calm just to irritate him.

"Oh, yeah? Did you tell her the rest of the job? About the smoke in your lungs, how that burns? Or how about the heat?

How it's so hot you swear you'll melt any minute? No, you did not. You didn't bother to tell her all that, because you want to be the hero. You want to save everyone. Well, how about you save her by discouraging the whole thing?"

"You know, Dhillon, I always knew you were overly cautious, but I never took you to be closed-minded." She put away the tool and stood to face him, sunglasses hiding her eyes. But he didn't need to see her eyes to know that they radiated defiance, just like the rest of her.

"The only closed mind here is yours." Dhillon threw his words at her like weapons.

"She's going to do this, either way. I might as well help her." She folded her arms across her body.

"She never even had the idea until she found out you were a firefighter." He wanted to move closer to her, to take off those sunglasses and see her eyes. But no good would come of that. If this was going to be her stance, they could never be together anyway.

"Are you sure about that, Dhillon? Because she was in that fire, too, as a child. She lost her father, same as you. Her life changed drastically that day. Not just yours." Riya dropped the rag and gave him her full attention.

"She was five."

"Old enough for memories." She shrugged.

Dhillon stepped back, exasperated. "Seriously, don't you even care about her? It's one thing to not care about yourself, but dragging her along? You know that she worships you. She'll listen to you. *Tell her no.*"

"You know what? I do care about her, and that's why I won't do that." She did that little chin tilt that told him she would never back down. The conversation was over.

He started walking away from her, still holding Scout. "If she does this, you're responsible."

Still fuming at Riya, his stomach clenching in fear and worry for his sister, in addition to the fear and worry he had for Riya, Dhillon stared at his house. All of his exhaustion was gone, replaced by adrenaline pumping through his body. Screw it. He hooked Scout to her leash and got back in his car, sent a text to Ryan and headed for the basketball court.

"Dude." Ryan was waiting for him, basketball in hand. "You didn't even change. You're going to play in scrubs?" The evening was warm, and the humidity still lingered.

"Just throw the damn ball." Dhillon took off his shirt and tossed it on the ground.

Ryan barely offered a reaction. They'd known each other since grade school, almost as long as Dhillon had known Riya. Which meant Ryan knew almost everything about Dhillon—most importantly, that he had always been in love with Riya.

"Okay. So it's gonna be one of *those* games?" He threw the ball. "Got it." Ryan was taller and leaner than Dhillon, and he had played basketball in high school.

Dhillon caught the ball as he walked onto the court. They were at the local high school, and the place was strangely deserted. A few kids played soccer in the distance, but the court was completely theirs. The evening sun still heated up his bare back, but he barely noticed with all the warring thoughts in his head.

He started dribbling as he got close to the net. Ryan tried to block him, so Dhillon turned his back and dribbled backward. He backed them closer to the net, keeping the ball away from Ryan before finally turning and taking his shot. It was wild, and he missed by a mile.

Dhillon chased after the ball, returning to a puzzled-looking Ryan. "What's going on?"

Dhillon shook his head and threw him the ball. "Just play."

"You texted at just the right time. I had just gotten out of the OR." Ryan started making his way to the net, easily getting by Dhillon to make a basket. "Burn case." Ryan was a trauma resident.

Dhillon got the ball. He was sweating and breathing hard. "Uh-huh."

"We ended up sending the patient to the burn specialists, then plastics."

"Uh-huh." Dhillon's mind suddenly filled with images of Riya getting burned. Then his sister.

"You'd think you'd be in a better mood after you got some."

Dhillon stared at his friend. *How the fuck does he know that?* He threw the ball at Ryan.

Ryan caught it with ease. "Please. I've known you for, like, twenty-plus years. Eighty percent of our conversations are about sex and ninety-nine percent of those for you are about— Wait. No way." Ryan's eyes widened, and a sly grin fell across his face. "Riya!"

Dhillon shook his head. "No."

"Liar!" Ryan grinned but then furrowed his brow. "You'd think you'd be happier." Ryan took a shot and made the basket.

Dhillon absently picked up the bouncing ball, shrugging.

"Was it that bad?" Ryan was incredulous.

"No, moron. She was…" Amazing. Wonderful. He was supposed to be here to forget the images of Riya in bed with him, but leave it to Ryan to bring it all up. "It doesn't matter. It was just a onetime thing." He took a shot and missed.

"You finally get her, and you're letting her go?" Ryan got the ball and held on to it.

"It's not up to just me. You know how she is. No commitment." Although, when he was with her, he hadn't got those one-night-stand vibes from her at all. Until she woke up. When she realized what had happened. The look on her face—she had been appalled. "Besides, she's a firefighter now. And I just can't do that."

"She's a what?" Ryan squinted his eyes, as if doing so would make him hear better.

"A firefighter. Throw the ball."

"Dude, that is so hot!" Ryan chuckled but did not throw the ball. "Literally." He laughed at his own pun.

"Says the emergency trauma surgeon who thrives on adrenaline."

"And sex." Ryan aimed at the basket and took a shot. It hit the rim and bounced off. Dhillon lunged for it. "Don't forget the sex."

"Yeah, we know all about your revolving door. No need to shove it in my face." Dhillon started dribbling the ball again, getting closer to the net.

"I barely have time for that revolving door anymore. Residency is a bitch."

"Is it? Doing exciting cases, saving lives, all the women, is it too much for you?" Dhillon kept dribbling.

"Wait. Are you seriously telling me that you don't think a woman firefighter is hot?" Ryan went on defense behind him, spreading his arms, trying to prevent Dhillon taking a shot.

Well, when he put it that way…there was definitely something sexy about her in the uniform. Or at least what was under that uniform. A memory flashed through his mind. "Not if it's Riya."

Ryan brought his arm around and stole the ball. But instead of dribbling it, he held on to it. "You're an idiot, you know that? You get these beautiful women, and then you find something wrong with them. Every. Single. Time."

"What?" Dhillon had no idea what Ryan was on about.

"What was wrong with Sharmila?"

"She left me."

"You never even went after her."

Quite frankly, he had been relieved. They'd only dated for six months before he'd decided he should ask her to marry him. "She said I was boring."

"I don't think those were her words, but—"

"You can't compare her to Riya." No one compared to Riya.

"Fine. Then go *after* Riya." Ryan threw the ball at Dhillon, hitting him hard in the gut.

"You're not listening. She's definitely not interested." Dhillon threw the ball at the net. "She made that abundantly clear. She couldn't get home fast enough." The ball hit the rim and bounced away.

He was just another guy to her.

seventeen
RIYA

"Hey!" Riya flung her arms around Roshni the best she could, considering her cousin's bulging belly.

Roshni squeezed her tight. "God, I'm so sorry I haven't been to see you in so long. Masi's all settled?"

"Yes." Riya stepped back, taking the bags of food from Roshni's hands. "You didn't have to cook." She was still processing her last turbulent encounter with Dhillon, so this surprise visit from Roshni was a balm to her soul.

Roshni followed Riya into the house. "Duh, Sebastian cooked." She smiled with that twinkle she always seemed to get in her eye when talking about her husband. "He made his special pasta that Masi loves."

Scout rushed to greet the newcomer, letting out a small bark and hiding behind Riya's legs. "It's okay, girl," Riya cooed to her. Then, turning back to Roshni, she asked, "Where is my little guy?"

"Anand is home with Sebastian." Roshni rolled her perfectly made-up eyes. "Terrible threes. But he's got a cold, and I didn't want him near Masi." She squatted down to Scout. "But once he finds out you have a puppy, he'll be pissed he couldn't come."

"Oh, this is temporary. Until I find a home for her." Riya walked Roshni back to the kitchen to empty the food bag. She left it on the counter and then placed her hands on Roshni's baby bump. She bent down. "Hi, baby. It's Riya Masi, your favorite aunt ever."

"What can I do?" Roshni looked around the kitchen.

"Just sit. Mom's sleeping. I sent Papa to the grocery store."

"Thank God. I'm exhausted." She plopped down at the small table. She was adorable in a peach maternity dress that hugged her baby bump just so. But Roshni always looked amazing—makeup done, black hair perfectly straight—all that with a full-time job and a toddler.

"Chai?"

"Duh. Yes."

Riya placed a pot of water on the stove to boil, then turned back to her cousin. She and Roshni were exactly nine months apart, and there wasn't much about Riya that Roshni did not know. Roshni was the only one in the family who had known when Riya had applied to become a firefighter. She was the one who talked Riya off the figurative ledge when she was at the academy and was convinced she'd never make it.

"I'm so sorry about Lucky. What timing, huh? Everything all at once." Roshni shook her head.

Tears burned behind Riya's eyes at the thought of Lucky. Not only had she lost Lucky himself, but the dog had also been the last thread in her bond with Dhillon. And after last night, everything was broken.

"Oh, sweetie." Roshni hugged her. "I know you miss him."

Riya leaned into her cousin's embrace for a moment. "I do."

"There's something else, right?" Roshni pulled back and studied Riya's face.

"No." Riya shrugged and grabbed the small stainless steel canister of chai masala and the matching medium and large canisters of tea and sugar. Scout left the kitchen and went and stood by the door. Riya followed, letting her out on the tether, and returned to the kitchen.

"Lie to yourself, sis. But don't lie to me." Roshni plucked a few leaves of mint from the small plant on the windowsill. "It's got to be Dhillon."

Riya snapped her gaze to Roshni. "Why would you say that?"

"Um, you're, like, living next door to him again. And you both just lost Lucky." Roshni snapped her fingers. "You were with him last night!"

"Well, we were both with Lucky." Riya busied herself with the chai.

"What happened? Did you accidentally sleep with him?" Roshni laughed.

The thing about besties was that they could read even the smallest hesitation. Riya's hand stopped for a second as she added the masala to the water, and Roshni stopped laughing. She clapped her hand over her mouth and walked a lap around the small kitchen. "Oh my God," she whispered. "You totally slept with him."

Riya forced herself to keep moving.

"You better start talking." Roshni opened the pantry and pulled out the container of chocolate chip cookies. She bit into one while Riya spoke.

"Not much to say. Lucky died. We were sad. I took Dhillon for karaoke and a canoe ride to distract us. Next thing we know, we're in bed."

"Sounds great so far." She grabbed another cookie. "Except for where Lucky died."

"Or the part where his sister called, and he lied to her about where he was?" Riya interjected.

"Do you really think strong-but-silent Dhillon Vora is going to tell his baby sister he's in bed with you?" Roshni pointed the cookie at her.

"It wasn't like that. He lied about where he was and then told her he was coming home. If he didn't want to get into it, he could have just said he was out with some random woman so he could stay with me. But he needed an out, and he went home."

"Riya…"

She held up her hand. "Don't. It's fine. It's not like I haven't had more than my share of one-night stands." She turned back to the chai and added the loose tea to the pot.

"But this is Dhillon." Roshni took one more cookie and put away the container.

"He's a caveman," Riya grumbled.

Roshni laughed out loud. "Dhillon Vora is a lot of things. Smart. Kind. Caring. Superhot."

Riya cocked an eyebrow at her.

"What? I have eyes. And that man is six feet of pure muscle and grace, and he loves animals. And that scruff he's been sporting is not hurting him one bit. I bet all the women pet owners love having him as their vet. Not to mention those teenage girls he and Hetal coach who probably only come to practice to watch him. But he is not a caveman."

"He hates that I'm a firefighter," Riya said.

Roshni furrowed her brow. "Hmm. Didn't see that coming. Wouldn't most guys find that hot?"

Well, not Dhillon, apparently. "Whatever."

"You can *whatever* me all you want, but you have loved that boy since you were both kids."

"How could you possibly even know that?" It was true. But still.

Roshni leaned toward her, a grin worthy of the Cheshire cat on her face. "Because I was there that Rakshabandan when the parents tried to get you to tie a rakhi on Dhillon as his *sister*. And you refused. You could not have been more than—"

"Nine. I was nine." Riya allowed herself a small smile as she added the milk and mint to the boiling mixture. "And I just didn't want to embarrass him if he didn't have a gift ready." That was her story, and she was sticking to it.

"Uh-huh."

"Hey, Riya!" Dhillon's voice boomed from the front door, sending a jolt of unwanted excitement through her body.

She swallowed hard and did her best to form her face into a mask of indifference, but warmth flooded her cheeks instead.

Roshni giggled. "Speak of the superhot devil."

"Kitchen," Riya managed to croak out.

"Scout has nearly chewed through this rope tether." Dhillon entered the kitchen, his sunglasses on top of his head and a very contented-looking Scout under one arm, the frayed rope in his other hand. He was still in his scrubs, but they were disheveled, and he was sweaty.

"Seriously?" Riya shook her head at the puppy. "You trying to get away? What am I going to do with you?" It was easier to talk to the dog. She could not think about what she wanted to do to Dhillon. Still wanted to do.

"Well, I brought home a tether from the office. It's in the car."

Riya turned to him. Honestly, why did she melt at the very sound of his voice?

"What? I'm a vet. I saw this coming." He arched an eyebrow as they made eye contact. "You sure you don't want to build a fence?"

Riya needed to stop looking at him and remembering what it had felt like to kiss those lips, to hear his voice whisper in her ear, to feel— "I'm not keeping her." She forced her gaze to the puppy. "It's temporary." She flicked her gaze back to him. If he was at all fazed by being in her presence, he did not show it. But why would he be? It was one night. One incredible, amazing night when she had felt loved and cherished and at peace. Yet he couldn't wait to get away from her.

"You still have to train her." He was in doctor mode, his voice clinical and detached.

"I know."

"Remember how we used to—" His voice caught.

Memories of training Lucky flooded her, driving hot tears to her eyes. She nodded, holding up a hand to stop him from continuing.

He ducked his chin and cleared his throat, peering at her from under his lashes. His next words came out soft, gruff. "Just do that."

She squeezed her lips together to hold back more tears. That had been a team effort.

"I'm home in the evenings," he offered, his voice soft again, no sign of Dr. Vora in it.

She nodded.

He turned to Roshni as he let Scout down. "Hey, Roshni. How have you been feeling?"

Roshni grinned. "Great. Thanks." Her voice softened. "Sorry about Lucky."

"Thank you." He rested his gaze on Riya before he turned

to leave. "I'll put the tether out so you'll be all set." He nodded at Roshni. "Good seeing you. Good luck with the baby."

Riya stood frozen in her spot until she heard the door shut behind him.

"Oh, yeah. There's nothing there." Roshni rolled her eyes.

That was the beauty and curse of a best friend: they knew when you were full of shit.

Riya peeked into her mother's room before heading back to Johnny and Leo for the night. Her mother was watching her Hindi soap operas with great concentration, her eyes glued to the screen, a spoon of yogurt halted halfway to her mouth.

Riya glanced at the screen and saw a beautiful young woman smirking, a decidedly evil twinkle in her eye. She was wearing the most gorgeous silk sari that was draped perfectly on her curvy body. The music was ominous, a great *dan-dan-daan* as the camera closed in on her expression. She had either killed someone or started a false rumor, causing strife in the family.

"I'm going to bed, Mom. Do you need anything?"

Her mother gasped as the camera zeroed in on the person receiving the evil smirk. This second woman was hopelessly doe-eyed, equally beautiful and fashionably dressed in an eye-catching beaded sari, with just the perfect pool of tears in her eyes to make the viewer feel for her. The victim. Either someone she had loved had died, or the evil one had insulted her cooking in front of her mother-in-law.

Riya couldn't tear her eyes away. A couple of moments passed as the camera zoomed in on the evil smirk, then the tear-filled doe eyes, back and forth, with no dialogue at all, just ominous music.

"Riya. What are you doing standing in the doorway like that? Come and sit," her mother chided.

The spell broken, Riya went in and sat on her mother's bed

with her back to the soap opera. Her mother raised the remote and muted the sound. "Going to bed so early?"

Riya wished she'd sat facing the TV so she had somewhere else to look. And because she did not, she found herself looking in the direction of the small mandir her parents kept in the room. A small glass Ganesha sat in the very front of the altar. "I have another twenty-four-hour shift starting at six."

"Okay." Apprehension from her was strong and clear.

Riya made eye contact with her mother. "Mom, I'll be fine."

Her mother shook her head. "You don't know that."

"True." She paused, took her mother's hand. "You remember that night?"

Her mother's head snapped up. "Of course. But—"

"Okay." Riya squeezed her mother's hand. She'd explain her career choices another day.

"We should have been home that night," her mother blurted out, eyes wide, bottom lip quivering.

"What? Mom, you were."

"No, we were out when the fire started. Remember?" Her mother's voice shook. Maybe this hadn't been the best idea right now.

"You were there when we got outside." Riya kept her voice even. She had been so happy to see them, she had almost forgotten that they had been out.

"We had just gotten there. We were late. We were supposed to have been home an hour before, but we were with our friends, you and Samir were grown, so we thought *what could happen?*" Her eyes filled with tears. "If we had been home…" She shook her head, tears falling down her cheeks.

"Mom, no. You know you can't do the *what-if* thing. It's not your fault." She squeezed her mother's hand. "There's no way to predict what exactly will happen in a fire."

Her mother swallowed and sniffled and looked at her, her voice stronger now. "Your father tells me your boss says you are doing well."

A small smile crept onto Riya's face. "Yes. That's true. But I'm new, and I'm a woman, so I have to prove myself."

Her mother nodded. "What about getting married?"

"Mom." The switch in topics was completely normal for her mother. Job and marriage. The final duties of a parent in getting their children to the promised land of Settled.

"You told Varsha Masi you'd think about it." Her mother's eyes were wide and alert. Clearly, she was excited at the prospect.

What the hell? Dhillon had made it abundantly clear he wasn't interested in anything further with her. Her new job wasn't helping that. And it would give her mother something to focus on while she recovered. "Yeah. Okay. Set it up. I'll meet someone."

eighteen

DHILLON

"Riya's going on a date," Hetal reported as she grabbed the bag of soccer balls from the trunk of the car.

Dhillon snatched up the fluorescent orange cones from the trunk as the news settled into his heart like a rock.

"Did you hear me, Bhaiya?"

"I heard you," he grumbled.

They carried the equipment onto the field. Dhillon had coached Hetal's soccer team since she started playing as a child. His dad would have done it, had he been alive, and Dhillon missed playing soccer, so he had volunteered. He wanted his sister to have everything she would have had if their father had been alive.

Hetal was busy with college and working at the clinic,

but she still loved it, and she volunteered as a coach, too, for twelve- and thirteen-year-old girls. Now Dhillon was her assistant coach.

"Well, don't you think you should ask her out?" Hetal dropped the bag of balls on the edge of the field. Dhillon started placing the cones out for the drills they were going to run that day.

"Why would I do that?" When she was clearly not interested in anything long-term with him.

"Oh my God, Bhaiya!" Hetal stopped him. "If you don't, she's going to meet someone and fall in love and get married and you'll still be stuck alone!"

"I'm not *stuck* alone. It's a choice." Sure it was.

"The point is, you need a life." She had her hands on her hips, and the look she was giving him could rival any auntie they knew. "You'll never get Riya if you don't try."

"I tried." He sounded more despondent than he'd planned on.

"You what?" Her eyes widened at this news.

He looked at his little sister, who wasn't anything close to a baby anymore, and repeated himself. "I tried. She's not interested. End of story." He knew it was true, but it didn't hurt any less no matter how many times he said it.

"*Not interested?* What does that mean?" She started stretching. "And what does *tried* mean?"

"Pretty self-explanatory." Dhillon copied her stretches. The girls might only be twelve and thirteen, but he got a workout coaching them, so he needed to warm up first.

Hetal narrowed her eyes at him. She opened her mouth to speak, but just then, the first of the girls arrived, so Dhillon was given a reprieve while she turned her attention to the players.

Riya was dating? Living at home must have made it easier

for her parents to pressure her, that was all. She was just going through the motions to make them happy.

Or was she? And what difference did it make? He had told Hetal the truth. Riya wasn't interested, and no matter what she had said that night about it not being weird, it was. Because every time he saw her, all he thought about was how soft her skin had been over her muscles, how his new favorite flavor was beer on her lips, how all he wanted to do was keep her safe.

"Dhillon!" His sister's voice jarred him from his thoughts.

"What?" He sounded more agitated than he'd expected.

"The team's here." She smirked at him as if she knew what he had been thinking about. "Can you start the drills?"

"Oh, yeah, sure." He nodded at the girls standing in front of him and forced himself into the present moment. "Let's do this."

Each girl grabbed a ball and followed Dhillon onto the field. He pushed all thoughts of Riya to a small corner in the back of his head as he directed the girls in the drill. Dhillon focused on critiquing their performance. After twenty minutes, they switched: Dhillon's group went over to Hetal's station, and Hetal's group joined Dhillon at his. Riya was all but out of his head when he heard the girls talking.

"Coach Hetal said she knows a female firefighter. We're going down to the station after this to meet her."

"What was that, Kayla?" Dhillon asked.

"We're going to the fire station to learn about being a firefighter. Coach Hetal knows one of them—a girl!" Kayla's eyes widened in awe and excitement. "We're going after practice today."

"Really?" Dhillon glared at his sister across the field. She had insisted they bring only the one car. So now, apparently, he was going to the firehouse for a lesson in fire safety and how great firefighting was. Fabulous.

"You're coming, right, Dr. Vora? Coach said you would." The young girl looked at him with wide, innocent eyes, and he had no choice.

"Of course. I'm your assistant coach. And don't forget—"

"You taught Coach everything she knows," they chorused.

Dhillon managed to make it through practice. The girls helped load equipment back into the car before getting into car pools with some of the parents. Dhillon had half a mind to call an Uber and go home. If it weren't for the fact that the girls wanted him there, he would have. His sister must have counted on that.

They arrived at the fire station to find Riya and a couple of other firefighters waiting for them. One of the others was also a woman. Dhillon did not remember seeing her at this house before.

The girls were chattering and laughing about whatever twelve- and thirteen-year-old girls chattered and laughed about. Dhillon's attention was drawn to a certain dark-haired woman in her firefighter blues, who was pointedly not looking his way. Not to mention that Hetal seemed so comfortable at the station. Talking to Riya's lieutenant. She was twirling the hair in her ponytail around her finger. *What?*

Dhillon tore his gaze away from Hetal and back to Riya, who stood next to her captain. The man was in dress uniform, while the rest of the crew were in their firefighter navy blue T-shirts and pants. He was a tall, solidly built man, a bit older, but easily as fit as—if not fitter than—his younger counterparts.

Riya had taken the floor, and the girls were completely captivated. "Hi, ladies. I'm Firefighter Riya Desai, and we here at Engine and Ladder 52 are thrilled to have you here. We'll show you whatever you want to see, but I just have a few things I want to say. First, if the alarm goes off, go with your coaches and get out of the way, 'cause we've got to go.

"Next, let me introduce you to my captain. This is Captain Davis. He has over twenty years of experience as a firefighter and is always ready to share that experience. Next, I'd like to introduce you to a new friend of mine, Lieutenant Katie Meringue. Lieutenant Meringue is visiting all the way from Engine 23 in Baltimore just to meet you all."

Lieutenant Meringue stepped up. "I am really excited to see so many young women here today to learn about firefighting. In the past, firefighting was left to men, but as you can see, that is no longer the case. I hope you will take what we have to say to heart and consider firefighting as a possible career."

Katie? That was who Riya had asked Daniel about. Daniel had helped facilitate this? Dhillon knew he hadn't liked the guy.

"And this is my lieutenant, Jeff Ambrose," said Riya.

The lieutenant stepped away from Hetal (*about time!*) and corralled the girls in a circle. He made a few introductory remarks and turned the floor back over to Riya.

Dhillon stepped closer so he could hear her better. Her eyes raked over him as he moved, but her gaze never landed on his. She knew he was there; she just wasn't going to acknowledge it.

Fine.

The girls nodded, intent on Riya's words. Dhillon couldn't blame them. Even her instructions had him spellbound.

"I'm so glad you all came out today so you can see that firefighting is a profession for women as well as men. It's hard, grueling work, but there's nothing I'd rather do. And let me tell you, if you *want* to do this, you *can* do this." She paused.

Dhillon glanced around. The girls were hanging on her every word. She split them into two groups, one with her and Lieutenant Meringue, the other with Hetal and Lieutenant

Ambrose. Dhillon considered following his sister and Ambrose, because the lieutenant was friendlier to Hetal than he needed to be. He ended up following Riya's group because—well, he was weak. He was careful to stay in the back and out of the way. She showed them the rig and the ladder and went over how they responded to a call. The girls asked pointed, thoughtful questions and were completely engrossed in her answers. She showed them the kitchen and explained how every firefighter had a duty in the house and how they rotated the chores. The two groups met up at the last stop. The locker room.

"This is where we shower and keep our clothes, since we do have twenty-four-hour shifts," Riya explained.

They started to walk past the locker room when one girl asked, "Can't we go in and see?"

Riya tightened her mouth into a small smirk as her gaze swept over the girls and her lieutenant. "Actually, no. That's the men's locker room."

The girl nodded. "So, can we see the women's locker room, then?"

"No." Riya sighed.

"Why not?"

"Because there isn't one." Riya let her gaze fall over the girls as well as over all the other firefighters there, the captain included.

Dhillon felt a grin creep over his lips. Leave it to Riya to find a way to make a point.

A hush fell over the girls, and then the indignant chatter began. These were young girls who had no idea what Title IX was because they had always been allowed to play all sports. Their mothers were doctors, lawyers, nurses, police officers, soldiers and supreme court justices. These girls were racing to shatter whatever glass ceilings remained.

Nina spoke up. "What do you mean, there's no women's

locker room?" She directed her question not to Riya but to the good lieutenant.

Ambrose scanned the room, looking slightly like a cornered animal, who knew he couldn't come out fighting. He rested his gaze on Hetal, but she simply waited for his response along with the girls.

"Um, well…" He let out a breath, looking deflated. "That's a good question. Desai is the first woman firefighter we have ever had at this house. You're right. It's something that needs to be remedied."

Nina stared him down for a minute, and Dhillon could almost feel the lieutenant's discomfort. His sister used to stare him down like that. Nina turned back to their hero. "So what do you do?"

Riya cleared her throat. "I wait until they're done. Or I go home and shower."

Dhillon watched the lieutenant. This was news to him. Just then, the alarm sounded. Saved by the bell, as it were.

Riya called out, "All of you can gather in the kitchen with your coaches. Sorry, but duty calls." She nodded at Hetal and Katie, and they got the girls together. Dhillon followed. Riya brushed by him, catching his eye for a moment. He couldn't read her expression. Then she ran.

nineteen

RIYA

Schultz had them running through tires, pushing tires, putting on turnout gear, taking off turnout gear and—the best part—sliding down that pole. Riya felt great. She was going to pass out any minute, but she felt alive and strong. It felt like they always had to train at the hottest time of day, but sweat and heat were part of her now, so it didn't really matter. That may have been the point.

In the middle of the drill, the alarm sounded. Riya ran into the locker room, strapped on her oxygen tank and grabbed her SCBA and helmet. She was on the engine two minutes after the alarm had sounded.

"Looking good out there, Desai," Schultz said and grinned at her. "Getting stronger."

Riya gave a grateful nod, and Schultz moved on to Evans. "You, too. I'm going to have to make drills harder for you two." Riya had never seen that wicked gleam in Schultz's eyes, as if he was going to enjoy working them until they dropped.

Alvarez piled in next to her. Schultz was the driver, as always. Ambrose was the last on, after he made sure the company on the ladder was set.

Ambrose grabbed the radio and got the details of the call. He directed Schultz. Multiple-vehicle collision on a highway. Injured and trapped civilians. Schultz parked the rig, blocking traffic, a slight distance from the scene. A point of command had arrived and set up and was already assessing the scene, assigning duties. Ambrose jumped off the rig, Schultz behind him.

Another firehouse had arrived first. The rest of them unloaded from the rig and began following instructions. Sirens blared, and people were shouting orders, firefighters and paramedics rushing to fill them. Organized chaos. Riya's heart pumped as she calmly absorbed the scenario, waiting for her assignment.

"All right. We've got four vehicles involved," Ambrose said, his ear to his radio. "Two still have people in them. Desai, you and Evans take the Jaws to the front car." Ambrose was barely done speaking when Schultz handed the tool to Riya and set up the generator.

"You're putting the rookie on the Jaws?" Alvarez was incredulous.

"She's practiced, but she needs to do it on scene." Ambrose fixed Alvarez with a stare. "And last time I checked, I made the assignments."

Ambrose made eye contact with her, and she saw something there she hadn't before. But there was no time to analyze. "Don't just stand there, Desai. Move."

"Yes, sir."

She picked up the fifty-pound Jaws with ease while Evans got the generator.

She must have had a slightly panicked look on her face, because Evans stopped her for a moment. "You can do this. We've done plenty of drills."

His calm confidence helped Riya relax. "Yeah. Okay."

"We got your back." He dipped his chin at her in encouragement.

She grinned. *Don't vomit.*

"Okay, then." Evans grinned. "Let's go save some people."

The two cars in the middle were smashed together, people trapped inside. The front car was in the other lane, and the back car was on the shoulder. Paramedics were on the scene, too, taking care of the victims who were already out of the vehicles. Police managed traffic.

Riya focused on her job, running to the front of the two smashed cars, barely even noticing the weight of the Jaws in her hands. An older man was trapped with his leg under the dash on the passenger side of the vehicle in front, but the back of the car was also crumpled in. A young woman with a bleeding gash on her head hovered around the car.

"That's my dad!" she screamed. "I don't know what happened. The car in front just stopped—I don't know, I don't know—"

Riya caught the eye of one of the paramedics already coming her way. "Ma'am. I need you to go with the paramedics and get that cut looked after. I'll get your dad out."

"I need to stay... He's old..."

The paramedic was at her side. "Ma'am, my name is Ariana. I need you to come with me so we can take care of that wound."

The woman touched her head as if noticing the blood for

the first time. She looked at Ariana. "But…my dad." Her lips quivered. "I can't leave him."

Ariana's voice was firm and soothing. "Ma'am, your father is in good hands. These men—" She stopped and did a double take at Riya. A smile fell across her face. "These *firefighters* will take good care of him."

"You'll get my dad?" The woman gripped Riya's arm.

"Of course," Riya replied, avoiding Evans's gaze. They weren't supposed to make promises; she knew that. Ariana directed the woman a small distance away to give Riya and Evans room to work.

Evans had started the generator. "You got a plan?"

Riya nodded. "Let's get the door off using the cutter and then use the ram to push back the dash."

"Copy that, ma'am." Evans nodded his agreement.

Riya nodded, then turned to the victim. "Fire department here, sir. We're going to cut the door off and get you out. What's your name?"

The man turned to her, blood dripping from a cut in his cheek. "Harvey. It's Harvey."

"Okay, Harvey. I'm Riya. This is Marcus. We're going to cut you out of here. I need you to stay still. Nod if you understand."

Harvey nodded. Riya flashed him what she hoped was a comforting smile, since her insides felt scrambled. She turned to Evans with a confidence she hardly felt. *Fake it till you make it.* "Start it up."

"Wait." Harvey looked at her. "*You're* going to cut this open?"

"We both are." She nodded at Evans.

Harvey motioned to the Jaws. "Shouldn't he be holding that?"

For a split second, the temptation was there. Evans was more experienced and could definitely cut this man out, whereas this was Riya's first time. *There's always a first time.* The words came to her from the recesses of her memories. *Samir.*

She gave Harvey the most confident smile she had. "I can manage." She put the tool in position just as Walsh ran over.

"Captain needs Evans," he said. Evans nodded and left.

"Walsh, this is Harvey. We're going to cut him out," Riya said.

Walsh nodded. "You got it, babe."

She shot a glare at him. "Not. Your. Babe."

"No need to get bent out of shape, sweetheart."

"Jeez, Walsh. I'm not your sweetheart, either," Riya shot back at him.

"Hey. You." Harvey looked at Ian. "You can't talk to a woman like that. Especially when she's got that machine in her hands. Let her work. I want out of this."

Walsh rolled his eyes and held the door. Riya grinned at Harvey and got to work. She brought down the shield in front of her face and powered up the Jaws of Life. The hefty machine vibrated in her hands, but she held it steady. After she made a few cuts, Walsh caught the door and removed it. Riya switched to the ram. She positioned it under the dash and against the running board, away from Harvey's leg, and started it up. The ram extended its arm, pushing the dash away, allowing room to free the man's leg safely. Walsh signaled the paramedics to come over, and once Harvey had been extricated, Riya removed the Jaws.

Elation flooded through her. Where there had been knots in her stomach, there was now excitement. She had done it. She'd used the Jaws of Life! Wait until she told Dhillon.

Oh. Or not.

"You did it." Harvey didn't seem surprised, just very grateful. "Young lady, you sure know your way around that machine. Thank you."

"Part of the job." Riya's smile was genuine this time as she moved out of the way to let the paramedics through.

Walsh slapped her on the ass. She swung around, jaw clenched, heart pounding. "What the fuck are you doing?"

"What? It's a compliment. Job well done."

She shoved him with her free hand. She was still holding the Jaws. "Touch me again and it'll be the last thing you do with that hand."

"Don't you shove me." His face darkened.

She narrowed her eyes and spoke through her teeth. "You're just lucky we're on scene right now."

"Hey, Desai! We need the Jaws back here. Now!" Evans called to her from the second car.

She made to move toward him. Walsh blocked her way. "This isn't over."

"Oh, it better be." She jogged off to help Evans.

"Everything okay?" Evans asked, glancing back at where Walsh was still seething.

"Nothing I can't handle." She turned her attention to the car and peeked in. Her hands were shaking in anger, but she called upon her previous elation as she leaned toward their patient. "Who do we have here?"

The trip back to the firehouse was a jovial one. Even the summer heat didn't faze them. Schultz and Alvarez had taken down a spontaneous car fire on the scene. Riya had got Harvey and two teenagers safely out of their cars with the aid of Evans and Walsh. Minimal injuries, no fatalities. It was a good rescue. Lieutenant Ambrose even smiled at her, albeit briefly. At least he wasn't glaring at her anymore.

"We got ourselves a new person to handle the Jaws," Evans declared as they disembarked the rig.

Riya bathed in adrenaline-fueled elation as the guys congratulated her. She hung up her turnout gear on the engine as they all started their postcall duties. As they finished up, the guys started getting ready to shower.

"Hold up," Lieutenant Ambrose called out, getting everyone's attention. "We have a situation that needs to be remedied. But until we do, Desai, you can have the locker room first. The guys'll wait till you're done."

"Seriously?" Her grin was huge.

Ambrose nodded. "Better hurry and get in there before they get too impatient." He leaned down and whispered in her ear, "I had no idea you had to wait. But before you go—" Ambrose stopped her, raising his voice so the guys could hear "—I think we can all agree that the rookie handled the Jaws of Life like a pro today. Apparently, cutting up cars is one of her talents."

Hearty applause passed through the room like a wave. Riya flushed with pride. She turned and headed for the locker room as all the guys headed in the opposite direction toward the kitchen.

Walsh was the last to pass. He grazed her shoulder with his, murmuring, "Want company?"

Her skin crawled. "Fuck off."

twenty

DHILLON

Dhillon changed his shirt for the third time. "What's wrong with this one?"

"I don't like the color on you." Hetal glanced at him as she went through his closet. "How about this?" She pulled out a solid navy blue button-down. "With the jeans you have on."

He did as he was told. Fourth time must be the charm because Hetal grinned at him and nodded. "Perfect."

Dhillon inhaled. Thank God. He was just going on a date, not to a wedding. "So can I go?"

"Where are you taking her?" Hetal asked in that little-sister singsongy voice.

"I'm meeting her in Baltimore for dinner." Dhillon put his wallet in his back pocket and his phone in his front pocket.

"Don't forget to open doors, et cetera. It's nice to do that," Hetal advised.

"I'm not an idiot."

"Just checking. I appreciate those things in a guy." His sister shrugged. "And you haven't been on a date in years."

Well, he wasn't even sure he should be on this one. But if Riya was really dating, then he seriously needed to put her in the past and move on.

"Whatever. Can I go now?"

Loud, angry voices reached them from downstairs. Their mother was arguing with someone. Hetal's expression reflected his own confusion. He nodded toward the steps. "Come on." As soon as he opened the door, it was clear.

Hiral Mama.

Dhillon bounded down the steps, Hetal close behind him. They both marched into the kitchen.

"What's going on?" Dhillon attempted to keep his voice neutral.

"Ah, Dhillon. Finally. Someone with sense." Hiral Mama addressed him. "Talk to your mother. Tell her how ridiculous it is that she is dating. She's on shaadi.com, for God's sake."

Dhillon's shock was so complete, he was momentarily speechless.

"Surely you understand. You also have a sister. You would not want your sister dating random boys, now, would you? It is highly inappropriate for a widow of her age to be seen with *men*. You see, don't you?" Hiral Mama asked.

Dhillon's mother was fighting tears. "Hiral Bhai, Rohun makes me happy!"

Hiral Mama did not even turn to acknowledge what she had said.

"Actually, Hiral Mama, Mom can make her own decisions.

As can my sister. Those ideas are outdated. It's time to open your eyes and see how happy your sister is," Dhillon countered.

Hiral Mama's eyes hardened. "It is not acceptable that Namrata Ben and Neha Ben approach me at the mandir to tell me about my sister's wayward actions."

"Wayward?" Dhillon was astonished. "I hardly think—"

"Obviously, you are not thinking." Hiral Mama turned to his sister. "I tried to reason with you. You won't listen. And neither will your son." He shot Dhillon a hard look before turning back to his sister. "I forbid you to bring down the family name and continue in this manner. Our parents would be ashamed of you."

At the gasp of horror from his mother, Dhillon fisted his hand. Uncle or no, Hiral Mama was begging to be punched. Instead, Dhillon spoke through clenched teeth. "Leave. Leave now."

His uncle turned to him, anger oozing from his eyes. "Show some respect."

"Earn some," Dhillon spit back.

Hiral Mama's eyes widened. "Such disrespect. What would your father think?"

Dhillon stepped toward his uncle. No way was he bringing Dhillon's dad into this. But before he could say anything, Dhillon's mother stepped between them. "Hiral Bhai, okay, fine. I'll do what you say. Just go."

Hiral Mama inhaled, calming himself. He nodded at his sister. "Wise choice. I knew you wouldn't hurt the family." He threw a glare at Dhillon and left, ignoring Hetal altogether.

Once the front door slammed shut, Dhillon and Hetal turned to their mother.

"You're not serious, Mom?" Hetal hugged her mother. "You can't just stop seeing Dr. Shah."

"I have to. You heard your uncle. It makes him look bad. It makes Dada and Dadi look bad."

"Mom," Dhillon said. "Dada and Dadi have been gone for ten years. And honestly, they would want you to be happy." Maybe it had taken him a minute to get used to the fact that his mother was dating, but she was so happy. She deserved to have someone she could share her life with if that was what she wanted. Dhillon was furious that his uncle failed to take his own sister's feelings into consideration.

She shook her head, swallowed tears. "No, it's too much. It's easier to just do what he says. It's years of tradition. I can't fight it." She gently pushed her daughter back. "Come on, now. I need help with dinner."

"Sure, Mom." Hetal pulled away and went about gathering vegetables and flour and spices to make the evening meal.

Dhillon just stood there, seething.

"I'll be fine." She smiled, though it was obviously forced. "You look nice."

"He's got a date," Hetal piped up.

His mother grinned. "Riya will love how you look, all dressed up."

Dhillon sighed. "It's not with Riya."

His mother glanced at her daughter, puzzled. Hetal shrugged. "Riya's dating someone else."

"Oh. Well." His mother turned back to him. "Lucky girl, whoever she is. Have fun." She kissed his cheek.

"Yes. Have fun!" Hetal called as she pushed him playfully out of the kitchen. She whispered to him, "It's okay. I'll be here. Ryan's on his way to pick up food. Go. Meet women." She gave him a gentle push to get him moving.

He turned to look back. His mother was already chopping vegetables. Hetal made a shooing gesture at him. He sighed and turned away again.

He glanced quickly at the framed photos of his dad on the wall. One of his favorites was of the four of them. His dad had Hetal, then a toddler, in a carrier on his back, and Dhillon stood between his parents. They'd been hiking and camping in Shenandoah. Another photo showed just him and his father—even then, Dhillon had been his father's *mini-me*. They had left his mother and sister to play at the campground and the two of them had gone white water rafting together for the whole day.

"It'll be an adventure," his father had said.

And it had been. Neither one of them was experienced in white water rafting, but they paddled and navigated the rapids, stopping along the way to eat their packed lunch of spicy tepla and peanut butter and jelly sandwiches.

Dhillon remembered how hard it was, but also how fun it had been to be on a true adventure with his father.

Even at thirty, Dhillon would not have minded having his dad around before he went on this date. He felt like a damn teenager.

"No need to rush home! Stay out as late as you want. Or don't come home at all. We won't worry," Hetal called from the kitchen.

"That's not what you said the last time I was out late," Dhillon called back. He cringed as the words left his mouth. *No need to bring up that night.*

"Yeah, but you said you were with Ryan."

"No, he wasn't." Ryan had just walked through the front door.

"He really wasn't with you?" Hetal had walked into the family room. "He said he was having drinks with you. The night that Lucky died."

"I did not—" Ryan started but stopped when Dhillon shot him a glare. "Oh, oh yeah. Right. Drinks."

"What are you doing here?" Dhillon changed the subject before his sister, the FBI interrogator, asked more questions.

"Your mom said she was cooking tonight. I need a home-made meal," Ryan said.

"Ryan," Sarika called from the kitchen, "if you're going to eat here, you have to help."

"Yes, ma'am." Ryan immediately started for the kitchen. "It smells amazing."

"Go, Dhillon. You'll be late," Hetal warned.

"Yeah, Dhillon. Go," Ryan echoed. "And then text me after."

His stomach was in knots. Did he really want to do this?

"Fine, I'm leaving." He took another step toward the door. "Don't forget to feed Lucky." The whole room went silent. Emptiness overcame him for a moment. This was his family. He could call and reschedule his date and just stay here with the people he loved and enjoy a fabulous evening in the comfort of his home.

As if he could read his mind, Ryan spoke. "Dude. If you leave her waiting, you'll never get her into—"

"I'm going, I'm going." Dhillon raised his hands in surrender. There was no need to allow Ryan to finish that sentence with his mom and sister right there. He walked out the door, keys in hand, down the steps to the driveway. He pushed the button to unlock his door when he heard Radha Auntie's car beeping open at the same time. Momentarily confused, he looked over and saw Riya standing outside it, key fob in hand.

She looked heart-meltingly good. There was no other way to describe it. Riya was tough, always had been. But she wasn't a tomboy. Dhillon had seen her dress up over the years, but her jobs required uniforms that were functional, and Riya was always happiest in jeans and a T-shirt.

Right now, she had on a cool blue summer dress that showed

off her strong arms. Between the short length of the dress and her high heels, her beautiful brown legs were gorgeous and curvy, muscular and defined. Dhillon had no idea about makeup, but Riya glowed, her lips sparkling. Her wavy dark hair was down and flowing to the middle of her back, despite the humidity being at nearly 100 percent and the sun beating down from a cloudless sky.

She was going out. And not with her pregnant cousin. She was going out on a date. He clenched his jaw at the thought of another man holding her hand or making her laugh. He couldn't even let himself imagine this other man actually *touching* her. If he was honest, he couldn't even stand the thought of another man even *looking* at her the way he was looking at her right now. Not to mention the thoughts that were swirling about in his head.

It didn't matter. She didn't want him.

"Hey," he called, because why not torture himself a bit before he went out?

twenty-one
RIYA

"Hey." Riya studied Dhillon much the same way he was studying her. He was looking at her like he'd never seen a woman before. Not to mention that he was most definitely not wearing his usual scrubs or shorts and a T-shirt. Dressed-up Dhillon was most definitely something. Navy blue button-down shirt, molded nicely across his broad chest, sleeves just tight enough to hint at what she knew were impressive biceps. The cuffs were turned up and folded a couple of times to reveal strong, roped forearms. He was almost as muscular as any of the guys she worked with. She drew her gaze down. Good blue jeans, which she already knew hugged his ass perfectly, and casual dress shoes. He had taken a minute or so with his hair and trimmed the scruff so it was the exact amount that looked sexy and not sloppy. She was certain if she stepped close to him, she'd be enveloped in his cologne, which always mixed so well with his natural scent.

He was going on a date. A fancy date. With a woman. Jealousy, instant and suffocating, pierced her heart. Nope. He didn't want her. Which was why she was going on a date, too.

He was also flushed, his jaw ticking, and he was fidgeting with his keys. "What happened?" Riya furrowed her brow.

Dhillon shook his head. "Hiral Mama just convinced my mother to stop dating. She finally found a decent guy. She was happy." He fisted his hand around his keys. "He just doesn't understand how to be a brother."

Riya was all too familiar with Hiral Mama's holier-than-thou attitude. She'd never really liked him. She frowned. Dhillon was right: his mom deserved someone to share her life with. "Sorry. Want me to ask my mom to talk to her?"

His eyes landed on hers, slightly hopeful. "Yes, sure. She always listens to your mom."

"Well, they're, like, BFFs." Riya did her best teenage impression, and it was awful. But it made Dhillon relax and chuckle, so mission accomplished.

"Hetal dressed you?" She smirked as she looked him up and down, hoping that the jealousy didn't come through.

"Yes." He raked his gaze over her, and Riya enjoyed that just a little too much. "You?"

"Roshni just left," she confessed.

"You look—" His voice was gruff, and he didn't finish his sentence, just cleared his throat.

"You, too," she managed. "You going to the harbor?"

"Yes. How about you and…?"

"Akash. Little Italy." She bobbed her head. This was ridiculous. She needed to get into her car and leave before she said something stupid. "What's your date's name?" *Like that.*

"Sonia. She's a doctor. Pediatrician."

Of course she was, the little bitch. Professional, just like him. Straight and narrow, most likely. They'd be perfect together and make perfect little doctor babies together. *Ugh.* "Nice," she said.

"And Akash? What does he do?"

Goddamn. She could not remember right now, not with Dhillon-V standing there looking cool as a cucumber and hotter than fuck all dressed up for some other woman. "Oh, he's in IT. Computers." Or something like that.

"Sounds great."

"It is," she added smugly, as if IT was *the* thing.

"Well, I should go." Dhillon opened his car door.

"Have fun!" She forced lightness into her voice. "I know I will."

twenty-two

DHILLON

Dhillon watched Riya drive off in his rearview mirror, then pulled out of the driveway himself and headed for the harbor. He tried not to think about Riya or how stunning she was tonight.

What the hell was that dress Riya had on? No. He shook his head and concentrated on what he knew about his date so he wouldn't sound like an idiot.

When he'd spoken to Sonia on the phone, she'd seemed like a very nice person. In addition to being a pediatrician, she loved cooking and hiking.

She had picked a place in the harbor that ended up being just a few blocks from the bar where he and Riya had sung karaoke just a few weeks ago. He hardly had to wait before a very attractive woman with soft brown skin entered, looking as though she was searching for someone. She looked just like her picture. Dhillon approached.

"Sonia?"

She looked up at him and smiled. She was gorgeous. Fabulous smile, taller than Riya. *Stop doing that!*

"Yes. Dhillon?" She laughed and extended her hand when he nodded. "Nice to meet you. Sorry I'm late."

"No, not at all. Let's get the table."

The hostess led them to their table. Dhillon waited while she sat, then seated himself. The night was warm, so he had requested outdoor seating to enjoy the view.

They ordered a bottle of wine, and the conversation flowed with ease. She loved outdoor dining and seafood. She was the middle child with brothers on either side of her, and her stories about growing up the middle sister of two boys were hilarious. She practiced in a small office in Baltimore and was on her way to becoming a partner.

Though Dhillon found he was enjoying himself, his thoughts drifted to what Riya was doing just a couple of miles down the road in Little Italy. Was she impressing her date? Of course she was. She had tales from being a paramedic, and now from firefighting. She was tough but warm and kind. She was beautiful. She had a dry sense of humor, but she was easy to get along with. As long as your name wasn't Dhillon Vora. Akash-the-IT-guy would be an idiot to not like her.

"That sounds great. Don't you think, Dhillon?" Sonia was looking at him. "Dhillon?"

The waiter was at the table. He had no idea what had just been said.

Dhillon glanced at the waiter for a clue.

"Dessert menu?" he asked, one eyebrow raised, as if he knew Dhillon had been thinking about another woman just now.

"Always." He grinned and turned his attention back to Sonia. *Yes. Focus on Sonia.*

The waiter left, taking his judgment with him.

"So did you have any pets growing up?" Dhillon asked, as he emptied the last of the wine into her glass.

"Hell, no." She scrunched up her face and picked up her wineglass. "Thanks."

Dhillon put the bottle down and paused. "What?"

She shrugged. "I'm not really a pet person."

Dhillon stared at her. "You know I'm a veterinarian."

"I do. That's fine. I just can't have pets of any kind in the house. They're messy, and they're a lot of work. Just not my thing." She sipped her wine. "Do you see your sister often? Seems like you're pretty close to her."

Dhillon was still reeling from the fact that she did not like pets. It was fine, right? Lots of people didn't like pets. "I live at home."

She paused with her glass halfway to her mouth. "As in, with your mom and sister?"

Dhillon nodded, a smile on his face. "My dad died when I was in high school, and I'm still there."

"Pretty traditional that way, huh?" She sipped again.

"No. Not like that. I just like to be there for them. How about you? What made you agree to shaadi.com?" He wasn't going to continue defending his living arrangements to someone who didn't like animals.

"Agree? It was my idea. Listen, I'm, like, twenty-eight right now. If I want to have kids by thirty-four, and I do, I need to find someone and get married in the next few years. I'd like to have some time being a newlywed before I'm a mom."

"You've got it all planned out."

There had been a time when he'd had his life planned out. He'd been almost engaged to a woman he thought he was in love with, he'd just bought the practice, and he'd been look-ing at houses to buy. Then she'd left. When he'd found him-self whirling from relief as opposed to devastation, he realized that maybe it was for the best. Since then, he'd been drifting.

Until Riya had come back. Who was he kidding? Riya had never really left.

"So tell me." He picked up his wineglass. "How do you feel about karaoke?"

"Ugh. Never. Not in a million years." She pursed her lips. "I mean, I can sing—don't get me wrong. But in a bar?" Her raised eyebrow spoke volumes about how she felt. "Please, no. How about you?"

Dhillon shrugged. "It's fun."

Next thing you know, Sonia will order fruit for dessert because she hates chocolate. What the fuck was his problem? Sonia was a perfectly lovely, intelligent woman. But when he looked at her—nothing. He was indifferent to her.

When he thought about Riya, his first reaction was anger. Then attraction. Then concern. Then he invariably found him-self smiling. She was not easy, by any means. She was the one who knew how to get him out of his comfort zone and take risks and live life. She loved deeply and gave her whole self. Which was why he still loved her, no matter what she was doing with her life. No matter that she did not love him back.

The waiter arrived with a sample tray of desserts, his judg-mental eyebrow raised.

Dhillon nodded at Sonia. "Go ahead. You pick."

twenty-three

RIYA

It was early, barely ten thirty, when she pulled into the drive-way. Dhillon's car was not there, so he was still on his date. Great. He was probably having a fabulous time. Good for him. Maybe he'd be out all night. That Sonia was probably as per-fect as her résumé. Riya was happy for him. Right?

Her date had started out fine. Akash was just the right amount of nerdy, not absorbed in explaining the details of his job to Riya, content to give her a general overview so her eyes didn't glaze over.

He pulled out chairs, opened doors and didn't order food for her. (One guy had done that, and it had been everything Riya could do to not punch him, then get up and leave.) He was handsome and funny and filled out his shirt nicely.

Riya could do nothing but think about what Dhillon was doing.

She had gone to the bathroom, given herself a stern but silent talking-to and returned to the table prepared to focus on Akash rather than pine over someone who did not want her. Between her self-lecture and the wine, she had relaxed and enjoyed herself. Akash was not at all threatened by her being a firefighter. Nor did he think her job was too dangerous for her to do, like *some* people she knew.

They enjoyed a lovely Italian meal and had just ordered the house tiramisu when it happened.

She'd heard some of the guys at the firehouse talk about *badge bunnies*, women who were attracted to the badge. Many of them wanted to be able to say they'd slept with a firefighter. Some of the guys didn't mind, but plenty of them did. No one really wanted to be treated like a conquest.

"You must be very strong." Akash had placed his hand on hers.

"I mean, I need to be properly fit to do my job." She removed her hand. Something about his touch was…unappealing.

Definitely not the fact that he wasn't Dhillon.

"That is so hot. Do you have any tattoos?" Something about his lopsided grin made her stiffen back into her chair.

She had a small Ganesha tattooed on the side of her shoulder that was currently covered by the cap sleeves of her dress.

Instinct made her lie. "No."

"You know, it's kind of a fantasy of mine to be with a woman firefighter." He said this like he was ordering food off the menu.

"Excuse me?" She was sure her voice had gone up an octave.

"I mean, come on. Firefighting is totally hot—no pun intended. But it's a real turn-on. Don't you think?"

Riya narrowed her eyes at him. "I mean, I know some

people think firefighters are hot, but our job is serious. People die if we don't do our jobs." She squirmed in her seat. He couldn't possibly...

"You're a gorgeous woman. You're a firefighter." Akash simply shrugged.

"So you thought, what the hell, let's see if she'll just sleep with me? Check that box?" Riya gave him her most saccharine smile. *What an asshole.*

He nodded, visibly relieved that she had caught on. "Yes. See, you get it."

She sat straight up, her eyes hardening. "Oh, I get it. But no, thanks."

"Come on. One night. You can't possibly be a virgin."

"What the hell is the matter with you?" Riya pulled out some cash and dropped it on the table. Then thought better of it and picked up the cash. Let the asshole pay. "I'm not interested. If you want to score a firefighter, get someone to play dress-up for you."

She stomped out and got into her car, shuddering. A shower was necessary. She was pulling into her driveway when she realized that she completely missed out on the apparently amazing tiramisu. Damn it. Why were men such assholes?

And now Dhillon was having a fucking fantastic time on his date. She sat in the driveway a moment and gathered herself before going back into the house. Her mom was getting better, but she'd probably need Riya around for a couple more weeks. She started to open the car door when headlights blinded her momentarily. She failed to ignore the little jump her heart gave.

Dhillon was home.

She suppressed a satisfied grin that he was home at the same time as her. He exited the car with a to-go box in his hand. She smirked. She'd bet her turnout gear that was chocolate cake in there. Dhillon had a sweet tooth, but his date didn't eat dessert.

"Hey," she called out.

"Hey." He sauntered over to her car, leaning against the hood next to her, and she was at once in the protective bubble of his scent. Wisps of his cologne and *him*.

"What's up?" she asked, nodding at the to-go box. "How was Sonia?" She tried not to say the woman's name with a tone, but she was probably not successful.

He opened the box, and sure enough, there was a huge slab of chocolate cake in there, along with one fork. "She's awesome. Intelligent. Funny. Very attractive." He nodded as if that said it all. He put a piece of cake on the fork and held it out in front of her mouth. "How about Akash?"

"Same." She opened her mouth and ate the cake. "Very handsome, he totally works out. Just the right amount of geeky."

The cake was light and moist, and the icing was chocolaty without being too sweet. In other words, perfection. And the fact that Dhillon was feeding her didn't hurt, either. Though, they used to do that when they were kids, sharing dessert. Who needed two spoons?

"You're home early," he said, as he fed her another bite.

She took the cake and was grateful for the full mouth so she didn't have to talk. She shrugged and swallowed. "So are you."

"She doesn't like pets."

Riya's mouth dropped open. "No! I'm so sorry." No, she wasn't. A little part of her danced a jig. She was excited that Little Miss Perfect Pediatrician didn't like pets.

He nodded as he ate more cake.

"Shouldn't that have been on her profile? Why did she even waste your time coming out?"

Dhillon held out another forkful of cake. She took it.

"What makes you think she wasted my time?"

"Because you're a vet." And she knew him. She remembered that every time they saw a stray or heard about a lost dog, Dhillon's heart broke. He had told her that an animal's love was pure. The way he had quietly tended to various animals over the years was a testament to how he felt about those who could not care for themselves. It was who he was. If Sonia didn't get that, she didn't get Dhillon. A spark of victory hit her heart. "I'm guessing she passed on dessert, so you ordered this piece of cake to bring home."

Dhillon shook his head and inhaled, his eyes incredulous. "She ordered the fruit."

She took the fork from him. "Are you saying she didn't waste your time?"

"I'll say whatever I have to to get you to give me that fork." He smirked at her.

She moved the fork away from him and cut into the cake. He met her eyes, then bent down and put his mouth over the fork, his eyes never leaving hers. She stopped breathing.

He broke off a small piece of cake with his thumb and forefinger. He brought it close to her lips and waited for her to open, still watching her. She was powerless to look away from him. She opened her mouth and allowed him to feed her, her lips grazing his fingers. He watched her, his voice that seductive mixture of gravel and honey. "Why are you home so early?"

He was so close. Their bodies not quite touching, the scant space between them charged with energy. She couldn't tear her eyes away from him, and she couldn't step away.

She could lean in and kiss him, and she could have him again. But it would only be for tonight. And she couldn't stand being with him again if it was only for the night. She replayed the night they'd been together over and over again. No. She needed to move on from him.

"He just wanted to nail a firefighter." She rolled her eyes.

"What? That's a thing?"

"So it would seem." She shuddered and made a face. "I need a shower."

His eyes glazed over, and she knew he was thinking about her in the shower. And she did not mind one bit. He cocked a half smile at her, and her knees went weak. "Totally his loss." He looked quickly away from her, as if he'd said too much.

His words warmed her, but she let them go and loaded up the fork. "Last piece." She paused, the fork in midair as though she meant to offer it to him, but instead, she ate it herself, wiggling her eyebrows in victory.

"Too bad." Their faces were inches away from each other. He brought his thumb to her lips and wiped. "Chocolate."

Silence floated comfortably between them. Riya would have been happy to bask in his attention and eat cake from his fingers all night. She just couldn't deal with the heartache that would result.

She moved back an inch, but it might as well have been a mile. "Thanks for dessert. I missed out on the tiramisu."

She stepped toward her house but then turned to face him. He was leaning back on his car, watching her. "For what it's worth, it's Sonia's loss, too."

Dhillon broke into a small laugh and nodded his thanks. "Good night, Riya-D."

She turned and went into her house.

twenty-four

RIYA

No sooner had Riya finished her nighttime duties and laid her head down on her pillow than the alarm sounded. She popped back up and stepped into her gear. She was assigned to the engine, so she hopped on. There was a spot next to Walsh, but there was no way she was going to sit there. She stepped over to Evans and motioned for him to scoot over.

Evans looked from her to the empty spot next to Walsh.

Walsh grinned. "She probably can't control herself around me."

"You wish," Riya spit out at him.

Evans scooted over. "Give it a rest, Walsh."

Walsh mumbled something, but Riya was concentrating on what Dispatch was saying. They were being sent to a neighborhood not far from her parents' house.

"Smoke and flames visible. Rescue needed."

Schultz leaned into the horn, sending about the blaring *baaamp-baaamp* to accompany the wailing siren. Adrenaline pumped hard and strong through her body. By the time they reached the scene, she was raring to go.

Being assigned to the engine meant working the line. Schultz pulled the engine up to the scene, and sure enough, dark smoke floated into the air surrounding the brick townhome. She disembarked, inhaling the pungent odor of burning wood and plastic while fitting her SCBA. The ladder was already there, trying to get roof access to the fire. More sirens screeched in the distance as other departments were called in. Schultz hopped out of the driver's seat and scurried on top of the engine to the pump panel. Ambrose shouted orders.

"Let's go," Ambrose said, nodding to another engine on the scene. "I need two for rescue, 71."

"Yes, sir." Two firefighters from 71 ran toward the burning building.

"Evans, Desai, grab the lines. Move in!"

"Yes, sir." Evans grabbed the line.

Movement swirled around her, as if in slow motion, as firefighters took their assignments. Her radio squawked. A man and a woman were trapped inside. Ambrose sent in another unit of two firefighters to aid the rescue. Paramedics stood close by.

Flames floated out from the windows over the garage. The floor above glowed orange in the setting sun. Smoke continued to rise. Sweat dripped down Riya's back, and she shivered as a chill slid through her body. Then she froze.

Everything slowed down and faded. She was fifteen, standing outside in her nightgown, her mother's arms around her. Her father had run toward the house.

"My son! My son! Inside! Undher ché. Bicharo, eklo ché!" In his fear and panic, her father had reverted to Gujarati, his English bro-

ken. *The firefighters had kept him out, assuring her father that they were searching for the boy. And they were. Young Riya had stood frozen with awe as two firefighters had gone into the house while the others had worked the line.*

One of the firefighters had carried Samir out. He was barely conscious from smoke inhalation, but he was clutching her necklace. A firefighter had handed the necklace to her before the paramedics loaded him and Riya's mother onto the bus. Just before they closed the ambulance doors, she saw them put an oxygen mask on his face. Relief had flooded over her. Her brother, her personal hero, was out of the fire. He was going to be fine. She clutched the necklace to her chest, knowing that their brother-and-sister bond could never be broken. She had these firefighters to thank for that. Her throat was sore, as she had also inhaled some smoke, but she wasn't scared anymore.

Two hours later, Samir died in the hospital, and when she found out, Riya felt the ground beneath her give way. She lived like that for years, no sure ground, no footing. She had held on to that necklace so she could feel her brother beside her.

The Rakshabandan when he had given her that gift was imprinted on her mind.

"Riya, this necklace took me a month to make," he'd said. "But I put all my love for you and all your love for me into it, so it's special. Even when I go to college, I want you to know you can always count on me. I will always have your back."

She had believed him. He had gone back into the fire for this, and now he was dead. She was unable to part with it, and she kept it as a reminder of his sacrifice and her responsibility.

The first time she had gone into a fire after that was where she had found her footing, her solid ground. She had been working as a paramedic, and her bus was first on the scene of a house fire. She had run in without thought and had brought a young boy out by the time the first engine had arrived. She had received more than a few lectures for that, but the next day, she had applied to become a firefighter.

"Desai! Desai! Grab the line!" a man was yelling at her. "Riya! Snap the fuck out of it."

She left that past fire as she felt strong hands on her arms, shaking her. Her breath was coming heavy, she felt tears on her cheeks, and acid churned inside her. She looked at the man as if she were in a dream. He was familiar: dark skin, blazing eyes filled with anger as he continued to shout at her. She failed to understand who he was or why he was yelling at her.

"The line, Desai! Riya! It's Marcus! Can you even hear me?" Panicked hazel eyes glared at her, and in a flash she was back. Evans. *Oh, shit!* She needed to take the line in with Evans. That was her job. She grabbed the line. She wasn't sure where they were supposed to be going, so she followed him.

"You with me now?" Evans yelled at her. His mouth set in an angry line, and rightly so. She had spaced out. Just a few seconds, but in a fire, seconds counted.

"Everything okay over here?" Ambrose eyed her, his brow furrowed.

"Yes, sir," she shouted back over the noise and turned her focus to the task at hand, afraid to even look at him. She had almost dropped the ball, not done her job. People died if she wasn't on top of her game. Lieutenant Ambrose had been right that day. She had to deal with her issues with fire.

"What happened out there, Desai?" The captain's baritone, while not harsh, demanded an answer. Ambrose stood behind her, giving her space. The captain had insisted the lieutenant be in the room.

Multiple firehouses had been called, the fire had been put out, and there were no injuries, no fatalities and only moderate damage. It was a good outcome. Once the engine had returned, they had set about cleaning and restocking the rigs. She was just contemplating the possibility of a shower when

Captain Davis had summoned her to his office. Her stomach had dropped. She'd been anticipating this. There was no way to hide what had happened. Ambrose had had to tell the captain that she'd frozen on the job.

She shook her head. "I don't know. I thought I'd dealt with it."

"With what?"

Riya looked into her captain's kind, dark brown eyes. She tried to forget that Ambrose stood just a few feet behind her. Her stomach roiled, and she swallowed hard, but she had to answer. "The house fire."

"What house fire?"

She was unable to meet his eyes. "I was fifteen. And there was a fire." She paused to breathe. "In my house."

Captain Davis nodded for her to continue.

"I lost my brother." She paused. "Today, that house—it…it looked like mine. The flames, the smoke." Her hands shook, so she fisted them in her lap. "I was standing in front of that fire again. And I could see him, being brought out…" Tears prickled her eyes. She broke off. She would not cry. Not here. This was not how a firefighter behaved. She cleared her throat and sat straight up. "It won't happen again."

"Damn straight it won't happen again. I'm recommending you check in with Psych."

Riya moved to the edge of her seat and leaned forward, dread filling her. *No, no, no!* "That's not necessary. I've got it under control. Besides, I passed the psych eval already."

He pierced her with those dark eyes again. "Check in with Psych weekly and you can keep your shifts."

What if the guys found out? "Isn't there another form of punishment?"

"This is not punishment." He shook his head. "This is ensuring that my team is fit to do the job."

She leaned in farther. "Captain, I'll look weak in front of the guys. They'll never respect me."

"They respect people who can do the job." Captain Davis paused. "Can you do the job, Desai?"

"Yes, sir. I can." She stabbed her finger into his desk to accentuate her point. "I was made to do this job."

He grinned at her, but it was a short-lived thing. "Glad to hear it. You can continue to do it if you report to Psych."

She opened her mouth to say more, but he raised his hand. "Dismissed, rookie. And if I was you, I'd leave while I was ahead."

Riya was screwed. The guys were going to find out she was going back to Psych, and they'd never think she was fit for the job. It was beyond mortifying.

She stood and turned, prepared to be assaulted by taunting blue eyes and an I-told-you-so smirk. Instead, her lieutenant looked at her with soft eyes and a closed mouth. She would have preferred the taunt and the smirk.

"I guess you were right, after all," she threw at him as she opened the door.

He caught the door and covered her hand with his, forcing her to look at him. "I was never trying to be right." He focused his gaze on her. "Go home, Desai. There's only a few minutes left on your shift anyway. Get some rest. We'll start fresh tomorrow."

He made sense, and she was suddenly weary from it all. She left the captain's office and marched out of the bays and straight to her bike. She couldn't face the guys right now. She just couldn't. Once they found out she had been ordered to Psych, they'd never look at her the same way.

She pulled into her driveway, barely remembering how she got there. The motion-sensor driveway lights flickered on, revealing a figure leaning against the brick between the two garages.

"Tough night?" Dhillon's voice was gravelly with sleep, and her reaction to it was as it always was: a thrill leading to her insides melting.

His hands were shoved into the pockets of his shorts, and he wore a fitted T-shirt. He pushed off the brick with his shoulder, his champal slapping the bottoms of his feet softly as he approached her. Didn't he have any loose-fitting T-shirts?

His grin slow and lopsided, he looked at her from beneath sleep-tousled hair. She had the feeling that if she stepped closer to him, he'd still be warm from his bed. "Sorry, I didn't mean to startle you." He didn't look sorry. He looked pleased with himself.

"What are you doing out here in the middle of the night?" She tried to sound accusatory to cover up whatever feelings she was having. "Is that a pink shirt?" Because that was what was important at midnight.

He looked down at his T-shirt as if he had no idea what he was wearing. "I think the important question is why your lieutenant is calling my sister in the middle of the night about you." He yawned. "But to answer you, Hetal bought it for me, but this color has some kind of fancy name."

She narrowed her eyes at him and shrugged. "Salmon? Tea rose? Coral?" It suited him. Just another thing to love about Dhillon: he could wear pink.

He shook his head like he couldn't be bothered. "What happened, Riya-D?"

Tears burned behind her eyes, and she stared at him, determined not to answer. Dhillon waited as if he had nowhere else he'd rather be. As if he hadn't been awakened in the middle of the night.

"I freaked out today." She sniffled. "Like, I froze and couldn't do my job."

He nodded, still looking at her.

"There was a fire. A townhome fire."

His eyes hardened, and he frowned.

"I was on the hose with Evans, and I froze. There were flames in the windows, Dhillon-V, and the smoke—like that night—and all I could think about was Samir. All I could see were flames in those windows." Tears flowed down her face, and she didn't even try to stop them. "It was like I was back there again. Like it was happening right now. Evans was yelling at me, and it took a minute before I even recognized him. I was… was…" She was loath to say the word, but it was true. "Weak."

Dhillon wrapped his arms around her, tucking her head in between his shoulder and neck, and held her while she sobbed. Only Dhillon understood what had happened. Only Dhillon could comfort her. And it felt good to be in his arms again. He waited for her to settle down before pulling back enough so he could look at her. "You are many things, Riya-D, but weak is not one of them."

"I have to go to Psych."

He shrugged, like this was expected, normal. "Good."

"Good? The guys are going to think—"

"Since when do you give a shit about what people think?" His arms were still around her. "This is the girl who has done what she thinks is right her whole life, people's thoughts be damned. Don't you remember when you came to the mandir still dressed in your soccer gear because there was no time to change?"

She chuckled through her tears. "Namrata Auntie was livid!" She did a mock Indian accent. "'What kind of girl comes to temple, sweaty and dirty?'"

"Your mother was mortified. Your dad just shook his head. You did not care." He pulled his arms away from around her and took her hand. "Remember what you said?"

She nodded. "'My heart is clean. It shouldn't matter if I'm sweaty.'"

"You impressed me, even then." He wiped away her tears with his thumbs, resting his hands on her face.

She tamped down her excitement at the thought that Dhillon was impressed by her in any way. Past or present.

"And every year, you sneak out of the yearly remembrance without eating." Dhillon spoke softly. "Everyone who attends, except our families, is certain of your disrespect."

"But you know why?" Her watery eyes met his.

His voice was deep and soft and reassuring, cocooning her in its warmth. "Because you can't stand to eat Samir's favorite foods without him."

His hand grazed her shoulder, soft and warm, sending oh-so-pleasant chills through her body. She looked up at him as he gasped, his eyes hooded over.

"I should get inside. Get some sleep."

Dhillon snapped his gaze up and pocketed his hands. "Yes. You should."

Neither one of them moved.

"Talk to the guys. Tell them what happened. They are good people. They'll get it," Dhillon said.

Riya shook her head. "I don't know…"

"Yeah, you do." Dhillon was firm. "You know what the right thing is here. You just have to let yourself be vulnerable enough to do it."

It was almost a command. Dhillon had never commanded her a day in his life. She knew he still hated the idea of her being a firefighter, but here he was. He could have played on her fears and insecurities and encouraged her to quit. Tried to talk her back into being a paramedic. That was what he wanted: for her to be safe. Instead, there he stood, giving her sage advice about how to keep doing what she was doing and do it even better, his own fears be damned. "This is who you are. Doesn't mean it's easy."

This was why she loved him.

twenty-five

DHILLON

Dhillon returned to his house to find his mother in the kitchen. Didn't anyone in this house sleep? She was in leggings and an oversize T-shirt, standing and staring out the window, almost in a trance, Scout in her arms.

"Mom?"

She started and turned toward him, and Scout wiggled free to get to Dhillon. She raised her arm to call him over, a small smile on her face.

"Why are you awake?" he asked, bending down to pet the puppy. Riya had asked them to take Scout when she was on the overnight shift, since her mother was still recovering. He came up next to her, trying to see what was so mesmerizing. "And why are you standing here?"

She shrugged. "Scout woke up when you left, and I couldn't fall back asleep. I keep thinking about…" She shook her head.

Scout curled up at his feet. He rested his arm around his mother's shoulders. "Dad? You're thinking about Dad?" Must be something in the air. The past was seeping into everyone's present.

She turned to him, teary-eyed in the moonlight, and nodded. "For the life of me, I don't know what he stayed back to get. You and I, we took Hetal. Lucky stayed with your father…" She squeezed her eyes shut, pushing tears onto her cheeks. "He just makes me so mad."

"Mom." The same thoughts haunted him all the time. What if he'd just pleaded with his dad to come out with them? Why hadn't he done that? At fifteen, Dhillon had adored his father. He and his dad had always enjoyed each other's company. They had rock climbed, hiked and watched old movies together. His father was the one who had advocated for Dhillon to get a puppy when his mother had been hesitant. He hadn't lived long enough for Dhillon to hit a rebellious phase or even roll his eyes at him.

"Sorry." She chuckled, but it was a cold thing. "Your dad could just be so stubborn sometimes. He couldn't simply come out of the house with us. If he had, we'd have him." She turned to Dhillon. "You would have had your father all these years. You two had such a special bond. I remember when you were a baby, he wanted to do everything—change your diapers, wake up with you, play with you. He had lost his father when he was very young, and he wanted to be the best dad to you."

Dhillon nodded, a small smile on his face. "He was the best dad."

She squeezed his arm. "Then, when Hetal was born, he didn't know what to do with himself. He said 'dil anand thi bharayi gayu' when he learned he had a daughter." She shook her head, smiling at some memory Dhillon could not see.

"I remember." His father's heart had filled with joy.

The instant his baby sister was born, Dhillon was in awe. She was so little, so fragile-looking, Dhillon's protective instincts kicked in with fervor. It was older-brother-love at first sight.

"Dad," he had said, "I get to do Rakshabandan this year."

His father had beamed at him. "Your first one. Let's make it special."

Dhillon saved his birthday and Diwali money and had got his father to take him shopping. It took Dhillon hours to decide on the best first Rakshabandan present. His father had patiently taken him from store to store. Finally, unable to decide, Dhillon had asked his dad what he had got for his sister for their first Rakshabandan.

"Dhillon," his father had said, a small smile on his face, "it's not about the gift. It's about the promises you and your sister make to each other."

"But she's just a baby." Ten-year-old Dhillon was practically a man compared to Hetal.

"True, she's just a baby now. But she will grow up, and you will grow up. Certainly, being a bit older, you can guide and watch out for her. But never underestimate the power of your sister to guide and watch over you as well."

Dhillon had simply shaken his ten-year-old head in disbelief. How could a little baby watch over him?

"I got my sister earrings for her first Rakshabandan," his father finally told him.

Dhillon had grinned. "Perfect. That was two stores ago."

Hetal still had those tiny little earrings. His mother had got him a delicate gold bracelet, on behalf of his baby sister, for his first rakhi. He still wore it.

"Your father would want you to be on your own—" his mother's words brought him back to the present "—instead of chained to this house by obligation or loyalty or whatever keeps you here. He'd want you to marry Riya and move on with your life."

"I'm not marrying her." But he'd got damn close to kissing her again the other night. He'd be lying if he said that didn't keep him awake at night.

"Whatever." She waved him off. "Even Hetal should be in the dorms, partying and enjoying life. Both of you stick to me as if I'm some weak old woman."

"And that's Dad's fault?"

"No. It's mine. I love having you both here, and I let that get in the way of doing what is right. You should be living your own lives." She inhaled. "I'm just tired of everyone thinking that just because I lost my husband, I'm not capable of living my own life. Do I miss him? Of course! Am I angry with him? Sometimes. I used to waste time wishing things could be different, but that just made me angrier. Now it just hits me in times of frustration." She looked out the window again. "You remember when we scattered his ashes?"

Not a day he would ever forget. It had been him, Hetal, his mother, Hiral Mama and his family, and the Desais. They had chartered a boat so they could scatter the ashes in the ocean. His dad had loved the water, and his mother was of the belief that if they scattered the ashes in the ocean, they might make it to India.

"We all went."

"Scattering his ashes… I was terrified on the trip home. It was then that I realized how alone I was. Hetal was barely five at the time. You were just a teenager, hadn't even gotten your driver's permit. Your father was supposed to teach you how to drive. That was our deal. I potty trained, but he had to teach you to drive. I didn't know how I was going to handle

working and providing, as well as raising the both of you."
She shook her head. "And missing him." Her voice cracked.

Dhillon put his arm around her and squeezed. She rested
her head on his shoulder a minute.

"It was a while before I could accept what my life would
look like without him." She side-eyed her son. "Your dad
and I had what was called a *love marriage* back in the day. Basically, it meant no one had introduced us. We used to sneak
off and meet at mandirs all over town. Hiral Mama found out
and told on us." Her eyes widened in mock drama. "It was
all very scandalous at the time. Luckily, we were in love, so
when Hiral told our parents, we were more than willing to
make it official and get married." She gazed out the window
again. "We dared to dream together." Her eyes were moist.
"It didn't work out exactly like we'd planned, but I'd dare to
dream with him again, even knowing what would happen.

"Anyway, I didn't know how I was going to work and take
care of you and your sister and everything else." She looked up
at him, pride in her face. "But you stepped up. Your father's
son all the way. I hated that you had to quit soccer, work extra
hours after school at the clinic, help with the girls. But we
needed that at the time."

Dhillon shrugged. He wouldn't have done anything dif-
ferently.

"We don't need it now, Dhillon." She brushed his hair out
of his face.

He stared at his mother.

"Live your life. I just saw you get up in the middle of the
night for Riya." She raised an eyebrow at him.

Dhillon rolled his eyes and shrugged.

The smirk on her face said everything. "Damn it, Dhillon. Go get her. Don't let the past keep you from your future." She took his face in her hands like she had done so

many times before. But she had to reach up to do it. "Dare to dream with her."

"I can't. I can't have dreams with Riya." He already had dreams of his life with her, but he never allowed himself to indulge in the fantasy that they could actually come true.

"Why not?"

He ran his hand across his scruff. "You know why. That night...we lost Dad, we lost Samir, we lost—"

"Dhillon, you need to let that go. We had no control over *who* went into the house. Or who came out. Riya is strong. She—"

"I can't, Mom. I cannot 'dare to dream' with her when I know the dream will end." The words—even his voice—sounded weak, but those were the facts.

She dropped her hands and sighed. "Take some risks, sweetheart. You bought that practice. You talk all the time about how you could make it better. Do it."

Dhillon just stared at her. She was right. He could take out a loan and redo the office to his liking. He knew exactly how it should be. But he simply did not think taking out another loan right now was wise, with Hetal getting ready for professional school. "Hetal's going to vet school..." Or at least she *was*.

"Forget about all that, Dhillon. We can all manage things together. You will continue to stagnate, living here in this house." She turned back to the window.

He simply stared out the window next to her and saw what she saw. Tommy Higgins's tree house. The one he and Riya used to sneak into before the fire. The one she went to after the fire. Alone. She'd been a mess today. But she had to get back to work; she would never forgive herself if she didn't. So he'd made sure she went back. Even if it scared him to death to have her fighting fires.

"Mom." Suddenly he was a little boy, his voice shaky. He

didn't remember the last time he'd allowed himself to feel so vulnerable. "Mom, I can't remember what he looked like." His eyes burned, and he was shocked to feel the prickle of tears. "I mean, we have all these pictures, but I'm forgetting what he looked like, what he sounded like."

"Oh, Dhillon." She squeezed him to her. "I'm so sorry you had to grow up so fast. You never really got to be a kid." She pulled back and reached up to place her hands on his face again. Dhillon remembered her doing that when he was a boy. Right now, he felt like that boy. "You only need to remember how he made you feel. Your dad made me feel like anything was possible. He made me feel like I could do anything. That was his superpower. How you make people feel is something that is never forgotten. That being said, beta, you must move forward with your life. Buy a house—" She put up a finger against his unspoken protest. "I know you can afford it. This house has been paid off for a few years now."

Her eyes filled with sorrow for him. She shrugged, letting him go. "Look at these pictures. Your father was always up for an adventure. Always ready to try something new. He's gone. Us pining away for him will never bring him back, Dhillon. It's time we took some chances, risked a little to live our lives."

She paused and turned to stare at the tree house. "I knew you and Riya used to sneak off to that tree house." She cocked a grin at him.

Dhillon was wide-eyed with shock. "You did?"

She nodded. "Your dad knew, too. We also knew it was Riya who made you go."

Dhillon tried to hide the smile that crept to his face with those memories. He and Riya would meet up after dark and take snacks up to the tree house. They smuggled up the requisite chocolate and cupcakes, but they also took spicy Indian snacks. Dhillon had to admit, there had been something ex-

citing about eating all that in a tree house they weren't supposed to be in. They had discussed the latest theories on *The
X-Files*, the validity of *ER* episodes, as well as the drama of
90210 and *Saved by the Bell*. They talked about school and what
they wanted to be when they grew up. Riya had changed her
mind every day.

"She's good for you. And you for her." His mother smirked
at him again, making him wonder what his face had just revealed. "Your father is long gone. He was a great man. But us
living in the past is never going to bring him back."

"Are you kicking me out?"

"I'm trying to." She stared again at the tree house, inhaling
deeply, as if gathering power from her breath. Her eyes were
bright and excited when she turned back to him. "You know
what? Screw my big brother. I can date if I want. Rohun treats
me like a capable woman. Which is more than I can say for
any other man in my life—including you."

"I think you're capable, Mom," Dhillon defended himself.

"Then why do you still live here?"

"To make sure you're okay." The excuse was starting to
sound lame, even to him.

"I don't need that." She turned to leave the kitchen. "Dhillon, if you want to know what your father looked like, just
look in the mirror. You look just like him." She smiled again,
the tears gone from her eyes. "Your sister and I love you, and
we will always need you. But we don't need you to take care
of us all the time."

She turned back to him at the doorway. "But I do want a
dog."

Dhillon nodded and looked out the window again. The
moon was full and high, and it lit what was left of Tommy's
tree house.

twenty-six

RIYA

She slept fitfully, going over and over Dhillon's words. She woke early and knew he was right. She arrived at the station early for her shift and found the guys already there, music blaring, laughter reaching her all the way in the parking lot. She parked her bike and inhaled deeply.

Evans, Schultz and Alvarez were laughing and singing as they cleaned and restocked. Her heart ached as she watched them. She wanted to be part of that. If this was what she wanted, she had to take it for herself.

She was mortified that she had frozen on the job, embarrassed that she had to report for psychological support.

The guys switched up the song they were singing and started singing about putting out fires they had never even started.

She inhaled and set her lips to join her company. They were all in the middle of cleaning and singing a Billy Joel song. They stopped singing as she approached. She joined Schultz in restocking the supplies.

"Hey." Evans approached her. "You came in." The anger was gone from his deep baritone, but there was no question that he required an explanation for yesterday's behavior.

She hesitated. She looked from Schultz to Evans to Alvarez. She owed them all an explanation. They waited for her to speak, their faces filled with concern.

She stocked a few things, while she gathered her words. Looked at them again. "I was in a fire. When I was fifteen." She shot a glance at them. "It was a townhome. Like the one yesterday." Tears burned behind her eyes. Ridiculous. She thought she'd dealt with all this. "When I saw those flames, I was back at that first fire." A tear escaped. She slapped it away, clearing her throat. "I should not have let it affect my performance on the job. And for that I apologize. Someone could have gotten hurt because of me. And I can't…" She swallowed back all the remaining tears and went back to work. That was all she had to say.

"Desai." Evans spoke first, his deep voice genuine with concern. "You lost someone, didn't you?"

She kept her lips pressed together, shrugged.

"Most of us have." Evans nodded, compassion in his eyes. "It shows."

Tears welled up in her eyes. She turned her back to them.

"If you tell us, it loses its power over you." Evans's eyes softened. "I lost a cousin. It's why my brother and I are fire-fighters."

Her heart ached for Samir and Dhillon's father. Their families had been so close, and Kishore Uncle had been more than just a neighbor to her. Seeing that fire last night had made it feel like she was losing them all over again. She turned her head halfway, speaking over her shoulder. "I lost my big brother. He said he'd always have my back. Now he's gone." Tears fell down her cheeks.

"Yeah. Okay." Evans nodded. "You can turn around and face us if you want to. You're not the first firefighter to cry."

Riya froze in her restocking. What was he saying?

"Firefighters have feelings. Yes, we are strong and tough, but that's because we have to be for the job."

She wiped at her eyes as she turned to face them.

Schultz smiled. "There she is."

The next thing she knew, he had her in a bear hug. Then Evans joined in. Lastly, Alvarez. When the guys finally let her go, her tears were gone, and she was smiling.

"I lost my dog in a house fire." Alvarez spoke up.

Schultz smacked him. "That's not the same. What's the matter with you?" Schultz shook his head at Riya, apologizing for Alvarez's insensitivity.

"No. I get it." She looked at Alvarez. "A loss is a loss. We almost lost Lucky in the fire. A firefighter carried him out." Something nagged at her then. Something she had not thought about since that fire. The firefighter.

"The vet's dog?" Schultz's question pulled her away from her thoughts.

"Yes. Same fire. We're neighbors. He lost his dad. I lost Samir."

She picked up a rag and wiped at the engine, cleaning imaginary grime away to distract herself. "I'm sorry." She swallowed. "I let you down."

"We're fine." Schultz squeezed her shoulder, forcing her to look at them.

"We have each other's backs here, Desai. That means you,

too." Evans grinned. "Besides, you're the best cook in the house."

She nodded, her heart filling with gratitude. "It won't happen again."

"Damn straight it won't." Evans raised an eyebrow at her and grinned.

Alvarez started drumming out a beat on the side of the engine, as he was known to do, and picked up the Billy Joel song again. The lyrics spoke of fires that burned before any of them were even born, and continued to burn even as they fought.

Each of the guys took a line, then motioned for Riya to take the next line. She shook her head, a smile popping onto her face.

Riya caved and sang her line, laughing.

The three men, her friends, her company, broke out into wide grins as they continued to sing about fires they hadn't started but fought anyway. Singing made the work go faster, and before she knew it, the rig was clean.

"Gotta tell you, Desai. You have great potential as a firefighter, and you're an amazing cook, but you can't sing worth shit," Alvarez said, laughing.

She shrugged. "Sad for you, because that has never stopped me. You can ask—" she was about to say *Dhillon* "—anyone who knows me."

They had made their way to the kitchen. "We haven't had breakfast yet, and it's your turn, Desai." Evans shrugged at her.

Lieutenant Ambrose was seated at their large dining table, reading the paper, a cup of coffee in his hands.

"We'll start the prep for your amazing omelets," Schultz said as the three of them made for the refrigerator.

She went and stood in front of Ambrose. "Lieutenant."

"Desai."

She waited for him to speak.

"Everyone has a moment when they freeze. And after what you've been through... In any case, Captain expects you to report to Psych, and so do I." He fixed her in his gaze and narrowed his eyes. "We're a small department here. We need all our firefighters ready to move. Am I clear?"

"Crystal, sir."

"All right, then." He stood and folded his paper. "Carry on." He walked away and left her standing there.

twenty-seven

RIYA

Ambrose was in a pissy mood, so they all had to do drills at the hottest part of the day in the middle of July in Maryland. In full turnout gear. They carried the hose, they carried tires, and lastly, they carried each other. Sweat had dripped and pooled into every crevice all over her body, and her muscles were screaming for nutrition.

She needed to get cleaned up. She had four female candidates for the academy coming by today, interested in her mentorship program. She and Katie from Engine 23 in Baltimore had a list of all the female firefighters in the area who were interested in being mentors. Every single woman they reached out to had said yes. Riya had the potential mentees fill out paperwork, and now she was going to match them to these experienced women. The visit today was so that Riya could meet them in person and give them their assignments. She was giddy with excitement. Even Ambrose's crappy mood couldn't deter her happiness.

"Hey! You look gross." Hetal was early. Naturally, she was one of the young women in the program.

"Yeah, well. Your boyfriend decided to kill us today by making us carry everything in the house," Riya grumbled. "Including each other." Who knew Alvarez was close to two hundred pounds of solid muscle?

"He's not my boyfriend," Hetal said.

"Well, why the hell not?"

Hetal pursed her lips and rocked her head back and forth. "I may have embellished my age, and he found out."

Riya widened her eyes. "Hetal! How old did he think you were?"

She shrugged. "Twenty-five."

Riya tried to hide her grin. "So now he knows that you're *almost* twenty-one."

"And he's twenty-seven. Which I don't think matters. I'm very mature for my age." Hetal glanced over to where Ambrose stood with Evans, the sad look on her face betraying her sassy tone.

"Maybe, but now *we* suffer. Thanks." Riya grimaced at her. "Let me go and grab the shower before the guys can move, so I'm ready when the other girls get here."

"You're just going to leave me here?"

Riya flicked her gaze to Ambrose, who was watching them intently. "Yep."

She ran to the locker room on rubber legs while the rest of the guys writhed on the bay floor. If she was first, they'd have to wait. She peeked into the locker room and called out, "Hello? It's Desai. I need a shower. Anyone in there?"

No response. *Yes!* She dumped her gear, grabbed a couple of towels and quickly stripped down. She hit the showers and reveled for a moment in the cool, fresh water. The shower was quick but refreshing. She dried off and wrapped herself in a towel before leaving the shower area for the lockers.

"Couldn't wait to get me alone, huh, Desai?" Walsh's voice came from behind her.

She jumped. "What the hell are you doing here? I announced myself." She tightened the towel around her. Nothing like being naked in front of a lech to make her feel vulnerable. "Leave. I'll be dressed in ten minutes."

"Come on, now." Walsh came closer, dragging his words, a sick glint in his eye. "You don't really want me to leave. No one has to know."

Her entire body stiffened and went on defensive alert, but she did not back away from him. "I really do want you to leave. In case I haven't been clear enough up until now, I'm really not interested." She stood firm and looked him in the eye. "Quite frankly, I've had enough of your harassment. I thought you'd back off if I ignored it, but you won't. It's time I pressed charges."

"Harassment? Charges? What the hell are you talking about? I have not harassed you." His sense of indignation was real. And pathetic.

"Sexual innuendo. Unwelcome touching." Her voice got louder and more agitated with each accusation. "Inviting yourself to my shower. All that is harassment." She was shouting now, her anger at him from all these weeks coming to a head. "This—" she nodded at him "—this is harassment in the workplace."

"Oh, come on. What do you expect, a beautiful woman like you, working with all these men?" His sense of righteousness was nauseating.

"I expect to be treated like a colleague. I don't see you making passes at Evans or Schultz," she shouted at him.

"If a woman is going to be around men, she has to learn to accept that she's going to attract some attention. Especially a woman who looks like you." He dragged his gaze down her body and reached out as if to touch her. Riya acted on instinct. She blocked him, grabbing his outstretched hand and pushing him away. She grabbed him by the neck and slammed him into the lockers. She held him there, squeezing his neck while he choked.

"Hey, what's going on here?" Lieutenant Ambrose shouted. He was the first one in. She heard the rest of the guys clamoring in behind her.

"I'm done with his bullshit. That's what." She squeezed tighter and relished Walsh's gagging sounds. *Please don't let the towel slip.*

Evans's soothing voice reached her. "Let him down, Desai. It's okay."

"It is not okay!" she grunted.

"You're right. But killing him will not help you." Ambrose's voice had an edge to it she'd never heard.

"Riya Didi!" Hetal's voice cut through. "He's right! Let him down."

She narrowed her eyes at Walsh. "You ever even look at me—or any future woman in this house—the wrong way again and I'll finish this." She released him only after he nodded weakly.

As soon as she let him down, Walsh started shouting. "You all saw that! She tried to kill me because I gave her a compliment."

Lieutenant Ambrose shrugged. "I didn't see anything." He turned to the men behind him. "You all see anything?"

They all shook their heads.

"No."

"Nope."

"Nothing, sir."

Ambrose turned back to Walsh. "But I did hear Firefighter Desai accuse you of improper behavior."

"I'm pressing charges," she growled.

"Charges? You little bitch." Walsh took a swing at her, his fist coming at her in slow motion. A memory popped into her head. She was seven and Samir was showing her how to make a fist.

"Look, Riya. Your thumb goes here." He had taken her hand and adjusted the thumb placement. "Got it?"

She had nodded. She wanted to be strong, like her brother.

"When you punch, pretend the thing you are punching is behind what you're actually punching. You'll power through every time." He had eyed her form as she practiced air punches.

"Good." His voice had got quiet. "But Mom and Dad are right. This is a last resort. If there's a way to solve something without punches, do that first. If not, then—" he nodded at her little fist "—take them down."

Riya easily blocked Walsh's wild punch and clocked him on the jaw. He went down, unconscious.

She stood over him, her breath coming hard and fast. *It had to be done, Samir.*

"You are one badass woman." Alvarez grinned.

She looked up to find the department watching her, admiration on their faces. Her heart raced, betraying her calm demeanor. "You all mind if I get dressed?"

Riya didn't really do Rakshabandan anymore. She didn't have a brother, so she just ignored the day. Which was easier when she wasn't living at home. Or when her father's sister wasn't coming. She told herself not to be so selfish. Her dad and foi had a fabulous bond, and they didn't always get to be together for this holiday.

It really was the best holiday. Riya had always made two sweets. One Indian and one not-so-Indian, and she tried different ones each year. Her mother had always insisted they dress up in their best traditional clothes, even though the actual ceremony only took about five minutes. Riya's mother would get the thali ready. On this platter would be vermilion powder, uncooked rice, a small lit diya, and the rakhi, which Riya always made herself from embroidery string.

At Riya's last Rakshabandan, she had made peda, a cardamom milk fudge. For her non-Indian sweet, she had tried macarons. It had been her first attempt, so they needed work. But Samir had acted like they were the best thing he'd ever had.

He had handed her the small box, and in her excitement, she had quickly ripped it open to find the beautiful filigree pendant inside. It was Ganesha and an ohm intertwined. It was beautiful, more so because she knew he'd made it.

Her mother was jabbering on about Rakshabandan prep as she chopped vegetables while Riya made the dhal.

"And guess what?" Her mother was beaming. It was hard to tell she'd had a heart attack a few weeks ago. "Rumit Mama is coming." There were tears in her eyes as she gushed about her younger brother coming for Rakshabandan. "Your masi is going to be practically living here."

For the first time since all this prep had started, Riya was truly excited. Rumit Mama was much younger than her mother, and Riya adored him. The house would be full again.

Riya grinned with genuine happiness. "We should make his favorite, peda!"

"Of course." Her mother hesitated.

"What?"

"I was hoping you'd make those macarons, too."

Riya stiffened and turned back to stir the dhal. She hadn't made any kind of sweet for Rakshabandan since the last time she'd made them. It wasn't often that they celebrated, so there hadn't been any need. Baking did soothe her, but she never practiced the macarons.

"Riya." Her mother touched her arm. "It's okay to move on."

Riya glared at her mother.

"Wash your hands," Riya's mother told her as she washed her own hands, with that mom voice that Riya hadn't heard in years. The one that compelled even thirty-year-old children to do as they were told. "Come with me."

Riya cleaned up and followed as her mother marched upstairs and down the hall to Samir's room.

"What're we doing here?" Dread, deep and foreboding, settled into Riya's stomach.

"We're going in." Her mother did not sound the least bit apprehensive.

"No." Panic rose in her voice as Riya shook her head. "No one's been in here since—"

"That's not true. Your father and I have been in here plenty. The first few times were the hardest, but now, when I miss my son, I come in here to feel close to him. I know he's never coming back to us, but at least I can remember him."

Shock didn't even begin to cover what Riya felt as she heard this. Her mother was infinitely stronger than Riya had given her credit for. Apparently, Riya could run into burning buildings without a thought, but going into her brother's room made her light-headed and nauseous.

"Come on." Her mother nodded at the doorknob. "You need to do this."

Riya placed her hand on the knob, her stomach in knots.

She closed her eyes, and Samir's face appeared clearly in front of her. He was young and handsome…and smirking at her as he so frequently had. *What's the matter? You scared?* She took a deep breath. *Yes, Samir. Scared and heartbroken. You left me.* She turned the knob.

She pushed open the door and stood in the doorway. The heaviness and disorder she might have expected from this room were absent. The air was clean, sunlight streamed from the window, and things were…tidy.

Riya's mom stood beside her, her mouth set and unyielding. "It's overdue for you, beta." She squeezed Riya's arm.

I never left you. I've been here all along, Samir said in Riya's mind.

Riya siphoned courage from her mother's touch and stepped into Samir's room. She scanned the space, not completely believing what she was seeing. Samir's art was everywhere. There were paintings and metal sculptures, wall hangings and wood carvings. Her necklace was a mini sculpture, and she saw its parent hanging on the wall. Paintings and sculptures of Ganesha were a definite theme, but Samir's art was more than that. Her gaze caught on a small, eight-by-ten painting of colorful cookies. Her macarons.

Samir was everywhere in this room. Tears flowed down her cheeks with abandon, but she found herself smiling. "Mom, what…?"

Her mother's face glowed with pride. "We were able to salvage more than we had thought we could." She stopped and looked around, tears filling her eyes. "He never had to go back in the house."

"What did you say?" Riya snapped her head around to look at her mother.

"Look at how much of his art we were able to save. The fire didn't take it. He came in to save it, and the smoke took him."

"He went in to get this." She pulled at her necklace.

"What?" Her mother furrowed her brow.

"He went back in to get this. He was holding it when they found him." Her lips and voice shook with the pain of saying these words out loud. "He had made it for me for Rakshabandan. Remember? He went back in because of me." Now her mother knew the truth.

Her mother's confusion turned to shock, and she shook her head. "No, no, no, beta. That's not it. That's not— Is that what you thought, all these years?" She caught Riya in her arms, the way that only a mother could. Riya couldn't remember the last time she'd let her mother do this.

"Riya, Samir was applying to art school," her mother whispered into her hair.

Riya pulled back. "No, he was going to engineering school."

"Yes." Her mother smiled, pride still shining through. "But he was applying to an art program as well. So he could have a solid degree as well as follow his passion. He loved engineering, too. He didn't want to have to choose, so we didn't make him."

"I...I had no idea."

"I think he was going to surprise you." She looked around. "But what I do know is that he came back in for this." She gestured to the artwork. "He needed some of these pieces for his application. He did not come in because of you." She squeezed Riya's arms as if she could squeeze understanding into her. "He did not die because of you. He died because he was trying to save his art. He was trying to save his dream." She paused. "Your room is at the top of the stairs. He must have simply grabbed your necklace on his way."

Her mother's gaze followed her as she wandered about Samir's room. Riya felt as if she'd traveled back in time. Her older brother's room had been off-limits to her as a younger sibling, which had simply increased its allure back then. But there had been those rare times when Samir would let her come in and they would chat about this and that, especially as they'd got older.

She distinctly remembered breaking in when she was about nine and finding his art. He'd been so angry with her when he caught her, she'd assumed that the art was a secret. She'd come to understand that his art revealed things about him that he hadn't been ready to share with anyone at the time. Ganesha was the Remover of Obstacles. What obstacle had Samir wanted removed? Now they would never know.

Riya turned to her mother. "Why did you bring me in here? Why now?"

Her mother shrugged. "It's well past time. Rakshabandan has been difficult for you since we lost him, and I thought that maybe if you came up here, it would be easier." She sighed. "I have been hard on you for choosing to be a firefighter because I am afraid of losing you. But it's your dream, it's part of who you are—like art was part of Samir. I'm so proud of you. Saving lives. Mentoring women who want to be in your field."

Her mother's hand on her shoulder was warm. "I wouldn't stand in Samir's way, and I won't stand in yours. I'll worry, but that's a mother's right." She smiled. "That's why I brought you in here, so you could see how your brother dreamed."

Riya had no idea what to say. She'd thought she could never go into Samir's room again. But now that she was here, a peace settled over her.

"Is this why there are Ganeshas all over the house now?"

"Yes. They are all Samir's."

"Even that garish thing in the kitchen?" Riya chuckled.

Her mother shook her head, but she was smiling. "That was

one of his firsts. A precursor to your necklace." She watched Riya a moment. "Take something."

"What?"

"He was your brother. His art just sits here. Take something. Replace Johnny Abraham or whatever in your room. Or take it back to your place when you go."

Riya had already picked out what she wanted before her mother finished talking. She had spied a watercolor Samir had done from a photo of the two of them. It was from that last Rakshabandan. They were hugging each other, their lips overflowing with sweets they had crammed into one another's mouths. Riya was looking at the camera. But Samir was looking at her. She remembered the picture being taken. She had felt so loved, so part of a family. She couldn't remember having had that feeling of family since then.

She picked up the painting. Her mother teared up looking at it.

"Come on, Mom. Those macarons aren't going to make themselves." She bumped shoulders with her mother.

They turned to go downstairs when a familiar voice carried up to them. "Riya? Riya? You home?" It was Dhillon, and there was urgency in his voice.

twenty-eight

DHILLON

Dhillon entered Riya's house, hastily removing his Crocs, Scout at his heels. His heart was racing. He could not believe what his sister had just told him. He called out again as he made for the kitchen. "Riya!"

"What?" Riya called from the steps.

He backtracked. Relaxed a bit when he saw her face. "I just talked to Hetal."

Radha Auntie came up behind Riya as they both descended the stairs. He fixed his gaze on Riya, unwilling to say more in front of her mother. Radha Auntie graciously took the hint and made an excuse to be in the kitchen. They waited until they heard the sounds of pots and pans clanging before resuming the conversation.

"What happened at the station?" Dhillon glanced at Riya's hand. Sure enough, her knuckles were red and scraped raw.

She shrugged. "I took care of a problem."

Dhillon couldn't help his smile. "So I heard." He nodded at her hand. "You okay? Need help with that?"

She looked at her injury as if just now noticing it. She grinned. "What're you going to do about it? You're a vet. I'm not an animal."

He rolled his eyes. "Basic first aid."

"Which I am more than capable of handling." She pursed her lips at him.

"Which you haven't done yet," he countered.

When Hetal had texted him, saying that Riya had punched Walsh, his mind had immediately gone to the worst-case scenario. He had been on his last patient of the day, and when the appointment was over, he'd left the office as quickly as he could.

"Come on." He tapped her shoulder. "I know where your first aid kit is." He started up the stairs, hoping she would follow. She did, but not until she let out an exasperated sigh.

The Desais kept their well-stocked first aid kit in the hall closet. Dhillon marched up the stairs and opened it, pulling out the container as Riya joined him and sat on the top step. Scout scooted around and tucked herself next to Riya's hip.

Dhillon sat down next to her, but not before noticing that the door to Samir's room was open. He pulled out antiseptic and took her hand. She had a solid scrape, and it would most likely be bruised by morning.

He tilted his head toward Samir's room. "You've had a big day."

She inhaled deeply, then exhaled. But she was more relaxed than he'd seen her in a long while. "I went in there." She met his eyes, and he could swear they lit up.

"And?" He moved each of her fingers to check for breaks.

"And he was getting ready to go to art school." Tears filled her eyes, but she was still smiling. "So he didn't want his art to burn, and that's why he went back in the house. Not to get my necklace."

Though she had never said as much, Dhillon had always

suspected that Riya had somehow felt responsible for Samir's death. He squeezed her hand.

"Ouch!" She pulled her hand away.

Dhillon exaggerated the roll of his eyes. "Please. You punched a guy in the face with that hand, and then you tackled Samir's room. No way my little squeeze hurt that much."

Riya smiled but still raised her hand to give him a playful smack. He caught her hand before it landed, and she tried to pull it away, but he brought it to his lips. "You are incredible. And much stronger than you think. In every way." He kissed her bandaged hand. "Tell me everything. I want to hear how you took that asshole down."

Riya grinned but did not pull her hand away, and Dhillon was reminded of sitting in the tree house with her as they gorged on snacks and told each other everything.

She filled him in on the details of her run-in with Walsh, and he forced himself to remain calm, though the caveman part of him wanted to hunt down and beat Walsh himself.

"Walsh went down like a sack of potatoes." Her eyes lit up. "Piece of shit that he is."

"Sorry I missed it."

She stood. "Come on. I'll show you something."

Dhillon stood and followed her to her room. He hadn't been in there in close to fifteen years. He stood in the doorway, as she picked up an eight-by-ten watercolor of her and Samir from Rakshabandan. He recalled that one clearly. Samir had been so patient with Riya. He was such a great big brother, and Dhillon remembered thinking he wanted to be just like him.

"Samir painted that?" Dhillon looked closer. The room smelled like Riya, fruity and clean. "It's beautiful."

"I know, right?" Riya was beaming. "I can't believe I didn't know he was going to art school. I mean, I'm relieved—" she tugged at her necklace "—but there was so much about him I didn't know."

"Well, we both knew one very important thing."

"What's that?"

"He was an amazing brother."

Riya looked at Dhillon, her eyes shining. "He really was." She placed the painting on her dresser, leaning it against the mirror.

They turned to go, and Dhillon took a proper look around. "Johnny Abraham, huh?"

"Shut up." She smacked his shoulder and pushed him out of the room.

Dhillon took off his shoes as he entered the mandir to the scent of incense and the soft chanting of prayers. He clasped his hands together without even thinking. Beside him, Riya did the same.

Today was his dad's birthday. Every year on this day, the Desai family joined his family to commemorate the day. The celebration was always simple. A few prayers, a donation in his father's name to the mandir, some tears and time to remember his dad.

Riya had not always joined them, claiming she had a shift, and of course, no one ever questioned her. This year, however, Riya had been dressed and ready as the families piled into their cars and headed over.

Hiral Mama was very active in the mandir, running the schedule for celebrations and prayer times and more. Not much happened here that he did not know about, and he took great pride in the work. He certainly did not seem to mind that his position also granted him some level of prominence, not only in the community he served there but in the larger surrounding community.

Upon the death of Dhillon's father, Hiral Mama became even more overbearing in his opinions as to what their little family should be doing. Sarika had drawn the line when her brother had suggested she take her children and return to India. After that, Hiral Mama had only bothered to voice his opinion when it affected him.

Dhillon had had enough of his uncle's meddling and was hoping to just commemorate his father's birthday as always and leave without incident.

The main hall was moderately full when they arrived, just in time for evening prayers. It was still sticky outside, but the air-conditioning inside the building was strong, and Dhillon shuddered in the sudden chill. Riya wrapped a shawl around her shoulders.

Front and center along the back wall were statues of Krishna and Radha. All around the periphery were statues of other deities, Ganesha among them. Dhillon side-eyed Riya. Traditionally, she'd had a love-hate relationship with Ganesha, the Remover of Obstacles. Today, she seemed lighter and happier, leaning more toward the love.

She caught him looking and leaned over to whisper, "Every Ganesha in our house was made by Samir."

Dhillon turned to look at her properly. She was stunning in her simple green salwar kameez, her gorgeous hair flowing around her shoulders. "Even that one in the kitchen?" Dhillon made a face, and Riya covered her mouth with her hands to hide her laugh.

"Quit gossiping. You two are worse than the aunties," Hetal mock-chided as two women their mother's age approached.

"Ah, Sarika." The tall one nodded. "I thought we might be seeing you here today."

Dhillon's mother pasted on a smile that her children—and Riya—immediately categorized as the politest *fuck you* smile ever. Dhillon subtly elbowed Riya and caught her smirk from the corner of his eye.

"Of course, Namrata Ben. Always good to see you as well." Sarika put her hands together in front of her in the traditional namaste greeting. "Rajni Ben, you as well."

Rajni Ben returned her greeting.

"It is good that you honor your husband so devoutly, even so many years after his death," Namrata Ben simpered.

"He was a good man." Dhillon's mother's smile was plastered in place. "Oh, I see a friend of mine. Please excuse me."

Dhillon tensed as his mother waved and walked over to a man who had just entered the mandir: Rohun Shah. Hetal and Riya were holding in giggles as Namrata Auntie turned and saw Dr. Shah grin broadly and walk quickly toward their mother. Even Dhillon found himself suppressing a smirk of satisfaction at the pure elation on his mother's face and the horror on Namrata Auntie's as Dr. Shah took both of his mother's hands in his in greeting, his face filled with complete adoration.

Hetal leaned into Dhillon, barely suppressing her laugh. "Good thing Riya Didi's here. Namrata Auntie looks like she might have a heart attack."

After spending a couple of minutes unabashedly staring at the couple, Namrata Auntie turned a vicious glare on Dhillon. "You should take more control of what your mother does. It is shameful how she is conducting herself."

Dhillon fixed her with a hard stare of his own. "The only thing shameful here is your judgment. My mother is free to live her life as she pleases. You would do well to mind your own damn business, Auntie." That should match his mother's polite *fuck you* smile just fine.

Namrata Auntie's mouth dropped at being spoken to in such a manner. She swept her gaze over Hetal and Riya as if each one of them was offensive for simply existing. Then she turned and huffed off in a flounce of jingling sari beads.

Before Namrata Auntie was even five feet away, both women burst out in laughter, Riya placing a hand on Dhillon's shoulder to support herself.

Prayers began, and they sat on the floor together, happily making room for Dr. Shah. His mother was already ostracized at the mandir because she refused to wear the traditional white-only wardrobe of the widow. While she was a woman of faith and proud of her culture, she did not always agree with all of it, and neither had her husband. Dhillon sat between his mother and Hetal, and he could feel Riya behind him. His mother's eyes were wet with tears that did not fall.

They finished their prayers and mingled with friends they knew. He was considering making his way over to Riya when his uncle approached.

Hiral Mama's jaw was clenched, and his eyes blazed as he approached his sister. "I just spoke with Namrata Mehta," he growled.

Dhillon's mother raised her chin at her brother. Sarika Vora was about five foot two, so her brother had more than a few inches on her, but she didn't look the least bit intimidated. "So?"

"So? That's all you have to say?" His eyes bugged out of their sockets, and a vein at his temple throbbed.

"Namrata Ben is the biggest gossip and busybody in town. I don't know why you listen to her or why you care what she thinks."

"She's a huge donor to the mandir, and she told me she saw you holding hands with a *man*." He spit the words out, complete disgust on his face.

"Yes, which you know. I haven't hidden anything from you." She met his gaze, unblinking.

"We discussed this. You said you would end it," he growled again.

"I changed my mind. It's my life. I'll choose to live it how I please. Not how *you* want me to." Dhillon watched his mother, and a smile spread across his face. She had known this confrontation was going to happen. She had come to the mandir tonight to meet it head-on. *Go, Mom!*

"She said he's *here*." Hiral Mama was nearly vibrating with indignation, which Sarika ignored.

"He is." Her face lit up for a moment, and she motioned to Dr. Shah. "You should meet him. Rohun, this is my brother, Hiral. Hiral, Dr. Rohun Shah." She looked pleased with herself, but Dhillon caught the challenge in her eyes. She was daring her brother to cause a scene.

The vein at Hiral Mama's temple was throbbing out of control, his teeth were clenched, and he was flushed. They might need Riya's skills today after all. "What are you doing?" he spit.

"I'm dating this man, Bhaiya." Though "bhaiya" was an affectionate and respectful word for *brother*, his mother said it with more than a tinge of sarcasm. "And I'm happy."

Dhillon swelled with pride in his mother for finally standing up to her brother. She really did look happy. She deserved that and more.

"But…but—" Hiral Mama was sputtering now "—you're a *widow*." He emphasized the word, as if Sarika had committed some crime by suffering her husband's death. "This looks bad."

Enough. Dhillon opened his mouth and stepped toward his uncle, speaking through clenched teeth. "Hiral Mama, this is how it is. I'm positive that a man of your stature does not adhere to the old notions of widowhood. Surely you understand how unfair and harmful those ideas are to women." Dhillon stared down his uncle until Hiral Mama nodded.

Dhillon grinned broadly, clapping his uncle on the back. "I thought so. Now that we've cleared that up, we will hear no more about it."

"You have a younger sister," Hiral Mama argued. "Would you allow her to do something that you knew was wrong?"

Dhillon opened his mouth to speak, but no words came out. He glanced at his sister and saw her lips were pursed and one eyebrow was raised. Was that what he was doing? Was he ultimately no better than his closed-minded uncle? No. That was different, wasn't it?

"I would want my sister to do what made her happy."

Dhillon's mother stepped in again. "Bhaiya, I have made up my mind. If you are concerned with appearances, consider this my last visit to this mandir. There are other mandirs in town I can attend." She turned to the group. "That is enough. Let us go."

They gathered at the Vora house for dinner. Dhillon trailed behind the group, lost in his own thoughts. Riya trailed beside him. Everyone went in, but Riya took a seat on the step and patted the area next to her.

Dhillon sat down. The evening had cooled, and a pleasant breeze went by; even the air was drier and less sticky. A perfect summer evening.

"You know I have to protect my mom and sister," Dhillon said, as if he was continuing a prior conversation.

"Why?" Riya's question was soft and without judgment.

Dhillon watched her for a moment, enjoying her face in the moonlight, her fruity scent. "I promised my dad. That night. He sent me out with Hetal and my mom, and he went to get— You know, I don't even know what he went back for. All I remember is that he told me to take care of them, to keep them safe." He paused. "It was the last thing he said to me."

Riya nodded, was silent for a moment. "Remember when we scattered the ashes? Your dad's?"

Dhillon nodded.

"His brother was there, and he said that your dad never played it safe. He took every chance he could, to experience life, love, whatever. It's part of why he fell in love with your mom in the first place. It's why he had the courage to leave India and come to the States and start a whole new life in a country where he knew no one." She paused and Dhillon felt her eyes on him. "I'm not telling you anything you don't already know. Life is about risks and chances. You take them all the time, yourself. You bought that practice when you were just a couple years out of school. You're so like him in so many ways, yet you put your loved ones in a bubble. Let them live, Dhillon. Just be there for them if it doesn't work out."

"Am I as bad as Hiral Mama?" The thought plagued him. He wasn't that unreasonable, was he?

Riya squeezed his knee, and in spite of himself, Dhillon gloried at her touch. "No one is that bad. But you can't protect them so much that they're unhappy."

"I feel like I'm failing my dad." Dhillon stared into her brown eyes.

"You are." No Riya sarcasm. Just honesty.

Dhillon pushed a breath out. "Tell me how you really feel."

"You're failing him, and them, because you won't let them live."

twenty-nine

DHILLON

"Dr. Vora, Rocky's here with his mom. Again." Hetal's voice was tight and formal as she stood ramrod straight in the doorway of his office.

Dhillon gaped at his sister as her words registered. "'Dr. Vora'? Really?"

She pursed her lips at him and nodded. Great, so she was still mad. He did want his sister to be happy, but he couldn't shake the fear he felt when he thought about her fighting fires. It wasn't safe.

"Thank you, Ms. Vora. Is that it for the day, then?"

"Shelly can give you an update on the surgical patients. Tristan is on her way for the overnight shift." Hetal turned on her heel, nearly bumping into Shelly.

"Sorry, Shel." Hetal smiled at the older nurse and walked around her.

"Seriously, Doc, this sibling animosity thing has got to stop," Shelly said.

"She's a nightmare, right?" Dhillon typed in a plan for the cat he'd just seen.

"No, Doc. You are," Shelly said.

"What do you have for me?" Dhillon asked tersely. Every single woman in his life was going to be the death of him.

"Nala, Coco and London are stable status post ovariohysterectomy but need to stay for observation. Tristan is running late, but your sister said she would stay with the dogs until she arrived."

Tristan was a first-year veterinary student who had worked with them while she was in college. She often did overnights, so she could study in between taking vitals.

"Perfect. Thank you, Shelly. You leaving, then?"

"Yes, I am. Grandkids are coming over, and they want to bake." She grinned widely. "I'll have treats in the morning. Maybe that'll improve your mood."

Dhillon grimaced at her. He stood, preparing himself for the last patient. "See you tomorrow."

Dhillon followed his still-distant sister into the exam room.

"Ms. Sullivan, how good to see you and Rocky." Dhillon looked at the chart Hetal had pulled up on the computer.

The lights flicked off, leaving them in the dark for a few seconds.

"Oh, my!" exclaimed Ms. Sullivan.

Before Dhillon could make a move to investigate, the lights came back on.

"Ms. Vora, make a note to call the electrician tomorrow. I don't like that flickering," Dhillon said. Probably another huge expense he wouldn't be able to afford.

"Sure thing, Dr. Vora."

Hetal and Dhillon coaxed Rocky onto the exam table, and Dhillon started his basic exam. Rocky was fine and up-to-date on shots, so Dhillon declared Rocky perfectly healthy.

Hetal checked them out as Dhillon went to check on Nala, Coco and London before leaving. Nala was a small hound mix, and Coco and London were Australian mini labradoodles.

All three dogs had been spayed that morning, and Dhillon liked to keep them overnight for observation. Tristan was as smart as they came, and it would be good for her to see, in any case.

Coco and London seemed to be doing just fine, but Nala had vomited a couple of times from the anesthesia. He cleaned Nala up and updated their charts for Tristan, even though Hetal would give her the rundown.

"Hetal," he called out, grabbing his backpack, "I'm leaving. Nala puked, but the others are great." He walked to the front. "Hetal?"

She was sitting at the desk, unnaturally still, her face contorted. Dhillon went into big-brother mode, instantly dropping his backpack and going to her. "Hey, Hetal, what happen—"

Dhillon stopped as he realized what had caused her reaction. A package had come from the crematory. Lucky's ashes. His heart fell into his stomach. He put an arm around Hetal, and she melted into him like she used to when she was little.

They stared at the package together. Finally, Dhillon cleared his throat. "I'll take it home. Riya—"

Hetal nodded and wiped her eyes. "Of course."

Dhillon waited while his sister composed herself. "You okay waiting for Tristan?"

"She just texted. She'll be here in ten minutes." She blew her nose.

He kissed his sister's forehead and grabbed the box and his backpack. "I'll make dinner."

"I'm going to finish pulling charts for tomorrow." Hetal paused. "You know you can get your own place, right?"

"You want to talk about this now?"

"I'm saying, we're all fine. You don't have to always take care of us. You're thirty years old. And you live at home with your mom and sister. You'll never get a girl like this."

"Well, I guess with Mom dating, it cramps everyone's style," he replied sarcastically.

"Exactly!" Hetal wasn't kidding.

"I went on a date. With a beautiful, intelligent woman."

"And all you did was find fault with her."

"She hates pets!" Dhillon waved his arms at his surroundings. "And chocolate. Come on."

Hetal rolled her eyes. "That's one girl. You're a nice guy. I've heard you are handsome—hot, even." She shuddered. "You can't live at home forever."

"You just want me gone so you can do whatever you want."

Hetal shook her head. "Kids need to be away from their parents at some point."

Dhillon just stared at her. "I'm not your parent."

She shrugged. "But you're not always just my brother, either."

Dhillon was speechless. His run-in with his uncle last night was fresh in his head. So was the talk with Riya after. He didn't know what to say to her.

He was lost in thought as he started the twenty-minute drive home. Of course he wanted to date someone. It was just that the person he wanted to date...didn't want him. He simply couldn't shake the memory of that night from his mind or his body. Despite all that Riya had said, when they had been together, it had felt like...more than a one-night stand.

He was barely ten minutes out from the office when his phone rang. It was his alarm company. He tapped the Bluetooth in his car.

"Dr. Vora, this is DVS Security calling. The smoke alarms are going off at 2354 Old Freetown Boulevard. We have notified the fire department. They are on the way."

Panic flooded through him. His sister. Tristan. The dogs. "Thank you. I'm on my way to meet them," he managed. He turned the car around and called Hetal. *Pick up pick up pick up.* She did not pick up. He called Tristan. No answer.

Damn it.

He gunned it all the way back to the office and was greeted by smoke, flames and the wailing of the sirens behind him. He parked next to Hetal's car. It was empty, as was Tristan's.

He got out of the car and ran toward the clinic. Tristan was just running out, coughing and clutching London and Coco.

"Go to the cars," Dhillon ordered, his heart racing. "Where is she?"

"Nala. She wouldn't let Hetal near her." Tristan coughed. "Ran toward the back. Hetal went to get her." She coughed again. "Happened so fast. Smelled smoke and then there were flames."

"It's okay." Dhillon left a coughing Tristan as he heard the sirens come closer. Still too far.

Smoke wafted from the building. Dhillon barely hesitated a millisecond. He had held back once and lost his father. It was up to him. Things might be different now if he'd had the courage to run in after his father. He pushed his way into the clinic and headed for the back.

Thick, gray smoke impeded his vision. He tried to use the visual cues so he wouldn't get turned around. The desk. The break room. Exam 1. Exam 2. His office. The surgical unit. The recovery, where the dogs had been. His eyes burned, along with his chest and lungs. He pulled his T-shirt over his nose as he coughed and went down on all fours. Didn't smoke rise?

He grabbed the extinguisher and tried to put out some of the flames as he searched for Hetal and Nala. Smoke started to fill his lungs. He couldn't breathe. At the sound of a bark, he turned. Wherever the sound was coming from, Hetal would be there, too.

In the thick smoke, he made out a form, crouched over, just a few feet away. "Hetal!"

"Bhaiya!" She coughed.

"Nala?"

"Can't—" *cough* "—find her."

In the distance, almost another world, sirens squealed and halted. The fire department was here.

"Just leave. I'll get Nala."

Another bark, from behind Hetal.

"I hear her!" Hetal ran after the dog.

"No! Hetal, I got her." Dhillon crawled over to where Hetal had been. He couldn't see her anymore. A wall of flames appeared, seemingly from nowhere, separating Dhillon from his sister. Voices drifted back to him from the front, and he tried to call out. He was coughing more, and it was getting harder to breathe.

The last thing he saw before he passed out was someone jumping the flames. *Please don't let it be Riya.*

thirty

RIYA

Riya had been in the middle of cleaning the ladder engine when the call came in. Her heart fell to her stomach as she immediately recognized the address.

Dhillon's clinic.

She was in her boots and turnout gear in seconds, the oxygen tank on her back. Though the team was more than efficient and quick, it seemed a hundred years before the engine made it to the clinic. What she saw upon arrival sent waves of sadness through her. This was Dhillon's dream. And it was going up in flames.

Flames and smoke were visible from the street. Not good. She recognized Dhillon's car, then Hetal's. They were still here somewhere. She looked around as her team prepped to fight the fire. Neither Dhillon nor Hetal was outside, which meant they were still in the building. A dog barked in the parking lot, and she turned toward it.

He must have had dogs post-op overnight. That meant— "Tristan!" Riya called as she spotted the young woman.

Tristan coughed as she held on to the two dogs in her arms. "Riya, thank God. Dhillon went in after Hetal." She coughed. "One more dog left, too."

Riya handed Tristan over to the EMTs.

She turned to her team. "The vet is in there. His sister and a dog." The guys all looked at each other. "I'm going in. Lieutenant, I need backup."

Ambrose nodded.

This was Dhillon. Her heart twisted at the idea that something might happen to him. She pushed the thought away. Not on her watch. Not ever again. She was already geared up. She fit her SCBA mask straps as she ran into the clinic.

She instinctively ran to the back where the recovery animals were kept. That was where Dhillon would be.

"Dhillon! Hetal!" she called out. *Please let them be okay.*

A dog barked not far from where she was, and she headed in that direction. Her stomach turned at a form on the floor. "Dhillon!" She knelt beside him. *Oh God oh God oh God. Not Dhillon. This can't be happening. Not again.* He was conscious, but just barely.

Screams came from the other side of the wall of flames in front of her. Riya looked around for a way to access Hetal while keeping Dhillon safe. From behind her she heard heavy, booted footsteps, and then Ambrose leaped over the flames, gaining access to the other side. Riya grabbed the extinguisher next to Dhillon and put out some flames to give Ambrose a path out. More sirens sounded in the distance. Other houses on the way to assist. It was worse than she had originally thought.

She wrapped her webbing, basically a thick strap, around Dhillon's chest, fastened it at his back, lifted his torso off the ground and started dragging him toward the exit. Luckily, the clinic had tile flooring, so she wasn't fighting carpet as well. She saw Ambrose holding an unconscious Hetal and a dog.

"Follow me, Desai," Ambrose grunted.

"Yes, sir."

She heard Ambrose radio to the captain that they were on the way out and they needed the chopper immediately because someone was burned. *Hetal!* Riya's body went weak for a moment. No, not her. Riya refocused her efforts on Dhillon. Nausea threatened to overtake her, but she needed to get him out.

Every step was agonizing. She could only see a foot or two in front of her, the smoke was so thick. Heat from the flames was almost debilitating. All the training she had done and she still felt as though she would melt. Sweat dripped into her eyes inside the SCBA.

She pulled Dhillon with everything she had. The fire could take the building. She'd be damned if she let this fire take Dhillon from her.

Her quads and back screamed and her shoulders stiffened, but she ignored all that. Pain was temporary. Pain was proof you were alive.

Already, Ambrose's form was blurred by smoke, but Riya followed the hose lines that had been put down by Evans and Alvarez. She concentrated on putting one foot in front of the other, the heat building around her. There was only one option here: to get them all out safely. Period.

She cleared the building and was greeted by a rush of relatively clear air. The paramedics had been waiting, and now two of them rushed over and took Dhillon from her as she fell to her knees and threw off her SCBA. She gulped in fresh air, humid and thick though it was. More sirens wailed, and the thunder of nearby helicopter rotors vibrated through her.

Dhillon was on a gurney. Her heart pounded in her ears.

Her muscles screamed. Her lungs ached for oxygen, but she stood, forcing her legs to support her. She needed to assess Dhillon's condition. He was still breathing, but he needed oxygen after inhaling smoke in the building. She had grabbed the oxygen mask and was placing it over his nose and mouth when a firm hand took hold of hers.

It was Mario, her old partner on the bus. "You're a firefighter today. We got this, Riya."

A fourth fire engine screeched to a halt, sirens blaring. Two flight medics in black uniforms disembarked and jogged toward the gurney where paramedics hovered around Hetal. Ambrose had stepped back and had thrown off his SCBA. He was bent over, catching his breath. Riya ran over to Hetal.

What Riya saw made her stomach bottom out. "No. No," she whispered.

Through the quick movements of the paramedics, Riya caught glimpses of charred skin. Everything slowed down around her. *No!* The air she had been so grateful for just a moment ago was now impossible to breathe. That could not be her beautiful Hetal, whose scrapes she had healed, whose hair she had brushed and who she had taught to cook. The sight of burned flesh and the stench it produced, coming from someone she loved, was too much, and she turned away and vomited.

She turned back, wiping her mouth. Hetal was unconscious. Riya's friend Daniel was there, along with his partner, Crista, as they were the flight medics. They were loading Hetal onto the bus to take her to the helicopter.

"Daniel! Crista!" Riya ran to them. "Take me with you! Take me with you!"

Daniel paused and nodded to Crista to continue. "Riya? Riya, what's the matter?"

"Daniel, you have to take me with you. That's my— She's like a sister to me...and it's my fault." She wasn't making any sense, but she had to be sure that Hetal was okay. "It's all my fault." She was crying again.

"You know I can't do that." Daniel was firm but kind. "We'll take care of her. I promise." He glanced behind Riya and nodded at someone. "We need to get her to the hospital." He jogged over to the ambulance that was his ride and hopped on, closing the doors as it drove off toward the chopper.

Riya tried to run to Hetal, but she couldn't move. Someone was screaming. Why couldn't she get to her? And who was screaming?

Strong hands gripped her arms from behind. "Desai! Desai!" Ambrose turned her to face him, his hands still wrapped around her biceps. "Riya! Stop!" His blue eyes were wide and fierce, coming from beneath his helmet and through his ash-stained face.

It was her. She was the one who was screaming. Tears streamed down her face.

"Let me go! Let me see her." Riya pleaded with Ambrose, tried to release his grip on her. But she was too weak. She'd spent all her energy saving Dhillon.

"They're taking her to the hospital." Something in her lieutenant's voice made her stop. There was worry in his eyes. Fear. For Hetal. "Desai. I need you to get a grip. That fire is still going."

Riya looked at Ambrose's grime-covered face. "She's burned. She's burned, and it's my fault." Her voice cracked.

Ambrose shook his head at her. "No. It's not. You helped save her." His voice was firm and unforgiving. "Come with me. There's a goddamn fucking fire eating everything in its path. The paramedics, the flight medics, they know what they're doing."

She stood, paralyzed.

Ambrose was in her face. "You saved his life, Desai." He

pointed to the ambulance that was loading Dhillon. "Now, let's see what we can save of his dream."

She nodded at Ambrose, replaced her SCBA. "Let's go."

He replaced his own SCBA and headed toward the hose. Riya followed close behind.

"About fucking time." Schultz's voice was grim as they approached.

As they grabbed the hose and attempted to douse the flames with water, Riya forced herself to focus on the fire and not what might be happening with Dhillon and Hetal.

The captain appeared at her side. "There's a woman asking for you." He pointed, and Riya recognized Sarika Auntie even from here.

"It's okay. I'm working." She couldn't face Auntie right now.

"She'll only talk to you." He put his gloved hand on the hose. "I'll take your spot."

Riya nodded and let go. She ran to Auntie, undoing her SCBA straps as she approached her.

"Where are they?" Sarika Auntie was close to tears. Riya had never seen her like this before.

"They're on their way to the hospital." At Auntie's stricken face, Riya continued soothingly, not knowing where the calm was coming from, "They're both okay. Dhillon took in some smoke. But Hetal is burned."

"Burned?" Auntie's eyes flicked back and forth as if she couldn't understand the word.

"Auntie." Riya fought her own tears, still managing to remain calm. "I have to take care of that fire. Call Ryan. Tell him to meet you in Trauma. Call Dr. Shah."

Sarika Auntie nodded, pulling out her phone.

"You good?" Riya squeezed her arm.

"Yes, I'm good."

"I'll find you later." Riya refastened her SCBA straps and returned to the line.

thirty-one

DHILLON

Dhillon opened his eyes to an unfamiliar face staring down at him. He inhaled, realizing there was an oxygen mask on his face.

"Hey, Doc. Welcome back!" The young paramedic's features came into focus. He was familiar. A former colleague of Riya's. Mario?

"Hey. Mario?" His throat was scratchy, and he was nauseous. He tried to move the oxygen mask.

Mario nodded and grinned. "Yep. But let's just leave that there for a bit, okay?" He replaced the mask over Dhillon's nose and mouth.

Dhillon nodded. "You picked up…Riya's mom…" It hurt to talk.

"Don't try to speak, Doc." Mario looked at his partner. "But yeah. I picked up Riya's mom that night she had a heart attack. This is Sarah. You remember her?"

Dhillon nodded.

"You took in quite a bit of smoke." Mario's eyes flicked to monitors. "So we're taking you to the ER. Want water?"

Dhillon nodded. He removed the mask for a moment to drink the cool water. "My sister," he croaked.

Mario made eye contact with his partner. Something passed between them. Dhillon tried to sit up.

"No. Lie down." Mario gently pressed Dhillon's chest to keep him on the gurney.

"My sister!" Dhillon repeated, as loudly as he could with his throat so sore.

"She's out of the fire and on her way to the hospital. That's all the info I have right now," Mario said as he concentrated on various dials and buttons.

Mario was lying, and everyone in the ambulance knew it. Dhillon knew the man wouldn't tell him more until he had facts.

"You know, Doc, Riya pulled you out."

Dhillon's eyes widened, and his heart rate increased. He could see it on the monitor. "She did what?"

"She saved your life."

thirty-two

RIYA

Hetal was injured. And it was her damn fault.

Riya had done everything right this time. She'd got backup, worked as a team, kept the big picture in front of her, followed orders.

Still, someone she loved was injured.

All because she had to make firefighting look amazing and glamorous. When really, it was hot, gritty and dangerous. Not to mention there were no guarantees for anything. She had made herself look like a hero and had empowered Hetal into thinking she could do the same.

What the fuck had she been thinking?

She attacked the fire with a vengeance. As if each flame had arrived to personally destroy her. She checked every ember to make sure it was dead. She was thorough like she'd never been before.

And would likely never be again.

Because she was done. She was no firefighter, and she'd proved it tonight. She'd enticed Hetal into being a hero, and she'd lost her cool in front of her colleagues. Screaming and crying and vomiting. *Professional firefighter. Ha! What a joke.* There was nothing professional about her.

Samir was never coming back. No matter how many people she saved. Riya was supposed to teach Hetal, keep her safe. But she hadn't done that. Her words had said one thing, but her actions had said another.

"Hey, can you watch Hetal? Mom's running late on shift, and I need to get to work." Dhillon hadn't even made eye contact when he'd shown up at her door. It was close to a year after the fire, after the kiss. And he still wouldn't look at her.

"Um, yeah. My parents are out, but I can watch her." Riya had smiled at Hetal, who was close to six years old by then. *"We'll go on an adventure."*

"Yeah. Okay. Just be careful." Dhillon had been awkward, hesitant to leave his sister.

Riya had played games with Hetal, then taken her outside for their adventure, which ended up being tree climbing. Riya did this all the time, and she had a favorite tree she liked to climb. She took the little girl to that tree and let her try it. She didn't let her go up too high, but Hetal had seen her do it and was excited to keep trying for higher.

Things were going well until Hetal slipped and fell. She'd only fallen from a few feet up, but her ankle was sprained. Riya had carried her back to the house, wrapped an elastic bandage around the girl's ankle, applied ice and propped it up on a pillow. They watched movies and ate ice cream until Dhillon came to get his sister.

When Dhillon came home, he was livid. "What do you mean you took her to climb trees? She's six!"

"We were climbing trees when we were six, Dhillon," Riya reminded him. "And we got hurt, too. She'll be fine."

"Well, that's different." His dark eyes had blazed accusation at her.

"How's that different?" Riya demanded. Climbing trees was a normal six-year-old activity.

"I don't know." He had raised his voice, which was rare. "It just is." Dhillon had picked up Hetal and taken her home.

What the hell had she been thinking? Trying to mentor others—she was still a rookie herself. It was her own damn pride that had kept her from seeing it. From admitting that Dhillon was right. Back then and right now.

She inhaled deeply and cleared her throat. She had to get back to work. The fire was out, but she still had to help the guys wrap up the hose and reload the truck.

Dhillon had worked so hard to make this dream a reality, but not much was left of his clinic. An image of a teenage Dhillon, scarfing down cold samosas in a tree house and declaring that he'd be a vet one day with his own practice, popped into her head. Her heart ached for that boy and the dream that was now ashes.

Even without the investigation, it wasn't hard to see that Dhillon pretty much had to start over.

Her phone buzzed in her pocket. Tristan. "I contacted the owners. They're on the way. I'm getting some pain meds for the dogs, and I'll make sure they're all settled safely."

"Hey, Tristan. Is there a colleague of Dhillon's who can take care of things for a day or so?" He would need some time to regroup. "Let them know what happened and where to go for care?"

"Yes. I'll contact Shelly and coordinate with her."

"That's great. I'm sure Dhillon would appreciate that," Riya said robotically.

"How are they? Dhillon and Hetal?" Tristan asked.

"Can't tell. I'm still on scene. But I'll update you as soon as I know." Riya ended the call and headed for the engine.

On the ride back, the men around her remained silent. They knew who Dhillon was to her. They knew who Hetal was to her—and their lieutenant.

"Desai," Lieutenant Ambrose called out to her.

She turned to look at him. Pained blue eyes pierced her through the ash and grime that covered his face. That covered all their faces.

"Well done." His mouth hardly opened, revealing no emotion. Every eye was on them. He swept his gaze over the company, landing back on Riya. "The vet's gotta weigh—what? One eighty, maybe two hundred pounds? Of solid muscle?" He curled his lip. "Impressive."

Congratulatory nods, thumbs-up from all around.

She should be elated. The irony of the situation did not pass her by. The respect of her peers was what she had wanted all along. It was misplaced.

They arrived at the station. Riya hung up her gear and helped clean up. "Hey, Desai," Evans called out. "You want the shower first?" He looked around at the guys. "We can wait."

"Nah. I got to talk to Captain. You all go ahead."

"You sure?"

She nodded. "Yes." She headed to the captain's office as the guys gathered their stuff and headed for the locker room to shower.

She knocked.

"Come in."

Captain Davis was already elbow deep in paperwork. He looked up, surprised. "Desai. Good work tonight. Glad you decided to be on the team." He shuffled some papers.

She took out her badge and laid it on his desk. "I'm not fit, Captain. I'm out."

The captain looked at her, his eyes wide. "What's this? You did good work tonight. Put that back in your pocket." He dismissed her with a wave and went back to work.

"With all due respect, no, sir." This was the hardest thing she would ever do. She wasn't backing down now.

"What's this about?" He turned his full attention to her, pulling off his glasses.

She shook her head. "It's personal. It may be that my head's not in the right place. It's just…I shouldn't be here. Out there. I shouldn't be fighting fires. People will get hurt."

"I don't understand."

"Neither do I, sir." Her voice cracked, and she willed herself not to cry. She had wanted nothing more than to be a firefighter. She wanted to save lives, change people's futures for the better, but clearly it was more than she could handle. "I can't do the job. Thank you for everything. I'm sorry." With that, she left without waiting to be dismissed.

She walked out to find Ambrose and Schultz standing outside the captain's office, turnout gear off but still grimy from the fire. They looked at each other as Riya came toward them, concern on their faces.

"What's going on, Desai?" Ambrose spoke as gently as he ever had.

She met the lieutenant's gaze. "I turned in my badge." Interesting how easy it was to say difficult things if you distanced yourself from them.

Ambrose narrowed his eyes at her, his jaw clenched. "Running, are you?"

"Call it whatever you want." She shrugged; the fight was out of her. "It's for the best, trust me." She started to walk away.

"People get hurt in fires, Desai," Ambrose called after her. "You deal with it."

"You're right. People get hurt in fires." She turned back to him, her heart pounding. "But they shouldn't get hurt by the people they trust to keep them safe. I'm a firefighter, and I let someone I love get hurt. If you hadn't been there…" Her voice broke again. "Not going to happen again."

She turned all the way to face her lieutenant, walking back to him. "And if you care about Hetal—" Riya tilted her chin up to look him in the eye "—you'll rip up her application when it comes your way."

If the anger Dhillon had shown when Hetal had sprained her ankle as a child was any indication, he would never forgive her for this.

Just as well. She'd never forgive herself.

thirty-three

DHILLON

Dhillon had returned from the dance, slightly giddy from finally having kissed Riya. He'd been wanting to for so long, but he hadn't thought she felt the same way. But she did! He was nearly floating. His parents had just got his little sister to bed and were enjoying a rare few moments of quiet when he had walked in.

"Someone looks like they had a great time." His father had chuckled.

Dhillon shrugged, trying for nonchalance. "It was okay."

His parents had shared a look and a small grin that Dhillon didn't understand. But they were always looking at each other and smiling. It was just part of their relationship, so he didn't pay them much mind.

Lucky had bounded to greet him as if he'd been gone for a month instead of a few hours. Dhillon had got on the floor to play with him.

"*Can you take Lucky out before you go to bed?*"

"*Sure, Papa.*" Dhillon had leashed Lucky and taken him out. He had considered knocking on Riya's door to see her again, but it was late, and he didn't want her to get in trouble. When he returned, his parents had fallen asleep on the sofa. He woke them, and the three of them went upstairs together.

Dhillon had fallen into blissful sleep, Lucky defiantly curled up next to him on the bed. He dreamed about kissing Riya. Wondered if she might want to be his girlfriend.

He was awakened by his father's urgent shouts. "*Dhillon! Dhillon!*"

Dhillon jumped out of bed to smoke and heat. He hurried out into the hallway and found his parents outside his sister's room. His father thrust a screaming Hetal into his arms.

"*Take her. Go with your mother and get outside. Keep them safe. I'll be right behind you.*"

Lucky was barking.

"*Take Lucky with you.*"

Dhillon held on to his sister and called for Lucky to follow. His mother was at the stairs. "*Dhillon!*" She grabbed Hetal from him.

He did as he was told, as smoke and flames raged around them. He followed his mother down the stairs, out the door and across the street, assuming that his father and Lucky were behind him.

Once they were out, it was clear that Riya's house was on fire as well. He stared at her door, willing her to come out. When she finally emerged with Samir behind her, his mother called them over. Riya had run over to them. He met Riya's eyes for a moment, both of them relieved to see each other.

But suddenly, Samir had turned around and run back into the house.

"*Samir! No! Come back!*" Sarika had shouted.

"*Samir!*" Riya echoed, attempting to follow him. But Dhillon's mother held her firm.

"Riya! You have to stay here. It's too dangerous," Dhillon insisted, just as her parents drove up. "Your parents are here." He nodded behind her.

Dhillon turned his attention back to his house. Where was his dad? And Lucky? "Where's Papa?"

Without waiting for an answer, he started toward the house. The fire engines were in the driveway.

"Papa! Lucky! Where are you?" He ran closer as his mother screamed for him to stay put. But he had to get to his father. "Papa! Lucky! Come out!" He started to get closer: he had to go in, get his father.

A firm hand on his shoulder stopped him. Dhillon looked up into the face of a firefighter. "Kid, you gotta let us work."

"My dad and my dog," he tried to explain, "they're still inside."

The firefighter nodded and relayed the information into his walkie-talkie. "We'll get them." A couple of firefighters entered the burning house. Dhillon was in awe of their bravery. Sure enough, a few minutes or an eternity later, one of the firefighters emerged, carrying Lucky.

Dhillon ran to Lucky, but the firefighter ran past Dhillon to the ambulance. Lucky's whines called to him, and he followed his companion.

"Stay back, son. Let us work," the paramedic had said.

Dhillon had stood there, powerless to help Lucky, powerless to get his father. He willed the other firefighter to come out with his dad. He stood there while water doused the flames of both houses. He stood there while firefighters called out to each other, chaos erupting around him.

No one came out.

Dhillon followed Riya to the waiting room at Hopkins where he assumed his mother would be. Riya had simply told him that Hetal was burned but had not uttered a word after that. He was too shocked to push it. Too angry to speak. Riya had saved his life, but Hetal was injured because of her. Besides, if Riya had decided not to talk, she wouldn't.

When they approached the waiting room, they found his mother pacing. Ryan sat in a chair, watching her. She looked up when the door opened.

"Dhillon." She ran over and put her hands on his face, turning him this way and that, checking her son to see what damage had come to him. "What happened? Are you okay?"

Before he could answer, she gave Riya the same treatment, adding a hug. "They said you pulled him out." She kissed Riya's ash-strewn face. "Thank you."

"We're fine, Mom," Dhillon rumbled. He looked at Riya. She met his eyes and looked away. Silence clanged in the waiting room.

Ryan finally spoke into the silence. "Hetal has second- and third-degree burns. Her left arm and thigh."

Dhillon stared at his friend for a moment as he processed this information. "How is she?"

"She's in surgery. They need to do grafts." His mother answered, clearly trying to maintain some professional distance, but failing.

"Ryan?" Dhillon looked to his best friend. As a trauma resident, maybe Ryan would have some answers.

"She'll be in the hospital for a few weeks. They'll do the grafts, make sure she's healing. There will probably be some physical therapy. It'll take some time, but she'll be fine," Ryan answered.

Dhillon nodded. She had to be. The waiting-room door opened, and a doctor in blue scrubs walked in, carrying two cups of coffee. It was Dr. Shah. Concern colored his face as he looked at Sarika.

Dhillon felt a small amount of relief that Dr. Shah could provide some comfort to his mother.

"Sarika," said Dr. Shah, handing her one of the coffees. "Hello, Dhillon. How are you? Can I get you anything?" He held out the other coffee to Dhillon.

Dhillon shook his head. "Thanks. I'm okay."

"Rohun." His mother took the coffee. "What are you doing here? It's the middle of the night."

Dr. Shah shrugged. "I was just finishing a procedure when I heard."

"That's not necessary. You've had a long day—" But the gratitude on her face belied her words. She was happy he was there.

"Your daughter is in the burn unit, and you're here. So I'm here."

Dhillon extended his hand. "Thank you for coming." He nodded at his mother. "It's very much appreciated."

Dr. Shah scrutinized Dhillon's face. "You've been better."

"I'm fine." His throat was still scratchy from the smoke, but a pit had settled in his stomach. He turned behind him, but Riya was gone. She left because she felt responsible. As she should.

thirty-four

RIYA

Riya shoved on her helmet and started her bike. She had no destination. She just needed to be away from Dhillon and Hetal and all that she had caused. Her heart ached, her muscles hurt, and she was still covered in ash and sweat since she hadn't even been able to shower before quitting her dream job.

It was no surprise that she ended up in front of Phil's Place, where she and Dhillon had sung karaoke the night Lucky had died. Whatever. This place wouldn't care if she still smelled like smoke.

She walked inside and sat down at the bar. The place was still open, but things were winding down. Annika greeted her with a smile.

"Hey, Riya." She was irritatingly bubbly for the late hour.

"Annika."

"You okay?" Annika stopped wiping down the bar when she heard Riya's tone.

Riya shook her head. "Saw your fiancé tonight."

Annika's eyes widened, as she nodded her comprehension. "The chopper." She studied Riya. "That's happened before. Part of the job."

"Yep. Part of the job." That she didn't deserve to have.

"Or not?" Annika poured Riya a beer. "Want to talk about it?"

Riya shook her head. What would she possibly say? Annika nodded and left Riya alone with her drink. The door jingled somewhere in the back of her mind, but Riya was deep in thought. What could she have done to keep Hetal from being burned? Every time, she came up with the same answer. She should have kept it real. Explained to Hetal the brutal reality of firefighting. Not told her how awesome it was to be a hero.

She vaguely registered someone pulling up a stool next to hers. For half a second, her heart lifted in the anticipation that Dhillon had come after her. But it was Daniel who sat next to her, grinning. As if Dhillon would ever forgive her for letting Hetal get hurt.

"Wow, I haven't seen disappointment like that since I told my nephew I couldn't buy him a car until he learned how to drive," Daniel chuckled. "You were expecting that guy from the other night?"

Riya shook her head. "Doesn't matter." She turned back to sipping her beer.

As Annika came back over, Daniel said, "Well, word on the street has it that this woman—" he poked a thumb in Riya's direction "—pulled a one-hundred-eighty-pound man out of a burning building tonight."

"I'm not surprised." Annika grinned at her.

"Nor should you be." Daniel shook his head. "Riya is very good at her job." He turned to his fiancée, his voice soft. "Hey, you."

Annika grinned and leaned over the bar to kiss him. *Ugh.* They were so darn cute.

"Aren't you on the chopper tonight?" Riya interrupted. She couldn't continue to watch the goo. No matter how cute. It made her want it for herself, and she'd never have it now.

"I was covering until Rick came in." He studied Riya, seeming to register her postfire appearance. "You okay? I thought you'd be at the hospital or still on shift."

"Nope." She was curt, as she forced away the burn of her tears. She instantly regretted it, softening. "Sorry about earlier this evening, the freak-out..."

Daniel waved it off. "Understandable. Even for those of us on the job. When it comes to people we love. We've all had our moments." He glanced at Annika.

Riya was failing to keep her tears at bay. She put some cash on the bar and hopped down, as she nodded to Daniel. "I should go." Her voice cracked.

Daniel looked concerned. "You sure you're okay? Listen, Riya, I'm not sure what happened there, but it's not your fault. We like to blame ourselves for things, but it usually isn't anything we can control."

She could unload her fears onto Daniel right now. He was a colleague, a friend. She just couldn't bear to say the words out loud. She shook her head. "Thanks, but no."

Daniel nodded. "Katie mentioned you were trying to get together a mentorship program for new women recruits. Kind of guide them through the process. She's really excited about that."

This was the most ridiculous thing she'd heard all day. Her, a mentor. What had she been thinking? She let out a derisive laugh. "Yeah. No. I don't think I should be mentoring anyone. Katie's fabulous, though. She should do it. I'm out."

The tears were ready to burst out of her. She turned before anyone could see and marched out the door.

The morning dawned early, bright yellow sun taunting her at six o'clock as she mounted her bike. She hadn't really slept: she had basically been waiting for the sun to rise so she could see in the daylight what the fire had done to Dhillon's clinic.

Of course she cared about him. She didn't even bother to tell herself that she didn't. Denying those feelings was getting too hard. And denying them wasn't making them go away. She'd just have to accept that she was completely in love with the one man who would never be able to love her back.

She parked her bike in the lot, and her heart sank. The sun revealed what the streetlights and moon could not. The clinic had been built decades ago, so the walls hadn't burned down. But everything else had. The brick walls were scorched, the ceiling partially intact, the occasional beam still offering a modicum of support, but the rest was blackened, broken, burned debris. Gray and white ash covered everything.

Dhillon's clinic was all but gone.

Her heart broke for him. His dream had indeed turned to ash. She analyzed as she walked closer to the remains. Most of the structure was destroyed, but a few beams still stood. Burned desks, monitors, supplies—nothing appeared usable.

"Hey." Dhillon startled her as he appeared from inside the wreckage. He had dark circles under his eyes, and his hair was standing on end. He was still in his scrubs. He hadn't gone home yet.

Her instinct was to go to him, wrap her arms around him and tell him it would all be okay. He could start over, design the practice the way he wanted it. But he wasn't hers. He didn't need her.

Correction. He didn't *want* her.

She couldn't speak. He just stared at her. "Thank you. For pulling me out."

She nodded. "It's my job."

"What happened in there, Riya? I have to know."

She cleared her throat. "Well, Tristan was able to get Coco and London. But Nala ran to the back." She looked away from him. "Hetal went after her. When we arrived on the scene, Tristan was just exiting the building. Lieutenant Ambrose and I entered. I found you, unconscious. A wall of flames separated me and you from Hetal and Nala. Lieutenant Ambrose jumped the flames and got to her, but not before she was burned."

His beautiful features transformed from shock to anger as he listened to her account. *"You."*

Riya nodded in agreement, willing the tears that burned behind her eyes to go away.

"I knew she was in there, so I had to get her out. We heard a bark, and I tried to go, but I passed out," Dhillon said. "Hetal was trying to save Nala. *You* made her think she could save those animals. You. With your stories of heroism." His voice was still smoke-gruff, but Riya heard him loud and clear.

"I'm sorry," she choked out over her tears. Those two powerless words were too little, too late.

"Why are you here, Riya?" he demanded.

"I, uh, came to see how bad the damage was." Riya couldn't meet his eye, but she couldn't stop looking at him. "You'll have to rebuild."

Dhillon shook his head, without looking at her. He picked up what looked like a monitor and threw it down in disgust. "There's nothing here that's worth keeping." He finally raised his eyes to her. "I'll have to start over completely. New building, everything."

"The walls are still good." She didn't sound convincing, even to herself.

He glared at her like she was ridiculous, his hollow eyes now fierce with fury. "That's what you have to say? 'The walls are still good'?"

Butterflies invaded her stomach. She cleared her throat. "How is she?"

Dhillon stood tall, harsh lines defining his face. He folded his arms across his chest and turned away from her to study the rubble. "She needs grafts, there'll be physical therapy... scarring." His voice drifted off as if he couldn't process what was happening. "I don't know."

He flicked his eyes to her for a brief second, then looked away. "What're you really doing here, Riya?"

"I told you. I wanted to see what was left." Riya frowned.

Dhillon raised an eyebrow in her direction. They stood in silence for a moment.

She sighed. "I was thinking about the time I babysat Hetal and we climbed the tree." She watched Dhillon study the ruins.

He didn't miss a beat. "Sprained Hetal's ankle."

"She'll get through this." Riya swallowed her tears. *She has to.*

Dhillon finally turned to look at her. "It's not exactly the same thing, Riya." The accusation was clear.

"I'm sorry, Dhillon. I'm so sorry." Her voice cracked. "I didn't think—"

"Damn right you didn't think." He raised his voice. "Always so gung ho to move ahead and do the next exciting thing, no matter what the risk. Or the cost." Waves of anger and disbelief emitted from him. "You want to risk your own life, you go ahead and do that. Stop risking the lives of people I love."

His dark eyes bored through her, paralyzing her. He had never spoken to her like that. In all these years, with all the things that had happened, he had always included her when he spoke about the people he loved.

She should tell him. Tell him he was right, that she was dangerous to the people she cared about. Tell him he was right not to be with her. The words wouldn't come.

Instead she looked around at the ash-covered remnants of Dhillon's dream. "You've been saying you wanted to modernize the office, be more efficient. Here's your chance. Don't blow it." She gave a sharp nod, the last of their bond turning to ash as she turned on her heel and walked away.

Things between them would never be as innocent as they had been before the first fire. This fire had burned away more than Dhillon's clinic. She might have saved Dhillon's life, but the fire had taken him from her just the same.

thirty-five

DHILLON

Dhillon strode through the hospital corridors, his heart heavy and his mind racing. His run-in with Riya a few mornings ago had drained him of the last of his energy. But she was right about one thing. He had a chance to make his practice into everything he'd ever wanted. This may not have been how he would have chosen to go about it, but it was a chance nonetheless.

Dhillon walked in to Hetal's room without knocking and stopped in his tracks. Lieutenant Ambrose—Riya's boss—was seated at his sister's bedside. He was on the edge of the bed, holding her hand in his, leaning over and talking softly to her, a smile on his face. As Dhillon reeled from what he was seeing, the lieutenant—Jeff?—tucked a strand of Hetal's hair behind her ear, his fingers lingering on her cheek.

His stomach filled with acid.

"What the hell is going on here?" Dhillon demanded.

The lieutenant turned to look at him and stood, still holding Hetal's hand. "Oh, uh, Doc..."

Hetal was glaring at Dhillon. He narrowed his eyes at her. "Hetal?"

Ambrose moved closer to the bed. The action infuriated Dhillon further; his sister did not need protection from *him*. But then he recalled Rohun moving closer to his mother as Hiral Mama fumed at her.

But this was different.

Isn't it?

His sister met his eyes and spoke clearly. "We're dating."

Dhillon knew his jaw had dropped. There was a part of him that registered that his sister being in love was a good thing, but he ignored that. "Excuse me? How is that even possible?"

"Well, Bhaiya," she said, as if speaking to a toddler, "when two people meet, they get to know each other—"

"Not funny." Dhillon folded his arms across his chest.

Hetal smirked at him. "I don't know. I thought it was pretty—"

"He's a firefighter!" They were talking about Ambrose like he wasn't even there, but Dhillon did not care.

Hetal's eyes blazed as she sat up in her bed. "This, Bhaiya, *this* would be one of those times you could be a brother to me." Her breath came hard and fast. "Just because you won't allow yourself to love Riya Didi—"

"Allow myself?" As if loving or not loving Riya was a choice he'd made. As if the fact that the one night he'd had with her hadn't ruined him for all future women. As if right now he wasn't torn between the fact that he was grateful to her for risking her life to save his, and upset that she'd taken that risk. Not to mention that Hetal was in the hospital because she'd emulated Riya.

He let out a sardonic laugh. "Little sister, I can't *help* the fact that I'm in love with her. I have loved her since we were children. I will probably never love anyone the way I love her. I *wish* I didn't love her. Because I can't be in love with a firefighter."

"You wish you didn't love me? What the hell kind of bullshit is that?" Riya's gravelly voice came from behind him.

Dhillon's heart stopped at the sound of her voice behind him. The voice that haunted his dreams and lifted him up all at the same time. He inhaled and turned to face her. Her arms were folded across her chest, one hip jutting out. But despite the anger in her body, he caught the hurt on her face before she could mask it.

"How much did you—"

"I heard plenty." She shook her head in disgust, but the flash of pain in her eyes broke him. "You *wish you didn't love me* because I'm a firefighter? Well, *fuck you*, Dhillon Vora."

She fisted her hands by her sides and leaned toward him, her breath coming hard. "I wish I didn't love you, because it turns out you're an asshole. I'm no longer a firefighter, but you are *still* an asshole." She turned on her heel and stomped away from him.

"You're in love with me?" Dhillon called. "Since when?"

She stopped and spun around. "Since always. But that doesn't matter, because we'll never be together. You won't be with me if I am a firefighter. And I won't be with you if I am not." She turned to leave again.

"Firefighters die," Dhillon shouted after her, glancing at Ambrose.

She stopped, her back to him, and turned so he could see her profile. Ambrose watched him.

Dhillon swallowed to ease his throat. He spoke to her back. "That night. The firefighter who stayed to help my dad—he never came out." Grief clogged his throat. "I found out later that the man had suffered a heart attack right then. My dad must have stayed to help or something—no one really knows the details—but that firefighter died that night trying to save my dad." He cleared his throat. "I found out his name, looked him up. He left behind a wife and two kids. He risked his life for my family, and he lost."

She turned her head toward him. Something had softened about her, but only for a moment, and then her eyes turned hard again. "Move on, Dhillon. I'm going to." She walked out of the room. Out of his life.

Dhillon just stared at the empty space she'd left. What had just happened? How had he screwed this up so badly? How had he just hurt the one person he loved the most? She was completely right. He *was* an asshole.

He turned to his sister. "I really fucked this up."

"Yes, you did," Hetal agreed. "Bhaiya, it's a risk, being a firefighter. It's a risk loving a firefighter." She looked at Ambrose, a small smile on her face. Ambrose smiled back at her. "You could lose her—it's true. But you might not. And if you love her, you also get to be with her for whatever time you have. Isn't that better than losing her and never even being with her?"

Dhillon listened—really listened—to his little sister and her wisdom. His father's words floated back to him from that first Rakshabandan. *"Never underestimate the power of your sister to guide and watch over you."*

"When did you get to be so damn smart?"

"I learn from the best." She grinned.

Dhillon raised an eyebrow. "Thank—"

"Mom, idiot. I learned from Mom." She shook her head

as if she were the older sibling. Well, maybe it didn't matter who was older. She was definitely wiser.

"So, I need to get back to the station. When you're done here, Doc, stop by." Ambrose nodded at Dhillon. "I have something I want to show you."

"I'm good."

"I'm going to have to insist." Ambrose leaned down and gently kissed Hetal on the lips. Dhillon looked away. He may not be trying to break them up, but he didn't need to see everything. Clearly Dhillon was mistaken about many things. Right now, his sister was happy. He was not going to be like his uncle and put anything above her happiness. If things didn't work out, then he'd be there for her. Like any other older brother.

"I'll see you later," Ambrose said to Hetal. He nodded at Dhillon as he left. "See you at the station, Doc."

thirty-six

RIYA

It was true. Firefighters died. That was why there was a wall at the firehouse that honored the fallen. Their pictures hung there as a reminder of the sacrifices made. A sacrifice any firefighter would make. Including her.

Well, when she'd been a firefighter, anyway.

She strode down the hospital hallways, trying to process what Dhillon had told her. How could she be with him if she *wasn't* a firefighter?

She'd always thought that if Dhillon loved her, it would make her happy. But his confession only made her heart heavy.

Riya had stormed out of Hetal's room, intending to go anywhere but where she was. She got as far as her bike before she stopped herself. She couldn't use this as an excuse to not talk to Hetal. No matter how much she dreaded that conversation.

She waited in the lobby until she saw Dhillon leave. Ambrose had left a bit before. She stepped onto the elevator and headed back to the burn unit.

Riya stood outside Hetal's room, her stomach filling with butterflies. The antiseptic smell of the hospital didn't help with the nausea that was rising in her stomach. This was Hetal. She'd played with her, fixed her scraped knees, taught her how to defend herself. There was no need for this anxiety. Except that there was.

Maybe she should come back later. Yes. Later.

"I can see you standing there. Come in if you're coming in," Hetal called.

Riya had walked into burning buildings with greater ease. She tried to inhale courage from the medicinal air as she stepped into Hetal's room. "Hey." She tried to sound casual.

"Hey, yourself. Where the hell have you been?" Hetal demanded.

"Wh—"

"Don't give me that wide-eyed look! I don't care what Dhillon said to you. I've been here for four days, and you haven't even come to see how I am. What kind of sister are you?"

"I didn't think you'd want to see me." She sounded weak.

"You didn't think?" Hetal's eyes bugged out, and then she rolled them, hard. "You were the one who was supposed to be my mentor, and you can't even be bothered to check on me?" She let out a derisive breath. "Nice."

"I checked on you. I know your nurse." Another weak answer. She was full of them today.

"Riya Didi, I swear…" Hetal narrowed her eyes.

"Don't work yourself up. You're injured." Riya put up her hands in surrender. Hetal was right, of course. She'd been a coward. "I'm sorry. I just didn't think you'd want to see me after all this."

"Why wouldn't I want to see you?"

"Because I'm responsible. It's my fault you're injured." Her vision blurred.

Hetal furrowed her brow. "What do you mean?"

"I mean, as much as I hate to admit it, Dhillon was right. Firefighting is dangerous, and I never should have made it sound glamorous or whatever. You had no business running into that fire. You have no experience at all. It was dangerous, and you never would have done it if I hadn't told you how great it was to save people and be a hero."

Hetal stared at her in silence, her expression unreadable.

After several moments passed with only the sounds of beeping and slurping machines, Riya spoke. "Say something."

"I'd like to, but I'm trying to figure what I could possibly say that could have the slightest hope of penetrating your big fat head." If anything, Hetal was more agitated than before.

"Excuse me?"

"Exactly how much power do you think you have over me?" Hetal leaned toward Riya aggressively. They must have her on some awesome pain meds.

Riya shook her head. "I don't understand."

"I'm not an idiot. I know fire is dangerous. I lost my dad in one—or did you forget? I may have only been five, but I have memories of that night. And I remember my dad. Sometimes I think it would be easier if I didn't remember him. Then I wouldn't know what I'd lost." She paused for breath. "You and my dumbass brother think I ran toward the fire without a thought. That's not true." She sat up and leaned even closer toward Riya. "*I ran toward living beings.* I ran to save innocent lives from certain death. Not to be a hero. And the truth is, I don't think your goal is to be a hero, either. I think you just don't want to lose anyone ever again."

"I don't."

Hetal nodded. "So why'd you turn in your badge?"

Riya just stared at her for a moment. The words would not come. But when they did, they gushed from her mouth. "I let you down. You're like a sister to me, and I let you get hurt because all I thought about was myself."

"That's not true, and you know it." Hetal rested back in her bed.

"Do I?"

"You dragged Dhillon's sorry ass out, didn't you?"

Riya nodded.

"Did you do it because you loved him, or because his was a life that needed to be saved?"

Riya didn't answer.

Hetal tilted her head, an irritating grin on her face. "That's pretty damn amazing. He must weigh like one sixty."

"Pssht." Riya shook her head. "More like one eighty to one ninety. Your brother is solid muscle."

"Is he, now?" Hetal's face filled with mischief. "And how would you know that?"

"Never mind." Huh. She didn't want to tell Hetal that she'd spent the night with Dhillon any more than he did.

"I do think I want to be a vet after all, though." Hetal lay back, relaxed. Apparently, Riya was forgiven.

"Really?" Riya narrowed her eyes. "What made you change your mind?"

"That fire is *hot*." She lifted her head up. "Some mentor you are! You never mentioned how goddamn hot it was in there."

Riya grinned and shrugged. "Work hazard."

thirty-seven

DHILLON

Dhillon pulled up in front of the fire station. He actually couldn't believe he was there. But he was curious about what Ambrose wanted to discuss, so there he was. At his mother's request, he'd gone home to get Scout. No one wanted to leave her alone quite yet, and he didn't have the energy to argue that being left alone was good for young Scout, so he picked her up and brought her with him.

Scout sat up in the seat as if she knew where she was. When Dhillon let her out of the car, she ran into the open bay. The firefighters were running drills, but they all stopped when Scout made her entrance.

Upon seeing the puppy, Ambrose looked out and nodded at Dhillon. "Glad you could make it, Doc." He nodded at one of the men. "Evans, take over and start from the beginning. Run it all the way through."

Dhillon followed Ambrose. He studied the brick face of the building, the four bays, the firefighters running their drills in the late July heat and humidity. Each time he went there, it seemed to get easier. He drifted back to the conversation with his mom. She was right. It was time to put the house fire behind him. It had defined him too long.

Ambrose led the way toward the captain's office. "We'll head back this way." Scout trotted alongside them.

Dhillon followed Ambrose back through the offices to an area he hadn't recalled seeing before.

"How's Scout been doing?" Ambrose asked as they walked down a hallway. They were in an unfamiliar area. The walls were lined with pictures of firefighters.

"She's great. She essentially lives between Riya's house and mine." *Like Lucky used to.*

"Not totally at your house yet?" He raised his eyebrows. "Your sister told me you'd eventually want Scout to come home with you. I just lost five bucks."

Dhillon shrugged. "Moving forward, you should know that if Hetal is willing to put money on something, she's going to win."

Ambrose did a double take. "Moving forward?"

"Yes. Well, it turns out, my sister is grown up. She can decide for herself who and what makes her happy."

"Anyway—" Ambrose's smile broadened "—this is what I wanted to show you." He nodded at the wall. "My whole family is in the fire service," Ambrose continued. He side-eyed Dhillon. "My sister, too. So whenever I was hard on Desai, it was because I wanted her to be the best she could be. Quite frankly, my sister had a hard time of it as a woman. I wanted to make sure that Desai was up for everything that was coming her way. It's my job to make sure my team can do what they need to do on scene." He paused. "I do wish she'd have come to me when Walsh first started to harass her, though."

"Riya likes to take care of herself," Dhillon said.

The wall held formal photos of firefighters, most of them old men. One middle-aged woman and a couple of younger-looking men.

"These are our fallen. They died in the line of duty."

Dhillon paused and looked at their faces. Brave people. "Why are you showing me this?"

"See this man?" Jeff pointed to one of the middle-aged men. His uniform was a little different from the others, his photo slightly faded.

Dhillon nodded.

"This firefighter died in a fire, saving a young woman. He left behind a wife and two children." Ambrose paused. "The young woman he saved ended up getting married a few months later. She and her husband had three children. One of those children became a firefighter. One is an optometrist. The oldest is a doctor."

Dhillon slowly let his gaze fall over each of the photos of the fallen. Most older, a few way too young. All of them heroes. This was who Riya looked up to. Now, seeing their faces, Dhillon was moved. These people had lives they had planned for. But they had sacrificed all that, willingly. And so had their families. Of course Riya wanted to do her best. Of course she didn't want to end up on this wall. But she wanted to help people. She wanted to do her part in ensuring that no one suffered what her and Dhillon's families had.

But Ambrose was still talking.

"I'm sorry. What was the last thing you said?" Dhillon asked.

"The child who became a doctor is working at the burn unit at Hopkins. She's the one doing Hetal's grafts."

Dhillon couldn't believe it. "Who was the firefighter that saved the young woman?"

Ambrose grinned, pride oozing from him, as he tapped the faded photograph. "That was my grandfather."

Dhillon was speechless.

"All I'm saying is that life happens," Ambrose continued. "And death happens. I'm sorry you lost your father. I'm sorry a firefighter's life was lost that day, too. I'd like to say I can't imagine it, but I imagine it all the time. We're a family of firefighters, and we love each other fiercely because we just don't know when our time is up.

"Desai is a good firefighter," Ambrose said firmly. "She has great instincts, and she's selfless. She just needs some experience. She has to trust her team if her team is going to trust her." Ambrose started to lead Dhillon out, Scout trotting along right behind them. "Listen." He turned his head to Dhillon, a certain look in his eyes. "I happen to know that the captain has not yet filled out her dismissal paperwork. Get her to come back before he does, and all he has to do is hand back her badge."

"You want me—" Dhillon pointed at himself "—to talk Riya back into being a firefighter."

Ambrose stopped walking and faced him. "You tell me. Is there anyone else who has a shot at getting her back here?"

"What makes you think I want to do that? How do you know I'm not relieved that she's quit?"

At this, Ambrose grinned. "Because you're in love with her." He fixed Dhillon in his gaze. "And you would never underestimate her."

"I don't know who you're talking about, but you should not be underestimating any woman," a female voice said.

Ambrose shook his head and chuckled. "Busted." Dhillon turned to see another firefighter entering the bay along with a civilian woman. The firefighter was tall and lean, blond and blue-eyed. The woman was equally tall, with brown hair and glasses. They were holding hands. The woman was carrying a tote bag that was emitting tasty aromas.

"Hey, Angie, Bill." Ambrose smiled and walked past Dhillon to hug Angie.

"Who did you underestimate this time, Jeff?" Angie poked him.

"Probably Desai, the new recruit," Bill chimed in.

"It's not me—it's him." He flicked a thumb at Dhillon. "I never underestimated Desai. Just had to make sure she could do the job, like any other rookie."

"Didn't she go through the academy, like you?" challenged Angie.

"She did," Ambrose sighed.

"Enough said, then." She smiled at him.

Ambrose grinned, clearly knowing when he should shut up.

Angie held out her hand to Dhillon. "Hi! I'm Angie. Bill's better half."

"Dhillon Vora." He shook her hand and pointed to Scout. "The vet."

Angie exchanged a look with her husband.

"What?" Dhillon asked.

She smiled and shook her head. "Nothing. Bill tells me your girlfriend is a firefighter here."

Dhillon narrowed his eyes at Bill. "She's not my girlfriend, no matter what Bill said."

"And why is that?" Angie folded her arms across her chest.

"Uh-oh," Bill said. "Now you've piqued her curiosity. It's over. She has no boundaries."

Angie rolled her eyes. "It's a simple question." She put an

arm around Bill's waist. "Firefighters are hot. Why wouldn't he want to date one?"

"No idea. I think we're pretty damn awesome," her husband answered.

Angie studied Dhillon for a moment. "She got a hero thing?"

"Don't we all?" Bill joked.

She laughed. "That's just a prerequisite for the job. She was probably punching bullies and saving animals as a kid."

Dhillon nodded agreement. Angie was right: that was pretty much Riya in a nutshell. Before he could say anything, a sound like a klaxon blared, resulting in a flurry of controlled chaos.

Angie gave Bill a quick kiss on the lips before he grabbed his gear and boarded the engine. She stood beside Dhillon as the firefighters left to answer the call. They were gone in a few minutes, the two of them left standing there with Scout, watching.

Once the last engine was off, its siren wailing in the distance, Angie turned to him. "Well, that's that. Off they go." She held up the tote bag. "I'll just leave this in the kitchen for when they get back. Cute puppy," she added, ruffling Scout's fur. "Nice meeting you." She turned and started for the kitchen.

Dhillon reached out a hand. "I can take that."

Angie grinned and pushed up her glasses. "So it's not just firefighters who are chivalrous."

In the kitchen, Angie set about emptying the tote, pulling out what looked like a couple of trays of lasagna.

"How do you do that?" Dhillon blurted out.

"Do what?" She pulled out bread and a salad.

"See him off like that. Aren't you worried?"

Angie shrugged. "Yes, I worry. But it's not a constant thing.

Do I worry that he might not return? Or that even if he does, he might be injured and not be the man I know?"

"Yes." These were his worst fears.

"I met Bill in college. There was not a time that he did not reach out to help someone who needed it. Not ever. It's part of why I love him. This job is part of him." She shrugged. "There's no separating the two. If I want him, and I do, then I have to be up for being the spouse of a firefighter." She stopped unloading her bag and looked Dhillon in the eye. "So I send him off to be a hero and hope and pray that he comes home safely each time."

Dhillon stared at her a moment as she organized the food. She moved with purpose. "This is how you cope," he said. "You cook and organize while he's gone."

She did not look up from her task. "Yup." She stopped and looked at him. "And I have a full-time job, and I volunteer at the hospital. I didn't say it was easy. I said it could be done."

Her strength was admirable.

She grinned, her blue eyes dancing with amusement. "Listen, if you love them, you love them, no matter what. If the job gets in the way, maybe she's not the right person for you." She folded up the bag, and they started to walk out together. "You can't take the firefighter out of her."

"Scout." Dhillon called the puppy to him.

"I heard she pulled you out of a fire?" Angie asked him softly.

"Yes." Risked her life for his.

She raised an eyebrow, a sly smirk coming across her lips. "That's…kind of hot."

thirty-eight

RIYA

"Hey! Look at you, all cute in your sundress." Roshni drew an approving eye over Riya's outfit.

"Thanks. Let me just finish getting all this out for Mom and Dad's lunch," Riya said, as she sliced cucumber, tomato and onion.

"I like you unemployed. More time for fun." Roshni grinned.

"Like you have oodles of time to *lunch*." Riya rolled her eyes.

"I'm the boss. I make my own schedule."

Riya shook her head at her cousin as she put out the fixings for DIY chutney sandwiches. Her parents could eat when they were ready. She washed her hands and placed them on

Roshni's prominent belly. "You're so big! Any minute now, huh? You sure you don't have twins in there?"

"One heartbeat, sister."

"And you really don't know the gender?"

Roshni shook her head. "Nope. It really is the one true surprise you get in life, so Seb and I decided to wait."

Riya quirked her mouth. "Made it impossible to buy baby-shower presents."

Roshni waved a dismissive hand. "Green and yellow are fine. And it's not like you don't spoil Anand with gifts. Now you'll have two to spoil."

Riya grinned. "I got him something cool!"

"A fire truck?"

Riya felt a pang. She *had* got him a fire truck, but then she'd returned it and got him a police car instead. Roshni was going to hate that siren.

"I'll bring it by next week," Riya said, "as a surprise for you both." She felt cheered at the prospect of seeing her nephew.

"Riya, why did you really quit?" Roshni looked her cousin in the eye.

"It was for the best. End of story." It was. What if someone died on her watch? What if it was her fault?

Roshni stared her down for a moment. "You worked so hard."

"Don't you need to eat?" Riya ignored Roshni's comment, walking past her to grab her cross-body purse.

Roshni shook her head. "Let's go."

Riya had just unlocked her car when Dhillon appeared in the driveway. He was dressed in khaki shorts and a button-down. Casual, but not so casual that he looked like he was playing basketball with Ryan. He must be meeting someone. Riya's heart fell.

But seeing him again softened her enough to remember

that he actually loved her, even if he refused to do anything about it.

Dhillon stopped when he saw her. "Hey."

She couldn't see his eyes behind his sunglasses, but his mouth looked guilty. He was definitely going on another date.

She pressed her lips together and got in the car without saying a word. Talking to him was never going to help her move on. She slammed the door shut and pulled out of the driveway.

"Whoa! Pregnant lady sitting next to you." Roshni gripped the dash.

Riya inhaled and calmed her driving.

"So how are things with you and Dhillon?" Roshni asked, with a smirk on her face.

Riya side-eyed her. "Not talking about it."

"The man is clearly in love with you. Didn't he tell you so?"

"No, what he said was he wished he wasn't in love with me."

Roshni rolled her eyes. "He loves you. And you are clearly in love with him. Do something about it."

Riya focused on the road. Her cousin was right. It was about time she did something about it. "Fine. Go into my phone to the dating app, and let's see if anyone interesting pops up."

"That's not what I meant."

"That's what I need to do. Find someone else and move on. Put Dhillon in the past. I think there was a part of me that believed that somehow, by some form of magic, we'd be together. But that will never happen. So—" she turned to look at Roshni "—start swiping."

Roshni rolled her eyes and sighed heavily to make her opinion known, but she did pick up Riya's phone and was just catching her up on the latest family gossip when they heard the wail of sirens as a fire truck came up behind them. Riya pulled over to let the engine pass.

"Isn't that your engine?" Roshni asked.

Sure enough, the fire engine bore the familiar number *52* in black script. "Not anymore." Riya set her mouth in a line to hide her pain.

More sirens sounded, so they sat for a few minutes while Riya shifted this way and that, trying to see what was happening. An ambulance passed them as well. Then another.

"Go," Roshni said.

"What? No. Don't be ridiculous. I'm a civilian now."

Roshni shrugged. "Fine. Don't go." She started swiping on Riya's cell.

Riya glanced outside. "Maybe I'll just go see what's happening. I'll just be gone a minute. Promise." She put her hand out for her phone.

"Uh-huh." Roshni slapped the device into her hand.

Riya strode onto the scene with the authority of someone who belonged there. Old habit. There had been a car accident on the bridge, and four cars were involved. Right now, two of them were dangerously close to the edge of the bridge. EMTs were on the scene, helping people from the other two cars. She stayed on the periphery, observing. The front right end of one of the cars was smashed into the guardrail.

Her former lieutenant was directing the scene, and she saw him notice her. Embarrassed, she made to go back to her car, but he called out to her.

"Desai! Desai!"

She couldn't just ignore him. She should have stayed with Roshni in the car.

"Lieutenant." She simply could not bring herself to call him Jeff. Unemployed or not.

"We have a situation."

She nodded her head. "Sorry. I just wanted to see if I—"

"Could help?"

The understanding she found in his eyes was comforting and annoying all at the same time. "Call Dhillon," he ordered.

She stared blankly at him. She must have heard wrong.

"We have a situation. We need a protective dog moved. That vehicle," Ambrose continued, pointing at the one that was crashed into the guardrail, "has an injured man in it. He's bleeding from the skull, and his leg is stuck under the dash."

Riya furrowed her brow and shrugged. "Cut off the door—"

"Thanks, genius." Ambrose stopped just short of an eye roll. "Problem is his German shepherd. Won't let us near him. We're just looking for management, a trank or something."

Riya's eyes widened. "You want *me* to call him?"

"A man is injured. And you're here."

Riya hesitated only half a second. She pulled out her cell phone and dialed Dhillon's number. Now was not the time for awkwardness. This was purely professional. She wasn't trying to find out what he was doing all dressed up on a Saturday afternoon.

"Hello." That voice that had brought her comfort and angst came through the phone without the warmth she was used to.

"Hey. Uh, Dhillon. It's Riya." Duh, he knew that.

"Yeah. What's up?" He was short.

"I'm at a scene, and we have a situation. Do you have any tranks for a dog in your vet-to-go bag? Looks like a seventy-pound German shepherd. Won't let the paramedics near the victim." She cleared her throat. "We need it quick."

"Where is the scene?" Dhillon's voice changed from hard and stoic to concerned.

"Bridge over Little Patuxent, but you'll have to walk in." *Keep it clinical.*

"No problem. I'm in the traffic backup. Be there in five."

Riya tapped her phone off and turned to Ambrose. "He said five minutes. He's here, in the traffic."

"Okay." Ambrose nodded and started to walk away.

"Anything else I can do?" Riya asked.

He turned and took in her appearance. "Not exactly dressed for the job, are you?"

She looked down at her sundress and shrugged. "I can manage."

"Not what I meant." He turned and went back to managing the scene. "Should have a trank here in a few minutes." He nodded at Evans and Alvarez. "In the meantime, get the generator out. Let's get the Jaws ready to go. Have EMTs standing by."

Five minutes was a long time for that poor man to be sitting and waiting. Riya made like she was going back to her car but cut across to the vehicle with the dog. She could at least give it a try while they waited.

She walked over to the car with the dog. Sure enough, even Evans was unable to get close enough to the door with the Jaws of Life. Every time someone tried to get close, the dog lunged.

Riya approached. "Hey, Evans, Alvarez."

Both men turned to face her, exchanging glances between them. "You can't be here," Alvarez said.

"The vet is on the way," she said as she got closer to the car.

"Yeah, but you can't—" Alvarez started.

Riya took a few steps closer to the car. The dog lunged again, barking, teeth bared. She had no food to distract him. She spoke softly and quietly, keeping her heart rate calm. The dog ceased barking for a second as he assessed this newcomer. She took another step, and he resumed his aggression.

"You'll never get in without food." Dhillon's voice came from behind her.

She closed her eyes. No matter how long she lived, or how often she heard it, the sound of his voice would always make her melt inside. *Damn it.* She nodded but didn't move.

"No sudden movements. He's going to have to ingest the tranquilizer for us to get past him," Dhillon said, softly and calmly.

She nodded again.

"I'm going to come up beside you. Then you can slowly retreat."

He tossed a treat to the dog.

"Okay." Out of the corner of her eye, she saw him take a few steps, speaking quietly. The dog responded to Dhillon, eating the treats and calming down just slightly. Dhillon got closer and closer, until he was within arm's reach.

"Damn." Alvarez's voice came from behind her. "He's good."

Riya swelled with pride as she turned to Alvarez. "He's the best."

Dhillon got close enough to pet the dog. In the same calm voice, he addressed the firefighters. "The dog is stuck in here, too. You'll have to work around me."

"Let's go! We got EMTs? This door comes open, Doc gets the animal, you all get the vic," Evans called.

Riya stepped out of the way, though every piece of her wanted to help.

Evans and Alvarez stepped slowly up to the car door with the Jaws. Dhillon did his best to keep the dog calm, though the big German shepherd lunged and barked at the two firefighters, forcing them to stop.

"Let me try," Riya said.

Evans shook his head. "You have no gear on. And besides, you quit, remember?"

"I remember, but we have a situation here. That man is unconscious and bleeding. And I believe I can get close enough to cut him out."

Evans eyed her, exaggerated patience in his voice. "You're a civilian. No way."

"It's okay, now. He's getting sleepy. But no sudden movements," Dhillon continued in that same calm voice, his eyes never leaving the dog.

Evans and Alvarez made their way to the car. The dog was indeed calming down. They were almost close enough when the dog barked.

Riya was unable to tear her eyes from the scene. Dhillon was incredible, and her heart overflowed with pride for him, even as she longed to be the one running the Jaws. What had she done, quitting like that?

Evans and Alvarez removed the door. Dhillon grabbed the dog. Mario and his partner moved in to treat the patient. Helicopter rotors whipped overhead. She looked up as she saw the chopper swing around, looking for a place to land.

"Who's the chopper for?" she asked.

"Not that it's any of your concern," Evans said, "but they're trying to get a child out of the back seat of that car." He pointed to the other smashed car on the bridge. He headed to Ambrose for further instruction.

She broke into a run without thought. Her bag slapped her side, and she was vaguely aware of Dhillon running right by her side.

If the child merited a chopper, there was something really wrong. She arrived to find another fire-station unit attempting to extricate the child.

The front of the car was smashed in, the child trapped in his car seat in the back, the car itself tipping dangerously over the guardrail that overlooked the street below. There was no way to access the child except from the street side, and that whole side of the vehicle was smashed. The child's mother was being treated by paramedics, crying hysterically for someone to save her child.

Riya quickly assessed the scene. If they carefully cut the driver's-side door open, someone could reach in and grab the child. The team was getting the Jaws ready. She went closer and watched. The side of the car was so badly smashed, only a small portion of it could be cut away. Leaving a very small opening.

She took a step toward them. "Hey. Need a hand?"

The two firefighters looked at her, one of them holding up his hand. "I'm sorry, ma'am. But civilians can't be here."

"I'm not a civilian." But she was. "I'm with 52." She pointed her thumb in the general direction behind her. "I can fit through that opening and grab the child." She kept walking toward them and the car.

"Ma'am, I do not care who you say you're with. Even if you are with 52, you're not in uniform." He glanced at her sundress.

"Do you want that child out or not?" Riya clamped her jaw shut and stared him down. "I can fit through a smaller gap."

"We'll figure it out. No way we're letting a civilian—"

"She's not a civilian." Dhillon's voice came from right behind her. Authoritative. "She's a firefighter." Proud.

Riya's heart swelled.

"And who the hell are you?" the firefighter asked Dhillon.

"Listen," Riya said to catch the firefighter's attention, "there's no time to debate this. Let me get him."

"Let her do it." This time the voice from behind her was Ambrose's. He approached, removed his turnout jacket and handed it to her. "She's just off duty."

Riya grabbed the coat, while the other two firefighters looked at each other. They came to some kind of understanding, because they moved aside so Riya could squeeze through the small opening.

Ambrose caught her eye. "Be as quick as you can, and watch that you do not go too far over to the kid's side. Your weight could tip the car over the rail."

"Yes, sir." She approached the car and saw that the child, not more than two or three, was awake. Good news. They may not need the chopper after all. She gingerly squeezed her upper body through the opening.

"Hey, there. I'm Riya. I'm going to take you to your mommy, okay?"

The child was crying, but he nodded.

"Great." Riya nodded, smiling. She slowly crept closer. The child appeared uninjured from her vantage point, but she couldn't be sure. She leaned toward him, her arm outstretched to reach the seat-belt release. The car creaked and shifted, jolting Riya and the child. The child started wailing for his mother, and Riya couldn't blame him. Her heart was racing, sweat pouring off her.

"Guys?" she called to the firefighters outside.

"Make it quick, Desai," Ambrose called back to her.

"Yes, sir." She shifted her weight so she was in farther, but not on the child's side. That gave her just the inch she needed to release the seat belt, and it did so with a satisfying click and whiz while it retracted.

"Got the seat belt undone," she called out. She reached for the boy. "Let's go to Mommy."

Thankfully, at the word *Mommy*, he reached toward her, and Riya was able to grab his arms. She pulled him from the car seat and rolled over onto her back as she held him toward the small opening.

"Grab him!" she screamed.

A pair of hands grabbed the boy and carefully maneuvered

him through the opening. Once he was through, Riya slid herself out.

The boy's mother, a bandage on her head, was running toward them. She passed Dhillon, then Ambrose, finally stopping in front of the burly firefighter holding her child.

"Kai! Oh, my baby." She examined him, tears spilling down her cheeks. "Thank you." She squeezed him to her chest. "Thank you so much." She glanced around the group. A paramedic came by and led her back to the ambulance to check out the child.

Riya sagged in relief. She glanced at Dhillon. His face was ashen, but his smile was broad. She took off Ambrose's turnout jacket and handed it back as they left the area. "Thanks."

Ambrose leaned in to whisper in her ear. "For someone who quit, you sure do work a lot. Now leave, before I get in trouble."

"Yes, sir." She started to walk away from the scene, hyperaware of Dhillon's presence beside her. Great. She was sweaty and dirty—in a dress—and she was walking next to Dating Dhillon.

Oh, and yeah. She wanted her job back.

thirty-nine
DHILLON

Riya's dress was ripped and laced with dirt. She lifted the tangled mess of her hair and secured it in a hair tie, but a few tendrils didn't make it, and they stuck to her face. Her makeup was smeared, leaving black smudges under her eyes.

She was stunning.

The whole thing: the dog, the child... Not once during either of those situations had she panicked. She had assessed and moved forward. She was the poster child for calm, cool and collected.

She looked like she glowed from within with satisfaction from a job well done.

He, on the other hand, had been a selfish asshole. *Damn it.* He hated when his sister was right.

But it was true: Riya was made to be a firefighter.

"Guess you're late for your date." She side-eyed him, a smirk on her face. Traffic was still at a standstill, but now that the worst was over, it would get moving shortly.

He was taken aback. "Who said I was going on a date?"

"Look at you." She appraised him top to bottom. "And you smell good."

He raised an eyebrow at her. "You think I smell good?"

She rolled her eyes.

They walked a few feet in silence. Dhillon saw Riya's car a few cars ahead. They both spoke at once.

"I was wrong."

"I was wrong."

Dhillon's head snapped up. She was fidgeting with her hands, her bottom lip in her teeth, brow furrowed. He stopped walking, and Riya faced him.

"What were you wrong about?" Riya asked first.

He looked her in the eye. "About you firefighting. You're a natural. You work on instinct. I saw you jump into action today without a thought. More than once. You went from one emergency to the next, completely composed. You're amazing. I'm sorry it took this long for me to see it."

"I miss it."

"So go back," Dhillon said.

"Well, I have burned that bridge. The team is pissed at me for quitting." She looked at her fingernails, then back up at him. "I can't say I blame them."

"They're pissed at you for quitting because they know that you belong there, with them. Working side by side." Traffic started creeping forward. He moved toward her car, and she followed. "Listen, I'm the last person to tell you what to do—"

"Hasn't stopped you yet."

"All I'm saying is you're made for that job, because it's more than a job to you. It's who you are. I believe you've been say-ing that all along. I'm the asshole who's just hearing it now." She belonged in firefighting. He could feel it in his core. In fact, he'd probably known it all along—he was just too afraid for it to be true. But that no longer mattered. "Just because you're not working as a firefighter doesn't mean you aren't a firefighter."

She just looked at him, doubt playing over her face.

"Might be worth a bit of groveling to get your job back. And who knows? If you go soon enough, maybe your paper-work won't have been filed yet." Dhillon widened his eyes and gave her an exaggerated shrug.

"Wait. What are you saying?" Her eyes danced with hope.

"I'm saying I hear things. Like from my sister's new boy-friend…"

Riya's eyes lit up, sending a contentment through him he'd only ever experienced with her.

"What were you wrong about?" Dhillon asked.

"I never should have made firefighting seem glamorous. Maybe—"

Dhillon held up a hand to stop her. "I never should have held you responsible for Hetal's actions. She's an adult, and she knows what she's doing. She's just as stubborn as they come."

"Runs in the family," Riya muttered.

"It does." He stood there, taking her in while she processed all that he had said. He tucked a wisp of hair behind her ear and trailed his fingers along her jaw, and she allowed it. Si-lence floated between them. Dhillon needed to explain how much he loved her and how sorry he was for all the things he'd said. But right now, all he could think about was how touching her made him want to touch her more, but that he'd probably never get that chance again. "Besides, any dream worth having is worth fighting for." He looked directly into her eyes. "I believe Samir told me that."

"He did?" She looked genuinely surprised. "When?"

"When I was begging my parents for a puppy."

He was rewarded with her laugh. "Sounds about right."

He softened his voice. "Applies to lots of things. Including wanting to be a firefighter."

"This is me." Riya stopped at her car.

"Think about it." He looked her in the eye. The spark was still there: she wanted her job more than ever.

"Hey!" Roshni opened the window. "If you two are done making googly eyes at each other, I'm having a baby."

Riya turned to her cousin. "We know you're pregnant! Did you even say hello to Dhillon?"

"Hello to Dhillon," Roshni mocked. "I know how bad you two have it for each other, and if it was anything else, I'd keep my mouth shut. But my goddamn water broke, and if you don't start driving right now, I'm going to have this baby in this car!"

"What? Are you serious?" Dhillon stepped up to her window.

"I'm coming." Riya moved with purpose over to the driver's side, still the picture of composure as she assessed the now-moving traffic. She got in the car, then popped her head back out, smiling at him. "Thanks, Dhillon. Really."

"Can we go?" demanded Roshni from inside the car.

forty

RIYA

Baby Diya was as gorgeous as her mom, and if her cry was any indication, she was also just as forceful as Roshni as well.

Traffic had opened up, and Riya had made it to the hospital in *plenty* of time for Roshni to give birth to a gorgeous baby girl, Sebastian by her side. Riya made sure mom and baby and dad were properly settled by the time Varsha Masi showed up with her bags of food and home remedies for postpartum recovery.

"I heard you went on a date with Namrata Mehta's son?" Varsha Masi said to Riya by way of greeting.

"You mean Akash?" Riya couldn't believe what she was hearing. Made sense, though, that her date was the awful mandir auntie's son.

"Yes." Her masi cocked an eyebrow.

"Well, that explains a lot. He's not a nice boy, Varsha Masi. Not at all," Riya said.

Her masi shrugged. "Okay. Next boy, then. Who is next?"

"Hey! You made it to the hospital on time?" Dhillon entered the room with a laugh and a smile, his hands full of balloons and a small stuffed dog.

Roshni grinned at Dhillon. "Riya drove like a maniac."

Varsha Masi raised an eyebrow. Riya had no idea what her face looked like, but from her masi's expression, she could only guess. She shook her head at her: no way. Her masi smirked at her and turned to Dhillon, who was fawning over Diya and making little goo-goo noises.

Just when she thought he couldn't possibly get any sexier.

Varsha Masi turned to Dhillon. "Dhillon, so good to see you. Sorry about your clinic and about Hetal. How is she?"

"She's recovering just fine, Auntie, thanks. We all are, thanks to Riya." He met her eyes.

Riya's heart thudded in her chest.

Varsha Masi looked from Riya to Dhillon. "Uh-huh." She cut her eyes to Riya, a knowing smirk on her face. "And your office? What will you do?"

"Well, right now, I'm doing some house calls, and I'll work from the veterinary ER for a time. But I have full coverage from insurance, so I'm going to rebuild the office and design it to my preferences. I had been talking about doing that for a while. Here's my chance." He threw another glance at Riya.

Riya was impressed. Dhillon, putting everything out there. God, she loved him. *Wait—what?*

"Anyway, Auntie, I should go. I had an appointment that was derailed by—well, many things." He glanced at Riya again, sending zings through her body. "Can I see you out in the hall?"

Riya nodded, purposefully not making eye contact with anyone as she followed Dhillon out of the room.

Dhillon stood close enough for her to catch his fresh-from-a-shower scent. "Lucky's ashes came."

"Okay." She nodded her head as she processed this, trying to hide the sadness that washed over her. "Yeah. So whenever works for you."

"How about the day after Rakshabandan?" His eyes on hers were intense. "Before sunrise?"

"Sure." Riya forced a small smile.

"Great." He held her gaze for a moment. "I really have to go."

"Sure. Yeah. See you later."

Riya stared at the space he'd left. Varsha Masi was at her side in a minute, watching him walk down the corridor to the elevator. She raised one eyebrow and gave a slight head-bob that spoke volumes.

Riya ignored her. She needed to get to the firehouse to get her job back.

The sun was setting when Riya rolled up to the station on her motorcycle. She'd gone home to change out of her by-then-grimy dress and don her usual shorts and tank top. Butterflies seemed to have taken up permanent residence in her belly. She took her time dismounting, removing her helmet and laying it on the seat.

The guys were out cleaning the rig, laughing and joking with each other. It wasn't just a job to them; it was a way of life. A way of life she loved.

Not having it for these past few days had made her rethink the whole thing. There was more to firefighting than saving people. Saving people was important, but that couldn't happen if she didn't have a team, if she didn't have her colleagues' backs, and they didn't have hers. Dhillon had been right about that. She could do the job, no doubt, but part of the job was trusting others, and being there so they could trust you. Working as part of a team was a strength, not a weakness.

She'd quit in a cloud of guilt and regret. It had been hasty, and she wished she hadn't done it.

She inhaled. *Time to do this.* She walked with purpose, entering the bay as if she'd never left. Evans was there, as were Alvarez and Schultz. No sign of Walsh.

Evans and Alvarez nodded at her, but it was Schultz who approached her. "Hey. Nice work this afternoon."

She nodded, flicking her gaze over Evans and Alvarez as they pretended to work. "Thanks."

"Come to pick up your check?" Evans gave her the side-eye. Of course he'd be pissed. He'd spent quite a bit of time giving her extra training, working with her on new techniques and equipment. Not once had he doubted her or indicated in any way that she was less than because she was a woman.

"Uh, no." Her apologies had to start here. "Actually, I came to beg Ambrose for my job back."

"You're doing *what* now?" Alvarez turned to her.

"I shouldn't have quit. It was impulsive and done in the heat of the moment. But I miss being on the job." She paused. "It's the only job I ever really wanted, but I didn't get that until I didn't have it anymore." She sighed. "You guys have always been good to me, had my back, and I let you down. Even Ambrose, being the pain-in-the-butt hard-ass that he is, was only trying to make me a better firefighter. I was too caught up in myself to even see that." She paused. "I'm sorry I bailed on you."

The guys nodded. Evans had a small grin on his face. Not exactly what she had been hoping for.

"Desai." Ambrose cleared his throat behind her.

She closed her eyes and shook her head, a smile spreading across her face. When she opened them, she said, "Ambrose was behind me the whole time?"

All three broke out in victorious grins. "Pretty much," Evans nearly cackled.

She turned to face her lieutenant. "Lieutenant Ambrose."

His face was devoid of emotion. Great. "Not bad work today...for a civilian."

"With all due respect, sir, I'd rather not be a civilian anymore."

His hard gaze never wavered. "You'll have to talk to the captain."

Riya nodded. With a glance back at the guys, she followed Ambrose back to the captain's office. He did not turn around, offering nothing in the way of support. Riya's hands were sweaty, and her stomach was fluttery. She was more nervous than she ever remembered being. What if Captain Davis wouldn't let her come back? She wanted this more than anything, and it had taken losing it to realize that. Like how losing Dhillon had only made her realize how much she really loved him.

Ambrose sauntered right back to the captain's office and knocked, opening the door without waiting for a response. He held the door for her to pass through, then closed it with a soft click after he entered behind her.

"Desai," her superior greeted her from behind his desk.

"Captain."

"You should know that charges are moving against Ian Walsh, and he is no longer part of this department." Captain Davis sat up in his chair, leaning toward her. "You should have come to us right away. I do not tolerate that kind of behavior—not for one minute."

Riya nodded. "Yes, sir."

He leaned back in his chair, glanced at Ambrose behind her and continued. "So with him gone and you gone, we're down a couple firefighters."

She cleared her throat. "Well, sir, that's kind of why I'm here."

The captain raised his eyebrows, piercing her with his dark eyes. "Mmm-hmm?"

"I made a mistake, sir, handing in my badge like I did. I was distraught, in the heat of the moment, and like many other times, I reacted without thought. I know a good firefighter has to be clear in thought and focused, and I am striving to achieve that." She paused. The captain just stared at her.

"I have a lot to learn...and I know that. But I am good at what I know how to do." She leaned in. "Give me another chance. Please."

The captain flicked his gaze again to Ambrose standing behind her. "Lieutenant, you got anything to say?"

"Yes, sir. In my humble opinion, Firefighter Desai is impulsive and reactionary. She takes risks and encourages others to do so as well. Sometimes people get hurt."

Riya's heart sank. Of course Ambrose would feel that way.

"However, she never asks anyone to do anything she herself is not willing to do. I have seen her calmly and effectively do her job in the face of personal danger. She is passionate about her work, but she still needs training, experience."

What?

"Lieutenant, did you ever finish that paperwork I asked you to start, regarding Firefighter Desai's leaving the job?"

Ambrose shuffled his feet behind her. She forced herself not to look. "My apologies, sir. We've had a busy few days, and I have not had a chance to get to it." He paused. "I'll get right to that." He made a move to the door.

"No!" Riya blurted out before she could stop herself. She

looked at the captain, who had his eyebrows raised at her. "I mean, please don't. I really would like to come back. I can be good at this."

The captain stared her down for a moment. Riya held her breath. He narrowed his eyes, fixing that fierce gaze exclusively on her. "You are rough around the edges, impulsive, aggressive, and sometimes you don't follow orders." He opened a drawer and pulled out her badge. "You need more training, and Ambrose, here, is going to make damn sure you get it." He pushed the badge toward her. "If you pick that up, you are agreeing to do whatever the lieutenant asks of you. You have potential, Desai. I'd like to see you reach it."

Riya did her best to fight the huge smile of relief that was bursting to get through. "Yes, sir. I'll do my best, sir." She reached forward, her heart light, and grabbed her badge before her captain had a change of heart. "Thank you, sir."

Captain Davis waved a hand at her. "Dismissed."

Ambrose opened the door and shared a look with the captain as Riya exited the room in front of him.

"Thanks for that. I appreciate it." Riya stopped and faced him.

"Just so you know, Hetal had nothing to do with this." Ambrose met her gaze. "And don't thank me yet. You have no idea what's in store for you, rookie." Ambrose walked off toward his office, but not before Riya caught him trying to suppress a smile.

"Yes, sir," Riya called out to his back. She didn't care what he threw at her. She had her job back!

The guys were waiting for her in the bay. She grinned at them, her friends and colleagues, and flashed them her badge. "Captain gave me my job back!" Though, she suspected Ambrose had purposely stalled on that paperwork.

They shook their heads at her, frowns on their faces, and went back to work.

"Guys. Seriously?" She moved closer to them. "I'm not leaving. Like, ever again."

Evans looked at Schultz, his mouth twitching into a smile. "She's going to hog those Jaws. You know that, right?"

Schultz shrugged. "She's also going to want to do all the crawling through windows." He rolled his eyes. "Alvarez, she's probably going to eat all the cinnamon rolls, too."

Alvarez stretched to his full six feet five inches and stared at Riya. "You have cooking duty for the first month you're back."

She was speechless. She just grinned at her boys, afraid that if she spoke, she'd cry.

Riya was back.

forty-one

RIYA

Riya's foi and mama had arrived over the weekend for Rakshabandan. Both her parents were thoroughly enjoying having their siblings around. Varsha Masi had all but moved in so
she could be with her brother and sister as much as possible,
which led to more conversations about getting married than
Riya thought was necessary.

Riya's dad reverted to little-brother status and was making a
full-time job of teasing his sister. The air was festive and light
despite the heat and heavy humidity of late August in Maryland. It was impossible to dread the big day, even for Riya.

Her mother was pretty much back to her normal activity
level, adding more exercise, eating less fried food. Even her
Rakshabandan party menu had healthier options along with

the regular comfort food. Riya could have gone back to her apartment a week ago, but she was enjoying her parents and basking in the warmth of her family.

"It really is nice having Riya around again." Her mother was talking to Varsha Masi in the kitchen as Riya entered. Foi and Rumit Mama would be coming over soon, too.

She smiled as she dropped a kiss on each of their cheeks. "I like being around, Mom." She didn't even close her eyes anymore when she passed Samir's picture. She and her mother were cooking together, and her father was forever asking questions about firefighting.

"Then why are you going back?" demanded Varsha Masi.

Riya smiled and occupied herself with making a large pot of chai for everyone. "I'm a grown woman. I like living on my own." She laughed. It was the truth. Mostly. She also did not want a front seat to whatever was going on in Dhillon's life. "But I promised to come for dinner every week."

Everyone was dressed up in their Indian clothes and had begun gathering in the family room. Since Riya was not actually participating in the ceremony, she wore a simple salwar kameez in a bright, festive cobalt blue. She finished making the chai and was arranging the wide assortment of sweets on a few platters in the kitchen, trading family gossip with her foi, when Dhillon's heart-melting voice at the door had her dropping a peda on the floor.

Why was he here? But then Hetal's voice reached her, as well as Sarika Auntie's. It seemed the Vora family was joining them. Interesting that her mother had failed to inform her of this. *Whatever.* She picked up the errant peda and focused on what her foi was saying. It made it easier to ignore the spike of joy that flushed through her.

"Hey. Hetal made these." Dhillon's voice could turn her to mush in an instant, and today was no exception. She turned her head to nod at where he should put them. Her breath caught at the sight of him, too. He was dressed for the occasion in a beautiful silk jabo the color of sand, which he had offset with a deep red scarf around his neck. The tunic fit him perfectly, just grazing his muscle, not too tight but certainly not too loose. The scarf did fantastic things for his skin. He wasn't smiling. He looked…hesitant. And drop-dead gorgeous.

She glanced at the tray, heat rising up to her face. "She made her truffles. Thanks."

"Yeah, sure."

He didn't leave.

"Dhillon, *beta*. Can you get that serving platter?" her foi asked, oblivious to the tension in the air.

"Sure, Auntie." He reached into the cabinet she was pointing to.

"No. Not that. Not that one, either. That one. No, next to it. The other way. Ah, yes." Finally finding what she wanted, Dhillon brought it down and handed it to her.

Just then, Riya's mother called from the family room. "We are ready when you are, beta." Riya picked up two trays, avoiding looking at Dhillon as best she could. Dhillon grabbed the third and they joined everyone in the family room to much applause.

"Let's do this," Rumit Mama shouted. They started with the older generation of sisters tying rakhi to their brothers' wrists.

Riya watched as her mother tried to shove no less than three pedas in Rumit Mama's mouth all at the same time. Rumit Mama took it in stride, bestowing a beautiful silk scarf on his sister for her gift. Riya's father nearly teared up as his sister wished him a long and happy life while tying his rakhi. Her father gave his sister a signed copy of her favorite book.

Then it was Dhillon's turn. He took a seat on the floor, and Hetal tied his rakhi. She still did not have full use of her left arm, but she managed beautifully. Riya watched them closely. Actually, she watched Dhillon closely. He was playful and sweet with his sister, as always, but the love shone on his face and in his eyes.

Whoever he did end up with was going to have to pass the sister test. They would have to love his sister as much as he did.

Dhillon presented Hetal with a large package. She opened it immediately and found inside a backpack similar to the one Riya took to work at the firehouse.

Hetal's mouth gaped open.

Dhillon dipped his chin at the bag. "So, no matter which way you decide to go—firefighting, vet school or something entirely different—you'll have everything you need with you."

"Bhaiya." Hetal's eyes swam with tears. "It's vet school." She put aside the bag and hugged her brother tight. "Thank you."

Riya allowed her eyes to fill with tears, too. Samir totally would have given a gift like that. Damn, she missed her brother.

With that, the ceremonial part of the day was over. Riya wiped her eyes and stood to offer the sweets to everyone again, but Hetal stopped her.

"Riya Didi, come sit." Hetal indicated the spot on the floor that Dhillon had just vacated.

"What?"

"Just sit," Hetal said.

Riya did as she was told. Hetal sat across from her. "What's going on?" She looked to Dhillon for an answer. He just shrugged his shoulders, jubilation playing in his eyes, a smile taking over his lips.

"Riya Didi, I know that traditionally, we tie rakhi to our brothers, wishing them a long and happy life, because brothers are supposed to love us and look out for us, always." She smiled at Dhillon. "So much so that, sometimes, they won't even move the hell out of the house."

This earned her a glare from Dhillon and a chuckle from the rest of the crowd.

"Anyway... Riya Didi, you've always been a big sister to

me. You've looked out for me and loved me like I was your own blood. I don't remember a time in my childhood where you weren't there for me." She paused. "One of my favorite memories was climbing trees with you when I was little."

"You sprained your ankle that day," Dhillon interjected.

Hetal's face lit up. "I know. But the climbing was fun, and Riya took such great care of me after. We had ice cream and watched movies." Tears sprang to her eyes. "Dad had been gone a little while, and I remember that being the first time I had fun in a long time."

Riya teared up again at the young woman's words.

"So I'm tying this rakhi on you today to wish you a long and happy life. Because sisters should be able to celebrate their bond, too." With that, she took Riya's right wrist and tied the rakhi around it. "This rakhi I made for you is the color of fire. So you'll be safe, always."

They fed each other sweets.

Riya studied the rakhi, and a tear dropped from her eye. When she found her voice, she looked at Hetal. "I don't have a gift for you."

Hetal hugged her, a playful smirk on her lips. "I'll take an IOU."

Scout wiggled and barked in the back seat of Riya's mom's car. Riya was running a couple of errands for her parents today. She was meeting Dhillon tomorrow to scatter Lucky's ashes and then moving back to her apartment. She wanted as much time with Scout as possible.

She'd just got a text from Ambrose requesting she stop by the firehouse for a minute. She'd been off for a few days, but she was on shift tomorrow night. Whatever it was apparently couldn't wait.

"All right, Scout. Let's go see the guys." She got out of the car and unhooked the puppy. Before she could get the leash on, Scout bolted out and right into the station. Riya followed.

Scout had gone directly to Ambrose, since the lieutenant spent most of his time off hanging out at the Vora house with Hetal while she healed. Ambrose got down on his knees to greet Scout, taking all the doggy kisses and tail wags she had to offer.

Alvarez came from the back. "We fed you, too, dog." Scout ran to him and jumped up and down to play. Riya walked back to Alvarez.

Schultz came up to greet Scout as well and ran back toward the locker room with her. Riya followed.

Once Scout had made the rounds, she settled in at Riya's feet. "So what's going on?"

"Well, we missed the dog." Ambrose nodded at Scout, his eyes filled with humor.

Riya was confused. "You see her all the time at Hetal's."

Evans spoke up. "Yeah. But we don't."

Something was up. "No way you called me all the way down here just to see Scout."

Ambrose looked around at all the men, then back at Riya. "We have something to show you."

"We—" he spread his arms out to indicate all the men "—are all brothers here. We take care of each other. We have each other's backs."

Evans looked Riya in the eye. "We're your brothers, too."

"So we always have your back," Alvarez added. "You should have told us how bad it was with Walsh."

"I was handling it."

"You don't always have to handle things on your own," Ambrose said. "We can never replace the brother you lost, but we're here for you. Always."

They were standing in front of the locker room. The men parted, forming an aisle for Riya. She looked at each of these men as she walked past them until she reached the locker-room door.

"Open the door," Evans said, egging her on.

"You want me to open the locker-room door?" Riya looked around at them.

"Yes," Schultz answered.

"Fine." Riya pushed it open and walked in. It looked smaller, because new walls had been built inside it, along with a separate door.

Riya walked through the second door and froze. She was looking at a smaller version of the locker room, with five lockers, a bench, a mirror and, just past it, two individual, private-stall showers.

"What am I looking at?" Riya's heart was pounding hard. It couldn't be.

"This is the all-new women's locker room and shower. That we built for our sister in fire and future sisters to come. We'll get a bigger one soon. But this is for now." Ambrose was beaming. He leaned down to her ear. "You're our sister, whether you want to be or not."

Tears threatened to fall from her eyes as her words of thanks got stuck behind the lump in her throat. She didn't even care. She looked up at Ambrose. "Well, then I guess that I'm pretty damn lucky."

"Aw, man. Are you going to cry?" Evans rolled his eyes.

"Hell, yes!" Riya said, as she reached up to pull him into a hug.

She let the tears fall as she hugged Schultz and Alvarez as well. "I love it! Thank you!"

She wiped her eyes when she got to Ambrose. "Lieutenant."

"Probie." He smirked at her, and she hugged him, too.

These were her brothers.

forty-two

DHILLON

Riya was waiting on the dock when Dhillon arrived. The sky was just turning pink with the sunrise, and the air was still cool over the water but promised a typical humid August day.

Her knees were folded to her chest, and she rested her chin on them as she seemed to contemplate the small ripples in the water. Her hair was down, and it shone in the rising sun. She was strong and beautiful, and his heart raced just looking at her. He could have stood there and watched her indefinitely.

"Hi, Dhillon," she called. Ashes had to be sprinkled in moving water, so they'd come out to the Chesapeake Bay. Scout was curled up at her feet.

He made his feet move toward her. "Hey."

She stood when he got close. Her gaze fell on the box he was holding.

"Let's get a canoe." He raised his eyebrows at her.

She smirked at him. "You want to steal a canoe?"

"Borrow," he chuckled.

They were silent as they *borrowed* a canoe and paddled out just a bit. Scout sat looking over the water, quiet and still, almost as if she understood the solemnness of what they were about to do.

"She's gotten so big." Dhillon nodded at the puppy.

"Yeah." She scratched Scout's head. "I'll miss her."

Dhillon nodded and opened the wooden box he'd brought. Lucky's ashes had come to him in a pouch inside it. He pulled it out and opened it.

He and Riya reached in at the same time. It should be the most natural thing for their hands to touch, but Riya pulled back as if burned by him.

His heart ached.

"You go ahead." She waited while he gathered some ashes in his right hand.

She reached in after him, and then they both sprinkled the ashes into the water and watched as the blue-green ripples took them away.

He heard Riya sniffle and caught tears in her eyes. "You know, somehow Lucky always knew when I needed him. After we had those dog doors installed, he always came over when I was really sad. Did you know that?"

Dhillon was quiet. They both gathered more ash and released it into the gently moving bay.

"Dhillon, did you know that?" she repeated.

He sighed. "Lucky was always there for you, wasn't he?"

She nodded, looked at her fingers. "He was. Especially

after Samir died. I was freaking out in my house. You—" She stopped. "Well, I used to wait for you in Tommy's tree house."

"I never showed." He stared out at the water as they sprinkled more ashes, returning Lucky to nature. The canoe rocked them in the calm waves.

"Nope." Some remnant of the pain she'd felt from his rebuke still lingered in her. Her pain, his guilt for causing it, burned like acid in his stomach. "I assumed you were too busy for me."

Dhillon reached into the bag and scattered more ashes. "I wasn't too busy. I didn't know how to be there for you. You seemed so strong, so capable at school, hanging with your friends, laughing."

She tossed her hair back. "Ha! As if! I was a mess. I thought that if I acted like I was okay, I would be. But I needed my best friend, Dhillon." Her voice cracked. "And you never showed."

He knew he had no right to wipe the tears from her face, to touch her. He did it anyway, soothing away her tears with his clean hand, whispering, "I sent Lucky to you."

She snapped her eyes to him. "You what?"

"Our rooms. We shared a wall. Sometimes I heard you crying. Or your parents yelling. I would tell Lucky to go find you—"

"And he always did," she whispered, surprised. A small smile grew on her face.

"It's not the same, I know." Dhillon wanted to apologize for all of it, but his words weren't enough, even to him.

"You sent Lucky. You thought about me." She bit her bottom lip, still smiling. "You were there, the best you could be." She shrugged. "We were just kids."

He rested his gaze on her. "Yeah. But still, I am sorry."

Silence settled in around them as they finished scattering Lucky's ashes. Tears fell down Riya's cheeks. Dhillon's heart was heavy as he washed his hands clean in the cool bay and put his arms around her, pulling her close. She turned her head and snuggled closer to him.

"Having Lucky, it was comforting."

Dhillon nodded.

"Thank you for that," she whispered.

After a time, she sat back and took his hands in hers. They were smaller than his, but her grip was firm, determined.

"Dhillon, I love you. I cannot remember a time when I didn't." She paused, looked him in the eye. Her normally raspy voice took on an almost velvety quality as she spoke. "I'm a firefighter. It's who I am." She squeezed his hands. "One thing we both know is that life can be too short. I want to be with you. There's no doubt in my mind that I'd rather be with you for whatever days, months, years I have left as opposed to not having you at all. That is how much I love you, Dhillon-V." She paused, bringing his hands to her lips. She kissed them, her lips soft and plush, before meeting his eyes again, her face fierce. "If you don't love me like that, then I want nothing to do with you. I can't watch you move on with someone else. Either we're together or we're out of each other's lives. This—" she waved a hand in the air between them "—is too hard. What we both deserve is someone who would rather be with us than not."

She let go of his hands and started rowing. "I'm moving back to my apartment."

Dhillon was speechless. This woman had a way of doing that to him, time and time again. Just when he thought he knew her, she surprised him again. He allowed himself a happy grin and a light heart as they paddled to shore.

They secured the canoe, and Riya headed for her bike.

"No." Dhillon took her hand. "Come with me. My turn to drive."

"Dhillon, did you not hear what I just said?"

"I did." He squinted at her in the bright sunlight. "Please."

She sighed and studied him. After what felt like an eternity, she relented. "Okay."

Her hand in his felt more than right. It felt like it had always been there.

forty-three

DHILLON

Dhillon pulled into his driveway and looked at Riya. She hadn't said much on the drive back, and he knew her patience was wearing thin.

"You brought us home?"

He grinned at her and got out of the car. She followed, Scout behind her. She secured Scout and handed the leash to Dhillon.

Scout was officially his dog now. She was completely house-trained and well on her way to learning more commands.

He took the leash. "Just walk with me."

She was gorgeous in her trademark cutoff denim shorts and tank top as she leaned against his car, her mouth pressed into a line. He was trying her patience. The idea made him smile. Her hair was pulled up in a ponytail, and she had on no makeup. She was beautiful. "I knew you'd keep her."

"Yeah, yeah. I'm predictable. Whatever."

"We're walking Scout? That's what you want me to do with you?"

"Yes."

She sighed and shook her head like he was ridiculous. "Let's do it, then."

He couldn't stop staring at her, suddenly nervous around the girl he'd loved since he was five. But the amusement in her eyes relaxed him instantly.

The sun was properly up, beating down on them, the humidity rising. Dhillon led them around the neighborhood, Scout in front of them, Riya beside him. He relished her presence.

"Do you remember when you moved in?" Dhillon asked, staring straight ahead.

"We were what? Five, six?"

"Five." He stole a glance at her. She was smiling as she remembered. "Samir would have been ten."

"Way too cool for us."

They chuckled.

She continued. "You were painfully shy."

"No. I had just never seen anyone as cute as you before." He caught her flush from the corner of his eye.

"Whatever. We were five." She bumped his shoulder.

He led them out of their neighborhood and into the next. A mere fifteen-minute walk. A community of smaller single-family homes. He stopped in front of one.

"That was the day." He looked at her.

"What day?"

"The only day that was better than the day I got Lucky was the day we became neighbors."

She tilted her head. "Dhillon… I…"

He turned toward the house, drawing her gaze to it. "What do you think?"

She shrugged. "Cute. Quaint. What is it, like three bedrooms?" She studied the house for a few moments in silence.

"Are you assessing the fire risk?" Dhillon chuckled.

She was unabashed. "Just practicing."

"Got an exit plan?"

"Well, I'd have to see the inside floor plan, but since you mention it…" And she was off. He listened attentively.

He remained silent when she stopped talking. She looked at him. "What?"

She looked from the house to him and back, a slow smile creeping over her face. "You bought it?" Her whole face broke out into a smile, and he couldn't help but join her.

He shook his head. "No. Not yet."

"But you're going to? You're moving out." She raised her eyebrows, confirming she was right. "Of the townhome."

He nodded. "About time, don't you think?"

"Hell, yes," she giggled. "Your sister is going to be sooo happy. Though this house may not be far enough away."

"She's pretty thrilled. I think she's already packing my stuff. If I wasn't so secure, it might actually hurt my feelings." Dhillon laughed.

"You'll get over it." Riya bumped his shoulder again. "So what's the holdup? Why haven't you purchased it yet?"

Dhillon started walking toward the door, avoiding the question. "Come on. Let's look inside. It's open." His real-estate agent, Wendy, had allowed him to borrow the key.

He opened the door, Scout close behind. Riya started wandering the first floor, checking out the eat-in kitchen, small family room and foyer. Dhillon unleashed Scout and led Riya upstairs, showing her all the little details he'd memorized when he'd walked through the first time. They finally ended up in the back, on the deck. They leaned on the railing, shoulder to shoulder. The sun was high, with nothing but green grass and trees to be seen. Below the deck was a small, fenced-in yard. Serenity.

"It's gorgeous." Riya's voice was low, as if being too loud might disturb the peace. "Plenty of space for Scout. And for Zeus, when your mom brings Dr. Shah's dog over."

"Sure." He kept staring out at the sky and the meticulously kept grass. Then he turned to face her. He thought he'd be nervous at this moment, but he was nothing but calm. "I haven't purchased it yet because I wanted to see if you liked it."

"It's gorgeous, Dhillon. If not well overdue."

"Could you see yourself living here? With me?"

She narrowed her eyes, confused. "You mean, like a roommate?"

"No." He laughed. "Not like a roommate." Even looking at her was an experience. Every feature, every expression—he was sure that even after a lifetime, she'd still be able to surprise him. "The truth is, Riya, that I do love you, and I have loved you as long as I can remember."

"You said you wished—"

"I didn't mean that. I was wrong to say it. I'm sorry. Forgive me?"

Riya looked up at him, eyes wide, and nodded.

"You do not hide from the world. Actually, you're the one who gets me to take risks, and you're the one who sees the possibility in everything. You're a firefighter, and I know that is who you are. I love who you are. You're a hero. And not just because you pulled me from that fire." He stepped closer to her, resting his hand on her cheek, and lowered his voice. "Though, that is so completely hot on so many levels."

She bit her bottom lip and smirked up at him.

"What I'm trying to say is I do want to be the guy who sends you off to save the world." He cleared his throat so there was no mistaking his next words. "But more than anything, I want to be the man you come back home to. You're everyone else's hero. Let me be yours."

He paused and reached into his pocket and pulled out a ring. "I'm asking you to live here with me as my wife. Marry me, Firefighter Riya-D."

forty-four

RIYA

Dhillon's face was inches from hers, the heat from their bodies mingled, electrifying the scant space between them. She was enveloped in his scent, which was now his shower mixed with the saltiness from the bay. He was proclaiming his love for her with that melt-your-insides voice of his, and he was holding a gorgeous diamond ring.

Oh, and asking her to marry him. And live with him in this adorable house.

Her heart stopped for a moment when she looked at the ring. Platinum band, gorgeous diamond that was set flush into the band. Nothing sticking up. It was perfect.

She snapped her eyes up to him. "Did you pick out this ring?"

"Yes."

"It's…it's…" Completely gorgeous and thoughtful. Clearly, Dhillon didn't want her ring getting caught in her gloves. He had thought about things like this.

"What? If you hate it, I'll get you whatever you want." He swallowed hard, and Riya swore there was a bit of panic in those dark eyes she adored. *Huh.* "But you haven't answered the question."

"I don't hate it, but rings are a hazard at—"

Dhillon's response was swift. "If it's not safe for work, I had another idea."

"What's that?" She cocked an eyebrow, excited that he seemed to have the whole thing thought out.

"Are you saying yes?"

She smirked at him. "I want to know the idea."

He raised an eyebrow and kissed her shoulder, where the Ganesha tattoo was. His kiss rocketed completely through her body.

"Tattooed rings?" She inched closer to him, letting her body just graze his. She tilted her head back, so his lips were barely inches from hers.

"That's right."

"It'll hurt," she warned, bringing her mouth closer to his.

"Not as much as not having you." He leaned down closer to her, and she couldn't help herself—her lips melted onto his.

"Is that a yes?" he asked when they broke for air.

"Is Scout moving in with us?" She bit her bottom lip as if this were the deal breaker.

"Riya-D. Will. You. Marry. Me?" He pulled her close so their bodies were touching and looked at her, his eyes filled with the question, begging for her answer.

This was her best friend, her confidant, the man she had loved since she was a little girl. This was her Dhillon-V. "Of course." She grinned at him, her heart light and filled with love. "Yes, Dhillon-V. I will marry you."

"Of course Scout's moving in with us." He placed the ring on her finger. "Wouldn't have it any other way." Then he pulled her into him and kissed her again. His hands cupped the sides of her face, and she was his, and he was finally hers.

She melted into him, surrendering her heart to the only man she could imagine spending her life with. Her very own personal hero.

epilogue
DHILLON

Dhillon pulled up to the fire station as his three-year-olds chanted, "Are we there yet?" The new house was exactly seven minutes from the station, and the twins had chanted for six of those minutes. No sooner had he parked than his son and daughter were clicking themselves free of their car seats.

"Hold up, you two. I'm coming around to help you."

Anjali was already standing, helping her brother. "We don't need help, Daddy. We can do it."

She was definitely Riya's daughter. Sure enough, by the time Dhillon walked around and opened the door, both kids had jumped out of the vehicle without even waiting for the door to slide all the way open. They had even unclicked Scout, who bounded out of the minivan behind them.

Dhillon checked the parking lot and saw his mom's car as well as his in-laws'. His sister must be on the way.

Luckily, their legs were short, and they couldn't get too far before Dhillon caught up to them. "Hurry, Daddy. We want to surprise Mommy." Samir took his hand and pulled.

Dhillon allowed his children to pull him into the fire station. They let go of his hands as Jeff appeared in the bay and they took off for him, ramming themselves into their uncle-to-be's legs in enthusiastic twin hugs. Scout bounded after them, trying to get her share of the love.

"Look at you guys! Samir, look how tall you are. You, too, Anjali. What are you now? Like, six?" Jeff was animated with the children in a way that he wasn't anywhere else in his life.

The children fell into fits of laughter. Samir held up three fingers. "We are three, Jeff Uncle."

"You were at our birthday party!" Anjali pointed a finger at him, scolding him for forgetting. "Remember?"

"Jeff Uncle is getting old, beti. He can't remember." Dhillon grinned as he mocked his sister's fiancé.

"Still younger than you, brother." Jeff laughed and pulled Dhillon into a hug. "How's it going?"

"Great. Excited about today." Dhillon looked around. "Is she on a call?"

"She's in the kitchen with the guys." He scooped up Samir and Anjali. "Let's go find Mommy!" Scout followed them.

The twins squealed with delight as Jeff carried them off. Dhillon started to follow but was stopped by someone calling, "Bhaiya!"

He turned to his sister as she walked up to the station. Hetal had just come from the veterinary ER, where she moonlighted on occasion. Tristan was holding down the fort in Dhillon's new clinic.

"Where are our little rug rats?" Hetal asked as she joined him.

"With your fiancé." Dhillon hugged her.

She grinned. "I feel like I haven't seen them in ages."

"They're huge now. Almost ready for college," Dhillon teased. "You saw them last week at their birthday party."

They passed the wall of fallen firefighters, Dhillon mentally thanking them and simultaneously grateful that Riya's picture was not there. They arrived in the kitchen, where everyone was gathered, and Dhillon caught sight of Riya holding both children, listening to their latest stories. She was on a forty-eight-hour shift, and the kids were missing her. Her hair was in its regular braid, a few pieces flying loose. She was completely attentive to whatever the children were saying to her, but she caught his eye and smiled a smile that was just for him. Warmth spread through Dhillon as it always did when he saw her.

His in-laws chatted with his sister. His mother stood close to Jeff, squeezing his shoulder and laughing at something he said. Rohun Uncle stood beside her, watching her attentively. Everyone important to Dhillon was right there in the room.

Marcus came and stood by him. "Big day for our girl."

Dhillon beamed with pride. "Yes, it is."

Bill came over, extended his hand. "Hey, Dhillon."

Dhillon shook it. "Where's Angie?" But as he glanced behind Bill, he saw her setting up a cake. "The kids are still talking about the cake Angie made for their birthday."

"Me, too." Alejandro sidled up.

Scout wandered about, going from person to person, playing with Rohun Uncle's dog, Zeus.

Dhillon approached Riya and held out his hands for Samir to come to him. The little boy reached from his mother's arms to Dhillon's. "Hey."

Riya narrowed her eyes at him. "What's going on? The kids, your sister, our parents?"

Dhillon raised his eyebrows and jutted his chin toward Captain Davis. "Listen."

The captain got everyone's attention. "Thanks to everyone who could be here. I'm going to make this quick, since that alarm could sound any minute. Firefighter Desai has passed the lieutenant's exam and is now our newest lieutenant."

Riya turned to Dhillon, pride in her eyes. "That's why?"

He nodded. Smiling, Riya wove her way through her family and colleagues to her captain's side.

"Firefighter Desai, I think it's an understatement if I say that this journey was rough." He grinned at her as a murmur of agreeable laughter floated through the kitchen. "But you have grown as a firefighter, you have worked hard and earned this rank." The captain paused. "Lieutenant Ambrose."

Jeff stepped up and pinned Riya's new rank onto her shirt. "Couldn't ask for a better sister in fire, Lieutenant Desai."

Dhillon swelled with pride as she accepted her new rank. Riya was amazing, and she was his. A huge round of applause erupted, and Riya flushed, catching his eye.

"Thank you." She looked around the room. "I couldn't have done it without everyone here." She paused to swallow, as tears filled her eyes. "But especially my brothers," she said, as she looked at Marcus, Bill, Alejandro and Jeff, "who always have my back. And I wouldn't want to do it without Dhillon, who is *my* hero."

"Mommy is a loo-tenny! Can we have cake now?" Samir had his priorities all set. Laughter and another round of applause, and everyone congratulated her.

"Sure," Dhillon said, laughing, and he made his way to where his mother-in-law was cutting pieces of the cake. He settled his kids with their servings and was trying to get to his wife when the alarm sounded.

Jeff left Hetal's side with a quick kiss. Marcus and Bill each shoved a bite of cake into their mouths and went to answer the call, Riya along with them. Dhillon picked up the children to keep them out of the way, holding one child in each arm. He followed the firefighters out to the bay.

Firefighters in action still looked like organized chaos to him. Riya was already in her turnout gear and helmet as she came over to them. "Sorry, kids, Mommy has to go. Have cake." She kissed each of her children on the forehead and gave them both a quick hug. "Love you guys."

"What do we say to Mommy?" Dhillon looked at his children.

They each raised a tiny fist and waved it. "Go get 'em, Mommy!" they chorused. Riya laughed.

Dhillon caught her eye. She still made his heart race. "Love you, too, Dhillon-V."

He leaned down and kissed her lips. "You go be a hero, Riya-D. I'll be right here, waiting for you."

★ ★ ★ ★ ★

Acknowledgments

This book started with a conversation I was having with a friend who is a New Jersey firefighter. I was researching my previous book when he told me his story. Now, this is not Nilay Patel's story, but he gave me the idea to have a main character be a firefighter who was Indian. So, thank you, Nilay, for sharing!

Many, many thanks to my editor, Brittany Lavery, who helped me kill some darlings so I could better tell Riya and Dhillon's story. Extra gratitude as well to my agent, Rachel, who continues to believe in me and the ideas I come up with (even when some aren't so popular!).

Special thanks to Sarah Storin and her husband, Richard Goddard, for answering all my fire and firefighter questions so I could be as real as possible. That being said, any errors in detail are mine, so I could have things turn out the way I wanted them to.

As per usual, I couldn't have done this without my tribe of writers, specifically Shaila Patel, Namrata Patel and Farah Heron, all of whom listened to me go on and on endlessly about how to properly tell this story. You ladies are the best!

I am blessed and grateful to have a varied and true tribe of family and friends who continue to support and encourage my dreams. Love and gratitude to you all. You know who you are.

Finally, thanks and love to my children, Anjali and Anand, two of the most fun people I know, and last but never least, Deven, my true-life romantic hero.